YOU
SHOULD
HAVE KNOWN

YOU SHOULD HAVE KNOWN

A NOVEL

REBECCA A. KELLER

CROOKED
LANE

NEW YORK

Copyright © 2023 by Rebecca A. Keller

Published in the United States by Crooked Lane Books, an imprint of The Quick Brown Fox & Company LLC.

Crooked Lane Books and its logo are trademarks of The Quick Brown Fox & Company LLC.

Library of Congress Catalog-in-Publication data available upon request.

ISBN (hardcover): 978-1-63910-260-0
ISBN (ebook): 978-1-63910-261-7

Cover design by Heather VenHuizen

Printed in the United States.

www.crookedlanebooks.com

Crooked Lane Books
34 West 27th St., 10th Floor
New York, NY 10001

First Edition: April 2023

10 9 8 7 6 5 4 3 2 1

To Bill and Aggie Keller, whose love, honesty and bravery with getting older helped inform this narrative.

"The meaning of life is that it stops."

—Franz Kafka

"Maybe all one can do is hope to end up with the right regrets."

—Arthur Miller

CHAPTER

1

I SCANNED THE MEDICATIONS on the cart: pills sorted into tiny cups made of pleated paper, sitting atop smudgy laminated cards, each marked with a name and apartment number. The cards took me back to my hospital days, reminding me of surgical drapes framing the place to cut. A few medicines were set apart in smooth plastic containers the color of swimming pools: Oxycontin, Vicodin, Hydrocodone, Tramadol. Powerful. Dangerous. Able to suppress respiration. Like morphine. Named after Morpheus, the god of dreams.

In Greek mythology, Morpheus lived by the river of forgetfulness.

There is a common assumption that the only thing old people do is forget. Or, conversely, that all we do is sit around and remember, dwelling in the past. These things are not mutually exclusive. In fact, they represent the twin requirements of old age: recalling who we are and what we care about, while forgetting—or at least pretending to forget—how much we have lost.

Remembering and disremembering: getting this balance right has become my main struggle. There are some things I can't let fade. I press on the bruise, keeping the memories alive and active. They are part of me. Besides, injustice—or rather, indignation in the face of it—is as good a reason as any for a person to get up in the morning. Somebody, somehow, has got to hold the world accountable. Maybe by the sheer act of insisting on it, justice might happen.

I looked down the empty hallway.

There is a lot of freedom in a place like this. One could get away with a lot, since no one expects anything of us. Allowed to remember or required to forget: either way, no one expects an old woman to *do* anything. Well, I reject that. My age offers me a measure of protection.

But Iris, though. Iris. The thought of my daughter holds me back. The memory of her pain and the fact that she seems to finally be able to make room for new memories, new life, makes me pause.

I sometimes wonder where to drop the pin on the time line marking the sequence of events that led me to the Ridgewood Assisted Living Retirement complex—and all the things that have descended from that. Did it begin when I fell and hurt my knee? Or further back, maybe the day Cal died? Or maybe the path that led me here began when Bethany was killed?

"*Ruthie, my darling cousin,*" I wrote, "*one thing is for sure. However I conceptualize the past, I certainly would not have foreseen what the last two months have led me to.*"

*   *   *

It was *not* a nursing home, as my son and my daughter kept reminding me when we went to take a look at Ridgewood Senior Apartments. "Mom, the people who live here are residents, not patients. They have their own apartments and as much independence as they want. It's perfect for you."

Mr. Alfred, director of Ridgewood, was explaining the various support services and conveniences as we stood in the lobby ready to embark on the tour. "Now Frannie, I'd like to show you—"

I interrupted. "Call me Mrs. Greene."

Iris, bless her, barely bothered to suppress a smile. Her dimples gave her away, and she aimed a quick wink at me. Charlie cleared his throat, and Mr. Alfred blushed. "My apologies." He hurriedly passed brochures to us, explaining that Ridgewood, an "innovative senior residence," featured numerous amenities. "Tenants can utilize our support offerings on an as-needed basis. The library, the craft room, the van that takes people shopping, and the organized outings are all yours to enjoy." He looked at me over his eyeglasses before continuing. "The majority of our residents take advantage of packages that provide varying levels of support. Most include meals in the dining room, but we also offer distribution of medications, cleaning—even help with bathing as people get older and might want more assistance." I turned away at that last bit. I could wash my own bottom, thank you very much. I was only seventy-two, and despite the recent falls that had quite literally landed me here, I was in good health and sound mind. I didn't need reminding that this might be my home for a long time.

* * *

Mr. Alfred droned on at my son and daughter—I could tell he had decided they were his main audience. I slipped down a hallway off the lobby to a small chapel, "open at all hours to residents in need." Near the entrance was a discreet notice about the monthly memorial "for those who have passed on from the Ridgewood community." Mr. Alfred didn't call quite as much attention to that.

I returned to where he stood with my children. Mr. Alfred was easily six and a half feet tall and blockish as a wrestler. His voice, as one would expect from such an oversized throat, was a booming baritone. It took only a minute to realize that his size was in inverse proportion to his charisma. He was as devoid of charm as boxed vanilla pudding or, perhaps, the box itself.

"You're very fortunate," he was saying, "Our units aren't available very often." Iris turned to me and lifted her eyebrow in that way she had, and I fought the sarcastic urge to say, "Yes, very fortunate indeed." I bit my tongue to keep from asking what happened to the last resident, because I didn't want to irritate Charlie. Besides, it wasn't too tough to guess. I suppose whoever it was could have moved to Florida, but I had a feeling the answer was more depressing. Though, judging from the visit I had made to an old friend a few years back, there might not be anything more depressing than retiring to Florida.

Iris sent me a warning glance before smiling at Mr. Alfred. "Yes, we're so glad something is available."

Much as I hated to admit it, she was right. Ridgewood was a nice place, and if I couldn't return to my condo, there weren't a lot of choices. When Cal and I had first moved to Willow Park, it was practically in the country, and the forty miles to Chicago made the big city seem like a distant shore, a destination for special outings. But now Willow Park was just another suburb. Rush-hour commuters clogged the road heading to the next town over to catch the Metra train, and ugly beige townhomes were springing up along the highway. Other than Ridgewood, the retirement apartments in the area were either expensive golfing communities, which held zero appeal for me, or repurposed sections of nursing homes, with nasty carpet and bad smells. Iris kept telling me how lucky we were that Ridgewood just happened to have something. I understood what she meant, but I didn't feel all that lucky.

Ever since Cal's death six years ago, Charlie had fretted and nagged at me about living alone in the condo. I tried not to be distrustful and assume he wanted to be rid of me, which is what the devil on my shoulder whispered in my ear when I felt sorry for myself. At one memorable "discussion" in which Charlie tried to convince me to move, I said as much. He looked like I'd slapped him. He had reddish brown, amber-colored eyes, like those of a golden retriever, and equally as expressive. "How can you say that, Mom?" He draped his arms around me and spoke into the top of my head. "I just want you to be around as long as possible. We've had enough bad things happen."

Once again the cloud of our family tragedy blocked out the sun. The wounds were deep, and the scars had formed in welted, jagged lines. Charlie was right. I was a terrible mother for thinking so ungenerously. But I didn't want to move, and Iris was sympathetic about that. She's tenderhearted, my daughter. Even more so since Bethany's accident.

But Iris changed her mind after my last fall. It was embarrassing. I went sprawling and injured my meniscus, and worst of all, I had a concussion. I had to lie in the dark for a week, no reading, no TV. Nothing to do but think. And when my head was finally healed, I had to spend three weeks in a rehab center for my knee. But it was after my knee was better that the hardest blow of all came. My children began insisting that I shouldn't go back to my condo. Which was rich, because the condo was where we moved so we wouldn't have to keep up our old house.

When Cal and I bought the place, its unusual size—three bedrooms *and* a family room—had been a selling point: we may have been leaving our big old house, but we still wanted plenty of room to have the kids over and entertain. But now, its size, and the fact that there were steps from the living room to the kitchen—where I'd tripped and fallen—meant that the social worker at the rehab center *and* my doctor *and* my kids all had decided I couldn't live there anymore.

So here I was, touring Ridgewood retirement apartments, trying to be taken seriously as an individual, somehow, against the backdrop of the industrial aging complex.

Mr. Alfred waved his enormous hand to gesture us down a hall, and we dutifully followed. Bland paintings dotted the pink-beige walls. Benches were discreetly placed in little nooks. Mr. Alfred talked about the exercise rooms, the library, the computer center. I wondered whether these were actually used or if the tennis court and game room really functioned as placeholders for people's former lives, reminders of what we once had done or been able to do. Maybe they helped the residents think that their days of gardening or painting, or playing tennis or video games, would continue. These offerings were big selling points, to judge by how they were emphasized.

As we passed apartment doors individually decorated with kitschy decorative plaques or "leave a message" chalkboards, I noticed several were flanked by ceramic sculptures of dogs or cats. Mr. Alfred saw me noticing them and smiled. "We don't allow pets, so the neighbors on this hallway got together and declared whether they had been dog or cat people before coming here, and to make a 'hallway menagerie.'"

Cute.

We arrived at a sort of knuckle at the end of the hall, with two apartments to either side. Mr. Alfred fitted a key into one of the doors. "This is one of our sunniest units." He swept us in, and I had to fight the urge to be impressed.

The place was washed with light. To the right was a small but serviceable kitchen, with a curved half wall forming a counter and separating it from the entry. The spacious living room was straight ahead. To the left there was a large closet and a hall leading to the bath and bedroom.

Iris turned into the kitchen, where I heard Mr. Alfred continuing his spiel. "The appliances are top of the line . . ." and Iris responding, "Yes, very nice. Mom? Mom? Come take a look."

But I ignored them and headed into the living room, drawn by the view. The grounds of Ridgewood border a nature preserve, and this particular apartment was situated where the building angled toward the wood. Huge windows framed a lawn sloping down to thickly shadowed trees, and birds darted by a pond blinking in the sunlight. Despite my best efforts to resist, I could see myself drinking morning coffee as I watched the swallows dip and scatter.

I willed the image away. No doubt Ridgewood was beyond my budget. Cal and I had worked hard to be able to put aside something just for our kids, and I was insistent that we not dip into those investments. So all week Charlie had been going over my finances and talking with my insurance company.

Charlie bent in front of me and said softly. "Mom? What do you think?"

"Well, it's a pretty view. But I keep telling you, I refuse to spend your and Iris's inheritance on something like this."

He looked terribly pleased with himself. "What if I told you we could afford it with just your pension and the insurance? The long-term care policy you and Dad paid into for all those years will cover most of this."

"What?" I frowned and moved my head sharply. Too sharply, judging by his reaction.

He looked hurt, and the creases he'd begun to develop around his forehead deepened. "But this place has everything you said you wanted." His shoulders sank. "I thought you'd be glad that we could swing it."

I blinked as sudden tears pressed behind my eyes. I turned away. What was my aim? To stay in my condo at all costs? It was a nice enough place, but when I thought of home, I pictured my real house, the clapboard Victorian where we raised our kids, and where Charlie and Pam and my grandsons live now. Was I just trying to prove I was strong and independent? To whom? To the people who had been visiting me in the rehab center every day, seeing me struggle to climb stairs? The truth was, I had agreed to this, but I didn't want to do it. I didn't want to move in with a bunch of old people. So I punted.

"Uh . . . um," I stuttered. "It's very nice. It's just that everyone I ever got in a dispute with at the library or school will be living here sooner or later."

Charlie was silent for a minute. Then he said softly, "Mom, we know you're strong. We know you're still sharp.

Whatever bad thing you think it means to be in an assisted living apartment—it doesn't mean that for you. We just want you to be safe."

Iris had come up next to me. She was almost as tall as Charlie, and now she curled an arm around my shoulder. "Mom?" Her dark eyes were luminous. She let her long hair curtain her face as she bent close and whispered, as if no one else was around, "I just couldn't bear it if something happened to you too."

In the aftermath of her daughter's death, we had come apart, Iris and I. After Bethany was killed, I'd been unable to help Iris, and she'd been unwilling to let me in. She pushed everyone away: her husband, Jimmy; her friends; Charlie; me. Maybe especially me. Displaced sorrow made us angry with each other. But my increased vulnerability had freed her. She had someone who needed her again, and she could focus her worry and energy on me instead of on the injustice of what had happened to her daughter.

How could I say no to the depth of love in her eyes?

She squeezed my shoulder, and we leaned into one another. Charlie encircled both of us in a hug, and spoke over my head to Mr. Alfred, "I think we'll take it."

But as they separated to talk to Alfred about the arrangements I couldn't quite share their smiles. I turned my eyes to the window and the woods.

* * *

The morning of the move, I was up at dawn. Most of the furniture was already gone. I sat at a folding table in the kitchen, waiting for my kids, and shocked myself when I glanced down at my hands curled in my lap. Years ago I had picked up a staph infection in my right thumb. The thumbnail blackened and fell off, but it grew back thicker and stronger. That morning it looked yellow and clawlike, my skin dingy and somehow fake. Like my hand was made of wax.

But all that is analysis, explanation. When I saw my fingers clasped in my lap that morning, my immediate thought was: *They look like the hands of a corpse posed in a casket.*

I remember reading somewhere that old age is like visiting another country and that you enjoy it more if you prepare. But how can you prepare for this? Okay—financially, sure. Legally, architecturally—sure. Updated wills and wider doors and shower bars. But emotionally? Spiritually? Intellectually? I have no idea how to do that, and I crossed the border into this country a while ago. Nothing can prepare one for this. It is simply perseverance. Or maybe stubbornness. Finding motivation to get up every morning despite the fact that no one really cares what I do once I'm up. So long as I don't die or otherwise cause trouble.

And this country, I was traveling through it quite alone. That day, for the first time in my adult life, I was moving without my husband, leaving behind the last home we made together, going alone into the future. At least Cal had had me.

But had he?

I pushed myself up and paced, leaning on my cane, overcome. He'd died six years ago, and still I wondered. Had I been present enough? Had we had the sort of heartfelt discussions we should have had? It always seemed one or the other of us wasn't ready. On the few occasions he seemed like he was wading into deep emotional waters, I would change the subject or busy myself with some pragmatic concern. He'd do the same when I was the one who initiated. I remember years ago, when I was getting ready to go in for surgery—removal of a benign lump after a breast cancer scare. He held me by the shoulders and searched my face with such profound tenderness in his gray eyes. But when I put a hand to his cheek and asked what he was thinking, he moved his head just a little, and said, "Nothing, sweetie. Nothing at all. Just wondering where I should take you for dinner on Friday." Then he took my hand from his cheek and gently kissed the inside of my wrist.

Maybe that was our way of talking: that look, my hand on his cheek. We were married more than fifty years.

Besides, I told myself, if I needed assurance of his inner romantic, I could always read his love letters—a few precious souvenirs from when we were courting.

Our letters!

Oh God, our letters! Where were they?

I hobbled to the bedroom. Next to the master bath was a walk-in closet where I was pretty sure they were stashed with other mementos, on a high shelf.

The letters were intimate, private. Erotic. For me, they represented the secret garden, the time when Cal and I had allowed ourselves to be young and lusty and foolish and vulnerable and sentimental. We were both too pragmatic, too much children of hard times, to let those qualities—or at least the romantic words—seep into our day to day. But once upon a time, when we had exchanged our letters . . .

Now Charlie and Iris were going to be packing everything up, sorting through those boxes. I hadn't decided whether I'd destroy the letters or leave them to be read by our kids after I was gone, but while I still breathed, there was no way I would allow anyone else to see them. Or even know they existed.

I looked around, considering options. The high shelves that had offered secrecy were a hindrance now. Then I remembered. After a near mishap on a stepladder a couple years ago, I'd purchased one of those can-grabber thingies, basically a wand with a retractable claw on the end, to help reach over my head. The phone rang, but I didn't have time to attend to it now.

The answering machine clicked, and there was Charlie's deep voice. "Mom? Everything good? I just picked up Iris, and we're heading over. Moving day! Are you excited?"

That meant I had only fifteen minutes. I looked behind a stack of plastic bins into which Iris had begun packing sheets and towels. Leaning against the wall was the grabber wand.

Okay, great. I'd found the thing I needed to help me reach the thing I really wanted to get. Now, where was the decorated box that held the letters? I scanned the shelves. It was there, somewhere.

The phone rang again, and again Charlie's voice was on the machine. "Oh, I forgot to tell you. Pam made a coffee cake for us. We can have it in your new kitchen! Be there soon."

I spotted a tiny trail of blue velvet, tied around a box wedged behind a plastic garbage bag stuffed with blankets. Carefully leaning against the wall, I raised the grabber over my head. I managed to hook the bag of blankets and pull it down. It landed with a thump on top of the bins Iris was already filling with bedding. Now I could see the box more clearly. Stretching my arm practically out of its socket, I caught a loop of the blue ribbon, and the box came tumbling. The lid was knocked askew and papers and pictures—and the precious letters—spilled in a slippery avalanche to the floor. I caught a distant whiff of the perfume they'd been dabbed with, Evening in Paris, which I had thought was the height of sophistication when I was twenty-three. I bent to scoop them up.

Below them were photos.

There sat I, holding baby Iris while Charlie played in the sprinkler.

And there was Cal, handsome in his wedding suit, his dark hair shiny with Brylcreem.

There was the farm where I grew up, so long ago now, pale specks of snow flying across the black and white landscape, fading at the edges. I closed my eyes and saw the long empty road, the wind blowing tendrils of new snow sideways across pitted gravel. My woolen scarf stiffened with my breath. My cousin Ruthie and my dad walked next to me. The sky, low and colorless; the field stubble brown, dusted with frost. My dad touched my shoulder. He was pointing. Down the road, a moose emerged out of the ditch. The powerful haunches and the swooping antlers dignified the ridiculous humpy body. The huge bull plodded in our direction. At thirty feet away he lifted his enormous head, saw us, and loped off.

I blinked through tears. My grandkids would never see that place, of course. It seemed impossible that something so solid could be wiped away in a generation—the winter-locked farm, stars frozen in nighttime skies so frigid no moisture could obscure their glow; the summertime shimmer of northern lights, the root cellar, the milk house, the emptiness, the cold. My God, the cold! The calf I raised, and then we sold it. The melty taste of baby potatoes newly dug, cooked within minutes of being in the ground. And the sweet corn!

I realized I hadn't eaten.

I opened my eyes and took a look around my disheveled bedroom. A small flutter filled my chest. It was my heart, a fist-sized clutch of muscle, registering . . . what? Trying, despite all ridiculousness, to find a smidgeon of excitement about a new place? Or was the flutter simply what happens, the way the body marks the moment when one has to let go, and grief is replaced with resignation?

I heard the elevator in the hallway. Charlie and Iris would arrive any moment. I bundled the photos and letters into the box and hugged it to my chest, ready to carry them with me to my new home.

2

IT WAS TWO weeks into my life at Ridgewood, but I really wasn't getting to know my fellow residents. However, I was becoming acquainted with some of the aides. Jannah, with a hint of the Caribbean in her speech, was friendly and helpful but aloof, and diminutive Graciela, who always offered a warm smile as she distributed the meds at night, were my favorites. They reminded me of myself when I was young and working my way through nursing school.

But mostly I kept myself to myself—a fact that drove Charlie crazy. "Mom, socializing is one of the reasons you moved here," he reminded me.

Charlie and Pam and Adam and Danny had stopped by, bearing take-out burgers and offerings of my particular weakness, French fries.

"No, socializing is one of the reasons *you* said I needed to move here," I corrected. But I realized his gentle nagging explained the French fries, because Charlie was usually the one to remind me I was not supposed to have them. The salty, crispy deliciousness was meant to keep me from noting his ulterior motive of checking on me. It was working.

As if he read my thoughts, seven-year-old Adam lifted two fries stuck together. "Here grandma! This one is extra good." He poked it in my mouth, smearing my cheek with ketchup. I laughed and stole another one from his pile. I said, "Besides, who needs old people when I can have visits from these two goofballs?" and brushed Adam's hair away from his face. Eleven-year-old Danny, whose adolescence was flickering into view, rolled his eyes. But he did it with affection.

Charlie shook his head indulgently. "C'mon mom. You need to learn to play with people your own age." He wiped his mouth, and swallowed. "I mean, at least make an effort. It'll be good for you to get to know people. You'll be happier here."

And that, of course, was the sticking spot. In some childish spot deep within me, I didn't *want* to be happier at Ridgewood. But I knew he had a point, as loathe as I was to admit it. I exhaled. "I know. You're right." I looked at Adam and Danny. "But can we not talk about it now? I'd much prefer a game of Sorry."

I could tell Charlie wanted to pursue it, but Pam, bless her, piped up and said, "Yes, let's play. I think a game is a great idea." Charlie lifted his eyebrows at his wife, but I smiled at her gratefully. Being a daughter-in-law can be a challenge, and I appreciated her diplomatic intervention on my account.

Toward the end of the third game, the boys started to bicker, and when Adam insisted on getting a new card because he didn't like the one he drew, it was clear it was time to go home.

Charlie stayed behind as Pam headed out to the car with the kids. He shrugged into his jacket, and stood, peering down at me, his expression oscillating between exasperation and affection. I tilted my head, waiting for him to speak.

Finally I said, "Thanks for coming. And thanks for the burgers."

He put his hands on my shoulders. "You know, you might enjoy it if you let yourself."

I dropped my gaze and nodded. "I know."

"Promise me you'll make the effort?"

I faced him, and seeing the wry, "come on, Mom" expression on his face, I couldn't help but smile. He was right.

"I will." I said. "I promise."

He bent and kissed my cheek, then whispered, laughingly, "Don't think I didn't notice that you didn't say how or when . . ." He straightened, winked at me, and headed out to the lobby.

* * *

According to the aides, the library was the best place to meet my neighbors. So I began going there to write letters and read the news. I thought it would be a good way to put my toe in the water and meet people without having to make a huge commitment.

I wrote about it in a letter to my cousin Ruthie:

> So far I have met the retired bank executive who resents how his kids moved him to their neighborhood rather than finding him a place in Chicago, and the pixie couple who look like they sprang from a Beatrix Potter book. Then there's the well-traveled pair who makes sure everyone knows which port of call her jewelry comes from. To tell you the truth, I am not so crazy about these people, but going to the library to read the paper gives structure to my day. I even looked into joining the book group. I know you are probably laughing at that, since you have been nagging me to join one for ten years . . .

My prediction that I would run into my kid's former teachers came true. One morning at the library, I saw Charlie's middle school math teacher. Sad to say, she was still wearing the unfortunate baggy dresses, appliqued with cats or owls, she had sported in the classroom.

"Well, hello! Mrs. Wildmer, isn't it?" I greeted her cheerfully, but her blank expression masking panic told me she had no idea who I was. I smiled. "I'm Francine Greene. You taught my son."

She nodded vaguely. "Um, yes, of course. Nice to see you." It didn't bother me that she didn't remember. Teachers must have to navigate running into hundreds of parents whom they met once or twice during open houses or parent–teacher meetings years ago. Plus, judging by the way the staff interacted with her, I think in Mrs. Wildmer's case that natural tendency might have been exacerbated by memory issues.

On the way to drop the letter to Ruth in the lobby mailbox, I walked past the music room. I heard Mozart's Rondo Alla Turca, confident and note perfect, flowing into the hall. I was flooded with the memory of Iris playing it for her recitals. I looked in. Perched at the piano bench, in textbook performing posture, wrists relaxed, shoulders down, sat a man in plaid shorts and a pink shirt, his skinny legs ending in—what else?—socks and sandals. I tiptoed to a bench inside, letting the memories flow and eddy with the music.

"Do you play?"

I opened my eyes and focused. The pianist was speaking to me. He had pale eyes behind big glasses and a few wisps of colorless hair breaking over his ears. I cleared my throat. "Ah, well. Not exactly. I did a little when I was young, but . . ." I stopped myself. This man didn't need to know how devastated little ten-year-old me had been when my parents sold our piano. I shrugged. "My kids took lessons, and my daughter was quite good. In fact, she used to perform that piece."

"Yes, it's a common piece for beginners," he said dismissively. "I use it to warm up."

I smiled politely and was about to say, "By all means, don't let me stop you," when something passed over his face—was it wistfulness?—and he said, "I wanted to be a professional, but my daddy put a stop to that. Especially after I found jazz." He sniffed. "Good thing too. Saved me from a life spent in nightclubs."

Why did talent so often come packaged with unpleasantness? I cleared my throat. "Well, you play very well."

"Thank you. I try to practice every day. But we only have a baby grand, and our living room isn't quite large enough for the sound to linger."

"You have your own grand piano?

"A baby grand. Like I said. Even though we have one of the largest apartments—up on the top floor—we had to get rid of the big piano when we moved." The way he said it: some sort of signal.

Oh. Of course. He was well off, and I was supposed to be impressed. Just like every other community, Ridgewood had hierarchies some people were very invested in reinforcing. This guy may have had musical talent, but he was tone deaf when it came to people.

He sounded a few more bars. "I like playing here better." He tilted his chin toward the tall ceiling and the windows framing views of the preserve. "Better acoustics." But I got the feeling what he enjoyed most was the chance for an audience. I felt an unpleasant prick of recognition, like glimpsing a half-forgotten, disliked acquaintance from long ago.

Graciela appeared in the door. "Sir," she spoke in her kind voice, "Your daughter is here." She approached the piano. "Can I help you to the lobby?"

He bristled at her offer, though as he strained to get off the bench, it was obvious he needed her hand at his elbow. When he was finally upright, he seemed somehow familiar. But no. All old men look the same: narrow shoulders, collapsing ribcages, thin hair.

I stood as well. "Thank you for the Mozart."

He nodded in so courtly a manner that I almost pictured him tipping a hat. "Thank you for listening." Graciela smiled at me before she walked with him out the other door, into the hall. She may have been tiny, but she was obviously strong and capable.

When I was sure they were gone, I took a seat at the piano, lightly touching the keys. I remembered my fantasies of a concert hall full of people rising to applaud me after I

mastered the beginner's version of Beethoven's "Für Elise."
Slowly, softly, I stroked those notes, which I still found
beautiful after all these years. After I'd grown up and knew
what it was to owe a mortgage and not have enough money,
I understood why my folks sold our beautiful piano. But
understanding hadn't erased the loss. I'd been thrilled when
Iris had taken so well to her lessons. While she practiced, I
would stand in the kitchen, ostensibly making dinner, but
really just listening. Bethany was even better, with a beautiful touch and sense of musicianship.

I picked my way through "Für Elise" as quietly as I could,
in her honor.

*　　*　　*

The next day I made a point of passing by the music room
on my way to the library. He was playing again, and again
I ducked in and listened. It was jazz this time. He bent over
the keyboard with eyes half closed, the light glinting off his
scalp through thin hair. After the last note rang to nothing,
he turned to me, as if he'd known I was there all along. "As I
said, I am especially fond of jazz."

"I don't know much about jazz, I'm afraid. But that
sounded familiar."

"Marty Paich. I doubt you've heard of him."

I replied evenly, "Well. You clearly know your way
around a keyboard. I'm Francine Greene, by the way."

He seemed about to answer when someone spoke.
"Nathaniel?"

I turned and saw an elegant woman in a blue linen tunic
smiling in the doorway. "Am I interrupting?"

His face softened when he looked at her. "Of course not,
my dear. I was just practicing."

She beamed at the man I assumed was her husband. "It
was lovely."

I cleared my throat. "Yes, it was indeed." And because I
didn't want his wife to think I had some sort of interest in

him—one hears about ridiculous late-life dalliances in places like this—I leaned on my cane and walked over to introduce myself. "I'm Frannie Greene. I happened to be passing and couldn't resist stopping to listen."

She offered a neatly manicured hand. "I'm Katherine. Nice to meet you."

In the awkward silence that followed, I noticed she was holding a book I knew. "Did you enjoy that? P. D. James is one of my favorites."

"Oh yes. Very much. In fact, I was just heading to the library to get another."

"Me too, until I got distracted by the music." Then, because it seemed rude not to, and because there was something about her that I liked, I added, "Should we walk together?"

Katherine looked to her husband, a question in her eyes.

"Yes, go ahead," he said. "I'm happy to keep playing a bit longer."

"Are you sure, dear?"

I was surprised. It was almost as if she was asking her husband's permission. Haughty as he was, would he really object to his wife visiting the library without him?

Then I chided myself. Who knew what they'd been through together? Maybe one of them tended toward confusion or unsteadiness, and relied on the other. Old wine in old bottles sometimes needs special tending. Lord knows if Cal had survived, I might have been just as solicitous of him, and I am not a particularly solicitous woman.

Katherine and I made our way down the hall. It was slow progress: I was no speed demon since my falls, but within a few minutes it became clear she was having difficulty.

"I think I might be coming down with something," she said finally. "I guess I should have used my walker today." She placed one foot deliberately in front of the other.

Since moving into Ridgewood, I had come to understand why the hallways were punctuated with upholstered benches. "Here, let's sit," I said. "I could use a breather."

She eased herself down. "It is kind of you to pretend." She dabbed her nose. Her nail polish was pearlescent, as tasteful and feminine as the rest of her. "I think I might be catching that cold that's going around. My heart is not good, so I need to be careful. Normally I'm not quite this slow." She drew a breath, pressing her left hand under her diaphragm. I could see the strain. Without thinking about it I reached out and wrapped my fingers around her right wrist, and looked at my watch.

She startled, then relaxed her arm. "Well. I guess I know what you did for a living."

I pulled back. "Oh! I'm so sorry. Second nature I guess. Please forgive me." I couldn't believe I had done that. And that gesture? That old-school pulse taking?

She patted my hand. "Not at all. It's good to know there's someone I can ask about medical things. How long were you a nurse?"

Iris would get upset at that. She'd remind me that I could just as easily have been a doctor, and that if I'd been a man, people wouldn't assume I was a nurse.

I gave a half laugh. "I have a checkered history. Started as a nurse, worked for a few years, and then went to medical school."

A spark of special admiration lit her eyes. Medical school is always a big deal, even now, but for women of our age? I cut her off before she could say anything else. "But then I got pregnant."

She knew what that meant too.

I went on, "It was just too much. Not that I'm complaining. I have two great kids." I always make sure to say that. If there is such a thing as karma, I don't want the universe to get the idea that I regret Iris or Charlie. "I went back to nursing—ended up in charge of surgical nursing at my hospital. So I can't complain."

"I'm impressed. A mom and a professional. People nowadays don't know how hard that was. Not that it's easy now, but when we were young?"

"No kidding. How about you? Did you work—outside your home, I mean?"

"Only a little. I was an interior designer when I met Nathaniel. I tried for a bit, but then his daughter came to live with us, and . . ." She broke off. "His work required a lot of entertaining. I couldn't keep up." Her voice grew pensive. "I often wonder if I should have tried harder." She folded her hands.. "I don't regret it. But I do admire women who found a way."

She seemed lost in thought. To summon her back I asked, "So you have a daughter?"

"Lisa is Nathaniel's child from his first marriage. She came to us when she was ten."

"That must have brought some challenges."

She looked at me with surprise, then spread her hands. "Lisa is great. But it wasn't easy. Nathaniel didn't always know how to deal with his daughter." She tilted her head. "Have you ever met anyone who is a 'one person' person? I don't mean romantically, necessarily. And not because of shyness either . . . Nathaniel isn't reserved in that way. I mean, someone who really only connects with one person emotionally?"

I nodded.

"Nathaniel is like that. When we were first together, it was flattering. But I didn't realize till later that it was a lot of responsibility, how much he relied on me. So when Lisa came along . . ." She fiddled with an expensive-looking bracelet as she let the sentence hang. "Not that he wasn't a good father. He went to soccer games and teacher conferences and all that dad stuff. " She broke off again and looked at me seriously. "This is going to sound silly, perhaps. But my word for it is that he never developed 'heartstrings' with her." Katherine had a slight Southern lilt to her speech, and the way she said it, the word was exactly, perfectly right.

"I've seen it," I said. "A person gets so deeply attached to someone, it takes up all their emotional room."

She leaned back a little. "That's it. You understand." I got the distinct impression she was used to this, to having to explain her husband's lack of social graces or apparent empathy.

Poor Katherine. There is such a thing as being loved too much. And the poor daughter. I could imagine what this meant to a child from an earlier marriage. The kid must've felt twice abandoned.

"So, you had to deal with a daughter who arrived as a preteen?"

She laughed. "Well, when you put it that way, I guess the arguments we had made sense. Lisa was a nice kid, but she needed stability. Her mom was a beauty queen who couldn't stay married. One of those 'in-love-with-love' types. She was on her third marriage when Lisa came to us. It was tough at first. But we eventually figured it out. I think she appreciated the fact that she could yell at me, and I wouldn't melt down or stop caring. By the time she left for college, we were close."

I risked an almost rude question. "Was Nathaniel jealous of your closeness?"

She turned, surprise in her eyes. "I used to feel like that sometimes. How did you know?"

"It isn't so unusual really, a man being jealous of sharing his wife's affection with a child."

She smiled. "I bet you were a good nurse. You're very perceptive." She sat up straight and patted my hand. "But I'm keeping you. The library closes at four, and at my speed, you'll get there by midnight."

"No worries. I was just going to put my name down for the book group discussion tomorrow. I've read the book, so even if I just show up, I doubt they'll turn me away."

"Well, if they do, I will help you storm the gates. I was planning on going myself."

"I'm glad to hear that," I said, and meant it. I hadn't met anyone I genuinely liked in a while. "We can go together."

She smiled and then moved her head to look behind me. I followed her gaze and saw Jannah striding purposefully toward our bench. There were little pink elephants printed on her scrub jacket.

"There you are! Your husband was worried." She smiled at Katherine. "Everything all right?"

Katherine nodded. "Yes. Thank you. But I think I'm ready to go home." She turned to me. "Thank you so much, Frannie, for letting me interrupt your plans." Jannah helped her to her feet.

I pushed against my cane and stood as well. "My pleasure. I got to hear your husband play and talk with you. I don't know how much more activity I could handle in one day."

Katherine lifted an eyebrow and said, "Right. If we don't pace ourselves we'll be overwhelmed with all the excitement." Both Jannah and I laughed.

On the phone with Iris that night, I reported that I'd made a new friend. As I described my afternoon, it occurred to me that it was sort of an inversion: the flip side of the way Iris used to tell me about her day when I drove her home from grade school. But I didn't care. It energized me that even at my age I could connect with someone new. I was alive and in possession of my faculties. It seemed like I owed it to Cal and Bethany to actually live.

3

I HADN'T HAD THE nightmare for almost a year, but that night it descended again.

I am trying to rush to the hospital after the phone call, but I'm strapped into my family's old tractor, a 1940 John Deere. The beast heaves along and I am desperate to make it go faster, but I can't remember how to work the clutch, and I keep stalling. I see the hospital, but as I approach, the tractor lurches and sways, and there are headlamps bearing down and horns blaring. This is where I wake up, sweating, chest heaving.

I knew it was pointless to try to go back to sleep. I rose and wrapped Cal's old bathrobe around me and sat staring out the window into the dark. *Stop it,* I told myself. *It is time to move on.*

The same words I had said to Iris, after which I almost lost her.

As dawn broke, I had my usual talk with the ghosts. Convincing them to leave me alone. I knew, of course, that they wouldn't. I didn't really want them to. It was one of the darkest threads woven into the fabric of my life, and that of my family, and as much as I wished it hadn't happened, I had to accept the pain as part of my memories. In the four years since Bethany was killed, I had learned how to cope, but every so often it emerged, prickly and sharp, and I was forced to relive it in painful detail.

But I had to regain my balance. This morning I really didn't want to be swamped with sadness, or anger. I wanted to cultivate the possibility floating around the periphery of my new life. I had met someone I enjoyed talking to. I had something to do that morning, and what's more, I almost looked forward to it. I long ago learned that part of living through the pain was simply keeping on. One had to act as if one had forgotten, even if the memories were always crouched in the background, ready to ambush.

I made myself eat a piece of toast. Then I located my copy of *Shroud for a Nightingale* and sipped my coffee as I paged through it. I hadn't lied to Katherine. I had indeed read the book. What I hadn't said was that it had been a year ago, and I remembered very little. I skimmed through it as I sipped my dark roast, so that I would at least know the main character's names, and considered how I might bluff my way through a discussion. I marveled at the fact that I actually cared.

I pulled out my nice red sweater that complemented the shade of my favorite lipstick. I was going to do as much as I could, even here. I would not sit and wait to die. I was going to view the library and the exercise room and the music room, not as reminders of my former self, cynically placed here to manipulate or fool us oldsters, but as harbingers of possibility. Life demands that we live.

*   *   *

The Ridgewood Library was a large room with wide French doors overlooking a garden. Tall bookshelves flanked the windows. A folding display easel was set up near the door. On it, a bulletin board proclaimed the "book of the week," with pictures of the cover and "fun facts" related to books and writers. It announced the *Shroud for a Nightingale* book discussion, and asked, "Guess which Shakespeare plays also contain mentions of nightingales?" Not for the first time, I noticed certain similarities between Ridgewood and a middle school.

I saw a group of people sitting expectantly around an oblong table. A paper in the center of it was folded into a tented sign saying "Book Group." Katherine was not there, but several other residents were seated.

I hesitated. Suddenly joining the small group seemed such a foreign notion. So not-me. But then the activities director, a woman named Marta, noticed me. Marta had the sunny no-nonsense demeanor of a sixth grade gym instructor. She said, "Ms. Greene, I'm so happy to see you. Please, take a seat." She patted the back of a chair.

Well, then. I had told Charlie I would participate, and here I was. I nodded at the others sitting at the table. Marta kept checking her clipboard and looking hopefully at the door for more comers. The woman next to me, with spiky hair, gave a broad smile and extended her left hand in an awkward gesture. Something about the way she held her body told me she didn't move her right side very easily.

"Hi. I'm Geri." She nodded at the man to her left. "This is Evan. And that's Lottie at the end."

Evan had thick silver hair, luxuriant and wavy. It was conspicuous in a place where almost all the men and even some of the women were balding. He half stood, in an attempt to be courtly, and shook my hand as he repeated his name, "Evan Landrum. Nice to meet you. Welcome to our literary club."

"Such as it is," added Lottie tartly. To me she raised an eyebrow. "I'm not sure mysteries count as literature."

"Lottie has higher standards than the rest of us," Geri interjected, smiling. "She is a former English professor." She said it with sarcasm, but also affection.

I wasn't sure how to respond. "I always understood P. D. James was quite respected as a writer."

Lottie tilted her head. "Being considered a decent mystery writer is not the same as writing literature." She shrugged. "But I'll concede her prose operates at a higher level than most." Something about the spark in her eyes as she said this made me think she was playing a part. Lottie was from the tribe of older women who will not be ignored: her membership declared by oversized glasses with geometric frames, the slice of magenta streaking her curly hair, and a necklace that the magazines in my doctor's office would describe as "chunky."

At that moment Katherine pushed her walker into the room. In contrast with Lottie's flamboyant panache, she was elegant and understated in an expensive-looking lavender sweater, with her white hair perfectly in place. She smiled at everyone, and Marta brightened. "I'm so glad you could make it."

After Katherine took her seat, we got started. Marta began by asking a few general questions, and bit by bit my tablemates started dissecting the book. Lottie had a lot to say.

"I thought the style was a little dry. It all feels very 'British,' if you know what I mean." She crooked her fingers in air quotes. "It's all very well done of course, but I prefer more muscular, inventive prose. Give me some Elmore Leonard or Sara Paretsky any day."

I looked at her, surprised. She met my gaze, raised her eyebrow with a glint of humor. "Just because I love my Shakespeare and Harding doesn't mean I can't enjoy an entertaining potboiler." Then she smiled at me. I decided to like her. She was slippery and unpredictable and entertaining.

As the conversation unfolded, the plot began to glimmer into memory. Thank goodness. But because the mystery centered on a student nurse in a training hospital who had been 'playing the patient,' and ended up dead, I was afraid Marta or Katherine, both of whom knew my background, would ask me about the procedure in question and expose my faulty knowledge of the book. I was so distracted by trying to formulate a response to their imaginary questions that I didn't realize at first that Evan was talking to me.

They were all looking at me, in fact. "Um, sorry. Could you repeat that?"

Evan said, "So, who did you think did it? Did you figure it out before Dalgliesh?" Thank goodness, he reminded me of the detective's name.

Then I saw my profession could also be a good excuse. I cleared my throat. "You know, as a former nurse, I was so interested in the picture she painted of the training system, I'm afraid I wasn't as focused on trying to figure out 'who-dunit.' Besides, I'm not usually very good at that anyway."

Katherine asked, "Evan, did you know who the killer was?"

He tapped his copy of the book. "I wasn't sure. But as I crossed people off my list, she became one of my top choices."

"Really?" Lottie interjected. "Do you usually do that? Try to read between the lines for clues, that sort of thing?"

Evan opened his hands. "I guess it's silly, since the author isn't about to give the game away. But I can't help it." He shrugged in an almost charming gesture. "I've been part of a lot of investigations in my time. I guess I have a suspicious mind."

What an odd way to put it: part of a lot of investigations? I wondered what and how he investigated. I was certain he wasn't a former cop. A journalist maybe? A lawyer? I was about to ask when Geri spoke: "I don't even try. They always throw in red herrings or withhold key information anyway, so it ends up making me angry. I enjoy it more if I just go along for the ride."

This topic drew a lot of comments, and our discussion turned from the story at hand to descriptions of the way each of us approached different kinds of books. Eventually the conversation wound down, and even Marta ran out of questions and prompts. She snapped the book shut, and said, "Well now. That was excellent, I thought." She stood. "Remember, our next book is by another English writer, Dick Francis."

We slowly filed out of the library. I had to admit, I'd enjoyed it.

Katherine joined me at the door. "If we head to the dining room now, we can be sure to get the pie before it runs out. What do you think?"

I pulled myself up short. "Did you say 'pie'?"

She laughed. "I forgot, you don't usually have lunch in the dining room, do you? Wednesday is pie day. You know the Oak Street Bakery? The owner's mom lives here. He always delivers some cherry pie on Wednesdays, but they usually run out." She smiled conspiratorially. "Nathaniel has to watch his blood sugar, so I try not to eat too many sweets around him. But I do love pie."

It sounded delicious, and I was hungry. "But will Nathaniel mind?" My guess was that he relied on her utterly for many things, and also that she completely conceded to his whims.

"He isn't here. He's visiting his brother in Springfield this week."

"Springfield! He's well enough to travel?"

She rolled her eyes in disapproval. "Nathaniel and his brother have this yearly thing they do. It used to be swimming and running a 5K, then it was golf tournaments, now it's chess. Honestly, it's like they're ten year-old boys. Everything is a competition. I tried to talk him out of it. But he wouldn't hear of it. I swear if he were on his deathbed he'd rouse himself to go. Especially since to him not going would mean his brother had won. Ugh! I think it's so silly, at this age. I keep trying to get them to call it off, but to no avail."

"You didn't want to go along?"

"It's all about them. I never go. Even when we host, I just stay in the background."

Her husband was apparently even more stubborn and imperious than I'd thought. I was almost impressed. "So he's traveling alone?"

"His daughter, Lisa, is with him. His brother has a daughter Lisa's age, and they've always been close, so she gets a chance to visit her cousin."

We had reached the elevator. Katherine said, "So. Will you join me?"

"Sure. To think all these weeks I've been missing pie. I have some catching up to do."

When we entered the dining room, Katherine beelined for the center table. It had the nicest view of the pond outside and was best positioned to flag down the staff. She claimed a spot without hesitation and stood behind the chair smiling at the server, a gawky teenager, who, after a second or two, understood what she wanted and hurried over to pull it out for her. Feeling very self-conscious, I rushed to sit before he got to my chair. After we'd ordered and the server turned toward the kitchen, Katherine called him back. "Oh, and please put aside two of the biggest slices of pie for us? And whipped cream as well. Thank you, Michael."

The young man nodded and hurried away.

I'd had Katherine pegged as a shrinking violet, but in this circumstance she embraced a sense of authority. She did it graciously, but she was definitely comfortable giving orders. I, on the other hand, was not used to these sorts of hierarchies. One of the biggest challenges I'd had in Ridgewood was talking with the staff. I didn't know what was appropriate. The aides didn't work directly for the residents, but still, they took care of us: personally, intimately. And I knew I would sometime need to make demands, but the lines felt blurry to me.

I ventured, "You do that so easily."

"What? Oh, you mean . . ." She lifted her chin at the server, now on the other side of the room. "I learned the best way is to be clear and direct. Nathaniel had high-profile cases, even when he was a young lawyer, so we could afford help. He insisted on it, actually. Not that I minded. I preferred to focus on other things—Lisa and volunteer commitments.

For years I was the biggest fundraiser for the Junior League. It was a lot of work."

So her husband was a lawyer. No wonder I hadn't liked him. "What were some of his high-profile cases?"

Faint pink washed her cheeks. "You're going to think I'm terrible. But the truth is we never talked about his work."

"Really? Never?"

"He always said he wanted his home to be a respite from the world. And that's always been fine with me."

"But weren't you curious?"

"He dealt with people at terrible moments. Acrimonious divorces, contested wills, and then, later, criminals. You can't imagine how nasty it all got. So we decided there was enough ugliness in the world without inviting it into our home." She fiddled with her ring. It appeared to be set with a diamond and several emeralds. It glittered and caught the light.

4

THE NEXT MORNING there was a knock at my door. I had just gotten off my morning phone call with Iris, and Charlie, who worked at a small engineering firm, almost never dropped by on a weekday, so I was surprised. I opened it slowly, and there stood Katherine. She held out a giant streusel-topped muffin. "Lisa dropped some of these by last night. I thought you might enjoy one." She smiled. "Hopefully, you won't hold it against me, luring you into temptation with more goodies from the bakery."

I laughed. "Hold it against you? Are you kidding? So long as you don't tell my doctor." I pulled open the door. "In fact, I just made coffee. Come in and join me."

As she settled onto one of the stools by the counter that separated my kitchen from my living room, I quartered the enormous muffin and set it out on a small plate. Then I handed her a cup of coffee.

"Oh this smells good." She looked at me over the rim of her cup. "I'll keep quiet about the muffin if you don't tell Nathaniel or Lisa about the coffee. I'm not supposed to have it."

I had recently made a partial concession in that regard on the insistence of my own doctor. I said, "Does it make it better knowing it is half decaffeinated?"

She sipped. "Sort of. But it's kind of fun breaking the rules. I get tired of having to be so careful all the time. When I was younger, I could eat whatever I wanted, and even if it was unhealthy, nobody policed me."

"I hear you. It's one of my biggest annoyances with my kids. Iris is always, 'Mom, don't eat this, don't lift that.' . . . So tiresome. Makes me want to eat onion rings covered in cheese and salt just to prove I can." I raised my mug and clinked hers. "Here's to transgression."

That's when the alarm went off on my phone. I blushed, reaching to turn it off.

"Do you have something going on?" She stood. "I apologize for just stopping by. Don't let me interrupt your plans."

I shook my head, tucking my phone in my pocket, and gestured for her to sit. "Oh no. I just . . ." I glanced at the living room, feeling suddenly open. "Well, speaking of transgressions, would you be interested in joining me . . ." I lost my nerve. I felt myself blush.

She looked at me peculiarly and glanced from her watch to the television. Then she beamed. "Oh my goodness, you too?" She lifted her eyebrows. "So, do you think Summer will end up sleeping with Kyle?"

She had guessed it, my guilty pleasure: *The Young and the Restless*.

I sighed. "It started while I was in rehab for my knee. My roommate insisted on watching it. At first I turned my nose up—I always thought soap operas were so ridiculous. But by the end of the first week, I was hooked." I picked at the muffin, feeling sheepish. "It's so silly."

She waved my embarrassment away. "Oh please. I've been watching it for years. Back when Lisa was young, everyone I knew watched it. You were a career woman, so it just took you a little longer to get hooked on the adventures of Nikki and the Abbots and the whole town. And besides, is it really that different from following some of those costume dramas on cable?" She slid off her stool and looked at the television in my living room. "Let's watch together. It's about to start."

*   *   *

That week Katherine and I ate lunch together nearly every day, and I got a fuller picture of her life. We were from completely different worlds. She grew up as the pampered daughter of a wealthy Savannah banker, and became the cosseted wife of a judge, with a housekeeper and gardener. I grew up milking cows on a farm in North Dakota, where there was never enough money, and the idea of household help would have been unimaginable. Deep in my heart of hearts, I've always looked down on women like Katherine, an attitude I'm not particularly proud of, but still. Maybe I was getting more open in my old age. Or maybe I was more lonesome than I'd realized. She fascinated me: she was the real deal, a bona-fide, drawling, Southern debutante. Gracious and well mannered, she was capable of letting someone know when they weren't up to standard with a raised eyebrow and a tone that was simultaneously dismissive and disappointed. She occupied her place in the world with a rock-solid certainty about the way "things should be." She reminded me of some of the privileged characters on the soap operas.

Both of us were early risers, and we began meeting in the lobby for a morning stroll around the halls or the sidewalk that encircled the parking lot. It was lined with trees and plantings, and if the weather was nice, it was a great way to start the day. Perhaps because we were old, we spent a lot of time talking about when we were young.

She told me about the first time she'd ever seen snow, or at least experienced enough of it to try to make angels. "I was fifteen. I was at the youth group in my church, which met in the basement. When we came out, it was early evening and the light was bluish purple, and the air was sparkly and full of glitter, like in a movie. It felt like magic." Her eyes shone. "At the time, I was trying to impress a boy in the choir with my sophistication, but we all ran around like excited children, sticking our tongues out, trying to taste a snowflake. I was jealous of my friend who wore glasses, because she could tip her face upward and watch them melt on her lenses, while I couldn't stop blinking as the flakes hit my eyes." She turned, her face aglow with remembered delight. Then she became self-conscious. "That must sound ridiculous to someone like you, who grew up with snow."

I lifted my chin, memories of my own flooding my mind. "To tell you the truth, the first snow is always a little magical." Suddenly my heart was in my throat, and it was late afternoon and the shadows were stretching violet across the fields, and the whole world felt like it was holding its breath, full of mystery and hush as the first flakes landed softly on my cheeks. I swallowed. "That first snowfall, especially the slow, sparkling kind—not the kind we sometimes got, where it felt like the sky was throwing bullets of ice at you, but the lovely soft soundless kind . . ." I paused, suffused with a sort of empty longing. "Well, even us northerners are not immune to a world full of glitter."

For a moment the emotion of those recollections hung in the air, its own kind of precipitation. We took a few more steps, letting it condense and settle. When I felt recovered, I said, as if in trade, "I remember the first time I saw a magnolia. More precisely, I remember the first time I smelled a magnolia in bloom. We took a school trip to Minneapolis one year, and on the University of Minnesota campus was the first hybrid that could survive the cold. I guess a professor there developed it. Generations of horticulture students have kept it going."

"They're marvelous trees, aren't they? I see a few of some type of magnolia planted around Chicago now. Must be really hard to keep them alive some winters." She tilted her head. "And of course, they're not as big or fragrant as the ones back home."

I smiled.

We walked by a lilac that had recently blossomed, and I breathed in the sweetness. "You may have had magnolias, but my house was surrounded by these." I closed my eyes and focused, trying to resist the tug of nostalgia and appreciate the here and now. I heard her inhale next to me and sigh. "Oh yes. So lovely."

I also began to understand her marriage. It was clear Nathaniel worshipped her, and the price she paid for his worship was accepting his bluster as well as adopting a—well, a certain willingness to overlook unpleasantness. He kept to his sphere and allowed her full reign in hers. It struck me as a distinctly old-fashioned and rather restrictive bargain. Then again, what did I know? The older I've gotten, the more I realize there is nothing more mysterious than a marriage.

That afternoon I wrote to Ruthie, telling her about Katherine and asking if she remembered the winter we saw the moose on the road with my dad. And asking if she ever missed the snow, now that she lived in Arizona.

* * *

For that entire week, I never saw Katherine at supper. She told me she felt uncomfortable having dinner without Nathaniel. Having lunch with a lady friend was okay apparently, but in her world, for some reason dinner was reserved for one's husband. Maybe because the attitude in the dining room seemed more formal then—some of the ladies put on jewelry and lipstick. At any rate, while Nathaniel was gone, Katherine spent evenings in their apartment. For all I knew, she indulged herself in junk food and more soap operas or reading something salacious.

Up until then, my usual habit had been to eat a late breakfast in my apartment, skip lunch, and go to dinner as soon as the dining room opened. It was why I'd never seen Katherine and Nathaniel, since they always ate late in the evening. But lunching with Katherine meant bigger midday meals, which meant I also started coming down for the evening meal later, when the dining room was more crowded.

When I'd first arrived at Ridgewood I had described my initial foray to the dining room to Ruthie by comparing it to entering a high school cafeteria. It's funny, though our school in North Dakota was so tiny we ate lunch together in the school basement, I had seen enough movies about high school with my kids and grandkids that I recognized the situation immediately, standing in the door, wondering if where I sat would affect my social standing. I chose a small table, tucked away and almost hidden by the door next to the server's stations, and very quickly came to think of this as my spot. Unlike when I ate with Katherine, who inevitably took command of the center table with aplomb, when I ate alone, I always went for my half-hidden nook. I rather enjoyed being unnoticed, discretely able to observe my fellow diners.

That's where I was a few days later when, partway through my dinner, Katherine and Nathaniel entered and slowly made their way to the center table. He must have returned early. I watched as she arranged his cane on the arm of his chair. Her back was to me, and I was about to call out a greeting, when Nathaniel gave an imperious nod and began speaking to the server hovering nearby.

Suddenly my soup, which I had been enjoying, curdled in my mouth. My heart began racing. Graciela, who just at that moment was bringing me my main course, put down the plate and rested her hand on my arm. "Are you okay?"

I stared into her dark eyes, focusing on gaining control, taking deep breaths. "Yes. I, I just . . ." I swallowed. "I'm okay."

"If you say so." Graciela looked skeptical. "But I'm right here if you need me."

I shrank further behind the door, intent on regulating my breathing. Slowly the panic subsided. I began picking at my food, telling myself I was okay.

But Graciela kept her eye on me. It was a good thing too, because just as dessert arrived, it happened again, and this time I understood—in a painful flash—what triggered the attack.

He had an accent: worn down and nearly buffed out, but evident in certain words, as unmistakable as linguistic DNA. "Thank you," he said to the server who was refreshing his decaf. "That will be adequate." He drew out the word, with Southern softness.

I jerked my head up, inhaling sharply. The noise in the dining room fell away.

Adequate.

"Your injuries are perhaps adequate in regard to limiting your freedom, but I am still sentencing you to house arrest with an ankle bracelet."

"You will participate in an adequately vetted twelve-step program . . ."

"He has been adequately punished."

It was him. Nathaniel had been the judge in the trial.

I began to shake. Everything was sucked into a swooshing whirl. Though I could see people all around me lift their glasses and clink their silverware against their plates and move their mouths in conversation, and though carts full of dishes rolled by, all I heard was the roaring inside my head. I recognized the symptoms in myself. I was in shock.

Graciela stood before me, water pitcher in hand. "Mrs. Greene? Are you all right?"

"Y-y-yes." I stammered. "Could . . . could you take me back to my room? Through the back way?" She looked at me with puzzlement. And concern.

"Please, Graciela. I can't explain. But I . . . I've had a shock, and I don't want people to gossip."

She pursed her lips and nodded. One of the things I liked about her is that she didn't treat me like some superannuated version of a child. She knew I was in my right mind and gave me credit. She knew that sometimes people have their own reasons, and it's their own business. And that folks do gossip.

She nodded and saw that I was trembling. "How about a wheelchair?" she asked. "Just to get you to your room."

She fetched a spare one they keep near the door and wheeled me through the serving station and out the back hall, so I could exit unseen by Katherine or anyone else, thank God. We didn't talk, but after we got into my apartment and I was settled on my sofa, she crouched down in front of me.

"Are you sure you're okay?"

I nodded.

"If you need anything, just call." She dipped her head to look directly into my eyes. "Promise?"

5

AFTER SHE LEFT, I steeled myself, and because I was so shaky, I used the walker from the rehab center that my kids had insisted I keep, to push over to my desk. There, in the bottom of the lowest drawer, buried as much as I could bury it, was the manila folder. I had to swallow hard before I opened it.

The clippings about the accident, and the scandal, were beginning to become brittle and yellow. I lifted them carefully. There was the picture of the car smashed into the tree. There was a photo of Bethany from her middle school yearbook, and another of her from a curtain call for that musical she was in.

Then came stories about the trial of Stinson, the man who did it. A picture of him in his wheelchair, in front of the court. And there was the name, in black and white: Judge Nathaniel Kearney. In the picture his hair was dark, and he didn't wear glasses. Grecian formula and contacts. No wonder I hadn't recognized him. It figured he was vain as well as pompous and greedy.

I remembered how he'd made such a show, performing his sympathy for Iris and Jimmy.

I sat staring out the window as the light faded. Images and sounds and words gelled into coherence as the horror unfolded in my memory, as it had so often before. A narrative constructed out of shards: what happened first, and what happened after that, and after that. All the way till the end. I always made myself remember it all the way to the end. They say stories lose their potency if they're rehashed too often, but that would not happen to this tale. Every time it washed over me, it was a stream deepening the channel.

"Ma?" I heard Charlie's fearful rasp when I answered the phone. "We're at St. Mary's. You need to come. Right away."

There was shuffling and then Jimmy was on the line. "Mom? It's Bethany and Iris. A car, it jumped the curb." Sobs in the background. "Please, you need to get down here."

I raced to my Buick, stabbing the key into the ignition. Jimmy's shaky voice reverberated, urging me to go faster. A horn blared. I careened into the parking lot.

Habit almost carried me to the staff entrance but I caught myself and ran to the ER. I barged in on a conversation between a nurse and the person staffing the desk. "They're upstairs, in surgery," the attendant said. I half ran, my body falling into the shortcuts I'd nearly forgotten, except I had to backtrack when I got to a door that required a hospital ID. I pushed through the sensation of being weighed down, like I couldn't move fast enough. Like swimming through syrup.

The elevator doors parted like a stage curtain, revealing a swarm of scrubs and lab coats. I almost collapsed in relief when I saw Iris. She seemed even taller than normal, her long brown hair piled in a bun that flopped as she nodded. Her eyes were enormous, dark mirrors fixed on the doctor who was speaking. She had a welt on her cheek, and her arm was in a sling, but otherwise she seemed okay. Jimmy, looking heartbreakingly young, had his arm around her. Charlie and Pam huddled behind them.

But where was Bethany? My heart thudded in dread.

I moved closer. I stood unnoticed, but I heard everything. Head injury. Brain bumping inside the skull. Surgery to release pressure. *Oh my God, Bethany.* Risk of blood clots. Rib and shoulder fracture, blunt force trauma to the chest. Won't know anything for a while yet. Iris swooned and collapsed against Charlie and Jimmy.

I stepped forward and cleared my throat.

"Mom!" Iris lunged toward me. She bent over to rest her head on my shoulder. She wept, just like when she was a child and she'd waited until she saw me to begin crying after some accident or hurt. Jimmy awkwardly encircled us with his arms. Charlie and Pam made another layer of hugs and bodies and tears. But it was Iris who formed the core, the gravitational center of fear and disbelief.

A young resident was talking about CAT scans, and I saw Iris wasn't taking it in. I could tell she wasn't making sense of what he was saying.

I leaned forward. "Maybe you should explain it to me."

He turned, speaking slowly. "I am so sorry. I know this is a lot. Perhaps you can take your daughter to the waiting room, and I'll talk to her husband."

Except Jimmy was in worse shape than Iris. He was crumpled on a chair fifteen feet away, his face in his hands. Charlie hovered next to him. Jimmy sobbed loudly. Iris rushed to her husband and held him, stroking his hair. They awkwardly rocked each other, perched together on the edge of the bench.

I stood up straighter. "I think you'd better give me the details."

At that moment the elevator opened. It was Sameer Gupta, the head of Neurology. "Frannie? I just heard." He hugged me. I sent a chastening glance over his shoulder at the resident. Sameer said, "I'll see what's going on and fill you in." He disappeared through the doors that separated the operating rooms from the surgical lobby.

I stood, mute, amid the squawk of call buttons and the telemetry machines receiving info from patient's rooms. Activity thrummed around me. Someone in a surgical mask came forward. I refocused. It was Sameer again. Over his shoulder I saw my daughter rush toward me. For a split second, I saw her as I would have seen the loved one of any former patient, and then—a shock like ice water—I realized the woman with the terrified eyes was my Iris, and this tragedy was my tragedy, and everyone I cared about were "the loved ones." I reeled, suddenly overwhelmed. Sameer reached out to steady me.

"Frannie, take a breath." He spoke in a low voice with such caring, I knew he understood it had hit me. He whispered. "Your family needs you." He was right. I pulled up straight again.

Iris pushed me aside and stood in front of Sameer. "What is it? What's happening?"

Sameer swallowed. He said, "She's in surgery now. She is young and strong, and they're doing everything they can."

His words made my stomach drop. Iris's voice climbed into a sob. Jimmy folded her into his chest, where she shuddered, wiping her face on his pale blue windbreaker, already smeared with mascara.

* * *

The next thing Charlie was patting my arm and saying, "Mom? Mom, wake up." I struggled to rise from the deep cushions of the chair where I had fallen asleep.

Charlie said, "She's out of surgery."

The clock near the elevator put it at almost two thirty in the morning. I arched and pressed my hands into the small of my back. "I'll go talk to the doctor."

"He went right into another surgery. Some guy with a spinal cord injury. Besides, he already talked to Iris and Jimmy. They're in the recovery room with her."

"I want to go in."

"No. Only parents."

"But . . ."

He put his arm around me. "Let's go home. There's nothing we can do now, and Iris and Jimmy and Bethany are going to need us to hold things together the next few days."

I noticed the bruise-colored shadows under his eyes. I put my hand against his cheek. "How are you doing?"

"Oh, Ma." He swallowed. "I can't believe it." He bent to gather my purse and balled-up tissues from the couch, before his jaw tightened. "I'd like to get my hands on that bastard."

We left my car in the lot, and Charlie dropped me at my place. But I couldn't go to bed. That felt too normal, somehow. I curled on the divan by the picture window and stared outside till the sky got light and the world began to wake up and go about its business. Cars driven by those who had early shifts rolled out of driveways. A woman with a briefcase hurried by, eyes glued to her phone. People with jackets over their pajamas slumped in the park across the street, drinking coffee as their dogs did their business. Ordinary life.

I realized that within an hour or two, almost everyone I knew, and certainly everyone Bethany and Iris and Jimmy knew, would hear the news. The principal and teachers at the middle school would confer in low tones about how to handle this. The girls in Bethany's classes would hug one another in the bathroom. Their parents, hearing what had happened and imagining the unimaginable, would call one another to ask for news and blink back tears as they drove their kids to soccer or picked up the dry cleaning. They'd drop off cake and brownies and casseroles and heartbreaking notes for Iris and Jimmy and Bethany. I hoped they would remember Bethany's allergy to peanuts.

We went back to the hospital. Iris was curled in a chair, her head propped against the wall. Her eyes were closed, and her left arm was still captured in a sling. The cut on her cheek had purpled, but otherwise her face was as pale as Bethany's.

Bethany's head was somehow flatter than it had been yesterday. Except if I stood in just the right spot in the corner near the window. From that one place she looked like the same dear Bethie. With lots of tubes coming out of her.

I stroked the curls off her forehead. Her long lashes cast shadows on her cheeks. The last time we'd spoken she'd complained about a pimple that had appeared, and how it was going to ruin her school photo. And there it bloomed, troubling the smooth skin of early adolescence, a minor blemish on her lovely perfect chin. I squeezed her hands, leaning over the bed, trying to stifle my sobs.

There was a sound behind me. I quickly wiped my eyes, taking a second to find my calm nurse's expression before I turned to Iris.

She stretched awake, rubbing her face with her free arm. Her eyes were shadowed and empty.

I stood to hug her. She stiffened at my touch.

I understood. In my years of nursing I had seen this too. I would be the vessel for the anger. Someone close had to absorb the fury, the unfairness, to be the sink into which the horror was drained. To embody the unjust universe. To be angry with.

I touched my daughter's hair. "Hi, honey."

She exhaled, slumping as her exhaustion took over. "Hey, Mom."

"Did you get any sleep?"

"No. Maybe. I guess I dozed." She looked at me, suddenly tender, and took my hand. We watched Bethany's chest rise and fall to the wheezing rhythm of the machine. Iris whispered, "It should have been me. I was right there. It's my fault, I didn't make sure she had her seat belt on. What am I going to do?" She sobbed again and bit her lip. I knew this pattern too: cycling between guilt, exhausted blankness, bargaining with the Almighty, and desperate panic. Thank God, Cal had died in a different hospital. I didn't think I could have taken all of my worlds colliding in one space.

I held her tight. She pulled back after a few moments.

I kissed the top of her head. "Where's Jimmy?"

"He's getting us some coffee." Pause. "He's shattered, Mom. He isn't strong enough."

No one is. No one is strong enough. It was meaningless to assure Iris she would survive this, because mere survival— of any of us—is not what we wanted. To have our regular lives back was what we wanted, our lives from before. Bethany, the same as always. Iris, never knowing this dark tunnel. Everything back to normal.

But normal was an illusion. I had prayed all night, but you have to be very careful with words when you pray. I looked at the machine breathing for our Bethie, the tubing carrying away drainage, and prayed for her to recover. Mere survival was not enough.

Jimmy arrived with coffee and kissed my cheek. "I'm sorry, I didn't get one for you." He held out his Styrofoam cup. "Do you want mine?"

"No thanks—I'm sure you need it."

He wedged in next to Iris. Somehow the way they squeezed onto the single easy chair, each leaning on the other, was too intimate to bear. I said, "But the coffee does smell good. I think I'll go get a cup. Do you want anything else?"

In the elevator, I wondered whether I'd have to settle for the terrible cafeteria brew or if the Starbucks near the gift shop was open yet.

"Frannie? Is that you?"

It took me a minute to place the freckled woman with thick glasses. Then it clicked. "Miranda?" I'd known her since she was a student nurse.

We hugged and she smiled, "Just can't stay away from us, huh?"

I didn't want to tell her. I couldn't face any more sympathy. So I waved my hand in an "it's nothing" gesture. "I'm visiting someone. When the elevator stopped at this floor I got off on an impulse to see if I knew anybody." I hurried to change the topic. "Do you always work this unit?"

"Not usually, but we got slammed last night. A car accident, and that crane collapse . . . you probably heard about it on the news."

I swallowed. "The car accident was on the news?"

"No, no. The crane collapse." She pushed up her glasses. "The accident was sad, though. Guy jumped a curb. Hit another car, with a girl and her mom. I hear the girl is in pretty bad shape. And the guy was soused. I got to Emergency just as they were bringing him in, and I could smell the booze." She exhaled in judgment.

"He's . . . the guy is here?"

She lifted her chin, motioning down another hall to the west wing. "Yeah, he needed surgery. Spinal injury—they operated, but his legs are paralyzed. He won't get movement back." She sniffed. "Not that I have much sympathy." Her pager buzzed and she looked down. "Oops—gotta go. Nice to see you," she called over her shoulder as she padded off in her quiet white shoes.

I slid onto the bench near the elevator, reeling. Of course. Of course the EMTs would bring them both here. It's the closest trauma center.

The elevator doors opened and closed three times while I sat there. I waited till the hall was empty, and ambled in the direction Miranda had indicated, checking out the little sign by each door and noting the equipment.

In one there was a man on a respirator. It had to be him. The monster who'd hit my Bethie. The name on the door said "Sid Latourno."

I looked up and down the hall before I slipped inside. I approached the bed. Sid was an old gray man. I leaned over, trying to find the evil in that face. Then he snorted and shifted his position, bending his knees and kicking.

Not him. I back out slowly.

Roger Stinson was two doors after that. A face that might have been handsome before dissipation. Thick hair. Legs deflated looking and inert under the blanket. I stood staring down at the man who had done such damage to my family. A bile-tasting fury rose, acrid in my mouth. My chest filled with cold fog. But through it all, the beeping of the ventilator echoed in my head, like a ruthlessly beating, remorseless heart.

According to the research, survival among patients after ventilator withdrawal is less than an hour. In my experience, it was usually much less. And Stinson was on a morphine drip, which depressed breathing even further. I stared at the machine. He might last ten minutes, if I'd had to guess. But then again, he was relatively young, always an advantage when fighting for life.

I exhaled sharply. It didn't matter anyway. Any interruption and the alarm would sound at the nurse's station. I inspected the infusion pump controlling the IV. It was one of the newer models. Once the IV tubing is threaded through the pump, a nurse can set it to deliver as little as 0.01 milliliter of medication an hour or as much as a liter.

But it was easy to make a mistake inputting the settings: simply leaving out a decimal point or adding a zero when setting the rate can result in overdose. Such events were depressingly common. The nursing journals were full of case studies in which some small action, like forgetting to add a decimal after being distracted while hanging a new bag, resulted in outsized, catastrophic outcomes. Post-op patients were particularly susceptible because they were on such strong medication. I had lived in fear of making such an error.

I fingered the IV tubes coming out of the pump, staring at the settings. It would be so simple. And it was nearly shift change, when fewer staff were on the floor. He'd go unattended for the few extra minutes it would take. But who would get in trouble? Would one of my former colleagues have to go home thinking he or she had made an error that resulted in a man's death? There'd be an internal inquiry, and some poor former student, maybe even Miranda, could lose her reputation and career. Everything would be looked at.

Oh my God: I had forgotten about the cameras! Were there cameras in the hall? There had been talk of installing them a couple years before, as a "quality-control" feature.

More like a staff control feature, but still. I hadn't checked. If there were, I'd have been recorded, entering Stinson's room. The thought hit me like I'd been dropped into a pool. What was I thinking?

The infusion pump beeped, indicating he needed more morphine. They'd come soon to hang a new bag. I thought maybe I should just give the busy staff a break and slow the drip to almost nothing. Delay the new medicine. It wouldn't kill him. Just give him a taste of real pain, of what my family was going through . . .

I turned and practically ran down the hall to the elevator, aghast. I found my way to the Starbucks in a daze. My hands were still shaking when I put the cream in my dark roast.

That's where I was when I heard them call the code and Bethany's room number.

I raced back to the floor. A nurse was herding them out of the room, first Charlie and Pam, whose arms were linked around Iris, who was collapsing but trying to claw her way back in. Jimmy was blocking her view, holding her while looking back over his shoulder.

She sobbed when she saw me, her arms extended toward the door. "Oh God! Please, Mom, please don't let them . . ."

I shoved my way in, into the controlled chaos of extreme emergency. Chairs were willy-nilly to make room for the urgent choreography: arms spooled cords and tubes around other arms and heads and shoulders, doctors called out meds, nurses ripped open steri-packs and hung new bags. Machine beeps punctuated air filled with the smell of plastic and alcohol. In the center I caught a glimpse of Bethany, pale as the sheets, her lips purple, her small figure inert as arms and bodies reached over and around her. A young doctor loomed above her, his face grim with determination as he pulsed with all his weight into her chest, pushing with such force he practically lifted himself off his feet with each compression. Behind him another doctor gripped the set of paddles. "Clear," someone barked, and I heard the *shoomp* of electricity being pumped into flesh, and Bethany's body lifted and pancaked down. "*Again.* Everybody, clear." I was being moved, and a resident—the same one as before—tried to keep me from seeing. I squirmed to duck under his arm, but he held me, saying, "No. No, please. Please don't . . ."

Shoomp. The irregular squealing continued, her heart wavering in fibrillation. The resident backed me out into the hall and nearly over Iris, who was sunk partway to the floor, with Jimmy half holding her up, half crumpled himself. The machine squeal continued, so loud it drowned out everything else.

Then all was silent. Though I could see the chaos around me, the carts and equipment wheeling, and techs and nurses and docs calling directions as visitors with pale fearful faces skirted around us and eased down the other hall, eyes averted, and Iris's hands covered her open mouth—all was quiet. And finally in this silence I heard someone say, "Call it."

*   *   *

I looked down at the folder in my lap. The final clippings layered there were tangled together, much less orderly. *"Judge and Lawyers Investigated for Corruption." "Lawyer Convicted of Bribery." "Corruption Probe Continues, Judge Claims 'Witch-Hunt.'"* According to the paper, it had been going on for years, prosecutors and defense lawyers bribing clerks to get certain judges, then paying those judges to make sure there was leniency.

Two lawyers eventually went to prison. And although Judge Nathaniel Kearney and a prosecutor were charged with accepting bribes to let Stinson, along with other drunk drivers, off easy, the charges were dropped because the evidence was deemed insufficient.

Inadequate.

The way the word came off his lips echoed through my mind, and the curdled taste of the soup again flooded my mouth. It's amazing what the body remembers. It was no wonder I'd dreamed about Bethany's death the day I met him. My subconscious knew. His face had awakened the ghosts.

Still, it wasn't surprising that I hadn't recognized him. During the trial we were so out of it, so numb. And the black robes and big desk and official setting mask the human being behind the apparatus. Maybe that's the reason the men here at Ridgewood seem so emptied out. They're used to their trappings: their business identities, their office plaques, their secretaries. The props of old women are more portable: jewelry and face lifts and the tasteful expensive clothes that some of them still put on, even here, just to come down to our dining room to be served boring food by workers wearing name tags.

I thought of Katherine's expensive ring. It was like armor, or a talisman protecting her from reality. Spoils of war, a bribe for companionship. From a man to whom I now had to listen play the grand piano.

CHAPTER

6

THE NEXT TIME Katherine called, I let it go to voicemail. I was not ready to face her. After a few days I realized I had to make some excuse, so I waited till I knew she'd be at her weekly hair appointment to call and leave a message. "I forgot to tell you I'm staying with my daughter for a few days while her husband is out of town."

I hid in my apartment, eating canned soup and sandwiches and past-the-expiration-date yogurt. My thoughts whirled around Katherine, her husband (I couldn't bring myself to use his name, even in my mind), Iris, Bethany, this ridiculous circumstance.

How could this happen?

How could we have ended up in the same place?

I could not bear this knowledge alone. I opened my desk and took out an earlier letter to Ruthie I'd abandoned because it was so boring, a dumb recounting of meals and comments about health and updates about the weather out my window. Well, it wouldn't be boring now.

Once I started, it poured out of me, my incredulity, my horror, my outrage. *How,* I wrote, *How could she be married to him? How could I be a friend of a person who is married to someone so reprehensible?*

I stared at my writing, noting that I'd answered my own questions. Except there wasn't really an answer.

I guess people just kid themselves. History is full of crimi-nals who are kind to their pets, war criminals who were loving husbands. How this can be, I have no idea, but it is true. We are able to be two things at once, I guess.

I had an inkling of what Ruthie would think when she read that: she'd say talking about war criminals was over the top. She'd say the situation was absurd enough, and I didn't need to cloud my thinking with drama. But what the judge did was no small moral lapse. It was capital C corruption.

And the other thing I knew she was going to write back—because she had a generous heart and didn't want me to be lonely now that Cal was gone and she was far away—was that Katherine probably didn't know. She'd point out that women of her background were carefully trained to not see anything that unsettled the social order.

That's what I thought too. At least, that is what I'd decided to think. But I paced to the window, my mind swamped by the bigger question, the familiar one at the root of all of it, which is, how could our Bethany have died?

I put the letter away. I wasn't certain I was ready to share this yet, after all.

I hobbled from one end of my living room to the other, unable to distract myself. I shuffled through the books stacked on my table. I checked the television listings. I looked out the window. I could not settle into anything. But the pain of the past reminded me of my resolution to connect more with my living grandchildren, who I think sometimes get shunted aside because of my anger and grief.

I fished out my phone and called my grandson Danny. "Hi, sweetie. Do you think you could convince your mom or dad to let me take you out for ice cream?"

"I doubt it, Grandma . . ." He sighed. "They'll say it's a school night.

"Well, tell them . . ." I exhaled. Danny is eleven and just getting old enough to become a partner in my schemes. "Tell your dad it is a hot fudge emergency."

He laughed. "Hang on." Then I heard him yell, "Mom! Dad! Grandma needs hot fudge. She says it's an emergency." In the background I heard Pam groan and Charlie say, "An emergency, eh?"

Despite the tears still stinging my eyes, I smiled. Danny liked ice cream as much as anybody, but I'd never known Charlie to resist a hot fudge sundae. Once the seed was planted, I knew it would bear fruit. Or ice cream, to mix a metaphor. There were muffled voices, and Danny came back on the line. "We'll see you in a few minutes."

I put my papers back in the folder and stuffed them back in the drawer. Enough.

*   *   *

But it kept coming back. The horrible pull. Absurd as it was, I wanted to be near them. I wasn't sure why. To understand? I felt captive to a force that I could not resist. All I knew was that there was darkness in it, a draw that felt deep and perilous. And impossible to deny.

It took me almost a week, but I finally managed to tame my churning stomach and go down to dinner. I loitered just off the dining room, leaning on my cane, pretending to read the bulletin board. Each time the elevator door opened, I felt a sickening lurch in my belly. After ten minutes of this anxiety, they finally emerged. I took a deep breath, squeezed the top of my cane till my knuckles went white, and managed what I hoped was an ingratiating smile.

Katherine returned it. "Well, hello. So nice to see you finally! How are you?"

She was as warm as ever. Why shouldn't she be? Nothing had changed for her. She gave me a hug. "I've missed you," she said, and after glancing quickly at her husband, she added, "Would you care to join us?"

The judge looked at his wife, startled. After a tiny pause he added, "Yes, do sit with us."

I realized that at some level this was what I'd hoped for. I followed them to their usual table. The judge's crisp linen shirt had probably fit him once, but now it hung loosely on his rounded shoulders. I saw he wore a ring that matched Katherine's. Katherine was tastefully put together as always, with an expensive-looking gold pin at her collar.

I was never one to feel intimidated by trappings of wealth, partly because growing up as I did, I was so naive and unfamiliar with money I didn't pick up on things like the expense of jewelry or the status of a car, and by the time I'd had enough experience of the world to understand their meaning, I was also secure enough not to care.

But tonight, these trappings further destabilized me. I was out of my depth, my various intentions bobbing chaotically around, like my psyche was a flooded basement and I was wading in the dark. I had no real idea why I wanted to eat with them, only that I had strong desire to watch them. Why I didn't want to scream at the judge, to denounce him publicly, I don't know, but to my great surprise, I had no desire to. Not then anyway. I knew it would simply make me look like a lunatic, especially in the face of his granite certainty and confidence.

I sat next to Katharine, and the judge was on her other side. There were other chairs available, but no one else sat down. I realized I had never seen anyone else dine with them other than a woman around Iris's age. "Does your daughter join you for dinner?" I asked.

Nathaniel lifted his chin, "Do you know Lisa?"

"Um, well, no. I mean, Katherine mentioned what a lovely person she is," I blathered. I cleared my throat and smiled at Katherine. "I just realized you never mentioned if she lived nearby."

Katherine inclined her head. "Yes, she's only a few miles away. She stops by often."

"You and Nathaniel seem very proud of her." Katherine's eyes widened briefly, and she flashed a quick glance at her husband.

He cleared his throat. "I prefer to be called 'Judge.'"

I should have known. "Oh." I nodded. "I see. Well, I'm sure it is a title you worked hard for."

He dipped his chin, glad I understood. It occurred to me to insist he call me "Nurse," but I realized sarcasm might not be the best approach. The absurdity of his insisting on that title in the dining room of an assisted living complex brought the ludicrousness of the situation home to me. I felt suddenly woozy at the surreal nature of it all. I took a sip of water and steadied myself. Katherine asked, "Are you all right? You seem a thousand miles away."

I couldn't do it. "Oh yes. I'm just tired. In fact, I think I need to go put my feet up." I reached for my purse. "But thank you. Will I see you tomorrow?"

And somehow I became a regular at their table. I couldn't stay away, though I excoriated myself for it. It was like pressing on a bruise or rubbernecking at a fire. Shameful and potentially dangerous, but how could I not, at least . . . well, I didn't know what. Try to understand? To intervene? Shame him? Certainly not forgive? Although Katherine, maybe . . .

Whatever it was, I could not resist the chance to observe them.

Every night I removed myself from myself. Some part of my consciousness perched on the ceiling like a gargoyle, observing, while the rest of me sat at the table and played the role of sidekick and friend to the wife, bearing witness as Nathaniel exposed his haughty nature. One evening when I entered, he was upbraiding Katherine because she'd given a check to a charity without clearing it with him first. "It's not the money, my dear. It is that you didn't tell me about it or ask me an appropriate amount." He stopped and plastered on a dry smile when he saw me. I don't think he liked me particularly, but he pretended. Katherine had signaled she wanted me there, and she was clearly the one in charge of organizing their social life. Despite his bluster he relied on her for almost everything, including—maybe even especially—interactions with other people.

It didn't take long before I met Lisa. She was a tall, rangy woman with reddish curls that appeared to be hennaed. She also had piercings running along the entire outer ridge of one ear, and several more on the other. At our second meal together, I asked her about them. Nathaniel stiffened, but Lisa smiled broadly. "I wanted to do *something* interesting when I turned forty." She tilted her head almost imperceptibly away from Nathaniel. "I figured they were less permanent than a tattoo, and if I ever needed to, I could hide them with my hair."

I liked Lisa.

Sometimes Marta, the activities director, would also stop by the table to chat, and once in a while another jazz aficionado, thin and always wearing a hat, also dropped by. I think his name was Carson, but he and the judge spoke solely to each other, totally absorbed in discussing Biederbeck, Bird, and Monk and ignoring everyone else. I could tell it bothered Katherine, but I didn't mind in the least. It spared me having to interact with Nathaniel. The judge observed social niceties as befitting his upbringing and background, but he did not make conversation easy. I sensed that even his daughter viewed him with more duty than affection. Without Katherine he would have been really alone.

I also saw how she had managed not to know anything about his professional life. She wafted above it all like some ethereal and benevolent presence in a well-appointed temple. How did the old saying go? A bird singing in a golden cage? I found myself wondering: If she had known what was funding her lifestyle, would those Junior League luncheons have been less palatable?

But then she would turn to me and ask me about my health, my observations of the deer in the preserve, my thinking, my work, my memories of Cal, and I'd be filled with affection. And guilt. Guilt for judging her. Guilt for liking her.

Nathaniel, however, did not improve with time. One evening I finally got him to talk about his work. He began to bloviate about how he believed in "the system" and how people might try to manipulate it, but it was really a shining example to the world, etcetera. I almost choked on my food— that is, until Katherine, with her reliably gracious manners, cut him off gently and steered the conversation toward me.

"I don't think you've ever told Nathaniel about your career," she encouraged. To her husband she added, "Frannie has an impressive résumé."

"Well, I don't know about that." I set down my fork. "But I did love my job. I began as a nurse. Then I went to med school but had to leave when I got pregnant."

Nathaniel interjected with certainty, "So you stayed home and dedicated yourself to your family." It was a declaration, not a question.

I cleared my throat. "Not exactly. I went back to nursing and specialized in surgery." I picked up my knife and delicately bisected a beet. "But of course medical knowledge helped when taking care of my kids."

Katherine smiled. "Do you remember the day we met, Frannie? We walked to the library together." She turned to Nathaniel. "My heart was acting up. Frannie noticed and made me sit. She even took my pulse." She smiled at me like we were the oldest of friends. "Oh, I meant to tell you what my cardiologist said . . . "

Her husband twisted in his seat and looked impatient. His gesture wasn't lost on Katherine, and in a turn of events that couldn't have been better had I planned it myself, she shifted the attention to her husband. "But I won't go on about me. You have a cardiac issue too, don't you, dear?"

He drew himself more upright and proceeded to tell me about the very special and unusual surgery that he'd needed.

Apparently everything about Nathaniel, even his heart trouble, was exceptional.

"You've probably heard of my specialist. Dr. Max Kunstler? Max—he's a friend now, we golfed together—is the best in the city, if not the state. We got to know each other because my case was so unusual. Because of some structural aspects of my ticker"—and here he pressed his chest—"and my rare blood chemistry. He was going to write it up for some peer-reviewed journals." Katherine interrupted him, patting his arm. "Yes, dear. Thank goodness we got that taken care of." To me she added, "As long as he remembers his pills, things are fine."

I saw a flare of irritation in his eyes. Clearly he didn't like being demoted from a once-in-a-lifetime patient, star of peer-reviewed journals and on a first-name basis with the best cardiologist in the state, to an old man who had to remember to take his pills.

A perverse desire to stoke his ego surged in me. "That sounds fascinating. I have worked with many cardiac surgeons." I had to struggle to stop myself from asking, 'How did you discover the fact that your heart was malformed, small and twisted?' But I bit my tongue and rephrased, "How did you first discover your heart's unusual structure?"

He sent a small triumphant glance at Katherine, and began to detail his conditions. As he went on, I found myself thinking, *Yes, please. Tell me all about your heart. And your other ailments as well. About your medications, and when you take them. I want to know about all the ways and all the places you are weak and vulnerable.*

That night I finished my note to Ruthie. I left my earlier expressions of fury and outrage, but I didn't go into any more detail. I just couldn't. I told myself I just didn't want to seem to be trapped in the past, after promising her how I was going to be thinking about other things. But a strong instinct told me to hold back, that this was not something I should talk too much about.

7

THE BOX WAS a brilliant idea. Iris was always making things, little gifts, cute stationery, crazy arrangements of what-nots in her yard. She's what we used to call crafty. And a few weeks after I moved in (and after she'd had plenty of time to hear me complain about the bland food), she and Danny and Adam arrived with a present they'd made.

It was a small wooden box decorated with old images and advertisings decoupaged all over. The cover featured a 1950s image of a woman in an apron, holding out a tray and saying, "Help yourself." Adam had proudly pointed out the section he had done, with awkwardly cut images and globs of glue that hadn't been brushed out. Of course, that made me like it even more.

The inside of the box was divided into compartments, each filled with small containers of various non-sodium seasonings: lemon pepper, the world's tiniest bottles of Tabasco, a small vial with garlic powder, foil pouches of ketchup and mustard and slippery plastic packets of lemon juice. They were particularly proud of those because they'd had to swipe them from a local take-out joint that offered them for iced tea. Apparently Danny and Adam would go in and help themselves to fistfuls while Iris ordered sodas for them all. The boys had gotten a big thrill from this undercover mission.

It made me happy that Iris was doing things with her nephews. It wasn't always easy for her to spend time with them, especially as they got older. Danny was already approaching the age Bethany had been when she died.

A week or so after I'd started eating with Katherine and the judge, I brought this little kit to the dining room with me, hoping to use it to improve the invariably insipid tilapia on the menu that evening.

Katherine delighted over the cleverness of it, crying, "Look, honey, she has Tabasco." She turned to me and explained, "My husband is from Louisiana—he likes his hot sauce."

I held it out, like a waitress offering tea, miming the woman on the cover. "Help yourself," I said as charmingly as I could. "This food must be especially bland for someone used to delicious Louisiana cooking."

Any recognition of his specialness was like catnip to him. He puffed up. "Well . . . maybe just a little dash." The Tabasco had come directly from Louisiana: the tiny bottles were purchased as souvenirs from the factory on Avery Island, where they make it. Iris and Jimmy and Bethany had stopped there on their road trip to New Orleans. It had been their last vacation before she died.

"You northerners simply cannot imagine how I miss my nana's jambalaya. There truly is nothing like it." His accent was clearer then.

*   *   *

I stared out the window for a very long time after dinner. That afternoon I'd received the invitation for the annual memorial, when Iris gathered all her women friends who'd known Bethany for tea and cookies. I knew some of the group thought she should just get over it already. But how can you say that to a person? How much grief is too much?

Iris always distributed another of her handmade gifts with the invitation—embroidered linen pouches filled with flower seeds, in remembrance of Bethany. I recalled the previous year's gathering.

I'd gone to their house to help. Iris sat tucked in the corner of her porch, waiting for her friends as Pam and I finished getting the tea ready. After putting the last tray on the dining table, I stood just inside the front door, watching the light fade from gold to indigo. The evening swelled with the scent of water on grass, the random spark of fireflies—all the ordinary loveliness of a September evening.

From where I stood, I saw Iris's friend Cynthia. She was across the street and halfway down the block, waiting. Another woman—it looked like her friend Dianne—was heading up the walk. She spotted Cynthia and waved. They were hugging when a taxi pulled over, and a familiar older woman emerged. It was Miss Suzanne, Bethany's first-grade teacher. I knew those silver curls.

The women formed a knot on the sidewalk. As I watched, Cynthia reached into her back pocket and pulled out the pouch. The others followed her lead, fishing in their purses. I wondered if they had noticed how much better Iris had gotten at the embroidery over the years. That year she'd stitched "For Bethany" in dark purple and green, with tiny flowers underneath.

The sky darkened as the group stood there, serenaded by the crickets. I watched as first Dianne, then Cynthia and Suzanne opened the pouches and emptied the seeds into their hands. They were rosemary, for remembrance, and daisies, for the innocence of children. They scattered the seeds on the parkway. They put their arms around one another. Then Suzanne said something, and Dianne gave a small laugh, and a warm murmur of conversation moved through the group as they started up the walk to Iris's house. I wondered if they ever recognized the gift Bethany still gave them, this yearly renewal of connections.

Iris stirred and moved from the corner toward the door. Behind me, Pam put her arm around my shoulder and said quietly, "You okay?" I nodded and we softly pulled back into the front room as Iris stood in the threshold, waiting for her friends.

I looked down at my lap. I opened the packet that came with this year's invitation and inhaled the scent that rose into the humid air.

*   *   *

I began bringing my little spice box to every meal as I sat with the judge and his wife. I tended to rely on the lemon juice. And the garlic powder. There are very few things that can't be improved by garlic, even if it is powdered. I also found myself taking note of which seasonings the judge used. I told myself it was because I wanted to let Iris know how popular her kit was, and ask for replenishments. I tried to ignore the fact that every time I made special note of what the judge favored—besides Tabasco, he was partial to oregano—I felt a twisting in my stomach.

*   *   *

It was right around then that Mrs. Collier arrived in the apartment across the hall, introducing some chaos into the orderly rhythm of my life at Ridgewood. Most of the time, Mrs. Collier was a nice lady with bright, unfocused eyes, who was given to occasional flights of confusion. But once in a while, especially in the evening, she took a bad turn and became argumentative. Difficult. She probably should have been in the memory care wing, but I have a feeling her family couldn't accept that. Or perhaps there wasn't a room available, and Ridgewood management had her on the wait list. No matter. On her bad days Mrs. Collier made medication duty a really tough assignment.

Every night at around eight, a knock sounded on my door. Until my new neighbor's arrival, this had begun a courteous sixty-second interaction, in which an aide—usually Graciela—handed me a little cup with my meds. I wished her good night, and she moved on, pushing a cart with medications, lined up according to room number and name, to the next apartment.

But that all changed when Mrs. Collier moved in.

The first time it happened I heard high-pitched, angry words in the hallway. I picked up my cane and opened the door. Mrs. Collier, thin gray hair springing loose from her curlers, stood glaring at the little cup of pills in Graciela's hand.

"What is this? Who are you?"

"Mrs. Collier, this is your medicine."

"Where's my Amanda? Who are you? What are you trying to do to me?" Then the poor lady became panicky. Her eyes, unfocused but bright blue, shone with worry. "I need to get the children to bed. Where is Amanda?" She looked down at her meds. "Who are you? Take this away."

Graciela was well named: full of grace, a patient and kind caregiver. She reassured Mrs. Collier, "Now, you don't need to worry. Amanda is fine. All your children are fine, I promise." Then she urged gently, "Can you take your medicine now?"

Mrs. Collier pleaded, "I have to get home. It's late." She swung her unfocused gaze toward me. "Who are you? Please, I have to get home."

Graciela, her long braided hair pinned around her head like a crown, nodded at me, and then spoke gently to Mrs. Collier. "I know. Let's go in your room and get you settled, okay?"

I was never able to be that sort of nurse—emotionally responsive, soothing. For me, it was the technical aspect of medicine that appealed. It was why I focused on surgical nursing. The complex interactions: anesthesiologists, radiologists, technicians, the instruments and equipment and technologies all engaged in a complicated ballet were what excited me. I hated to admit that I preferred my patients to be out cold, but it was true. Things were less complicated that way.

Graciela gently eased Mrs. Collier back inside her apartment.

The medication cart was unattended in the hall. I leaned over to check out the medicines. "Kearney, Apartment 300" caught my eye, partly because I recognized the pills. All too well. Cal had been on digoxin too. Another thing Katherine and I had in common. Looking at them, I became a wife again, not a nurse.

But I wasn't a wife anymore, and she was.

*   *   *

I couldn't sleep. I kept trying to ignore the vague notions troubling the edges of my mind. As soon as I turned to examine them head-on, they'd slip away, like the mice that had sometimes appeared in our old house: glimpses of shadows, a darkness sluicing across the floor. But when I turned, there'd be nothing. At least nothing I could name or look at, nothing I could root out and defend against. It was as though something I couldn't get rid of was chewing away at me, at my foundations.

When I finally dropped off, my dreams were full of Cal. I was ironing his shirt, and he was angry because I had burned a hole in it, but the hole was teeny and shaped like a valentine, and I couldn't understand how that particular hole had happened with an iron. Then I was crying, and he kissed me and said, "It'll all be okay. You did it because you love me." In the dream, we were in our house, but it wasn't like our real life house at all. Right before I woke up, I was suddenly at his funeral, with Iris and Charlie holding me up.

CHAPTER

8

THE SCANDAL BROKE a year and a half after Bethany's death. The news reports described a pattern of easy sentences for drunk drivers, detailing the payoffs to clerks, and the collusion and kickbacks between the prosecutors and the defense attorneys. And judges. According to the papers, Stinson had sent someone to the hospital two years before he'd killed Bethany. If he'd been put in jail then, my granddaughter would still be alive. As more information came out, it revealed how Stinson had bribed his way out of consequences that first time, allowing him to do it all again. And to repeat the same scam in the second trial, for killing Bethany. With the same judge and prosecutor.

Of course, we were aware of none of that at the time. As horrible as losing Bethany was, in the immediate aftermath we managed to grow together, comforting one another. It was the legal proceedings that nearly did us in, setting us adrift, without even a clear outcome to hope for, besides some sort of ill-defined sense of justice. It sucked us into a whirlpool of constantly frustrated expectations. Iris coped by appearing at every court date—which were capricious, impossible to plan for, and frustrating, since mostly they consisted of incomprehensible mumblings between lawyers and judges and whispered exchanges between attorneys and clients. The "family of victims" blogs on the internet said that it was important to keep showing up, to remind the court of the damage this man had caused. Bit by bit, the goal of "getting justice for Bethany" became Iris's mission. It became her mantra, her reason for being.

And during all the months Iris was organizing her life around court dates, the guy who murdered Bethany was not in jail. His lawyer argued that Stinson was not a flight risk, since he was in a wheelchair and had a lot of medical troubles because of his damaged spine. ("As if people in wheelchairs can't get on a plane," Iris had sniffed.) An attorney friend of ours explained that because he was not incarcerated, it was in Stinson's interest to employ every means he could to drag out the process. And this, more than anything else, chipped away at Iris, at my family. We spent mind-numbing hours waiting for the case to be called, only to find that Stinson's lawyer was asking for another continuance because "Mr. Stinson had to have a procedure," or because the arresting officer was not available to testify, or because some paperwork had not yet gotten to where it needed to be. I soon understood that Stinson's lawyer knew exactly how to orchestrate all this, while still preserving the appearance that he, upstanding member of the bar, was in complete compliance. I came to loathe his lawyer almost more than I detested Stinson.

Television trains us to think that trials are full of tension, the courtroom charged with outrage. But that was not what I saw in the months that this played out. In reality, people were simply worn down by the boredom, the delays, the mundanity of it all. No wonder the neighbors and friends who had volunteered to accompany Iris to the hearings gradually stopped coming.

Who could blame them? They had jobs and families and daily lives: the imperatives of getting to the grocery store or their son's soccer match superseded the need to make sure that they were in the gallery whenever Stinson was due in court. As months passed, I saw that in her neighbors' eyes, Iris's resolute insistence on "justice for Bethany" began to seem like a stubborn refusal to move on.

"Move on." What a cruel term. How does one do that, I wonder, when the entire future one imagined has been destroyed?

But I wanted it for her too. It was necessary.

A year after the accident, I was sitting in Iris and Jimmy's kitchen. The trial had still not been scheduled. I was trying to get Iris to think of other things, so I had dropped by, hoping to take them to dinner. To feel normal for an hour or two, to do something other than mourn or curse the lawyers. No one was home yet, so I sat in the kitchen to wait.

The refrigerator door still displayed a schedule of events from the middle school. An outdated permission form for a field trip Bethany would never take poked out from under strata of expired coupons. A palimpsest of a daily life, completely altered now. I moved a take-out menu, and there, affixed to the door with a butterfly magnet, was a heartbreaking drawing of the three of them, in front of their house, that Bethany had done as a fourth grader. Tears stung my eyes.

The door opened and Jimmy entered the kitchen, arms full of groceries. "Ma!" he exclaimed as he set the bags on the counter. Despite everything, there was still something youthful about him. Maybe it was his freckles. Then he leaned down to kiss my cheek and I saw the shadows in his eyes, their surface closed over the pain. "This is a nice surprise."

I squeezed his shoulder. "I thought I could take you two out for dinner. Someplace fun. Maybe that barbecue joint?" The choice was strategic. Before she died, Bethany had become a vegetarian, in what Iris had decided was a form of rebellion in her meat-loving family. So they would never have eaten there with her.

I could see in Jimmy's face that he knew exactly why I'd suggested it. He nodded. "Sounds terrific. Just let me put these groceries away." He hoisted the bag. "I always welcome an excuse not to cook." Apparently it still fell to him to figure out what was needed from the market and make dinner.

Poor Jimmy. He was just as devastated as Iris. But somehow he had to keep going to work every morning and dealing with the outside world, the world of offices and traffic jams and signing for packages and paying the bills. The world Iris had withdrawn from. I thought it was a form of bravery to somehow keep facing the world as if your private universe weren't in collapse. But Iris sometimes acted as if Jimmy's carrying on with daily life was some sort of cowardly caving-in, a refusal to foreground their catastrophe, to insist that the world account for it over and over again.

"Where is Iris?" I asked.

He was reaching to put a box of cereal on a high shelf, and I saw his shoulders tense. He didn't look at me while he answered. "Um. Probably still at her group. But she usually calls if she's going to be late."

"She's still going?" Dismay tinged my voice.

I was the one who had suggested that Iris join a support group. Now I regretted it. When I'd first mentioned it, she'd resisted. At that point she was so shattered and so insular that any way to get her out of the house and take steps back toward life seemed like a good plan. I had reached out to someone from MADD, the Moms Against Drunk Driving organization. They seemed so admirable. These women channeled their grief to a purpose, working to make sure no one else would go through what they had.

But Iris went in another direction. She finally said yes, not in response to my suggestion, but to a "grieving for lost children" group that had reached out to her. I'm not sure how they got her name—maybe they kept track of potential new members in the papers. At any rate, I went with her, thinking it might help me as well. I attended four times before I realized not every such gathering is healthy. And that some things don't really count as "support."

I had imagined such groups existed to help people put their lives back together. I'll admit, maybe even that horrible phrase "moving on," and all the things it implied, was part of my thinking. Because, well—life. Life demands that we live in the present and construct our lives with the materials we are given. And Iris and Jimmy and everyone in our family were faced with somehow incorporating this lousy, horrible sadness into the fabric of our every day.

But that didn't seem to be the focus of this support group. At the first meeting we attended, the grievers—all women—perched on a folding chairs arranged in a circle in the basement of a local church. A table along the wall offered a package of cookies, a thermos of hot water and a basket of tea, instant coffee, creamer and sugar.

I went to get something to drink before the meeting began. As I opened the packet of Lipton's, one of the participants, a thin older woman with papery skin and gray roots, hugged herself and started to sway. Soon she was shaking, weeping like a child, with snot running down her face as she railed against the injustice of the world that had taken her son. The others caught her emotion and began to call forth their own loss. Within minutes the entire group was sobbing, like some sort of grief orgy. I thought of religious ecstasies and mosh pits . . . places where emotions are magnified and reflected, spiraling upward toward extravagant release. I gaped, horrified.

My shock must have shown, because a person at my elbow said, "It's something, isn't it?"

I turned. A woman with glossy dark hair sipped some instant coffee and nodded at the lady who had kicked things off. "That's my mom. My brother drowned two and a half years ago." She pressed her lips together. "I'm Rachel, by the way."

"I'm so sorry for your loss." I lifted my chin toward Iris. "That tall woman with the slipping ponytail is my daughter.

Iris. We lost Bethany—her daughter—last year." I hesitated. "Iris was driving. She blames herself. They were arguing, and she didn't make Bethany put on her seat belt."

Rachel's eyes signaled sympathy and recognition. As we spoke, another griever, a young woman in a yellow dress, began hiccupping, "If the doctor had done his job, Peter would still be here."

Rachel continued in low tones. "She lost her son to meningitis. Next to her—a genetic disorder. The one with the scarf lost her daughter in a diving accident, and the other one's kid had cancer." She cleared her throat. "That's really all they know about one another. That's how they identify. They come here to crank up their sadness—to pump one another up."

I whispered, "I thought . . . I expected there to be coping strategies. I don't know, talk about moving forward or something."

Rachel inhaled. "Yeah. You and me both."

I saw it clearly. This was a place where these women could simply *be* grief, elemental and raw.

As she drove home, Iris kept sighing in exhausted, shuddering breaths.

I cleared my throat. "So. What did you think?"

She exhaled. "You were right about joining a group. For once I was around people who know what it's like. They understand what I'm going through." She dabbed her eyes. "Did you know some of them lost their kids more than four years ago?"

The sentence put a chill in my heart. It reinforced my fear that Iris was in danger of defining herself solely as "a woman who had lost a child."

I said, "That's horrible. But . . . well, I wonder if maybe the people who run the group need to challenge those folks a little."

I felt her stiffen. "Challenge?"

"Well, you know. For some of them it's been years, and there is still such . . ." I let myself trail off, afraid to say more.

Her voice rose as she took one hand off the wheel. "What more challenge do we need, Mom? Getting out of bed is a challenge. No one who is grieving needs more of a challenge. How can you say that?"

I twisted in my seat and pleaded, my voice rising. "But no future was being developed. Don't you see? All that did was amplify your sadness. It was like people were performing their pain, not creating a new life beyond it."

"Oh my God." Her voice cracked in anger. "I can't believe you." You're the one who nagged me about joining a group. So I do, and now you don't approve."

"I meant . . . something worthwhile. Something that will help you put the pieces back together."

We came to a red light, and she turned to glare at me in evident disbelief. "I'm the one who gets to say what helps me. And that did help." She was furious. "God, Mom, how can you say stuff like that?"

I couldn't believe me either. It wasn't my place to judge. I was appalled at myself.

"You're right." I reached for her hand resting on the seat between us. "I'm so sorry." I swallowed, ashamed. But she pulled her hand away and turned from me to stare out her window.

* * *

Months later, as I sat in my daughter's kitchen and Jimmy sorted away the food, I said, "I didn't know she was still going to those meetings." At one point Iris would have discussed everything with me, but apparently not anymore. My throat tightened.

Jimmy busied himself with washing his hands before meeting my eyes. "She says it helps her." I could tell by his tone it wasn't helping him, or them.

There were footsteps on the back porch. Jimmy turned, his face rearranged into a practiced hopeful expression as Iris came in the door.

"Hi, honey." He bent to kiss her cheek.

She was distracted and puffy-eyed. "Hi." Then she saw me. "Mom . . . What brings you here? You should have said something—I would've made sure I was home." As was usual lately, she wore no makeup, and her hair hung in a lank braid.

I smiled, feeling like I was caught in some guilty act. I often felt that way around Iris. She was so fragile, and so angry. "I thought I'd take you two out to eat. There's that barbecue place I've been wanting to try."

"Oh." I could tell she was uncertain how she should respond. More and more I had the sense that there was some criteria Iris carried in her head, some rubric that she had to consult before allowing herself to do anything. In my mind it was directly related to the support group. Would a truly grieving mother go out to dinner?

Jimmy adopted a forced cheerfulness, but I could feel the tension underneath. Just like me, he didn't know what to do or say to make things better. He put an arm around her shoulder, trying to knit the two of them into a united team. "That sounds like a great idea. It's a nice evening, and I hear they have a patio."

I quickly stood and adjusted my jacket. "Great! It'll be fun. Do you some good."

It was the wrong thing to say. Iris flared. "Do me good? What do you mean?"

I leaned back. "Just—it's nice to get out once in a while. Change of routine, see what's happening in the world."

She pulled away from Jimmy and stepped toward me. "I don't need to know what is happening, Mom. What difference does any of it make to me? Do you think I don't know what you're doing?"

"For goodness sake, Iris." I lifted my shoulders, and opened my hands. "It's dinner. You make it sound like inviting you to a restaurant is trying to pull something sneaky."

"You're trying to make me feel better. But I'm not going to feel better. *I'm* not about to forget my daughter. It's barely been a year. Just because it's inconvenient for everyone if I'm sad, I am not going to pretend it's all okay just to satisfy you."

"Iris! You know better than that."

"You're just like everyone else. Wanting me to 'get over it.'" She made air quotes as she spat out the words. "Well, I'm not. I refuse to."

"So what are you saying? That you'll live in perpetual misery, with no purpose except to be sad? No one is forgetting Bethany. No one ever will. But we are still here. We need to somehow move on. Go forward."

"Go forward?" She glared at me. "You have no idea. *You've* never lost a child."

I felt like I'd been slapped.

"Iris! Stop!" Jimmy stepped forward, his voice loud and wavery. "For God's sake, I lost her too. Frannie lost her. You think you're the only one who feels it? Like you're the queen of grief?" He was fighting for composure, his mouth trembling.

Iris's face drained of all color. "I'm sorry." She pressed her fingers to her mouth and looked down. "I'm sorry."

Jimmy lost his battle and tears filled his eyes. He turned his back to her, his hands gripping the counter.

Iris stood in the middle of the kitchen, like the still upright mast of a foundering ship. She floated over to him and gently put her hands between his shoulder blades. Her voice was anguished. "How could God do this to me?"

Jimmy stiffened. "You've got to stop, Iris." When he turned, his face looked broken, but his voice was hard. "I mean it. You've got to stop. It isn't a punishment, and there isn't a reason. God does not murder little girls."

Iris looked up at him, her mouth half open. Then she swallowed and backed away for a few steps before turning and rushing out of the room, hands over her mouth. I tried to follow, but she yelled, "Just go away. Why can't you just leave us alone?" and slammed their bedroom door.

I returned to the kitchen, where Jimmy still stood over the sink, his face a mask of bleak despair. I squeezed his arm before letting myself out.

*   *   *

That night Jimmy called me in a panic. He had found Iris on the floor of the bathroom, barely conscious, empty pill bottle in her hand. We rushed her to the hospital, where they saved her life.

After that, she refused to see me. She didn't talk to me for three months.

It ended when another parent I had gotten to know from all the hours sitting in court called. He, too, had lost his daughter—to another drunk driver. "Where are you? Don't you want to see the sentencing?"

"What do you mean?"

"It was added to the calendar for today. It's happening now."

"What?" I couldn't believe the prosecutor hadn't let me know. I called Jimmy from the car. They too were rushing to get there so the judge could see my daughter's tear-stained face and sense her shattered heart and understand Stinson needed to be sentenced to the harshest possible punishment.

I ran into the building from the parking lot, but when I reached the courtroom door, I hesitated, suddenly uncertain. I tiptoed in and sat in the back. I wasn't sure Iris would welcome me.

That is how I came to hear the words that dispensed the "justice" for my granddaughter's death.

Stinson slumped in his wheelchair, shriveled and pathetic looking. His lawyer stood next to him, and across the aisle was the incompetent prosecutor, who hadn't bothered to have us testify and hadn't even notified us that the hearing date had been changed. The judge lectured Stinson, in a sonorous accent, about his behavior and his irresponsibility and the grief of our family. He spoke about how "the life you took can never be replaced," while looking with dramatic sympathy at Iris and Jimmy. Then the judge became stiff and officious. "But I do not believe the taxpayers should be made responsible for providing ongoing medical care, as they would be if I were to sentence you to prison. Your injuries are perhaps adequate in regard to limiting your freedom, but I am still sentencing you to home confinement with an ankle bracelet." He paused and looked down at the paper in his hand, and spoke words that later would torture my memory. "You will participate in an adequately vetted twelve-step program and work with schools to show young drivers what can happen if they make the same poor choice you did. You will also pay an eight-thousand-dollar fine." Then it was over.

Stinson sat up straight in his wheelchair, suddenly looking more robust. He pumped the hand of his lawyer and grinned widely at the judge, who shot him a glare back and shook his head.

I sat gape-mouthed, unable to process this travesty. Iris jumped up, her voice breaking. "Wait. Wait! I want to testify. Don't family members get to speak?" The prosecutor turned to cut her off, throwing a signal look at the guards, who moved forward. The judge, who had been halfway out the door, paused and held up his hand. The guards surrounding Iris stopped. She pleaded with the judge, "Please. Please let me tell you about my daughter." Her voice was ragged. "This isn't right."

The judge took a step toward her and spoke like he would to an upset child. "We are sorry for your loss." He adjusted his robe and nodded at the defense table, now empty. "It's all over now. He has been adequately punished. You should go home and rest." To Jimmy he said, "Take care of your wife." Iris sank into the bench, staring from him to the prosecutor, in disbelief.

Jimmy wheeled on the prosecutor, asking, "What the hell was that?" But the prosecutor was already rushing out of the room, his face pink, like he couldn't get away fast enough.

That night, I was staring, unseeing, out my window, my heart aching for my daughter, and wondering if she would survive this, when I heard a key turn in the door. Before I could throw off my afghan and get up off the couch, Iris appeared in my living room, eyes swimming.

"Oh, Ma," she cried, and dove for my lap. I stroked her hair while she wept.

Aᴍᴏɴᴛʜ ᴏʀ sᴏ after I landed at Ridgewood, Iris dropped by with an armful of brochures and paint samples. She was excited, but also a little nervous. "We found a contractor. Do you want to see the color scheme we're considering?"

We were sprucing up the condo because we'd finally decided to put it on the market. Surprisingly, I didn't have much emotion about it, particularly. Maybe it was just a case of not letting myself feel it. Because if I allow myself to go too far down that road, I have to face the fact that that Ridgewood is probably my last place . . . if I am lucky. More than any attachment to the condo, that is the hard thing to swallow. But it is also not something I can change. So, when my kids tentatively, gently raised the idea of selling, I focused on the practicalities. I realized it made no sense to keep paying the condo fees and taxes.

I said, "That's great honey. I hope the contractor isn't too expensive?"

"He is an old friend of Jimmy's. He's giving us the 'family price.'" Iris smiled. "How about we look at these over lunch at that new cafe on Central Street?" She winked. "You mentioned to Charlie you had a coupon?"

But I didn't want to go. "Thanks, but can I take a rain check?"

Iris was immediately alert. "What's wrong? Is everything okay?"

I just wasn't in the mood. Maybe my feelings about losing the condo and the independence it represented were deeper than I cared to acknowledge. Or maybe—just everything. Lately, I had been roiled with emotions I thought I'd dealt with long ago, anger and sadness bubbling up like a fresh spring. Plus, I'd slept badly. I didn't have the energy to summon the positive and healthy and forward-looking attitude I tried to embody when I was with Iris.

I gestured away her concern. "I'm fine. Just feeling a little out of sorts." I could see in her eyes a familiar mixture: worry, wondering how worried she should be, wondering if she should say something and risk annoying me.

I held up my hands. "Honey, don't fret. I promise everything is okay. Take Jimmy. Or go with a friend. We'll do it another time."

She leaned forward and her eyes moved over my face, evaluating. "You sure?"

"Yes, I'm sure. Really. I think I'll just take a nap before lunch." She looked at me for another moment, then bent to kiss me. "Okay. I'll call you later."

I put my feet up and closed my eyes.

*　*　*

The knock surprised me. I startled, dropping my feet to the floor. When I shuffled over and peered through the peephole, there was Katherine, smiling. I hadn't seen her in several days.

I opened the door, feeling awkward. Like I'd told Iris, I wasn't in the mood for company. Especially Katherine's. But despite myself, when I saw her face, I felt a faint surge of friendship. I said, "Hello stranger."

"I hope in this case you won't 'beware of strangers bearing gifts.'" She had one hand on her walker, and with the other she offered me a bakery box containing two luscious-looking croissants. As she held it out, I noticed her left hand trembled, and her color seemed off. But the social code of Ridgewood dictates that one does not mention such things, and as a nurse, I'd learned long ago not to ask unless I wanted to hear more than I'd bargained for. And her smile was bright, the waves in her silver hair as carefully done as ever.

It reminded me of the first time she had visited, bearing a muffin. Then I realized. I glanced at the clock. Yep, the timing was correct. I turned to her and said, "Let me guess. You want to watch The Young and the Restless?"

She nodded sheepishly. "Nathaniel has a cold and is cranky. And to make it worse, he's on the phone with his brother, who is so hard of hearing that Nathaniel has to shout. It makes it hard to catch the whispered secrets on the television. But mainly, I really needed to get out of the apartment." She pulled her mouth to the side and lifted her eyebrows.

Despite myself, the humor on her face lifted my spirits. I led the way to the living room and gestured her to sit. "Should I make us some tea?"

But she had already picked up the remote and was aiming it at the television. She made polite responses to my attempts at conversation, but Katherine was clearly most interested in finding the correct channel. Apparently she was more of a fan than I realized. I set some plates by the croissants on the side table and noted in the bright light of my living room that yes, her color was definitely off. Still, I decided to mind my own business and settled into my chair as she adjusted the sound. I claimed my croissant, savoring the flaky layers that shattered at first bite.

But I hadn't watched the program in a while, and my pleasure drained away as I figured out what was happening. There was one plotline in particular that troubled me, a complicated story of personal vendettas and lies. At the heart of it, someone was bribing a lawyer.

I fidgeted in my chair.

A commercial blinked on. Katherine muted the program and turned to me. "Interesting twist. Though I have to say that there are times when the writers should do more home-work, make the plots more realistic. I feel like they just take on a convenient target."

I swallowed. "What do you mean?"

"That part about lawyers. Everyone loves to hate lawyers—and it seems like the program has gone for that kind of story a lot over the years. It's just lazy."

I said, slowly, "Well, they probably figure that law-yers have power and that power corrupts. And lawyers are exposed to lots of criminals. It might make it easy for their moral compass to be shifted a few degrees." My heart rate was rising, and I could feel my pulse in my throat.

She sat up straighter. "People have no idea how difficult the job is." She lifted her eyebrows at me in assumed com-plicity. "Believe me, I know. People on the outside are always ready to jump in, criticizing, acting like they know what jus-tice should look like, when they don't have all the facts."

I opened my mouth, trying to figure out how to protest, when the program came on again, and Katherine immedi-ately clicked the remote to bring back the sound.

The screen was filled with the image of a judge entering the courtroom. Then the trial began. The ne'er-do-well son of an important family, prominent in the social universe of the program's fictional town, had been accused of assault by a woman of "poor reputation." I squirmed as the defendant claimed that any "out-of-character" behavior in the past was due to his former addiction, but that it didn't matter any-way because the woman was lying. The woman jumped in outrage, but the judge shut her down, and her own lawyer—the one who'd been bribed—sat mute and ineffective. In the end the judge gave the assaulter the lightest of all possible sentences. He referenced the accused's good family and his bright future ("I trust he will go on to do great things once this unfortunate incident is behind him . . .") as well as the "he said, she said" nature of the accusations. The woman—whose "loose behavior" had been prominently featured—ran out of the courtroom in tears. The last scene in the episode featured the victim, her face forlorn and mascara streaked, stumbling onto a bridge.

Katherine clicked it off and turned to me, smiling. "Well, I guess it turned out all right in the end."

I stared at her, trying to focus. To be watching this with Katherine, in my apartment, was so absurd a circumstance, it was worthy of a soap opera plot line itself. But this was real life. My life.

I swallowed "Turned out all right?"

"Yes, you know. Justice was served. The kid was from a good family, after all, and it's not like he got off scot-free. Hopefully community service will teach him to be more careful."

"But . . . what about the woman? What about what he did?"

She shrugged. "Well, anything that woman says has to be taken with a grain of salt. She already has a baby and doesn't know who the father is, and we know in the past she used men for whatever she could get."

Blood thundered in my temples. I sputtered, "But . . . none of that proves he didn't do it. It was all glossed over. Her lawyer took a bribe instead of defending her. No one at the trial even attempted to get to the truth."

She waved her hand. "No doubt the young man learned his lesson, so what was the use of putting someone like him in prison? It's important that people believe in the system, and the general public would not appreciate nuance. Her lawyer had probably saved her reputation from further damage . . ." She warmed to her subject, parroting the lawyer in the program. "It was just a case of 'he said, she said,' after all."

I was astonished. I couldn't even begin to untangle the circularity of this argument.

She glanced at me and her face changed. "Frannie? Are you all right?"

I had no idea what to say. Confront her? Tell her what her husband had done? Did she know?

I stood and hobbled to the window.

"Frannie?" She sounded concerned, puzzled.

I tried to keep my voice even. "It sounds like you are excusing bad behavior so long as the person has connections." I trailed off, stunned and inarticulate in the face of the poisonous attitudes contained in her comments.

I returned to my chair. "Imagine if it had been Lisa who was attacked. I'm sure you wouldn't be okay with this sort of outcome, even if her attacker had been someone from a 'good family.' The young woman was so devastated it looked like she was going to throw herself off the bridge. Do you think that's okay?"

"No, of course not!" She looked genuinely shocked. "Suicide is never okay! I believe it is a sin against creation."

I looked at her, beyond stunned. I had been expecting her to comment on the sentence for the attacker . . . but she was judging the actions of the despairing young woman? The cluelessness of asserting such moral certitude when she was in the process of defending corruption struck me momentarily speechless.

She leaned forward, her eyes troubled. "Oh Frannie, I've disappointed you. I'm sorry. Really. I guess I did come off as unsympathetic. It's just that I feel like I need to defend the system from people who don't understand a lawyer's job."

"Are you saying that it is part of a lawyer's job to take bribes?"

She flushed a vivid pink, and her eyes opened wide. "Frannie!" She pressed her open hand against her chest. "Of course not! How could you even suggest such a thing?"

How could I indeed? I stared at her, trying to figure out if her response was straightforward outrage, a blatant charade, or a more complicated reaction, a response to a potential rift in the tightly woven fabric of her self-deception?

Katherine swallowed and then offered diplomatically. "To tell you the truth, I guess my reaction comes mostly from the fact that soap operas are more fun if you take sides—sort of like my version of sports!" She smiled, trying to get me to return it. When I didn't, the corners of her mouth sank, and she leaned in closer. "*Of course*, in real life, in a real trial—when the people were real and not characters in a story—*of course* I would be sympathetic to the young woman. As you say, I have a stepdaughter to think of, and the world isn't always kind to us females." Then, having struck this ringing blow for feminism, she looked at me and leaned back. "I can tell you were a good nurse—you are so compassionate. You remind me how easy it is to be sucked in and get on my high horse."

I was completely at a loss as to what to say. She patted my hand. "Are you sure you're okay?"

I nodded. Her fingers curled around my hand, and she squeezed gently. "And . . . are we okay?"

I blinked at her, trying to focus. "Um, yes. I . . . I just . . ." My cell bleeped, and a picture of Iris lit the screen. I practically dropped the phone I snatched it up so quickly. "Hi!" I cried to Iris, enthusiastically. "Yes, I'm ready to discuss the new counters."

Iris said, "Um, Mom?"

I interrupted, "Honey, can you hang on one second? Katherine is here with me . . ."

"But Mom . . ."

"Okay. I'll call you right back."

I put the phone in my pocket and turned to Katherine. I had regained my composure, at least enough to know I could not continue the conversation with her. I needed her gone. Now. So I could process this. So I could scream. I inhaled deeply, more in control of myself.

"I'm sorry, but Iris needs me to help with some renovation decisions. Did I tell you we're putting my old condo on the market?" I stood to send a clear signal that our get-together was ending.

I must be a better actress than I'd thought, because she seemed completely unaware of how flustered I was. Either that or she had cultivated whatever armor was necessary to keep such conversations from leaving a mark. "Oh, no need to apologize. I barged in on you, after all." She leaned into her walker to stand up. "In fact," she offered, "I was a decorator for years. I'd be happy to help if you'd like any assistance."

"Thank you . . ." I moved toward the door. "But in this case my creative daughter has definite ideas. It is why I want to jump at this chance to offer an opinion."

She smiled at that. "I understand completely." She gave me a look that seemed to say, *"Let's put any unpleasantness behind us,"* and then replied, "Your Iris is so creative, but people aren't always good at seeing the viewpoints of others."

The absurdity of that comment, coming as it did from someone who had just demonstrated such utter cluelessness and self-delusion, led me to the most surprising thing of all in a morning full of surprises. I started laughing. In fact, as my guffaw burst out, I realized I was on the edge of one of those near-hysterical bouts, laughter as a response to the absurd. I bit the inside of my cheeks to keep myself from sliding into a howl.

Puzzlement passed over Katherine's expression, and I saw the question rise in her eyes, wondering if I was having some sort of an attack. Seeing this, I swallowed hard and managed to shake my head and regain my composure. I flattened my hand against my midsection. "Oh my." I exhaled slowly. "I'm sorry. It's just, well, if you had any idea about how your comment regarding Iris intersected with our history . . ." I let my voice trail off. "I didn't mean to be rude."

"Of course not!" she exclaimed, as if she couldn't imagine me ever being rude. Then she smiled warmly. "I'd love to hear more family stories. Iris seems like such an interesting person." A moment before, this would have added to my absurd laughter, but suddenly, the full understanding of what it would mean if Iris knew I had become friends with the wife of the judge who she considered responsible for Bethany's death descended like a wet shroud. I swallowed again, this time against tears. What was happening to me, rapid cycling through emotions like this?

Katherine continued to look worried. I reassured her. "Really, I'm fine." I mustered a fake smile. I seemed to be reassuring people of my emotional fitness a lot lately.

She nodded. "If you're sure . . ." she said, and opened the door.

* * *

After she left, I returned to my chair, drained. I felt like I was observing myself from a great distance: watching dark clouds develop on the horizon, or the thickening bands of a storm in a distant state flash across the map on the weather channel. I looked down at Katherine's untouched croissant. She *must* have known about the investigations.

How could she not have?

I'd been telling myself that she somehow had maintained a protected, vaporous remove. A scrupulous ignorance. But it had been in all the papers. She had to have known at least something.

I wondered how I would have reacted if Calvin had been accused of doing something so wrong. In my heart of hearts, I had to admit I probably would have stayed with him, publicly anyway. Especially if there were journalists nosing around, as there were around Nathaniel. But in private? I would have excoriated him. And after the hubbub died down, I probably would have divorced him.

But maybe I'm kidding myself. How many excuses do people make for those they love? Maybe he just denied it, and she believed him. And why not?

The stern voice of Sister Marie-Clotilde, the principal of my old convent school, echoed inside my head: *"Refusing to see sin is the same as sin."* In her uncompromising view, forgiving the people we love is one thing. Looking the other way and enabling them to do evil—especially evil we benefit from—is another. Those nuns who survived being sent from

France to the North Dakota prairie, and warmed with little more than their faith, had backbones of steel. There was no room for shades of gray in their moral repertoire. She would have scoffed at such a failure of conscience.

Then again, mere humans rarely measured up to the frosty standards of the good sister. She didn't really have the capacity for overlooking errors that loving someone requires.

The next day there was a note slipped under my door. It was from Katherine. In shaky handwriting it said, "I want to thank you for your friendship. I'm afraid I'm not feeling great lately—some old trouble acting up, nothing to worry about—but I might not be able to come down to the dining room so much in the next few days, and I wanted to tell you how much I value you. Thank you for being such a good person."

I stared at the note and realized my hand was shaking too.

THE NEXT TIME I heard Mrs. Collier make a fuss, I opened the door, thinking maybe I could help. But Graciela was ushering her back into her apartment, getting her settled. When the door closed behind them, I was once again drawn to the med cart. I stood peering down for a while. The way it was laid out didn't make sense to me, and I tried to discern why things were organized as they were.

"What's so interesting?"

I jumped and whirled around.

It was that guy with the thick silver hair, from the book group. What was his name? Evan?

He held up his hands. "Sorry—I didn't mean to startle you. I was coming home"—he nodded toward the top of the corridor, where the entrance to my hallway met the lobby—"and I saw you standing here. You seemed to be looking so intently."

I straightened. "Yes, well," I cleared my throat. "I was just . . . remembering. I started my career as an aide, doing exactly this sort of work. I was wondering if things had changed very much." I shifted the subject. "And you? What are you doing out and around at this hour? Usually, by this time of night everyone is in their apartment watching television."

"My daughter took me to the grand opening of a new ice cream shop." He waggled his eyebrows. "I had chocolate ripple. It'll probably keep me up, but I don't regret a single bite."

A friendly-looking woman leaned around the corner and called, "Dad? We're holding the elevator." She smiled in my direction, obviously not wanting to be rude.

Evan called, "Be right there." He inclined his head toward me. "Frannie, isn't it? Nice to see you again. Have a good evening."

I nodded at him and melted back into my doorway, watching as he ambled down the hall in his dated but fashionably patterned sweater. But after he was out of sight, a powerful urge nagged at me. I stepped back into the hall. Though I couldn't have told you precisely why, I opened the camera on my phone—just like my grandsons had taught me—held it over the med cart, and took a picture. I didn't question the urge too closely. Some instinct told me I might want to have it. For future reference.

*　*　*

Katherine had the flu. At least that's what Jannah told me when I entered the dining room and noticed their usual seats were empty. Remembering her pallor, I asked, "Is she okay?"

"I think so. The judge had been sick for a few days, and she was tending to him. But I guess it caught up to her. She's not so strong herself."

"The old fool should let the staff help," I said under my breath as I pulled out my chair to sit down.

But Jannah heard me. "I know. That's why we're here. But he is stubborn." She pressed her lips together to stop herself from speaking ill of a resident. Her dark eyes flashed. "He wants her to be the only person taking care of him."

I sighed. I knew Katherine saw looking after her husband as her main task in life, but still. "Will she be okay?"

"I heard she got worse, but I don't know anything else."

The next morning at breakfast, Nathaniel sat stone-faced, and Lisa sat next to him. Even when seated, she was taller than Nathaniel, but today he seemed almost shrunken, and Lisa hovered over him as he stared at his breakfast. He looked distinctly unwell.

I approached their table. "Good morning," I said. "I heard you have been ill. I hope you're feeling better." I looked around. "Will Katherine be coming down?"

Lisa sent a worried glance at her father before gesturing for me to sit. Her graying chestnut hair was pulled back, fully exposing all her piercings. "Katherine's in the hospital. They both had the flu. But it hit Katherine harder. She was having a difficult time, so we took her in last night."

"I'm so sorry." I turned to Nathaniel and added loudly, "I'm sorry to hear Katherine is not well. If I can help, please let me know." I knew the words were pale and useless, but it seemed rude not to offer.

He lifted his chin and spoke with his usual aloof formality. "Thank you, but Lisa is here. I'll be fine." Then perhaps realizing he should offer some comment about Katherine, he added, "I understand she is resting comfortably." His hand trembled as he lifted his water glass and looked away.

Lisa blushed at his curtness. "We're heading to the hospital in a few minutes." Bending her head nearer to mine and dropping her voice, she said, "I apologize if he seems rude. He's at a loss. He relies on her. But he likes to pretend it's the other way around."

I patted Lisa's arm and gave her the most understanding look I could muster before rising to return to my table.

I went to sit in my usual seat, half hidden in the corner. While I waited for my coffee, the server brought Nathaniel his breakfast, and Lisa pulled in close to him. "Try to eat something, Dad," she said, and put a piece of toast in front of him.

He pushed it away. "I'm not some invalid."

"Please?" She lifted a spoonful of cereal to his mouth. To my astonishment, he accepted the spoon meekly, like a child, before turning his face away.

Lisa let her glance linger on his head. Then she smoothed his back and said, "Come on. We should be able to get in to see her now."

* * *

There was no sign of them in the dining room the next morning. Walking through the lobby after breakfast, I almost didn't recognize the judge, curled into himself at the bench by the elevator. Worry had done its work: he was diminished and prickly, a desiccated husk of misery. I steeled myself. For a long time after Cal died, I thought he'd been the lucky one. You hear it all the time in a place like Ridgewood: those of us left behind suffer more. For a solitary and unfriendly man like Nathaniel, the misery and emptiness of life stretching ahead would be even worse. Having experienced that loneliness, I was sympathetic—even to Nathaniel Kearney.

The only thing worse is losing a child, I reminded myself. He didn't deserve my sympathy. But still. It reminded me of how punishing the pain is when one is left behind.

I approached him gingerly. "Any news?"

He shifted, eyes unfocused and blurry. For a second I thought maybe he didn't know who I was. "The doctors have nothing useful to say, as usual. If she can just fight off this bug . . ." He pressed his lips together.

"Dad?" Lisa rounded the corner from the hall. She nodded hello at me, then folded her tall frame to squat down in front of her father. "Ready to go to back to the hospital?"

I watched them slowly make their way out the door, her bright blue raincoat against his gray sweater.

I was supposed to attend the book club that morning. We were scheduled to discuss Jane Eyre. Katherine had chosen it, surprising everyone. I'd never enjoyed the story particularly—like everybody else I had read it in school—though I looked forward to hearing why she had picked it. But now that she wasn't going to be there I didn't really want to go.

Katherine and I hadn't talked in the week and a half since we'd watched the soap opera together. In the immediate aftermath of that incident, I had decided that I was done with her and that no friendship was possible. But I realized I missed her. Despite everything. Maybe I just missed having a buddy. She was the last new friend I would make in this life, most likely. One of the things that happens as you get older is that friends dribble away, just when you need them most. After Cal died, some of our couple friends had acted like widowhood was catching, and became much more distant. My old pal Sylvia and her husband, Bob, were crisscrossing the country in a Winnebago and were hardly ever in touch. Another former colleague to whom I'd been close was busy building a new life with a second spouse. My kids were wonderful. But they were my kids. Certain things I would never talk about with them, and certain things they were too young to understand. Thank goodness, I had Ruthie. Even though she was far away, my cousin was a faithful correspondent and my oldest friend.

In fact, I had sought her advice about Katherine. In my pocket was a brief note from her, in which she had replied exactly as I had expected. She scolded that I shouldn't be so quick to criticize (a comment she often aimed at me, even though she herself could more accurately be accused of it) and that finding friends at our age isn't always easy. I turned and went back to my apartment. Maybe I'd pour my craving for connection into another letter.

But it was no good. I managed a few lines, but I couldn't focus. Especially when my stomach growled. I had only picked at my breakfast eggs, which had been cooked to rubber, and now I realized how hungry I was. And not for any of the boring, healthy things I had in my refrigerator. I set aside my pen and paper and called Pam. "Hey! Do you know that new café on Central? Can I take you and the boys out for an early lunch? My treat—I have a coupon!"

* * *

It took a few days, but there they came, Katherine and Nathaniel slowly entering the dining room together. Katherine had grown even thinner and less upright, but she was still elegantly put together. She wore extra blush on her pale cheeks, and her sweater hung loosely on her frame. Lisa was with them, holding Katherine's elbow. The judge glanced around like an eagle, proud and ornery. After they were settled, Katherine kept glancing sideways at him, with tender eyes.

Her vulnerability touched me. She gave me a welcoming smile when I approached their table. I bent down to hug her, and she was so frail I was afraid my gentle pressure would hurt. "So glad to see you back."

She squeezed my hand. "I'm happy to see you too. Will you join us?"

The judge cleared his throat. "My dear, I don't think that's wise. You shouldn't get yourself overly tired." Then he looked at me directly and said, "I hope you'll understand it should be family first."

I turned to Katherine, expecting her to say, "Oh nonsense. Please, sit down." But though she flushed at her husband's attitude, she didn't say a word. Her eyes flickered away. Lisa's cheeks went deep pink.

I lowered my head slightly. "Of course. I just wanted to welcome you home."

Katherine's eyes were soft when her gaze lifted to mine. "Perhaps we can get together soon."

Cheeks burning, I retreated to my seat near the coffee nook. I watched her, pale as she was, fret over Nathaniel, arrange his cane on the back of his chair, and pull close his sweater. He waved his hand and dismissed her. "It's perfectly fine. Please stop fussing."

She put her hands in her lap. "Of course. You're right."

What was this? She was the one who had been sick! I wondered how much the effort of maintaining the charade of everything being "perfectly fine" was costing her. The whole scene: his dismissal of my welcome, her apparent acceptance of his imperious attitude, his irritation when she was obviously trying to show him affection . . . Ugh. I wasn't sure which of them I was more annoyed with.

He leaned over to pick up a dropped napkin and immediately let loose a cry of pain. "Aargh," he groaned. "My back."

Lisa stood. "Oh no, not again." She exchanged a look with Katherine. Nathaniel moaned loudly as Lisa helped him up. "Let's get you upstairs. You can take your medicine, and we'll call the therapist." An aide hurried over with a wheelchair.

Katherine spoke to her stepdaughter. "Go ahead and get him settled. I'll have one of the staff bring me up in a little while."

After Lisa pushed the grimacing Nathaniel out of the dining room, Katherine sat marooned at the table by herself, looking small and helpless. I decided to try again.

She glanced up as I drew near, and immediately smiled. I indicated the chair next to her. "Perhaps I can join you for a minute?"

"Oh yes. Of course!" Her voice was weak, but warm. "Now we can catch up."

"I hope Nathaniel is all right?"

"Oh . . ." Her hand fluttered near her face. "He has these back issues. It's painful, but he has pills for it." She sighed. "He'll be fine in a couple hours." There was something wistful in her voice. And perhaps a whiff of bitterness?

"How are *you*?" My tone let her know I really meant the question, that it was not just passing-the-time small talk. "You were the one in the hospital, after all."

"Oh yes. I . . ." She touched her nose with a tissue. Something passed over her face, and she glanced away. Then she pulled her lips into a brief smile that didn't really reach her eyes. "You know how it is. Day to day." She tilted her head. "It doesn't get any easier, does it? Getting old, I mean. And everything we have to deal with."

I half chuckled. "No. No, I guess it doesn't. But I'm glad for every chance to get better at getting older. If you know what I mean." I thought it was a funny formulation. But she seemed far away. When she didn't say anything, or even smile, I cleared my throat. "So—will you be joining the book club meeting next week? I was hoping to sway your vote when we choose our next title. The others keep picking mysteries, and I want some biographies."

"I'll do my best." She again glanced away for a second. "Frannie?"

Her tone surprised me. "What is it?"

"I've . . . really enjoyed doing things with you."

"Me too." At that moment I really meant it. "I enjoy your company." I corrected the tense, for emphasis, and squeezed her hand. Her face was sincere, but there was an opaque quality. Was she offering some sort of half apology for Nathaniel's rudeness, or her distance? Was she thinking about bringing up our conversation about the television show? Or was it something else?

"Are you all right?" I asked.

She smiled with forced sunniness. "Yes, of course!" She put her other hand on top of mine, tentatively at first. Then she patted it. "Do you remember when we first met? You took my pulse! It seems so long ago now." Her voice grew pensive. "Time flies. It is hard to know the best way to make use of one's energy."

It felt like we were talking at cross currents, like she was saying something I couldn't pick up on. I matched her exaggerated brightness with my own, trying to get her to be more committal. "Well, I advocate for time with your friends. And reading more books, of course." She smiled and squeezed my hand again. Behind her I could see into the hall and caught a glimpse of Lisa getting off the elevator. I said, "Really, I miss you. Let's get together. Maybe we could arrange another 'pie lunch.'"

Her eyes were moist when she returned the smile. Vivid, but also sad. "Oh yes! I'd like that."

Lisa arrived. "So you got to chat after all." She bent down to kiss Katherine's cheek. "Ready? We should get back to Daddy before too long. I'll have them send up our lunches." Katherine pushed against the armrest of her chair, and Lisa helped her up. As they left, Katherine looked over her shoulder at me. "It would be lovely to eat pie with you again, Frannie. Someday soon." I watched her go, full of annoyance and puzzlement. And I had to admit, affection that persisted despite my reservations.

Still. I often felt, after talking to Katherine, that I had missed something. That if only I were more refined, more in tune with the charm school way of saying things, I would know better what she was talking about. She spoke in an allusive and indirect fashion, one refined, socially astute people understood and could respond to in kind, but indecipherable to a blunt kid from North Dakota.

* * *

Later that week I was walking through the lobby when someone called my name. I turned. It was Evan Silver Hair. From the book group. He hobbled toward me, somehow giving off the impression of spriteliness, although he was using a cane. He smiled. "Going to the library? Perhaps we can go together?"

He seemed a nice enough guy, but my lifelong tendency to resist kicked in. What was his real interest? And why did he always materialize out of nowhere? He said he'd been some sort of investigator, but maybe he was just a snoop.

"Ah, thanks but—"

He interrupted. "I'm glad you're part of our reading group. I'm especially curious to see what you'll suggest for our next picks." We were standing in the window-filled main lobby, and over his shoulder I saw a flash of bright color. I realized it was Lisa, running though the parking lot to the door. It was raining outside, and her yellow umbrella was bright against her ultramarine trench coat.

I held up my hand, this time interrupting Evan and nodding out the window. "Thanks, but if you'll excuse me, I'd like to catch her." I gestured in Lisa's direction and turned before he had an opportunity to respond.

I positioned myself so I was standing just inside the door when Lisa entered. I smiled at her. "You look like you've stepped out of a painting."

She held out her sleeves and umbrella and laughed. "I guess I do!"

I gestured to a nearby bench. "Can you sit a second?"

She looked surprised, but not unpleasantly so. "Um, sure—I have some time."

I carefully lowered myself onto the pale upholstery. She finished closing her umbrella and took a seat next to me. "What can I do for you?" she asked.

"I just wondered . . . Is everything okay? I haven't seen your folks since Nathaniel hurt his back."

Lisa nodded. "They're doing okay. I mean, of course, Katherine is not terribly strong." She paused. "You were a nurse, right?"

I nodded.

"Well, so then you know her trouble isn't reversible. But the doctors say just keep doing what she loves. Like that book group. She always enjoyed it."

"We're picking new titles now." I paused, hesitant to ask. But my last conversation with Katherine had felt so odd. "I hope I haven't offended her for some reason? I haven't heard from her."

Lisa's eyebrows shot up. "Oh! Please don't think that." She twisted toward me. "She'd be upset to hear that. It isn't anything to do with you, at all." She opened her hands, and slumped a little. "In all honesty, I'm a little annoyed with both of them. Dad is doing his thing again."

"His thing?"

"Actually, I should say *they're* doing *their* thing again." She crooked her fingers in air quotes. "Dad sort of hems her in. Insists she stay at home, not participate in activities, and he controls their schedule. And she seems to almost relish it. I guess she likes him playing her protector."

"I would never have guessed she'd submit to that so easily."

Lisa shrugged. "When things are going well, she's the one to set the agenda. But this is their pattern when things go wrong. Her recent bout in the hospital scared him. He feels helpless. And his response is to control whatever he can. As for her, she seems to almost be flattered by it. Like she has some weird princess syndrome." She shrugged. "That's what my therapist says, anyway."

I considered for a minute. "I never quite believed she was such a shrinking violet, even when she acted the part."

Lisa's chuckle was humorless. "I know. It's an aspect of her character I could never fathom." She shifted toward me. "Their whole marriage has been like this. When everything is chugging along smoothly, Katherine's life widens. Her world gets bigger and bigger, even though my dad is always at the center. She'll develop independent friendships, do volunteer work, that sort of thing. Even travel with her stepdaughter . . ." She flashed a rueful smile. I could see her trying to find the words. "It's like—I always picture her life as a rubber band that slowly stretches longer and longer. And they both seem fine with it." Lisa gestured with her arms, opening them wide. "But as soon as something upsets the regular order—" She paused. "Some trouble at my dad's job, for example . . ."

My chest tightened.

"And the elastic snaps." As she said this, she clapped her hands together loudly. I almost jumped. She went on. "Then Katherine reverts to this 'Southern lady' role. Totally deferential, letting dad dictate the terms of their life. Her friendships and external commitments all fall by the wayside. It has happened over and over again. It used to drive me nuts until I got old enough to see the pattern." She shrugged. "And to talk about it with my shrink."

"I imagine sometimes it was you who upset the order."

She smiled. "You don't miss much, do you? Yes, as close as Katherine and I were, if it came down to a choice between me or my dad, I never doubted who she'd pick. Or which of us my dad would choose, for that matter." She swallowed. "This is going to sound harsh, but I don't mean it to. Katherine was really great to me when I was a kid. In some ways more supportive than my biological mom. But the thing is, my dad didn't really have headspace for anyone other than Katherine. And whatever else she felt or thought, when push came to shove, she'd always stand by her husband. No matter what, she never challenged his actions, even when he—" She stopped short and pressed her lips together. "No matter what."

No matter what? I tried to read her expression, but she had turned away from me, and her profile gave no clue as to what she meant. How well did she know her father? How much attention would she have paid to any scandal? I thought of the yellowing newspaper clippings in my desk drawer. I wondered, would Iris believe anything bad about me? Wouldn't she dismiss such stories outright, out of love or loyalty?

Perhaps the only way we can survive is to be willing to believe the best and overlook the worst. And when it comes to family, I wonder how many of us really feel like we have any choice which side we are on.

I tried to phrase my question neutrally. "Is Katherine . . . one of those wives who believe their husbands can do no wrong?"

Lisa seemed to be looking inward. "Hmm." Then she exhaled. "What she actually believes deep down, I couldn't tell you. But let's just say women like Katherine don't see things that are *inconvenient*." My hands were balled in my lap, and I squeezed my fingernails into my palms. I thought of the army of do-gooding women, the wives of powerful men staffing the ladies auxiliaries and church sales, volunteering at hospital gift shops and museums and drop-in programs—how many of them were performing compensatory labor? Paying the karmic debt for comfortable lives built on the back of greed or corruption or injustice? I had known, of course, that Katherine was married to a reprehensible person. Once again the mystery rose up. Was she guilty merely of not knowing what he did? Or was it a deliberate refusal to see? Facts don't always reveal who we are. But our contradictions? That is where we show ourselves. We find a way to believe what we need to believe.

Lisa cleared her throat, startling me out of my thoughts. "Anyway, please don't take it personally. It's just that for now anyway, she's letting him call the shots." She shrugged. "She just seems so tired. Too tired to resist him."

* * *

The following day I observed Katherine and Nathaniel again from my seat behind the serving station door. Lisa pushed Katherine in a wheelchair while Nathanial, on his walker, inched with careful slowness alongside them. She looked even more pale and thin, but he, as always, reminded me of some ancient bird of prey, craning his head around before he landed. Katherine fussed, patting his arm like a newlywed. Wrapped in her cashmere and jewelry. I wanted to yell at her. I excused myself, too agitated to eat.

As I was getting ready to leave the dining room I heard her saying to the server, "No thank you," and the judge interrupting her, "Katherine. You will eat." To the server he said, "Yes, bring Mrs. Kearney the potatoes."

If Cal had done something like that to me, he would have received an icy glare, a kick under the table, and an earful when we were alone.

Katherine said, "Yes, of course, you're right. Thank you, dear."

I lurched away on my cane as quickly as I could.

CHAPTER

11

FOR THE FIRST year after Bethany's death, Iris rose at six every morning and headed to the bench in a nearby park. It was where Bethany used to meet her friends before walking to middle school. There Iris would wait, sipping coffee from a thermos, until light filled the sky and the first few sleepy-headed students, those on the swim team or going in early for makeup tests, would straggle by, trudging under their backpacks. After she finished the coffee, she'd wander past the corner where the elementary kids waited with their moms and dads at the bus stop, the same corner where she had once chatted with her fellow parents. Then she'd return home and go back to bed, crying herself to sleep over the world that had been taken from her.

When Bethany died, Iris lost not only her beloved girl but also her social place. Motherhood, the only career she had ever really wanted, and that she had achieved at great cost, was torn away. She'd built close friendships with some of her neighbors who had children Bethany's age—friendships based in part on shared experiences of parenting. The awkwardness that pervaded those relationships now reminded me, and worse, I know, reminded Iris, of the painful span when she'd been unable to conceive. Jimmy and Iris had tried for years before finally getting pregnant with Bethany, through IVF. Her miracle baby. I remembered the brave face Iris put on while all her friends had baby showers and bought strollers, and how some of them were disturbed by how urgently she wanted to be included in those conversations— just as they found her desire to join in on conversations about parenthood awkward now. Her longing marked her as out of step, uncomfortable.

The painful reminders extended to our whole family. Before the accident, Danny and Adam were often at Iris's. Bethany babysat for her young cousins, and the two families had game nights and dinners together. Given the unlikelihood that she'd be able to have another child, Iris was thrilled that Bethany loved playing with her nephews. She told me once how much she hoped Bethany would stay close with Danny and Adam, and how glad she was that after she and Jimmy were gone, Bethany would still have family.

But that all changed after the accident. Charlie and Pam kept inviting Iris and Jimmy over for games, or to the boys' soccer matches or recitals. And they would go, and Iris would put on a brave face and try to be present and happy. But often as not, she'd melt away from the room, seeking the shelter of the bathroom to cry in peace. Danny and Adam were young enough where they didn't quite understand what had happened or why Auntie Iris never had them over anymore. To their credit, Pam and Charlie continued to try, but I once overheard Pam explaining to Danny: "Well, you know it is very sad what happened to Bethany. Auntie Iris is still feeling really bad. I don't think we'll be going over there as much." Under her breath I heard her say, "She needs to pull herself together." There was a touch of exasperation in her voice.

When she turned into the hallway and saw me, her face fell. I saw in her eyes that she realized how unkind she sounded. I gave her a little shake of my head, but I couldn't really blame her. Pam's own sister lived a couple hours away and also had two boys, nearly the same age as Danny and

Adam. They'd started spending more and more time with her family. How could I find fault with that? Even though I knew Iris longed for closeness, she was too deeply mired in grief.

* * *

"The days are long, but the years are short." Someone said that to me about parenthood when I first had kids, and it stayed with me. Long after they were grown, after long exhausting days and eyelash-whisper, blink-short years, I understood the truth of it.

And I grasped it again, differently and more deeply, when I saw Iris struggling with her loss. For her the equation has flipped, and she is aching through long years without Bethany, and remembering the too-short days she had with her, all too well.

Iris wasn't the only one who'd had difficulty getting pregnant. During her fertility struggles I knew exactly what she was going through, because I had experienced it myself. But Iris never gave up. Unlike me.

In my case, after years of tracking my ovulation and having sex on schedule and praying every month, and feeling with rising exhilaration the swelling of my breasts and nausea, only to wake up with blood in my underwear, I had accepted the bitter fact that becoming a mom might not be in my future. But I wasn't as honest as Iris. I pretended it didn't bother me. I insisted I was focused on my career. But the truth was, I longed to be pregnant.

I was still working the ER then. One day a sixteen-year-old came in, pregnant and terrified. It was one of those cases you hear about: a kid who didn't know what to do and so simply did nothing. No, her parents didn't know. No, she hadn't seen a doctor. No, she hadn't made any plans. Maybe she should just marry her boyfriend? (As if that was somehow an answer.) No, she hadn't talked about it with him. She was six months along and had hardly been eating, starving herself in the hopes of hiding her growing midsection. Almost passing out at school had finally scared her into getting some medical attention.

My hands trembled as I put my stethoscope on her belly. Shelly, the other nurse I was working with, shot me a peculiar glance. Later, she approached me in the break room as I poured myself a coffee.

"Are you all right?' she said.

"Yes, of course." My voice was sharp. "Why do you ask?"

Another nurse in the room spoke up. "Well, you have to admit, that was ridiculous. Silly girl. As if ignoring it would make everything all okay!" She paused, "Especially when so many would welcome a baby." Her tone invited me to share, to acknowledge what apparently had been obvious.

Instead, I glared at her. "Are you assuming I want a child?"

She blushed. "Oh. Um . . ." she stammered. "It's just that you seem upset."

"Well, of course. Foolish girl." I lifted my voice. "But I'm going to medical school. A baby isn't in the picture." A thought that had been half formed in the back of my brain had chosen that moment to burst forth.

Both of them cried out, "Medical school! Really? How exciting!"

Well, why not? If I was going to be denied pregnancy, something an idiotic sixteen-year-old girl could achieve, I was going to account for myself in a different way.

The word spread among the nursing staff, and suddenly, instead of asking when Cal and I were having kids, I was asked about my application. My colleagues—all women— saw me as striking a blow for our collective ability. Any talk of kids was forgotten as they helped me with my organic chemistry flashcards in the break room. The day after I got accepted, they all chipped in on a decorated cake. It was what we usually did when one of us had a baby, but instead of a baby name in icing, surrounded by pink and blue rattles, it featured a caduceus on either side of my name, the snakes climbing up white icing to the wings of Hermes. In a box somewhere I have a photo of that cake. In the same box is my acceptance letter and a beautiful congratulations card from Cal, also addressed to "Dr. Greene."

Medical school didn't feel like a defeat or a fallback plan. It felt like the place I was meant to be. When I got my grades at the end of the first semester, I cooked Cal a special dinner: steak and mushrooms, mashed potatoes. Chocolate cake. I even splurged on some expensive wine.

"It smells great in here," he called as he walked in the door, and his eyes lit up when he spied me wearing my best red dress and makeup beside the candlelit table. He poured us each some merlot and lifted his glass. "To my wife, the doctor-to-be." We clinked. I sipped.

Suddenly my stomach lurched like I was rounding the apex of a roller coaster. I bolted for the bathroom, spilling wine all over myself. Cal ran after me. He held my hair back as I retched, kneeling over the toilet.

I sat back, wiping my mouth. "So much for my fancy dinner." I blinked at Cal.

He kissed my forehead. "You better get out of that dress before the stain sets."

He helped me up, and I lifted my hair for him to assist with the zipper. I had to suck in my stomach for him to slide it below my ribs. "Seems like this dress has gotten tighter." His voice was funny.

"I know. I had to struggle to zip it up." I sighed. "But don't worry, I won't let a med school diet make me fat." He managed to get the zipper open. Then he put his hands on my shoulders and gently turned me toward him.

His eyes were shining. He put one hand on my belly. "Frannie?"

It had never occurred to me that the exhaustion was anything other than study-induced sleep deprivation. Or that the occasional nausea was from anything other than too many cafeteria sandwiches. But all it took was one dinner, and Cal figured out what his nurse and aspiring-doctor wife had missed. I was pregnant. We did the math. I was probably six weeks along.

That night Cal fell asleep hugging me. I lay in the dark, eyes open. Overwhelmed. How could something I had wanted so badly finally happen when I had stopped hoping? I had a different ambition now, one I was in love with.

* * *

The next day Cal brought in the mail. He held up a notice from the medical school. "I guess you won't be getting these anymore," he said exuberantly. "You'll have to call so they won't bill us for next semester."

I swallowed. "We'll . . . have to see, I guess."

His eyes flickered with a momentary recognition that maybe I was saying what I was, indeed, actually saying. "But you're pregnant!" He hugged me, the doubt pushed down, replaced by a stubborn insistence on us both being deliriously happy.

I inhaled. "I'm not sure I want to give up med school."

His whole body stiffened.

"What do you mean??"

"Just . . . I'd like to keep going. At least to try."

He looked like I'd slapped him. "But we've been praying for this. You've wanted a baby for years. Now suddenly you don't?" He blinked at me like I was crazy. "You're having a child, for goodness sake. Our baby. Isn't that better than anything?"

I buried my face in his chest. "But I've come so far. And what if something goes wrong?"

"What if the exhaustion makes something go wrong? Can you live with that?"

I turned away. He stood watching me, waiting for me to engage. Finally he lifted his shoulders and sighed in frustration. Then he went into the front room and closed the door.

I went back to school. As my pregnancy became obvious, I was more and more isolated. One young man accused me of "wasting" a spot in medical school since I was going to be a mom. But worst was the silence between Cal and me. We kept trying to talk, but every time I said how unfair it all seemed, all he heard was my willingness to risk our child. The tension between us deepened as my belly grew. Anger, confusion, and fear were growing within me as well.

*   *   *

One Friday as I was leaving class, I felt a tightening around my waist. *Rectus abdominis*, the Latin name for the muscle, immediately pinged in my brain. Then it twisted into stabbing pain, and I had to grip a chair. This was no twinge or baby kick. I swallowed my terror. Early labor. I was not quite six months along.

I made it to my car and drove in panic to the hospital. My former colleagues in the ER were happy to see me for the mere second before they realized I could barely stand.

The PA system crackled with the stat page for obstetrics as they whisked me into a room. I knew before the OB came running that I might lose the baby. At that moment, I felt like my life would end as well. Even if Cal could forgive me, I wasn't sure I could forgive myself. A life of heartache unspooled in my imagination. I'd be too crushed to continue in school. Cal, bereft and angry and distant, would leave. I would lose my career, my family, and my marriage all at once. Desperate pleas rose, promises and bargains with God. I prayed with a fervor I didn't know I had.

*   *   *

The way women respond when I tell this story is determined by their age. Women of my generation assume as a matter of course that I left med school, while women in their twenties and thirties are surprised that I was even forced to choose. Women in between, those around my daughter's age, who at one time would have been outraged that I had to make a choice, fall reluctantly into a middle ground. As they have gotten older and had kids and come to know the limits of energy and time and attention and money, they seem mainly regretful for me. They understand that there are dilemmas for which there are no easy answers and that sometimes life imposes choices, either one sacrifice or another. But sacrifices, nonetheless.

In the ER that afternoon, Cal came running. The fear and love and terror on his face mirrored my own. I bawled like a child, snot streaming down my nose. He held me till the drugs kicked in. By some miracle, the contractions stopped. The baby that was Charlie quieted. The next thing I remember is opening my eyes to see Cal asleep, slumped in a chair next to the bed. He lifted his eyes when he felt my gaze, and took my hand.

I was on bed rest for the rest of the pregnancy.

*   *   *

The years are short but the days are long.

The demands of parenthood felt endless. A daily tornado of stress, responsibility, conflict, argument, sarcasm, laughter, playfulness, mess. The struggles to get them out of bed and to school, worries about friends and then romances and then sex and jobs and driving—oh God, teenagers driving. Some days I arrived at work feeling simultaneously like I'd just run a marathon, cried my eyes out at a funeral, and had a shouting match with a hostile neighbor: physically and emotionally spent.

And then they left.

The day Charlie left for college was it for me. I stood in his empty bedroom, marooned among the discarded posters and old books, the flotsam of childhood, and bit my lip. Iris was in her room, getting ready to spend her last summer at music camp. Both of my children would be far away. Full of tears and love and nostalgia, I crossed the hall and opened her bedroom door to ask her if she wanted to go out for coffee or shopping.

"Mom!" she yelled as she pushed her boyfriend off her, mortified and embarrassed.

I think of that day often when I remember Bethany, and how Iris didn't get to wrangle with her through the stop—start, herky-jerky dance of growing up. She never lived through the leave-taking and letting-go, seeing one's child move into adulthood. Of knowing you've done your job and raised them, but also that they will be home at Thanksgiving. Of being able to see an empty bedroom through the golden filter of nostalgia.

Iris cannot indulge herself in a warm bath of memories. She is too easily drowned.

12

As I walked into my living room, my cell buzzed in my pocket. Jimmy's number. My chest filled with icy dread as I fumbled to answer.

"Mom? Iris is in the hospital. But don't worry, I mean, there's no . . . She's okay. But come. She needs you." He cleared his throat. "Charlie is on his way over to get you."

I grabbed my purse and hurried to the lobby. I was scarcely there two minutes when I saw Charlie's silver Camry pull into the parking lot, bumping awkwardly as he took the speed bump too fast. I rushed outside to meet the car and was waiting for him as he pulled up to the curb.

Charlie ran around to the passenger's side to help me in. He was in exercise gear. His hair, which he usually kept carefully combed since his hairline started receding a few years back, was sticking out around his ears, with a few locks flopping down his forehead. His eyes were stormy and afraid. "Hey, Ma." He kissed me and held my elbow as I lowered myself into the car.

"What happened?" I asked as soon as he got in.

He put the car in gear and inhaled. I saw his hands tighten on the steering wheel. "She tried it again."

I was pretty sure I knew what he meant. But I had to make sure. "Did what?" My voice quivered.

"You know. She . . . tried to hurt herself." His voice wobbled too. Poor Charlie. I looked at his handsome profile, so like his dad's, and in sudden clarity I wondered what was it like for him. For so long now I'd been focused on Iris, her crises and her pain, that I had taken Charlie—his strength, the way he quietly held everything together without drama or demands—for granted. Did his kids feel like they were not as important as Bethany, their lost cousin? Tears welled in my eyes, and I resolved to pay more attention to them, and to him and Pam. I reached out and smoothed the hair jutting over his collar. "I love you, son."

He braked at a stop sign and turned to me. He squeezed my hand. "I love you too, Mom." His Adam's apple bobbed, and I saw the emotion. "I'm scared," he said quietly. The car behind us gave a little beep. He exhaled and accelerated.

When we arrived at the hospital, Jimmy was waiting for us. I said, "How is she? What happened?"

Jimmy shrugged and opened his arms in a gesture of helplessness. "I thought she had the flu. She'd been sweaty and nauseous, even had a little diarrhea." He stopped himself. "I came home and found her curled up in the bathroom, with some sleeping pills and a bottle of gin on the vanity. Just like before. But this time she didn't go through with it. She didn't swallow them all or drink so much." He paused. "I guess she stopped her antidepressants cold turkey. That's why she was sick."

Iris had been on a mild dose of Prozac for years—even before we lost Bethany. After Bethany's death and Iris's suicide attempt, the doctors shifted dosages and added something additional to address her anxiety. She'd been leery of the increases, but they helped. Perhaps too much, if she thought she could just stop them. I'd seen it before. People decide they feel so well they didn't need their meds anymore.

Jimmy said, "But she's been doing so great. We even began having fun again." His voice cracked and his eyes glittered like shattered glass on the highway.

Iris was in a bed in the ER, looking much as she had in the first months after the accident. Lank unwashed hair, gray skin. I reached out to stroke her cheek. "Oh, honey."

She allowed me to put my arms around her shoulders, and even leaned her head against me, but she didn't make a sound. She was far away.

Jimmy sat at the end of the bed, rubbing her ankle. I lifted her chin. "Sweetie, what happened?"

She turned her face away. I repeated, tenderly, "Honey?"

She swallowed. "I was forgetting, Mom," she whispered. "I was forgetting."

Jimmy cleared his throat. "We went out last weekend and dropped by some friends. Their daughter came home from play practice . . ." He inhaled and swallowed. "Afterward we went to dinner." He looked at me, pleading in his eyes. "We had fun."

Iris lifted her head and choked out the words. "Fun! We had fun. What an obscene thing to do. We should have been going out with our own daughter after a recital. Instead, we were laughing in a restaurant."

She cried, sweeping her eyes around the bed at us. "It's the drugs. It's all fake. I *should* feel bad. It's wrong not to. The accident was *my* fault." She stared at me, eyes wide. "I'm afraid I can't keep . . ." Her voice trembled, and she pressed her fingers over her mouth.

"Oh, Iris." I had to tread carefully. I stroked her hair off her forehead. She began weeping into my sweater. Finally I said, "Talk to your doctor. Maybe he can taper you off. But stopping cold turkey . . . It makes everything seem worse. It's dangerous to stop taking your medicine so suddenly. That's why everything seems horrible."

She snapped her head up, her eyes burning. "Everything *is* horrible. That *medicine* is what is dangerous. It lets you lie to yourself so you can feel okay." She covered her face and choked out in a strangled whisper, "How can I laugh and have fun? What kind of person am I that I could do that?"

Jimmy wrapped her in his arms.

I had lived through this after Cal died, and then four years ago, after we lost Bethany. Actively mourning someone is a way to keep them in our lives; it keeps their presence vivid and real. But eventually, life tricks us. The days pile up, separating us from the dead, and somehow, yes—that hoary phrase again—we move on. But letting go of active griev-ing is another loss, in a way. An important moment in the long process of saying goodbye. Iris had gone right up to the edge. But standing where she could glimpse a post-Bethany life and any happiness other than what she would have shared with her daughter—she retreated. Re-embraced the familiar pain rather than step into a future lacking the daily, familiar habit of her grief.

Later, I told Jimmy that next time I thought she would walk through the gate. Embrace the future. That this setback was really a symptom of the fact that she was getting better. I prayed it was true.

*   *   *

After Charlie took me back to Ridgewood, I lay in my bed in cold terror that Iris might have succeeded. She was in good hands now, I told myself. She hadn't hurt herself, or really even seriously tried. I squeezed my pillow and took comfort that she would be seeing the clinical psychologist first thing in the morning. They would be making arrangements with a therapist and reestablishing her meds, and Jimmy was taking some time off work.

But knowing these things didn't make me less afraid. Iris had her grief, but I had been cursed with fear. I'd lost Cal and Bethany, and almost lost Iris. Now, whenever Danny or Adam went swimming, or Charlie or Pam or Jimmy or Iris got on an airplane or went skiing, I had to stuff down a disproportionate, soul-chilling dread. I wasn't sure if I could survive another loss. But it wasn't just fear. It was also anger. After Bethany's death I lived with deep, corrosive fury at what had happened, at the judge, at the "system." I tried to contain it because I knew it could poison my whole life. But there were days, like today, when it boiled up.

I felt so lonely. I wished desperately I could talk with Cal. In times like these his absence was like a phantom limb, a piece of me missing. Being the surviving half of a long-term couple is anguish. The left-behind partner has to face mortality twice . . . and in between, to learn to live with an essential part of one's self gone. It feels like a punishment, unfair, unjust. I used to wonder what I had done to deserve such sadness.

A shudder wrapped my spine.

Who deserves anything? What is justice, anyway?

Who gets to decide?

Judges, a sardonic voice came back.

Right.

Stinson, destroyed by alcoholism and addiction, had crashed into Iris's car. He was the one who couldn't stop drinking. Who, in the grip of dangerous sickness, wasn't *forced* to stop, or at least removed from situations where his sickness could hurt others.

So where did the responsibility lie, really? I closed my eyes as tears slipped down.

With Nathaniel, that's where. The circumstances he set in motion caused our suffering as much as if he'd done it himself. As surely as someone who put a loaded needle in an addict's hand would be responsible for what came after. If Nathaniel had enforced the law the first time Stinson hurt someone, Bethany wouldn't have died. Iris wouldn't be blaming herself, guilt and grief eating away at her soul. Stinson would have been in jail or in treatment. Instead, Nathaniel had allowed an obviously out-of-control drinker to go free and do it again, this time to my family. And Nathaniel did it for money. He wasn't starving, wasn't impoverished, wasn't buying bread for his hungry child. He had plenty; he just wanted more.

I couldn't understand the greed. Was there ever enough? Did he tell himself: just one more time, just the next payoff, just the next bank deposit?

Or was it the emotional charge, the adrenalin?

Then, in a stab of insight, I understood. What had Lisa said about wanting to control things? It was the power. The fact that he could affect the outcome of a trial in whatever way he wanted. Whatever else—the money, the rush of transgression—he was persuaded to do it as an expression of his power. I could even imagine that in his vanity he convinced himself he was actually correcting an unreasonable or inflexible system.

The realization was as hard and cold and true as any I've ever had. "Bastard," I hissed. Then I turned over in my bed and punched my pillow. "Please, God," I whispered. Praying once again to a God I didn't quite believe in, but couldn't ignore. "Please let Iris be okay."

* * *

Jimmy and Charlie and Pam, along with some of Iris's oldest friends, arranged to be sure she was never alone. Iris agreed to go to a therapist—someone wise and smart and experienced—replacing that so-called support group and the internet grief blogs she haunted. Thank goodness. And she would get her medications reestablished.

So Charlie became my grocery-shopping, errand-running companion. And when he came a few days later, I told him I needed to go to the condo, to gather some things.

"What do you need? I can get whatever it is."

I answered, "No—you'd never be able to find it. I need to go."

"But Mom, the place is a mess."

In order to get it ready for sale, the condo was being repainted in neutral colors, outfitted with new curtains, bathrooms updated. He was worried that seeing my former home all torn apart would make me feel bad, but I didn't care about the condo. Not really. Our old clapboard Victorian, where he and Pam and their kids were living—that's the place I thought about when I thought about home.

"Charlie, please. It isn't asking much. If you can't drive me, I'll get the desk to call a cab."

He sighed. "Okay. You win. But just remember it's a work in progress." Once we were in the car on the way over, he pressed, "What is so important you need to fetch?"

"Just my box of stationery, that's all. I need some nice note paper, and I have a special card I want to send Ruthie for her birthday."

"Ah, Cousin Ruthie." Charlie exclaimed. "Are you aiming for a blessing or an absolution?"

Ruthie had once studied to be a nun, and when my kids were young, I had apparently developed a habit of quoting her on matters of right and wrong—until they became old enough to tease me and roll their eyes. I laughed. "Don't be such a heathen. Besides, she's one of the rare people who actually writes letters these days. It's nice to get something in the mail. The day is coming when no one will do that anymore."

He smiled indulgently, and his teasing voice reminded me of Cal. "I'm happy that you and Ruthie keep the post office in operation."

*   *   *

We pulled up to the door of the condo. Charlie seemed nervous, but also a little excited. He said, "Wait until you see how it looks," and opened the door, with a sweeping gesture. "I hope you like it. And just so you know, Iris chose the colors."

I hesitated, then stepped inside. Though I generally hate beige—as does Iris, who I am sure chafed at the real estate wisdom of insisting on generic blandness—the living room did look great, with new off-white curtains and freshly brightened walls the color of toasted bread. Charlie smiled in relief when he saw I approved. "Let's go see if the painters have finished the kitchen," he said, and headed down the hall. But instead of following, I veered into my old bedroom, pulled by memories and curiosity.

"Oh! For cripe's sake," I heard Charlie yell. "They used the wrong color." Then, loudly, "Mom, I've gotta call the contractor." I heard him plop down on a stool. He would be busy for a while.

Though most of my furniture had come with me when I moved, the bedroom set I'd inherited from my folks, too big for Ridgewood, was still there. Iris had yet to take it. I ran my hand over the nightstand, tracing a few faint rings made by baby bottles and coffee cups on the old wood, the gouge left when my dad dropped his hammer while hanging up a family photo. I opened the top drawer to look for the initials Charlie had drawn with sharpie on the inside corner when he was six. I remembered how upset I had been, scolding him as I scrubbed at the indelible ink, until his trembling lower lip melted my anger. I ran my hands over the little boxes of safety pins, earrings missing their partners, notepads with mini-pencils attached. I stopped when my gaze fell on an empty plastic bottle.

Cal's digoxin. He'd started on it shortly after Bethany was born, eager to do whatever his doctor ordered so he could have as much time as possible with his grandkids.

A dim image flared. The medication cart at Ridgewood.

Digoxin was a very common medication. Both Katherine and Nathaniel were on it.

I swallowed. Ah yes, arrogant Nathaniel. Darkness bubbled up, clouding the reflection, like oil spilling in a stream. *"Adequate."* The anger swelled, conjuring Iris clutching the empty bottle on her bathroom floor, sitting on a cold park bench every morning at dawn, watching other people's children go to school. Trying and failing to have fun with her nephews. My eyes cleared.

I looked down at the empty container in my hand. Cal had been on a very high dose. I remembered thinking at the time how fortunate it was that I was a nurse, because digoxin is such a tricky drug. The line between efficacy and toxicity is thin, particularly for older folks. Our kidneys don't clear it from our system so efficiently, so the drug can build to lethal levels pretty fast. Back when I worked ER, a digoxin level was often one of the first tests we ran on seniors.

My chest tightened. Where was the rest of his medication?

Maybe I'd put it with the other things I brought home from the hospital. I swallowed, pushing the memories of Cal's last days out of my mind. I blinked away the tears that were gathering, and swallowed again, the lump so big it ached.

Where would I have stashed them? I scanned the room. Then it came back to me. I put everything that came home from the hospital in the hall bathroom, in the cabinet where he kept his cologne and his shaving cream. Somehow it seemed that was where the last things he'd used belonged.

I went into the hall. Charlie was still on the phone, pacing in agitation, his back to me. "But we specifically said we wanted Pale Ocean Gray for the kitchen." His voice was exasperated.

I slowly walked the eight feet or so to the bathroom door. This area was being updated as well.

I pushed. There was resistance. I leaned against the door and shoved. It moved a bit, then swung free as it cleared the shard of broken tile that had gotten wedged under it. Thank goodness I had a good grip on the doorknob, otherwise I would have pitched face-forward.

The vanity had been pulled out from the wall and bits of tile scattered the floor. I managed to angle myself inside.

Behind the door was a narrow cupboard, useful for linens and toiletries. I braced myself. This little cubbyhole, almost more than any other place in the condo, reminded me of Cal. It was a shrine to his love of cologne, the storehouse for his fancy shaving creams, repository for countless Father's Day gifts of soaps on ropes and body powder.

I opened the cabinet. The scent of my husband, my partner of a lifetime, poured out in a wave. Here were his combs, his handkerchiefs—he still used cloth hankies—his favorite powder. His medicines. The sorrow that had been kept in abeyance hit me, and I put my hand over my mouth.

In some ways, my life ended the day Cal died. I know that sounds maudlin. I am not saying I haven't lived since then, haven't felt pleasure since then, or that my life was only meaningful in conjunction with a man. But that was the moment when the life I had planned and built came to an end. When the choices I made, about career, about where to live, and with whom, about what to do and where to shop and what to eat, were mostly in my control. It seemed like ever since that day, the circumstances of my life have been determined by a lot of other things in addition to my wishes.

Of course, I know control is an illusion. If nothing else, Bethany's death made that very clear.

The thought brought me up short. I wiped my nose with my sleeve and inhaled.

There, in the back. The large envelope with Cal's "effects." My eyes flooded, and I knew it had been pointless to think I could look through this cupboard without a meltdown. I was pulling the huge weight of my past behind me, and once in a while I just had to allow myself to feel it. In tears I opened the envelope. There it was: the refill that had come in the mail after he'd been admitted for the last time. A cry broke free. I turned the bottle over and over, feeling the heft.

"Mom? What is it?" Charlie was peeking in the door.

Our eyes locked. His grew luminous with understanding. He squeezed into the bathroom and put his arm around me. "I miss him too," he said softly. "Let's go home. I was afraid this would be too much for you."

I became rigid. "Please don't treat me like a child."

Charlie stopped. He knew me well enough to hear the warning in my tone.

"I'm sorry. I didn't meant to sound like that. But—it's got to be hard." His eyes flashed to Cal's cabinet. "Especially this."

"I . . . I really appreciate that you didn't clear it out."

He exhaled. "It seemed the sort of thing you would want to spend some time with."

I nodded and swallowed, trying to get control of myself.

He searched my face and seemed to be formulating a question when his phone buzzed. He patted my arm, and hurried to answer it. "Did you find the invoice for the correct paint?" he said as he turned, easing out of the bathroom.

I shoved the pill bottle in my pocket.

Charlie was pacing in the living room as he talked with the contractor. I headed to the desk in what had been our spare bedroom, because I still hadn't found the box where I kept my fancy stationery and the supply of nice greeting cards I'd accumulated, picking a few up whenever I found them on sale.

This room was Cal's retreat, his "office" after he retired, where he would watch his baseball games and play solitaire on our old computer. It was lined with photos of him with his grandkids. On the desk was the last picture taken of him and Bethany, displayed in a white ceramic frame patterned with hearts and "World's Best Grandpa" written in gold. She'd had it in her bedroom, and Iris gave it to me after she died. As I picked it up, the pills rattled in my pocket. I opened the drawer, and sure enough, there was the box of stationery.

Charlie appeared in the doorway. "They found the invoice, and I was right. They're going to redo it with the right color." He lifted his eyebrows. "Now—you ready to go home?"

I lifted the stationery and nodded.

We headed out to the hall. As Charlie pulled the door shut behind us, he said, "Be sure to tell Ruthie hello for me."

He winked. "Maybe go to some more book groups so you have something to write about."

I rolled my eyes. "I'll send your love," I assured him, patting the box. The movement jostled Cal's medicine, heavy in my pocket.

13

DIANNE, ONE OF Iris's oldest friends, had a country house in Wisconsin and offered to have Iris come and stay with her and her family when Jimmy had to go back to work. Iris's therapist thought some time away was a great idea, and it appeared to be working out. Iris seemed so positive during our phone calls, so like herself, I thought we had gotten through the crisis, dodged the bullet. Until the morning Jimmy knocked on my door, his expression as nervous as I've ever seen it.

Coldness filled my chest. "What? What happened?"

He patted the air reassuringly. "Nothing happened. Iris is fine." He nodded toward my living room. "But can I come in?"

I pressed my hand into my stomach and gestured him inside, frightened at his manner. As soon as he sat, I burst out, "What is it? What is this about?"

He opened his mouth to speak, then inhaled and wiped his hands on his jeans. "Oh, this is hard." He faced me. "Iris's therapist thinks . . ." He stopped again. "Iris and I have been talking." He squared his shoulders. "We've been looking into moving to the city."

Without meaning to, I lifted my hand to my throat. I heard myself inhale. Jimmy hurried on, standing and pacing.

"Everyone we know in Willow Park is a parent. They live here because of their kids. The schools, the playgrounds . . ." He shrugged. "Their social lives, the way they organize their time—it's all around their kids."

He looked at me and opened his hands. "Her friends are lovely. You know that. They care about her. But how can she move on when everyone she knows is constantly talking about their children, and all of her friends are the moms of Bethany's classmates? It's keeping her stuck."

He strode back to his chair and sat, leaning forward. "Our life has changed. We aren't parents anymore." His voice caught. He cleared his throat. "This time away has convinced us, we need to make a new reality. If we move to the city, nearer my job, we can go to pubs and bike the lakefront, go to concerts. Iris could get a job, at an art gallery maybe . . . someplace where she can be anonymous. Be just herself, not always the tragic lady who lost a daughter."

I inhaled, my heart racing. Of course he was right. Hadn't I been the one to talk about moving on? Hadn't I wanted her to expand her circle? Jimmy's eyes brimmed with pleas and unreadable emotion. I cleared my throat. "Why isn't she here with you?"

He exhaled and looked away. "She's still in Wisconsin. She was afraid of what you'd say." He reached out and took my hands. "You know she loves you more than anything. Please don't feel like we're abandoning you. We won't do anything without talking it over more, making sure we can get here, and you can get there." His voice rose, trying to convince himself—and me—of the possibilities. "You can come for the weekends. We can go see plays, visit museums. All the stuff you were complaining about, the stuff you couldn't do if we shut you up in Ridgewood." He offered me a tremulous smile, hoping I'd return it.

It was time, once again, to be a grown-up. Time to be an unselfish woman and to once again remember that the word "mother" is also a verb, the way I did when my kids were younger. Bethany had died four years ago. Whatever time and whatever distance Iris needed, she *needed*. I nodded at him with what I hoped looked like a smile, though I was struggling not to cry. "I understand. It makes perfect sense." I squeezed his hand. "You know I want whatever is best for her. For both of you."

But once he left, the tears fell. There were many ways I had imagined losing Iris. To suicide. To her drowning her guilt in drinking or drugs. To cutting me out in pain or walling herself off in anger. But I'd never thought she'd abandon me.

I pounded the armrest. *You are not being abandoned,* I scolded. *Cut the melodrama. This isn't about you.* I wiped my eyes and got up and paced. Chicago wasn't the other side of the moon. There was a commuter train. True, the station was another town over, but I could take a cab, couldn't I? Didn't people make the trip every day, as a matter of course? Wasn't I always saying Iris needed to rebuild? As I should have learned by now, I didn't get to dictate how she went about it.

*   *   *

A day later Jimmy stopped by again. He brought some brochures of new condos in downtown Chicago. He pointed out how close they were to the train and how many amenities and coffee shops and galleries were nearby. "You can take the Metra in for the weekend, and we'll check out new restaurants and go to concerts in the park!" He held up a commuter train schedule.

Willow Park was at the outer edge of the metropolitan area, barely captured in the map of the system. I knew this already—I had checked. There were a few inbound runs on weekday mornings—really early, to accommodate all the stops between here and downtown, and still get folks to their office towers on time for their morning meetings. Then a few returning in the afternoon rush. Hardly any on weekends.

But I swallowed and nodded, trying to keep my voice even. "Of course." Then I paused. "What does Iris think?"

"She's excited."

I looked at him. "Really?"

He reached out and took my hands. "Mom, she needs this. We have to make some change, shift the focus somehow."

I saw the hope and fear in his face. How selfish was I to want her near me when being near me also meant she'd have to drive by the place where her daughter died, every day?

I squeezed his hands and nodded. "Like I said before, if this will help, I'm all for it." I forced myself to smile. "Just promise me I get to pick which museums you'll take me to when I visit."

I managed to hold it together until he left to go back to work.

I dropped onto my sofa and stared out my window. I knew what would happen. At first there would be determination, and we'd both make huge efforts to connect, with me on the train telling myself, "See? This isn't so bad," and Iris making the long traffic-filled drive out to see me. But winter storms and road construction would happen, I'd keep getting older, the train would get harder for me to navigate. Iris would build a new life and get busier. Gradually the time between visits would grow longer, the context of stories offered in phone calls less understood, the details of our daily lives less shared. I swore in frustration. Not at Iris or Jimmy. At the world. I knew it was shameful and weak and absurd, but I didn't care. For once, I gave in and stewed in self-pity and anger. Not only had I lost my Cal and my Bethany, but now I was losing Iris as well. I pounded my cane into my carpet in frustration. Maybe I should call Charlie and Pam. Invite them for dinner. Offer to babysit, so they wouldn't leave too.

I called, but got the voicemail. Charlie texted me back saying, *What's up? Everything okay?*

As I was trying to text him back—honestly, how did people text so quickly on these tiny keys?—the little animated dots started dancing on my screen, and another text from him came in: *We're at a water park outing with the kids. Let me know if it is urgent, otherwise I'll call tomorrow.*

I went back to my chair. I noticed that Jimmy had left the brochures and train schedules atop a haphazard pile of folders and papers on my desk. Thank God, he hadn't realized the folders contained clippings and stories about Bethany. Nearly obscured by the stack of folders was the bottle of Cal's old pills, alongside the photo of Bethany and Cal, and another of Charlie and Pam and their kids with Iris and Jimmy and Bethany grinning happily into the camera in front of a Christmas tree. Images of my formerly intact and happy family in a messy, dusty still life.

Or *nature morte*, as the French would have it.

On top of another pile was the box of stationery. I decided to distract myself and begin Ruthie's birthday card.

Dear Cousin,

Happy Birthday! Do you remember when we were kids, that lemon pound cake your mom used to make for your party? I loved that. Do you still have the recipe? Though neither of us should probably have that much butter now . . . Is the rheumatism still bothering you? I'm sure the Arizona weather is helpful. As for me,

I paused, suddenly unsure of how much to share. Ruthie and I have always been close, but she didn't have children, and she hasn't always understood my relationships with my kids. She was not always generous about Iris's struggles, for example. I tapped my pen. I decided to smooth over the recent crisis, which I didn't want to talk about anyway, and write about the possibility of Iris and Jimmy moving, which I really did need to process.

I have some news. Iris seems to be on the brink of really turning the corner. However, as part of that, she and Jimmy are now considering moving to the city. They want a fresh start, away from bad memories—etc. Of course I can visit them via train, and it isn't like Chicago is the end of the world.

But Ruth, I hate to say it—I don't want them to go! I want her to be happy, but . . .

Am I a terrible mother?

I wasn't sure what else to write. I set the card aside. I bit my lip as I stalked around the edges of my living room, toggling between self-pity and shame. It was true, I didn't want them to go. But that was selfish. I was agitated. I needed to get outside, breathe some fresh air. Listen to the birds. I grabbed my walker—as upset as I was, the extra support would be wise—and pushed into the hall. When I passed through the lobby, the sound of jazz played on the grand piano flowed from the music room. I knew exactly who was playing, and this time I remembered the composer. Marty Paich.

I lifted my chin toward the room. "Go to hell," I muttered under my breath.

"Wow, what did you say?"

I turned to see who was speaking. And there again, not four feet from me, was Evan, with raised eyebrows and an evaluating smile. For goodness sake, was he spying on me? Did he hang out in the lobby to ambush people? And how did he always materialize like that?

I glared at him, letting him see the full disdain on my face. "I was sending someone to hell. Any questions?"

His smile faded. He dipped his head and backed away. "No. None at all."

I found a seat in the patio garden. A few minutes in the fresh air calmed me, gave me some perspective. The other thing I wrote to Ruthie was also true. I *did* want Iris to be happy. A change of scene would be good for her. And Chicago was *not* the end of the world. Iris loved me; she was not going to abandon me. I took in the smells of the flowers planted near the benches. I would call Danny and Adam and invite them for a sleepover. Maybe it was time to focus on them for a change.

Feeling better, I reentered the lobby. All was quiet. No one was around. It was that time of day when everything seems to be suspended, waiting for the evening. Here in Ridgewood it meant the afternoon activities were over, and the residents were in their apartments, waiting for the dining room to open. Back when my kids were young, this quiet moment was the half hour or so before I had to start thinking about what to cook for supper. In businesses it is the time when workers start looking at the clock, when drivers calculate how long before rush hour kicks in. I could hear muffled exchanges behind the closed door of Mr. Alfred's office, and the whirring of a copier. If I listened carefully I could make out the distant clatter made by pots and pans and plates and silverware in the kitchen.

But there was no sound of jazz or anything else coming from the music room.

I realized that ever since discovering who Nathaniel was, I had avoided the piano. This even though I had resolved to reconnect with my playing when I first moved in. I chastised myself. Iris was building a new life. Maybe I should too.

I ambled toward the music room. But when I reached the doorway I glimpsed the ultramarine blue raincoat thrown over a chair. Though I couldn't see her, I heard Lisa speaking.

"Dad, you've been down here all afternoon. Katherine would like to get ready with you. She wants to go to dinner. She needs your help."

"I don't think we should do that."

Lisa didn't say anything for a second. Finally, she said, "Why are you acting like this?"

Nathaniel answered, "I have discussed it with her already. I don't think it is a good idea."

Lisa exhaled, a note of pleading in her words. "Dad, come on."

His tone was adamant, even as his voice wavered. "I have one more piece I'd like to practice."

"Katherine asked me to come find you. She wants you to help pick out her jewelry."

His voice was strained, peculiar. Like his throat was constricted. "But I . . ." And here his voice cracked. "You're better at it than me."

Now Lisa's voice quaked. "I can't believe how childish you are being. How self-indulgent." I heard her moving, and I eased away from the door. But not so far that I couldn't hear her say loudly, "Fine. I'll do it. I'll send one of the aides to find you and bring you to dinner." When he didn't say anything, she said, "Why are you so stubborn?"

She stalked out of the room and turned toward the elevators without seeing me.

I had been planning on eating in my apartment, but now I changed my mind. It may have been petty, but I wanted to see what was going on.

*   *   *

I took my seat in the dining room early and brought a book. I hoped to appear to be reading so I could sit as long as I wanted and eavesdrop. When Katherine arrived, she was leaning on Lisa's arm. She still looked frail, but she was smiling, and there was something ethereal about her. I was struck more than ever by what a beauty she must've been when she was young. Lisa helped her to sit, and then pulled out a chair next to her. I started to go over and say hello, but just as I was about to rise, Nathaniel appeared in a wheelchair. He looked as stiff and hawkish as ever. Once he was stationed at the table, he at looked at Lisa and nodded, then gazed at Katherine. "Hello, my dear," he said. He managed to convey both affection and disapproval.

Katherine was very pale, and her rouge looked too bright against her skin. A string of pearls draped down her front, accentuating the thinness of her neck. But she replied with warmth, "I'm so glad you're here." She reached over and took his hand. "Isn't it nice to be out of the apartment together?"

Nathaniel held himself upright and slowly patted her wrist. But he said, "You know I disagree with this." He pulled his hand away and reached for his water. "Nonetheless, here we are." He lifted his glass toward her in a motion that was half toast, half a gesture saying, *Are you happy now?*

"Dad, *please?*" Lisa's voice was once again pleading, concerned.

He turned to her and held up his hand. "Enough," he said sternly.

I couldn't listen anymore. Whatever disagreement they'd had, it no longer interested me. He was an arrogant, controlling jerk. I hurried out of the dining room. How did Lisa put up with him? For the thousandth time I wondered what Katherine saw in the domineering SOB.

Unbidden, the image of her emerald ring came back to me, and the way she played with it as she told me they never discussed Nathaniel's work. I looked down at my simple wedding band.

I had left my phone in my apartment, and when I got back I found a voicemail from Iris. She said "Mom? I just . . . Can you, uh . . . just call okay? I need . . . I'm afraid . . . I'm just having a hard time. Please call."

It rooted me in terror. The words were chilling enough, but it was her voice that stopped my breath. I knew the shattered huskiness, that edge. It was the voice from before, when she had been in the hospital. Fighting panic I called her number, but she didn't answer. I tried Jimmy. I tried again. A few seconds later my phone buzzed with a text from his number: *Mom, just sit tight. I'll call you soon.* I dialed both of them again and again, but the calls went right to voicemail.

My stomach churned.

She was in good hands, I told myself. She hadn't tried anything. Jimmy would have said. Wouldn't he? Reaching out was a good thing.

I went to the window and pushed my face hard against it, flattening my cheek against the glass.

How did this keep happening?

How ridiculous, how absurd, how *unnecessary* it all was. If only Nathaniel had done his job. I wanted to scream. Suddenly the coldness of the glass seemed to enter my bones.

*　*　*

When I was a girl, there had been another ring.

I was desperate to get out of North Dakota to go to nursing school. But we had no money. I took a job helping a neighbor with housework. One day I saw a glint in a crack in the floor, a momentary flash. I got down on my knees and looked closer. There, wedged in a gap in the floorboards was a diamond ring. My employer had lost it the year before, and I knew she'd given up ever finding it. I dug it out and held it in a blade of sunlight to watch it sparkle.

The woman was outside, weeding the garden. I could hear her tuneless humming through the open window. My fingers itched to slip the ring in my pocket. It would have paid my tuition. Instead, I felt a surge of righteousness, and in that moment I did what the nuns had taught me to do. I whispered the old incantation: "Get thee behind me, Satan."

And it worked. The temptation to steal lifted like parting clouds. I ran to the window calling, "Mrs. Thorson! I found it!"

I remembered that moment now, and those old words, as my thoughts swirled and eddied around the cold hardness of my desire. But this time I didn't say the words.

Instead, when I heard the commotion in the hall, I picked up Cal's old pills.

14

WHEN I PEERED through my peephole, Graciela was there with the medication cart, and Mrs. Collier was experiencing her sundown confusion again. "Where are my children?" she pleaded, fear and bewilderment in her voice. "Amanda?"

Graciela, patient as always, tried to calm her. She gently took Mrs. Collier by the elbow and led her into the apartment.

I opened my door and peered down the corridor. It was empty. I stood for a moment, gathering myself and setting aside my cane before stepping carefully into the hall.

I scanned the top of the medication cart. As usual, there were the laminated index cards, inked with information and arranged into rows, topped with the pleated paper cups containing capsules and tablets. Some medicines were segregated into cups of aqua-colored plastic, and a few were in blister-packs. These were the pain meds: Oxycontin, Vicodin, Oxycodone. Powerful. Dangerous.

I knew Ridgewood used a double sign-off system: both the medication aide and the supervisor counted out and organized the meds, and both signed off before the cart left the locked drug room. Then, after the cart returned, drugs were counted, and any that were left undelivered were noted and the reason given. The sign-off sheets were registered and filed.

It occurred to me how easy it would have been for someone to skim some of those pain drugs, the Vicodin or Oxycontin, which had a substantial street value, once the cart left the med room. Maybe the good managers of Ridgewood figured they could rely on the residents to complain if something seemed missing. Or maybe they believed our small town was safe from those sorts of problems.

It didn't matter. As a nurse I knew that any drug protocol, even those that required scanning bar-coded IV bags and sophisticated electronic monitoring, could be defeated by a cheating staff. Just as simple precautions are sufficient when staff are honest and do what they should.

Still. Those were very powerful drugs.

I shook my head. As tempting as they might be, I was not interested in them. The pain pills would be too much like . . . well. One of the things I have learned over a lifetime of nursing: the line between a medicine and poison blurs easily.

I felt Cal's pills in my pocket.

I steeled myself, braced against the cart. I knew Cal's pills looked almost exactly like Nathaniel's. They *were* the same, really, just stronger. Same drug, three times the dose. The way I figured it, I was just opening the door to possibility. The digoxin wouldn't look suspicious in an autopsy: it would be expected. And by using Cal's leftover tablets, there was no paper trail to follow; nothing could point to me ever having the drug.

I scanned the cart again, not seeing the right card. Suddenly my own heart started racing. I heard footsteps in Mrs. Collier's apartment, and Graciela's muffled voice just on the other side of the door. The handle began to turn.

I scrambled backward into my own place like an awkward crab. Thank God, I'd left my door open. I slipped inside and managed to get it nearly closed before Graciela emerged. I didn't dare push it all the way shut and risk the telltale click. I stood on my tiptoes, and watched through my peephole, still as a tree.

Graciela was speaking to Mrs. Collier over her shoulder. "Yes, yes, I'll be right there," she said as she grabbed the clipboard hanging off the edge of the cart. She glanced quickly down, picked up a pen, and went back inside. As the door closed, I heard Mrs. Collier call, "Amanda? Is that you?"

I puffed my cheeks and blew out slowly. I waited for a count of ten, till Graciela was further from the door and the murmur of voices from Mrs. Collier's rooms faded.

I stepped again into the hall. My mouth felt like it was lined with sand, and I was afraid I would pee on myself. I couldn't focus. My glance seemed to be almost physically deflected from the surface of the cart, as if my attention were a battle plane trying to land in a hostile field. Then all at once my vision cleared: *Kearney, Apt 300*. But my hand hovered over the pleated cups. I wasn't sure I could go through with it.

Iris's voice rang in my head. *"Mom . . . I'm afraid . . . I'm having a hard time."*

The world tilted, and I had the whooshing sensation I'd experienced the first time I cut into a cadaver, the first time I held a retractor inside a living child, the first time I assisted in a C-section. I became all efficiency, my hands doing what I told them, just as in surgery, when there was no room for doubt. I lifted Nathaniel's pleated paper cup, and with adept fingers dumped the tablets quickly into the left pocket of my sweater.

Except I missed. Instead of sliding neatly into my pocket, the pills hit the edge of the fabric and bounced to the floor. Damn.

I stopped for a moment. Should I retrieve them? They were under the cart, and Graciela probably wouldn't notice. I'd leave them. Better to take care of the business at hand. Rushing now, I took Cal's old pills from my right pocket. But my hands were shaking and this sight of my own nervousness further rattled me. Two of the three pills slipped out of my hand and also dropped on the carpet. Now I had no choice. I needed them to ensure a large enough dose.

Grunting, I eased down to kneeling position. I began clawing underneath the cart, raking the carpet for Cal's old pills.

A tablet had lodged just behind the wheel. I managed to pick it up and examine it. The fact that Cal's pills looked so similar to Nathaniel's had been one of the beauties of the idea, but now I was forced to waste precious seconds trying to make sure I had the right one. Then I found the small mark on the tablet: it was definitely the larger dose, one of Cal's. But where was the other? Frantic, I flattened against the carpet to squint in the shadows under the cart. Then I saw it.

It wasn't under the cart. It had bounced and landed almost directly in front of Mrs. Collier's door.

I decided that while I was on my hands and knees, I should try to locate the three smaller tablets of Nathaniel's I was replacing, figuring I should scoop them up and hide them. Thank God, two of them had landed near one another, right next to the cart, nestled into the impression it had left in the carpet. I recovered them. Hopefully, wherever the other had landed, it wouldn't be spotted by Graciela.

Knees aching, I pulled myself upright. Now all I needed was the tablet of Cal's that landed in front of Mrs. Collier's door. The errant pill glowed white against the carpet, a beacon pointing to my guilt. I had to retrieve it. Besides, it was necessary to make the dose large enough.

I worked my way around the edge of the cart, steadying myself. I didn't want to drop to my knees again and risk looking like I'd fallen if Graciela happened to open the door. So I grabbed the cart with my left hand and stretched my right arm practically out of its socket. I managed to brush the tablet with my fingernail. It jumped a little but came no closer. I heard Graciela's voice on the other side of Mrs. Collier's door. She would reappear any second. Desperate, I plucked one of the pencils from the top of the cart. Reaching one more time, I managed to nudge the pill closer. I got hold of it and pulled myself upright, shaking with exertion and fear. Mrs. Collier's voice was closer now.

A rush of adrenaline came to my rescue, and my hands flooded with confidence. Moving quickly, I deposited the stronger pills in the paper cup, and placed it back in its correct spot on the cart. I double-checked one last time. The card was labeled "Kearney."

I retreated to my own doorway just as Graciela opened Mrs. Collier's door.

"Mrs. Greene!" Graciela frowned slightly. "Is everything okay?"

My cardigan was twisted and my reading glasses were askew, and no doubt my hair was sticking out in places. I knew I must look disheveled and crazed and undone.

"Yes, I'm fine!" My forced grin hurt my chapped lips. "I was going into my kitchen, and I heard you out here, so I thought I'd save you the trouble of knocking."

It didn't make a lot of sense, but she didn't say anything. She looked at me closely for a moment as she approached the cart. She inspected it quickly and then plucked my prescription from the top, handing me my thiazide and potassium. "Here you go."

I tipped the pills into my hand, then lifted them one by one to my mouth, hyperaware of every movement. I motioned to the pitcher of water on top of the cart, and accepted the Dixie cup she handed me. I swallowed, hard. "Thanks," I croaked.

"Have a good evening." Then she paused, peering at me. "Are you sure you're okay?"

My smile felt showy, so forced and wide I probably looked like a lunatic. "Yes! I'm terrific!"

I shut my door and placed my forehead against the jamb, blood thudding through my temples. I waggled my hands from my wrists and inhaled, trying to steady my breathing.

It was over.

Relief flooded through me, along with something weirdly close to satisfaction. Success. Accomplishment. Certainly it had been challenging. My knees ached and my back twinged. I leaned against the wall and closed my eyes, breathing in and out, in and out. Trying to slow my heart. To clear the adrenaline blasting my system.

It wasn't working. I waggled my hands again. I tried to swallow, but the lump in my throat wouldn't go away. There was a band around my chest, twisting tight. I made it to the bathroom and stared at myself in the mirror. My eyes were big and weirdly shiny. My hair was plastered against my head from when I had knelt on the carpet and looked under the cart, and my sweater was pulled around me, awkward and crooked. I stuck my hand in my pocket to straighten it, and my fingers curled around the pills. Around Nathaniel's actual meds. I pulled them out and looked down. Suddenly my dry mouth was flooded with saliva, and I lurched forward as a retch gripped me.

My God. *What had I just done?* Oh God. What had I done? Sister Marie Clotilde's voice mingled with the roaring in my ears: *"Francine, what have you done?"*

"Justice," I croaked into the mirror.

Justice?

I gagged, a stream of bile rising in my throat. The vomit shot out almost pure liquid. I noted my undigested meds in the sink and gagged again, fighting down panic. I began to shake violently.

Oh God. Oh God! What had I done? *Get thee behind me Satan, get thee behind me.*

I must stop Graciela from delivering those pills. Could I stop it? I cried out and rushed to the door, yanking it open.

There was no sign of Graciela. No doubt she was hurrying to make up for the time she'd spent with Mrs. Collier. I grabbed my cane and hustled as best as I could to the elevator. I knew Katherine lived on the third floor because the judge was always reminding everyone they lived in the "penthouse." As I madly pounded the "Call" button, I realized that despite my friendship with Katherine, I had never been invited.

The elevator wasn't coming. Nearly in tears, I jabbed at the button again and again.

Maybe I could call Katherine, tell her to get rid of his meds? Maybe say that I suspected Ridgewood had made a mistake? But how would I justify my knowledge? Could I pull off some lie? I didn't want to do anything that might trigger an investigation. But what could I say? How could I convince her?

As I fumbled with my phone, trying to think up the right words, the elevator whooshed open. I rushed inside and stabbed the button. I'd go to their apartment. I'd invent something. Say that I had tried to help Graciela and screwed up. Maybe I could pretend to faint and knock the pills from his hands. I prayed for luck—or divine intervention. As if they weren't really the same thing.

It took a lifetime to get to their floor. Finally the elevator opened and I hobbled down the hall, chanting, "Dear God, dear God, dear God," out loud.

I pounded on the door. After a moment I heard someone approach. *Please let it be Katherine,* I thought. *Please, please, please.* Some seconds later, Nathaniel appeared.

"Yes?" He spoke gruffly and seemed to have no idea who I was.

"Hello!" My voice wavered, though I tried to appear sprightly. But he glowered at me, so I immediately changed my tone. "It's Francine . . . Katherine's friend? You know, we've had dinner together, um, and, well . . ."

"Yes, I know who you are." He cleared his throat. "What is it you need?"

"Ahh. May I come in?"

"We are not in the habit of receiving guests."

"I normally wouldn't intrude, but—"

"This is not a convenient time." He began to close the door.

"Wait!" I cried, struggling not to scream. "It is impor-tant. Really."

His eyes were cold, but a little hazy. Oh God, had he already taken them? "Mrs. Greene, I am about to retire and Katherine is already in bed."

"But . . . please, you must . . ."

He waved his hand distractedly. "Good night." He closed the door.

I stood there, hollow.

It wouldn't matter anyway. I realized if they were ready for bed, they'd taken their meds. I slowly made my way to the elevator, which, of course, now came right away. My guts were churning.

My God. I had taken leave of my senses. How could I live with this? I had to clap my hands over my mouth to avoid vomiting again.

I slowly reentered my apartment, but I didn't turn on the lights. I sank into my chair. I was shivering cold. I wrapped myself in a blanket and sat by my window all night. I clutched my phone in case Jimmy called. In case Katherine called. In case there was news. Staring into the darkest dark. Terrified.

*   *   *

The next morning their table was empty. I took my old spot behind the door. It felt like I was playing a part, watching myself trying to figure out where to place my eyes, how to make small talk with the staff. I stared at my plate, coffee roiling my stomach, and listened.

"Mrs. Collier was so upset." I heard Graciela's distinc-tive voice, always warmer when she was talking with Jannah. "What a night."

"I know. The ambulance came to the Kearney's this morning." She dropped her volume, but not by much, since everyone here was deaf. Or practically everyone. I held my breath, listening hard. Jannah said, "Things aren't good." Then her beeper went off, and she hurried to the elevator.

I got up quickly. Oh, what had I done? I rushed out, struggling with my cane in the hall, feeling a frantic disconnect between my racing mind and my clumping body. I almost knocked over the small sign near the elevator telling people which way to the music room, which way to the lobby. Which way to the chapel.

I nearly ran there, if you could call my harried shuffle running.

By the time I arrived at the chapel, my panic was so intense I thought I was having a heart attack. I collapsed into a seat and gripped the back of the pew in front of me, trying to breathe.

For the first time in years, I slid onto a kneeler, clasped my hands together, and prayed. Fervently. Passionately. Unbelievably, I prayed for Nathaniel.

I tried to remember Cal, and my parents, my kids. All the years we went to church together, all the prayers we mouthed. But there was no answering sense of comfort. Everyone I knew on the other side of the cosmic divide seemed to have turned their face against me. Even Cal. All I sensed was an anonymous, hollow roar, like a furnace set to full blast, reverberating inside my head.

I'd wanted justice. To take advantage of being old and invisible, to get revenge for my Bethany, my Iris, my family. Nathaniel was a vain, dishonest, horrible man, sick and according to Katherine, not long for this world anyway. But who was I to make such judgments? Who was I to take a husband from Katherine, a father from Lisa?

And now I couldn't hear Cal's voice in my head any more. I didn't deserve to hear his voice, the sense of his presence. I was being punished.

In horror I pushed myself up, and stumbled out of the chapel, so disoriented I could hardly walk straight. I bumped into one of the hallway benches and sank down into it, trembling. From where I sat I could see into the parking lot.

An ambulance was pulling away. But it was driving slowly, apparently in no rush.

I was starting to hyperventilate. As I scanned the lobby in alarm, the office door opened, and there was Lisa, ghostly pale. I watched in slow motion as Mr. Alfred patted her shoulder. His face wore a practiced sad expression, and I saw his mouth form the words *"I'm so sorry."*

Some panic propelled me, and I was on my feet, mouth open. I must've made a sort of choking sound, because Lisa turned. She hurried over and took my hand.

"Oh, Frannie, you've heard." Her voice caught in her throat, and she blinked quickly. Tears started falling, and she lifted a crumpled Kleenex. I looked wildly at her. Mr. Alfred, accustomed to these scenes, stepped forward and spoke in a low, soothing pitch.

"I'm so sorry, Francine. I'm afraid Mrs. Kearney died last night." When he moved, I saw behind him an aide pushing a pallid Nathaniel in a wheelchair.

The room went blurry, and I clutched at Mr. Alfred as I went down.

"M OM? MOM?"
I slowly opened my eyes. Jimmy's face, staring worriedly into mine, gelled into focus. I sat up and looked around. I was sitting in my living room. Somewhere water was running.

Jimmy called over his shoulder. "She's awake!"

Iris came running in from the kitchen. "Oh Mom!" She knelt in front of me. "We were so worried."

"Iris! You're here." At the sight of her, a wave of relief, followed by worry and fear, washed over me. But I couldn't quite remember why.

I blinked, trying to clear the cobwebs. "What happened?"

Iris slid next to me and put her arm around my shoulders. She handed me a glass of water.

"You fainted. In the lobby."

"The lobby?" Then it hit me. At first just the feelings: overwhelming dread, fury, worry, guilt. Horror. Then the details floated up, in disconnected pieces. Iris's voice on the phone. Mrs. Collier.

The cart.

Katherine.

Oh God. I covered my face with my hands.

"Mom?"

But Iris was here—and safe. I lifted my hand and touched her cheek. "Are you okay? I got your message, and I was so scared . . ."

She covered my hand with hers. "Yes. I'm fine. Dianne and I had a falling out while I was up in Wisconsin, staying with her, over something she said to her daughter. I just . . . well, it sent me into a bit of a tailspin." She swallowed and looked at Jimmy. "But I pulled myself together. I have . . . I'm learning to deal with these things. I'm okay. Really."

Jimmy reached over and rubbed her forearm, love on his face. "You're doing great."

Whatever had happened, she seemed grounded. Focused. Sad, but not hopeless, not despairing. Thank God. I felt my spirits lift until I remembered. Then my heart rose to my throat. I turned to her.

"Katherine?"

She pressed her lips together and nodded. "I'm so sorry, Mom."

Jimmy sat on the ottoman in front of us. "You had just heard when we walked in. At first we thought you fainted because of us. Until Mr. Alfred explained." He leaned over and kissed my cheek. "I'm sorry about your friend."

*   *   *

I don't remember much about the next few weeks. Time passed slowly. There was a memorial service for Katherine, which I feigned illness to avoid. I looked so wretched—skinny, pale, wan—no one doubted me. I was so despondent I had no desire to even eat, much less converse. When I tried to go to the dining room, Katherine's empty chair haunted me. Guilt and shame robbed me of my appetite for anything. Once or twice I caught sight of Nathaniel in the lobby, looking hollowed out and pale—sightings that sent me reeling and drove me to hide in my apartment, staring dully out the window. Iris and Jimmy and Charlie and Pam took turns visiting. They nagged and cajoled, trying to interest me in eating, exercising. Into living, really.

One day Charlie and Pam brought over Adam and Danny and pizza and Monopoly, in an effort to lift my spirits. While the kids were setting up the game and getting out the paper plates, Charlie pulled me aside. "We're worried, Mom. What is it?" He tilted his head, perplexed. "Look, I get that you and Katherine were friends. And I understand sometimes things just hit hard . . . but, I mean, you'd only known one another a short time. Is there something else? Did something happen?"

I looked over his shoulder at the boys shoving one another over who got the Monopoly shoe, and instead of laughing, I wanted to weep. Of course something had happened. I had traded my well-being and joy for bleak remorse and guilt in an attempt at vengeance—an attempt so clumsy and inept it had missed its target. I forced myself to face Charlie and tried to be at least somewhat transparent about what I was feeling, if not its source. "I'm sorry. You're right—it hit me hard. I guess I just realized that might be the last time I make a close new friend. And on top of everything else that has changed"— I made a vague gesture around my apartment—"it just got to me." I reached out and patted his shoulder. "But I'll be fine. Seriously. I will take myself in hand."

After that, I did try, especially when my kids were around. I woke up enough to notice their worried glances and whispered phone conversations. I saw that if I didn't pull myself together, I could end up in the forced evaluation of a shrink. Worse, I realized with an upwelling of shame, I was derailing all the progress Iris had been making. *Selfish*, I chided, as my dormant soul stirred.

So I willed myself to eat, to feign caring about my appearance, powder my nose. To show engagement, or at least a pretense of it. I tried to seem like I was pulling myself together. I knew Iris and Jimmy had been planning a road trip after Iris felt better, as part of their "new lease on life"—a time to take stock, think things through. Discuss the move. Imagine a new future. I had to manage to do better, for her sake. Or at least appear to do better. I refused to hold her back.

I started calling Iris and telling her about the trips to the library, my conversations at dinner. My walks on the nature path. She didn't need to know they were made up.

The gesture that finally persuaded Iris and Charlie I would be okay was when I dug out an old copy of "Dad jokes" that Cal had kept in his desk. My kids were sitting in my kitchen, having coffee and cookies and another low-voiced conversation, probably about me. I shuffled over, leaned on the counter and asked if I could have some coffee. Charlie looked surprised. He said, "Of course!" and jumped to get me a mug. I took a seat at the table. Charlie filled my cup, and as I reached for a cookie, I asked if they knew what the bartender said when a ham sandwich walked into a bar and tried to order a beer.

They glanced at one another. Iris lifted her eyebrows. "No, but I have a feeling you're going to tell me."

I nodded. "He said ,'Sorry, we don't serve food here." I smiled. "Ba-dum boom." Their laughter contained relief.

* * *

The morning Iris and Jimmy left, they stopped on their way out of town, with a bouquet of flowers for me. It made me happy to see how excited Iris looked. I waved as they drove off.

But the effort wore me out, and it must've shown, because when I ran into Lottie by the elevator that afternoon, she asked if I was feeling all right. The magenta streak in her hair was now a darker purple, and her chunky bracelets clanked when she reached out and patted my hand. I felt a brief flash of envy that she was so free of other cares she could spend energy on self-decoration. But immediately after thinking that, I chided myself. It was a cranky, ungenerous response, springing mainly from the fact that what I was worried about was the state of my eternal soul. That, and the lonely reality that both Katherine and my daughter were gone.

I tried to muster a smile and assured her, "I'm fine. It's just been a tough time."

*   *   *

I continued to occupy my little table tucked away in the corner of the dining room, even though I often only managed to choke down a few bites. These days, whenever I entered, I made a point of nodding at the judge, but he scarcely registered my existence. Lisa had started coming in almost every day to have lunch with her father. She sat in silence and chewed, dutiful and uncomfortable. The judge didn't say much either, but when he spoke, he was cold.

"Lisa, more coffee," he said. At one time his imperious tone would've made me angry. Now everything made me want to cry.

Lisa set down her fork. "Anything else, Dad?"

He didn't answer—whether because of bad hearing or curmudgeonliness, it was impossible to tell. Lisa crossed to the serving station and returned with the coffee carafe. She refilled his cup. He nodded at her. Then she returned the pot to the warmer and sat down. She was once again cutting into her meatloaf when he lifted his cup and made a face. "You forgot I take milk."

Lisa's back went stiff. I looked away.

And there he was, seated on the other side of the dining room. Evan Silver Hair, staring at me again.

I tried to pretend he wasn't really watching me, but I couldn't kid myself anymore. I had noticed it before, and it was clear that was exactly what he was doing. He didn't even bother trying to hide it. And it was clearly not a flirtation either. The stare was both knowing and completely detached, akin to evaluating a curiosity in a museum.

I tried to stare him down. He was sipping water and tipped his glass in my direction, a small toast.

Blood pulsed behind my eyes, and I turned away. Lost my nerve.

The server placed my food in front of me. As I tasted the first forkful of meatloaf, I heard Nathaniel. "Take this away. Can't we ever have anything decent around here?"

"Dad, please."

"Well, it's true. What's wrong with these people?"

Lisa cut him off. "It's okay. I'll run to the store. I'll get cupcakes. We'll get any kind you want."

"Don't patronize me. I'm still your father." He was agitated, his voice threatening to rise into a rant. "Don't they realize—"

Her chair scraped as she got up and hurried behind his wheelchair. She began awkwardly maneuvering, trying to get him out of the dining room. All the while he was wheedling, "Wait. Lisa, I'm not, don't . . ." His voice fell from imperious to pleading. "Please stop." I caught a glimpse of his face, reddened in anger and, beneath it, despair.

I turned and saw Evan was observing intently. As the judge was wheeled out, our eyes met and he lifted his brows. His gaze pricked like a blade.

The food turned to chalk on my tongue. I managed to swallow, but what little appetite I had disappeared. I pushed my plate away. The server, a friendly young man whose name I couldn't remember, asked if everything was okay.

"It's fine." I said. "Not hungry today, I guess. I'll just return to my apartment."

But instead, I went back to the chapel and sat by myself for a long time. I woke slumped over the pew, my forehead on my hands. I'd fallen asleep on my knees, trying, against all my cynicism, to pray for forgiveness. To remember prayers from the days when I believed. Now that it was too late.

* * *

That afternoon I was trying to find some pleasure in the sun on the patio when a young woman appeared in front of me, blocking the sun.

"Mrs. Greene?"

I startled. "Yes?"

"Hi." She extended her hand. "I'm Sandra—I think we've nodded at one another in the lobby." I roofed my eyes with my left hand so I could see her face. She looked vaguely familiar. She went on, "My father—Evan Landrum—lives here, and I have been delegated to ask if he could take you to lunch or dinner." She seemed sweet, and her eyes telegraphed to me not to be alarmed. But it didn't work.

"Does your dad do this often?"

"You mean ask people out?"

"I mean send you to do the asking. Especially of people he barely knows."

She blushed. "Oh. I . . ." She blinked at me. "I'm sorry. I'm so used to the way Dad operates, I guess I didn't stop to think."

"No need to apologize. But your dad should issue his own invitations."

She nodded. "Yes. I believe you're right."

We faced one another awkwardly. She was clearly flummoxed. Finally, she stuck out her hand again. "Well. I'm sorry to bother you. I'll tell my father if he wants to invite you somewhere, he should speak to you directly."

"Wait." I could probably dodge him indefinitely. But if I wanted to find out what was behind that gaze of his, this was a golden opportunity. It didn't really feel like I had a choice. Not if I ever wanted to dine in peace again.

I looked up at her. "You know what? I might as well go. I'll tell him in person what I just told you."

She lifted her eyebrows. "Oh. Okay. How about this evening? We can meet in the lobby. I'll drive."

I hesitated. I needed time to prepare for this. "Not today, I'm afraid. But lunch tomorrow works."

*   *   *

Sleep was elusive that night. What was behind this invitation? And why was he always just *there* somehow? What was his interest?

A memory jolted me. Evan had seen me looking at the medication cart once before. Months ago.

I sat upright in bed.

I had been about to take a photo of it when he came up behind me, appearing in that annoying way of his. He said something about having been out for ice cream with his daughter and noticing me in the hall. I'd forgotten because at the time I wasn't planning anything, not consciously anyway.

Another memory, his words when we first met: "I've been part of a lot of investigations."

I threw the covers off, got up, found my walker tucked into my front closet, and pushed myself from one end of the apartment to the other and back again, trying to calm down, to think rationally.

He couldn't *know* anything. I was sure of it.

There'd been no rumors, no suggestion of anything untoward about Katherine's death. No one had given it any special attention at all. Dying is commonplace here: every month there is a service for the people who have passed. Katherine had come and gone, one of many. For most of us, this is our last place, if we're lucky and don't end up in the Alzheimer's wing or on a ventilator in a hospital. I'd been careful. No whispers had floated around the library or the lounge, and no one had any suspicions.

As far as I knew.

Besides, what was there to discover? Katherine's heart was bad—had been bad for a while, I reminded myself. Her heart trouble would have led to her death relatively soon anyway. Maybe it was even a mercy, I tried to tell myself.

My cheeks burned with shame at the thought of what Sister Marie-Clotilde would have said in response to that.

I stared out my window. I knew the pond and preserve lay beyond the inky blackness, but what I actually saw was my own ghostly image. Well, I decided, if Mr. Silver Hair thought he knew anything, had any suspicions, he'd best be careful, because no one would believe him. People would think he was senile. I would see to it, if I had to.

*   *   *

In the morning I put on lipstick and my favorite earrings, like I was getting ready for something I was looking forward to. Unbidden, the memory came of the first time I'd met him, at the library, when I'd been joining the book group and developing a friendship with Katherine. I blinked at my reflection. I took off the earrings and wiped away the lipstick.

When I entered the lobby, he was sitting on the bench, peering around while his daughter read a magazine next to him. When he spotted me, he pushed himself to his feet and smiled broadly. "So glad you agreed to join me."

We set off lumbering down the hall. His daughter took my arm, and he walked on the other side. He said, "I hope the local country club is okay." I suppressed my impulse to roll my eyes at the thought of a country club. Obnoxious golfers in stupid pants. Nathaniel in his plaid slacks, sitting at the piano. I inhaled sharply.

Evan nodded. "I know, I'm not crazy about country clubs either. All those self-satisfied business types. But this place has good food, and I've discovered they're very patient with a slow old man if I go during the middle of the day."

In the car we chatted about the weather, the lack of rain, the relative merits of the desserts at Ridgewood . . . the kind of bland chitchat people fall back on when they don't know one another enough to have actual conversation or, even more intimately, to allow silence. His daughter pulled into the club's handicapped parking spot.

She helped Evan out of the car. He took a moment to steady himself and then smiled at me with a touch of mischief in his eyes. "I usually use a walker, but I hate that contraption. And I'm fine without it, especially when I have this." He waved his cane jauntily with his left arm.

Sandra helped me out too, handed me my cane, and kissed her dad. "Call when you're ready to be picked up."

I took Evan's elbow, and together we formed a slow moving H shape: joined in the middle and using our canes on the outside. It was nice to have someone to steady myself against and to be escorted to a window table in a restaurant. In my mind it was less a lunch date than a reconnaissance mission, a counter-espionage undertaking. But the similarities were pleasurable all the same.

The waiter handed us a beverage menu. Evan ordered a Sam Adams.

Wanting to keep a clear head, I said, "I think I'll have coffee."

We looked out the window at the manicured lawn, covering artificial hillocks, until the waiter returned with the drinks. When he walked away, Evan cleared his throat. "I hope my invitation wasn't too forward."

"It surprised me. Why did you have your daughter ask?"

"I thought you might take it the wrong way otherwise. You know how things are. Have you heard about the commotion on the third floor?"

He was referring to a source of gossip in our little world, in which some supposedly innocent overtures were misinterpreted, and loose talk about a romance spread. I nodded. "You're single, I'm single, and you wanted to be sure I wouldn't make assumptions."

He flushed, "Not that that you're not . . . I mean . . ."

I held up my coffee. "No worries. I appreciate the attempt at discretion." I looked around. "And it's nice to get out and about."

"I noticed you've been eating by yourself at Ridgewood. Didn't you used to eat with the judge?"

So I hadn't been imagining his attention. But I was surprised at how he just jumped right into it. I set my cup back in the saucer so he wouldn't see my hand shaking. "I was friendly with his wife." I forced myself to meet his eyes, trying to fight the incipient blush I felt building.

His gaze was evaluating. One silvery eyebrow hair was longer than the others and shot off at an alarming angle. Finally he said, "Yes, what was his wife's name? Katherine? It was tragic that she died so suddenly."

"Tragic—at her age? I wouldn't put it quite so dramatically," I countered, perhaps a shade too quickly. "She had heart trouble, after all. Serious heart trouble, I understand."

"Oh, was that it? I hadn't heard. About the cause of her death, I mean."

"Well, I presume that was it." I knew I had lost the battle and that my cheeks were flushed, so I opened my menu and looked down so he couldn't see my face.

He was quiet for a moment before adding, "I thought he'd be the one to go first. It's kind of too bad, in a way. He's so miserable now. Women handle being alone better."

What an absurd thing to say. A switch flipped. My bravado returned. I lowered the menu, to face him squarely. "So, why did you ask me to lunch?"

"I was curious about you. You seem so detached. Plus, I heard you were a doctor."

I blinked in surprise. "Where did you hear that?"

His long eyebrow hair glinted in the light. "The judge. He told me you went to medical school."

Why would he talk to the judge about me? To buy time, I poured cream into my coffee, even though I drink it black. I fiddled, freeing the spoon from the napkin it was rolled in, and stirred. Without looking up, I explained, "Not really. Not for long. I started off as a nurse and went to medical school for a semester. But after I got pregnant, it just didn't . . ." I shrugged and set down the spoon. "Going back into nursing was more practical given the circumstances."

"All that must come in handy."

"All that?"

"Oh you know. Medical knowledge. When your kids get sick, or in case you have to maybe monitor somebody's medication or something."

The print on the menu blurred. Wow. He really wasn't bothering with subtlety. Or was I being paranoid? Wasn't that a comment I'd heard a zillion times about the usefulness of being a nurse when one has kids?

I took a sip of water and put on my nurse face. I regarded him like he was the relative of a patient I knew was not going to make it, but who had yet to be told that by the doctor. "Well, of course it was helpful when my kids came down with something."

"I bet it helps now too. I tell you, when I see that cart go by in the evening and how many pills some of us take . . ." He swirled the beer in his glass as he looked at me, a challenge in his eyes.

I couldn't hold his gaze. I turned, craning my neck. "I wonder where our waiter got to? I'm starving."

He motioned to the host, but he didn't let the topic go and went on without missing a beat. "And what about your husband? Forgive me for asking, but if your husband got sick like my wife did, being a nurse must have made things a bit easier."

Enough of this. I looked him full on. "Why do you assume I was married?"

That threw him. He flushed and fumbled. "Oh! Well, I just . . ."

I lifted my coffee. "Just kidding. Cal and I were officially married June ninth, 1968. Stayed that way for almost fifty years." I gave him a deliberately cool smile before taking a sip.

The waiter arrived, finally. I ordered a BLT and fries, and again declined his offer of wine or beer. As much as I would have loved a glass of merlot to calm my nerves, I asked for more coffee instead. Better to be alert than relaxed. I wanted to take control of the conversation. I wanted to get him talking about himself. I remembered something Jannah had told me about him. As soon as the waiter left, I asked, "And you? I heard you were a teacher."

He looked up, startled. "Um, yes. A long, long time ago. I taught fourth grade for a few years. But how did you know? I almost forget about that myself." He looked at me, half smiling but curious.

I sipped my coffee, enjoying having knocked him off guard. "I always think teaching is underappreciated. My daughter is still in touch with her fourth-grade teacher— they're friends on Facebook now. A good one can really make a difference." Banal platitudes, but I didn't care. I was fishing.

"Like I said, it was a long time ago." He shrugged. "I left teaching for law school. In fact, my experience is sort of like yours: I didn't end up being able to practice."

"What happened?"

"My . . ." He cleared his throat. "I mentioned my wife got sick. When she died, my girls were little, so the idea of trying to establish myself as a lawyer and at the same time take care of them just seemed impossible. So I went to work at a law firm. Doing research." So that's what he meant at book group when he said he'd been part of a lot of investigations.

"That must've been tough."

"You can imagine. Sandy was only seven, Amy and Brenna were nine." His eyes lit up. "But they have turned out to be terrific young women, if you'll permit a proud father to brag a little."

I opened my hands in an "of course" gesture. "What better thing for people our age to do than brag about our families?"

"Tell me about your daughter? Iris, right?"

Oops. What was I doing? I had just opened a dangerous door. What better thing to do than brag about our families, indeed. I cleared my throat. "Um, how did you know my daughter's name?"

"I met her one day in the lobby. I thought she looked familiar."

I did not like this. "Familiar?"

"Yes, I thought for sure we had met someplace, so I introduced myself. But we decided it must just have been that she looks like you." He met my eyes, smiling blandly.

I really did not like this. Iris doesn't look anything like me: she is the spitting image of Cal's mother.

Thank God, the waiter appeared at that moment, placing my sandwich and fries in front of me with a flourish. It was a complete indulgence, full of sodium and bad cholesterol, and it smelled delicious. I dunked a salty, crispy fry in the little silver bowl containing ketchup. You can tell a restaurant has pretensions when it feels it must "present" ketchup.

He had ordered a virtuous salad topped with grilled chicken. As the waiter set it down, I seized the initiative. "So, did you enjoy it?"

"You mean my work?" he asked as he slathered butter on a roll. So he wasn't so virtuous after all. "Yes and no." Then he set down the roll with a peculiar expression. "I learned that the law doesn't always work and that a lot of people who do bad things get away with them. Especially people with power."

Shit. Was this man going to ruin all my meals?

I still had my nurse face on. I willed my paranoid inner voice to silence because I wanted to remember exactly how he answered. I said, "That sounds very mysterious. What do you mean?"

He propped his elbow on the table and gestured with the fork in his hand. "I started at a firm that did pro bono work for the wrongfully convicted." The piece of lettuce on the fork quivered, and he took the bite. "Turns out, I had an instinct for investigation. I ended up doing work for the state attorney's office."

The state's attorney. Was that the office that investigated the judge? I couldn't remember. I forced my voice to be nonchalant. "That must've been satisfying. But how did you do it? A single dad with three young daughters? Did you have family around to help?"

As it happened, he did. He had grown up in the city—only a few miles from Cal. We started recalling favorite hangouts, malt shops, the sad day when they closed the Riverview Amusement Park, and then our talk shifted to whole categories of places from our youth that were no longer around: Woolworth's, soda fountains, neighborhood taverns. I had to admit, even though I'd launched the trip down memory lane as a diversionary tactic, it ended up being a genuine exchange of fellow feeling. And of course, we talked about parenting. As a single dad, he had a perspective most men of our generation didn't share.

I finished my sandwich and polished off my fries, relaxing into the afterglow of bacon. The waiter cleared my plate and added, "I'll be back with some more coffee." Then he handed us a menu. "Perhaps you'd enjoy some dessert?"

What the heck? Maybe I'd even have a glass of wine to finish off my meal. I opened the menu and was weighing what would be better at a place like this—tiramisu or cherry pie?—when Evan said, "So, tell me about your grandchildren."

The bubble burst. What was I thinking? Was I so lonesome that a little pleasant conversation had tricked me into lowering my guard? I set down the menu. "On second thought, maybe I'll skip dessert. I've violated my doctor's orders enough as it is." I looked at my watch. "Oh my. I didn't realize how late it was. I better be getting back."

"What's your hurry? Most folks at Ridgewood don't exactly have a packed schedule."

"My daughter is supposed to come by this afterno—" Shit. I inhaled and pressed my lips shut. "My daughter is coming over" had become my default excuse at Ridgewood whenever I wanted to get out of some outing or sing-along or craft activity, but anything to do with my daughter was exactly what I didn't want to talk about with Evan.

I corrected myself. "My daughter-in-law said she might stop by with my grandsons."

He leaned back in his chair. "Oh yes, you were telling me about your family. I feel like I monopolized the conversation, bragging about my girls. Tell me about your grandkids."

"My son has two boys—Adam and Danny. They are great kids. Adam is seven, and a goofy, funny, affectionate kid. Loves soccer. Danny is almost twelve. He's a sweetie, but he's definitely becoming a 'tween.' I've seen flashes of the beginnings of adolescence." I blushed, feeling somehow disloyal. "Not that adolescents can't be sweet."

He nodded, laughing. "I understand—the sweetness gets more complicated. Believe me, I get it."

His expression shifted ever so slightly, and he nodded, almost more to himself than to me. He leaned back, and his gaze was once again impersonal and evaluating. "What about your daughter? Does Iris have children?"

"No she doesn't, sad to say." Then I sighed, doing my best to sound like a mom exasperated by a fact I don't like, but accepting of my child's inexplicable choices. As if being childless had been her choice. *Forgive me, Iris.*

He polished off his beer. "So, no granddaughters to spoil then?"

Once in a while the sense of loss rises suddenly, as if it were still fresh. I swallowed hard, turning away so he wouldn't see the tears stinging the back of my eyes, and pretended to cough.

"No. No granddaughter."

Forgive me, Bethany. Forgive me, Charlie and Pam and Iris. Feeling ashamed and missing my family, I resolved to call my grandsons when I got home.

16

I DIDN'T GO DOWN to the dining room the next day. Why should I give Evan more opportunities to make me feel guilty and paranoid? I was doing just fine on my own in that department. I canceled my appointment at the beauty shop and skipped taking my books to the library, even though they were overdue. Too bad.

I was hungry, though. I went into the kitchen, intending to get a yogurt, but a package of chocolate chip cookies caught my eye. Why the hell not? I pulled at the stubborn cellophane package until it burst open and cookies went flying across the counter. I put a few on a plate and heated up the last of the coffee in the microwave. I'd clean up later. I sat by the window, eating cookies, drinking burnt coffee, and looking into the nature preserve.

The preserve was the best thing about being here. After I moved in, Charlie brought over a bird feeder Cal had made for our old house and hung it on the closest tree. I fretted over it—like a foolish old lady, wondering if it was okay, if we needed to get permission. Charlie snapped, "Mom, it's a bird feeder. Why should they care? If they object, we can take it down."

Of course, it was a stupid worry. I was still recovering from my fall then, and that day I was using a wheelchair.

Charlie squatted down to talk to me. I could tell he felt guilty for snapping, because he became very gentle. "I'm sorry," he said. His eyes were kind as he squeezed my hand. "I know today is a tough day." Then he hugged me.

But I had forgotten. Until that moment I had forgotten that it was Cal's birthday. In here, dates are unimportant. The outside world drops away, and one needs only remember the internal schedule—which day the van goes to the grocery, when they'll serve the cake and ice cream for that week's birthdays.

Now, looking back, I knew that I hadn't forgotten, not really. Not in the deep part of myself. It was why I'd started crying when Charlie hugged me, and why I had felt so small and sad and helpless that I—a woman whose lifelong motto had been "ask forgiveness, not permission"—had worried about approval for a bird feeder.

The feeder stayed, and no one made any comment at all, and every few weeks Danny and Adam help me refill it. We huddle at the window and spy on the birds bickering over the new treats.

This morning I watched as a greedy squirrel tried to steal the seed. I have a grudge against squirrels. They tore up the attic in my old house and chewed through a box of family photos. Rats with fluffy tails. Now that Charlie and Pam live in that old house, it is their turn to complain about the squirrels. But they don't do it in front of Adam, because he loves them. "Grams, look how funny they are," he says. He is just like Bethany, with a tender spot for all animals, including the rabbits that eat the strawberry bushes in the garden and destroy the basil. Once, when Bethany was little, I had to stop her from chasing after a possum that lumbered under the porch, the animals' pale, tufted fur glowing in the twilight. I think possums are creepy, but to Bethany, and now Adam, they're adorable. I still have the toy stuffed opossum I gave Bethany perched on my bedspread. I supposed I should give it to Adam. But maybe I'll buy him another one.

A movement caught my eye, and I made out a deer, hidden at the edge of the ravine in the nature preserve. So beautiful and watchful. I held my breath as it looked around, sniffing the air.

I was startled out of my reverie by my phone. It was Charlie, again. He'd called earlier, and I hadn't answered then either. I didn't feel like talking to anyone. Especially since the aide would be knocking at my door soon, telling me I really should go down to lunch. They begin rounding us up so early, it drives me nuts. I know it's because the elevators can only take so many at a time, but really, going down to lunch and dinner shouldn't take up most of my day. I suppose they think we don't have anything else to do.

Besides, there was no reason for me to go to the dining room. The tears started behind my eyes again when I thought of Katherine and our shared lunches. I guess karma had all sorts of ways to play out.

I got up, feeling lonely, and so shaky and unsteady I grabbed my walker to push over to the hall closet. It was a huge walk-in—practically a small room. I had gotten rid of so much stuff when I moved that the closet was still half empty. But in the back, on top of a low dresser, behind a scarf hanger, was a little tabletop shrine Cal and I had used for observing Lent when the kids were little. It was a crucifixion scene. On the base an array of votive candle-holders fanned out in front like a half halo. Cal's mother had given it to us. Mother Greene. Bless her, she'd been a true believer. A couple of rosaries she'd brought back from Rome (*"Blessed by the Pope himself!"*) were draped around the cross.

I fingered the rosaries, remembering all the years of prayer. Cal had inherited that capacity, that ability to believe. But after he died, I fell very quickly off the religion wagon. Would those prayers protect me now? Would all the good and right things I'd done tip the scale in my favor? For a long time I'd hoped fervently that there was some sort of accounting on the other side of the divide, a hell for people I considered evil: a pit of suffering and retribution.

Now the idea that there might be such a place filled me with dread. In recent years, I'd begun to hope for a place where I might see Cal and Bethany and my mom and dad again—a giant reunion party in the sky. What a horrible irony: imagining a happy afterlife now that I'd lost the right of entry. Probably theologians would find this view of heaven naive and silly.

But what the hell do they know?

I turned the shrine to face me. I had a sudden desire to light the row of votive candles, to feel quiet wrap around me, to pray. It seemed very important. But I didn't have any matches. I tried to take one of the candles into the kitchen so I could light it with my stove. But the candle was stuck fast in its built-in glass holder.

I remembered how I used to light my cigarettes when I was out of matches, back in my smoking days. I went to the kitchen, rolled a piece of scrap paper into a tight wand, and poked a toothpick in the end. I held this makeshift match in the flame of the stove burner until the toothpick caught, and holding it by the roll of paper, turned to take it to the closet. But there was a flaw in my plan: I couldn't carry it and also use my walker. I debated. I could probably make it on my own. But then again, I didn't want to risk falling while handling fire, and I certainly didn't want to have to call for help and be caught in the process of lighting an altar candle.

I snuffed out the flame. Then, still leaning on my walker, I nudged three kitchen stools into position at strategic points along the route between the stove and the closet, like mile markers on the interstate. Once I got the stools in place, I left my walker stationed where I'd need it, right in front of the altar, and slowly returned to the stove, using the stools to steady myself.

I picked up my jerry-rigged match, lit the toothpick again, and very carefully made my way to the closet, keeping near the stools in case I needed to check my balance. I only realized I was holding my breath once I'd made it all the way back to the altar and lit the candles. I exhaled in relief and put the toothpick out. The smell of beeswax began to fill my closet, and suddenly it was ten o'clock mass at St. Rita's.

I closed my eyes, trying to summon the right words. But I couldn't find them. The old prayers had left me.

My eyes filled, and I simply stood there, letting the years wash over me. My gaze rested on the image of the anguished Virgin Mother at the foot of the cross, and I whispered, "Forgive me." But who, exactly, was I asking? Cal, for all the times I let him down? Iris and Charlie, for when I was impatient, too crabby, too busy? God? The universe?

Katherine?

Forgive me, for I have sinned. Forgive me, for having lived past all usefulness. I closed my eyes.

I jumped at the pounding on my door. It seemed like hours had passed, but based on the amount of wick that had burned away, it could only have been a few minutes. I considered ignoring the knock, but I knew the aide would get a key and come in to make sure I was okay if I didn't answer.

"I'm fine." My voice creaked like old timber. I cleared my throat, hastily wiping my eyes and pushing into my foyer. "I'm fine. Thanks for checking. But I'm not hungry, so you can go back to work."

"Mom! Open the door."

Charlie? Oh for crap's sake. "Um. I'm not dressed for company." I wasn't dressed any differently from usual, but it was what sprang to my mind.

"I don't care how you're dressed. Let me in. I don't have my key." I was trying to think of how to make him go away when he scolded, "If you don't open the door, I'll get Graciela to unlock it, and then the whole place will be talking about it."

He was right. Gossip was like currency around Ridgewood. I sighed, flipped the lock, and he rushed in. His tie was loosened, and he looked exasperated. He put his hands on my shoulders and looked into my face.

"Are you okay? Why aren't you answering your phone? I got worried." Then he looked down at my sweater. "And you seem dressed just fine . . ."

"Sorry. I was in the bathroom, and I couldn't get to the phone when it rang."

"Then why not call me back?"

"I–I didn't know it was you . . ."

He walked over to the counter, grabbed my phone from where it was plugged in, and held it out to me. The display showed his missed calls.

I shrugged. "I forgot I could check that. I'm sorry."

He stared at me. "I had to cancel a meeting to come over here." Then he sniffed. "Did you burn something?" His brow furrowed as he looked around, and I saw the place as he saw it. The closet door behind me was half closed, thank God, so he couldn't see in, but the stools along the route from the kitchen to the closet were willy-nilly in the entry hall. In the kitchen, in plain sight from where we were standing, the microwave door hung open, and the yellow light on the coffee maker announced the machine was still on, even though the pot was obviously empty, the dregs baking onto the bottom of the glass carafe. There were broken cookies and crumbs all over the counter. There were also some cookies on the floor—I hadn't noticed them until now, seeing Charlie see them. On his face I could trace the mental calculus that always lurked below the surface. *Is she okay here? Do we need a live-in aide? How much will that cost?*

Charlie leaned down, his hands holding my elbows as he looked directly into my eyes, trying to read my mind, or perhaps see if I was still in possession of it. "Mom, are you sure you're all right?"

I met his eyes and summoned my "don't question me" nurse's face. "Of course I'm all right. What are you talking about?"

I couldn't remember if I had blown out the candles. How close was the flame to my scarves, hanging on the wall? How many old folks would die if I caused a fire?

Charlie gestured with his head at the mess in the kitchen, and the stools. "What's all this?"

"I . . . I . . ."

"Knock-knock!" someone called from the open apartment door. We both turned.

It was Evan, smiling. I wondered how long he'd been there.

He hobbled in. "Oh, gosh. I'm sorry that took so long." He smiled at me, then extended his right hand toward Charlie, leaning on his cane with his left. "You must be Charlie! Your mom has told me so much about you. I'm Evan."

For once, Charlie was speechless. His mouth opened and closed, like a fish's. I was equally confounded. Evan glanced around the kitchen. He turned to Charlie, "Your mom was having us to coffee. Like the old days. You know, a coffee klatch. Until Ida Gerstein had one of her spells and dropped her cookies on the floor." He looked at me. "Sorry—it took me longer than I thought to take her back to her room."

Charlie turned, flummoxed, back to me. Over his shoulder I saw Evan make a "roll with it" gesture.

I found my voice. "Um, y-yes. The old days. Yesterday we were talking about them, about the old days. And one thing led to another. So we were having a coffee klatch," I repeated inanely.

My son looked from me to Evan. I straightened, feeling my brain kicking in, finally. "Evan was going to help me clean up. In fact, I was just about to get a broom." I turned around and scooted as fast as I could into the half-open closet, pulling the door closed behind me. In the hall, Charlie was saying, "Mom? What are you doing?" as I blew out the candles, frantically waving away the smell. I licked my fingers and pinched the wicks to make sure there were no live sparks, then hid the altar, with the rolled-up-paper-burnt-toothpick gizmo hidden behind a basket.

I hurried to the door again. Evan was behind Charlie, but I maneuvered to block them, hands on my hips. "Can't a gal have a little privacy in her own closet?"

Charlie looked both irritated and confused. "I thought you were going to get the broom?" Then he lifted his nose. "What *is* that smell?"

"I forgot. I moved the broom." I pushed outward, forcing Charlie to back away, and closed the closet firmly behind me. "It's in the kitchen."

"Hello? Mrs. Greene? Excuse me?"

Now all three of us turned to the still-open apartment door.

There stood Graciela. "I came to see if you wanted help going down to lunch," she said, clearly puzzled by the confused expressions on the faces of everyone in this little mise en scène, all but Evan, whose bemused calm was really annoying me.

I took charge. "It's a long story, Graciela. But I'm not quite ready for lunch. Why don't you take Mr. Landrum down while I tidy up, and then you can come back and get me?" I couldn't think of any other way out of this situation, and I wanted Evan and Charlie out of my apartment.

Charlie didn't let her answer. "Mom, go ahead down to lunch. I can clean up."

"That's not necessary, Charlie."

"I'm happy to do it."

"No. I don't want you to clean up my mess. I'm perfectly capable."

"No one is saying you're not capable. But—"

"How about if I do it?" Graciela interjected. "You three can go down for lunch, and when you come back, it will be all cleaned up."

"Perfect," Evan said. I sent him daggers with my eyes.

Charlie smiled, "That's a great idea!"

"Actually, I'm really not hungry." I crossed my arms. I wanted these people out of my apartment.

Evan cleared his throat, and it seemed like he was finally picking up on my signals. He turned to Graciela. "Well, in that case, Graciela, do you think you could bring us some lunch trays up here?"

There is a charge for that service. Smooth how he was spending my money. I glared at him, but before I could object, he continued, "Neither one of us is quite hungry yet, so we can finish our interrupted conversation and relax a little."

"But what about the mess?"

Evan twinkled his eyes at her. "Mrs. Greene's son has volunteered to clean it up."

Graciela, bless her, turned to me and asked what *I* wanted. As much as I hated to admit it, Evan's idea about lunch being brought here seemed like a good one. "That sounds fine. But just a single wrapped sandwich for me, please. I plan on eating by myself." I aimed a smile at Evan.

"Okay." She still looked skeptical. "I'll bring it as soon as I can."

Charlie had begun picking up the cookies. He rinsed out the coffee pot, closed the microwave, wiped the counter and squeezed the sponge with an air of authority. "There. I'm not sure what's up with you . . ." He flashed a fond smile and kissed my cheek. "But please. Just be careful. And as much as I'd love to stay and have lunch, I think I really should get back to work." He nodded at Evan. "Nice to meet you." Unbelievably, he winked and nodded toward me. "Keep an eye on her."

Of all the impertinent condescending nerve! I wanted to strangle him.

Charlie and Graciela left together. I closed the door, finally down to just one unwanted visitor. I whirled on Evan. "What is going on? What are you really doing here?"

"You usually come to the library. When I didn't see you, I decided to stop by and see if everything was okay."

"I'm just fine."

"Unlike your kitchen." He had the gall to smile. "Did you like how I covered for you with your son? I've had trouble with those stupid cookie packages myself. And last month I destroyed a coffee carafe by forgetting to turn the machine off when it was empty."

I wanted to strangle him too. I crossed my arms and glared.

He appeared not to notice. "One of these days you'll have to tell me what was really going on in the closet." Before I could object, he limped into the living room and lowered himself into my chair by the window. "Nice view. Can we bring our lunch trays over here to eat?"

"Look, I appreciate your concern, but I really would prefer to be alone."

He didn't answer, just sat staring out my window. The air became suddenly still, like before snow.

"Mr. Landrum?" Silence. His strong profile was silhouetted against the light. "Evan?"

He pointed out the window, and his voice was quiet. "I remember climbing that ravine one winter with a cop who was giving me information. We took our kids sledding to avoid suspicion." He rubbed the top of his cane. "Now look at me. Takes me forever to climb stairs."

The ticks of the clock that Iris gave me filled the apartment, and the rest of the world felt far away. He didn't even move his head.

"Mr. Landrum? Evan? What are you really doing here?"

He turned his evaluative gaze on me, and I involuntarily drew in my breath at the sharpness in his eyes. "My knees may be bad, but my powers of observation and deduction are still quite sharp." He tilted his head. "I think we should talk."

I T WAS UNAVOIDABLE. This guy was not going to be put off. My best option was to figure out what he was up to. I went into the kitchen.

"I'm making tea," I announced as I filled a mug and put it in the microwave. When it bleeped, I dropped in a bag of Lipton's. I awkwardly edged myself into the living room, bumping my cane forward and guiding it with one hand while I balanced my tea in the other. I had learned by now not to fill it too full.

"Don't I get some?" he asked, a touch pathetically. I rolled my eyes, set my mug down, and limped to the kitchen without my cane.

Two minutes later I came back out and put his tea down on the table next to the sofa. Then I stood in front of him. "That's my seat."

He raised one eyebrow at me but pushed himself up and moved to the sofa.

I sank into my chair and realized with a shock how long it had been since the cushion had been warmed by another. But I wasted no time. "You wanted to talk. So talk."

"Right." He leaned forward and stared out the window at that hill again. Without looking at me he said, "When

I worked for the state's attorney, I heard about a lot of bad things. A mafia situation. Gangs holding neighborhoods hostage. Rip-offs of old people."

"I can imagine."

"I don't know about that. I'm not sure anyone can, any more than I can really know what it is to put my hands inside another human during surgery." He fell silent again.

Exasperated, but trying to figure out what was going on, I said, "It must have been hard to go home to your daughters after dealing with the worst of humanity all day. Especially without your wife to balance things out." The knowledge that he'd raised three daughters alone always tempered my opinion of him. And I wanted him thinking about what a parent might do for a child.

"Did I ever tell you about my wife's death?"

Where was this heading? Could it be that he was just lonesome?

Then I remembered how he'd mentioned his powers of observation, his razor-sharp glance. "No, Evan." I summoned my patience. "You did not."

"It was a long time ago. I was just finishing school and working as a junior researcher for a law firm. They were going to take me on as an associate when I passed the bar. My mentor in the firm had me looking into some coincidences he was suspicious about. Totally off the books, unofficial. But I loved it. Digging around, trying not to arouse curiosity or tip anyone off."

"And? What does this have to do with your wife's death?"

He shrugged. "I had just discovered something. A little detail. A pattern of changes in trial calendars and courtroom assignments. When I told my mentor, who was a partner in the firm, it made him curious. Really curious. He had me show him the files, asked me all sorts of questions. We were onto something, I could tell. I wasn't sure what it all meant, but I sensed it was big.

"Anyway, I rushed home all excited. But something was wrong. The kids were already at the table, almost done eating. Terri had a drink in her hand, which was unlike her. She shooed the kids upstairs as soon as I had my coat off. I knew it was something terrible."

I felt my stomach knotting. I'd lived through my own version of this.

He cleared his throat. "She'd been to the doctor. I remember the breeze coming through the open window while she told me, and for some reason I was hyper-aware of the shadows the curtains made on the floor. I didn't want her to say anything because I knew from her face and the sound of her voice that the next words were going to be really bad."

He paused and I had no desire to say anything either, remembering the afternoon we got the call with the results of Cal's tests. What is there that can be said?

"The cancer was aggressive. Something they didn't have good treatments for." He swallowed. "I tell you, during the next few months I often wished I'd gone to med school instead of law school. It was a crash course on the hospital system, chemo protocols—not to mention insurance. Caring for Terri and the kids was all I dealt with. She lasted nine months."

I didn't know what to say, or why he was telling me all this.

"I'm so sorry. It must have been tough to help your daughters through that."

He glanced at me. "Yes, but they also kept me sane. I decided that their existence was evidence that there was good in the world, and I couldn't ruin my life with bitterness. I couldn't bring my anger into the house." He rotated his palm around the top of his cane. "For a bit I tried to manage by going out with the boys, drinking before I went home. Then I saw, in the other cops and the lawyers I was drinking with, how that turned out, so I left that behind. I became a running addict instead. That lasted until I blew out my knee." He straightened his left leg.

"The whole time my sister and brother-in-law watched the kids, gave them stability, made excuses for me never being home or being buried in work when I was. Then my sister got pregnant herself. She sat me down. Told me I had to grow up and be a parent."

He shifted in his seat, and now I think he actually saw me. "So I had to somehow figure out a way to not be contaminated by the slime I was wading through every day, or I would turn into a bitter horrible person my daughters were afraid of, or an alcoholic."

For some reason my eyes filled with tears. My Cal had his struggles, including drinking. He stopped, thank God, after the time he raised his hand to Charlie. I'd watched as Cal slapped him, hard, right across the face. He split Charlie's lip. The color leached from Cal's face when he saw the blood. That night I told him either he got sober or he got out. He promised me he'd get help, and he did. Sometimes I want to ask Charlie if he remembers that day, but I am afraid to.

Evan kept looking out the window, his focus so intent that I turned to see what he was staring at. But there was nothing that I could make out.

He turned back to me and said, "Francine?"

I was startled that he'd used my first name. "What is it?"

"Remember, I said that I took my kids sledding here, with a cop?"

"Yes. You made it sound very mysterious. Very cloak and dagger."

"The cop was my brother-in-law."

I had no clue where this was heading. "Mr. Landrum, is there a point to this conversation?" That sounded so stiff that I corrected myself. "Evan, I mean."

He rolled his cane between his hands again. "Like I said, my brother-in-law was a police officer. One day he mentioned something—just a little detail, meaningless in itself. But the info fit into a bigger picture of a case I was working on. I got more out of him while the kids were sledding. The thing is, after he saw my interest, he clammed up. He wouldn't let me use it or take it any further. It was about another cop, you see, and bribes. After that he refused to tell me things, refused to talk to me about work."

"How come?"

"He was a cop above all. His first loyalty was to the police force." He cleared his throat. "To tell you the truth, I started to be afraid he was willing to look the other way—to condone it. Or maybe even be a part of it."

"So what happened?"

"After that, it was like every conversation was haunted. I couldn't look at him or my sister the same way, thinking maybe he'd allow something to go on, out of loyalty. And the idea that my sister would condone it . . ." He inhaled. "But they thought *I* was the disloyal one, especially when I started working for the state's attorney." He held his cane with one hand and tapped the top of it with his right palm, lost in thought. "It left me estranged from them." He turned to me, and I saw the hurt in his eyes. I remembered my anger at the complicity of Katherine.

The silence descended again, and I let it stretch on, hoping he'd go on. Finally, I asked, "Evan, I sympathize with all you've been through. But why are you telling me this?"

"It's my unfinished business. Somehow it's all connected." He swung his gaze at me. His eyes were no longer hazy with memory. The look was pinprick sharp, but calm. He said, "I am curious about what happened to your friend."

My stomach dropped. "What are you talking about?"

He lifted both eyebrows. "Your friend Katherine? The judge's wife?"

"I know who Katherine is. Or, rather, was." I swallowed. "But what in the world are you getting at?" I gave him the most perplexed face I could muster—but the confusion was not really feigned. Connecting the dots in this conversation required mental gymnastics, and I was not that nimble. I leaned forward and adopted the tone I used to deploy with recalcitrant staff at the hospital. "I'm not sure why you're telling me this, but I think we can assume they forgot our lunches. And I am ready for a nap." I pushed against my walker and stood. "So if you'll excuse me . . ."

"Sit down."

Well, he had some nerve. "Do I have to remind you? This is *my* apartment."

At least he had the decency to blush. He lifted his eyebrows. "Sorry. But please, Francine. I'm just trying to tell you. I recognized Nathaniel. I know about him."

I sank back into my chair and glared at him. "I want you to leave."

He glared back. "You have to hear me out. And you know it."

The furnace roar had started up in my ears again. "All I know is you come in here and ramble on about your past, trying to get my sympathy, and then insinuate something about my friend's death. What sort of ridiculous mystery are you imagining? I am totally confused and completely out of patience. And tired. Please, go."

He exhaled like the put-upon parent of a teenager. He leaned back in an exaggerated show of patience, but also of stubbornness. "Kearney is the unfinished business that connects all of this. He was one of the judges we were investigating."

"Why are you telling me this?"

"I saw you with Iris. I recognized her immediately and realized you were her mother. Then I noticed how much time you spent with the judge and his wife. The only explanation I could imagine was that you didn't realize who he was. After all, in this place people's memories are unreliable. But you seemed so sharp. It made me curious. And when I get curious, I start watching."

I didn't say anything, just stared out the window. I felt disconnected, untethered, like I was floating above the maples in the wood.

"Kearney had a history of dodgy behavior and a reputation for, let's just say, cutting ethical corners. He was one of the folks that I flagged to my mentor, except when Terri got sick, I set it aside. Let it go. Until a couple years later, when my brother-in-law let slip with the rumors. After a little digging, I saw that every drunk driver with money hired the same lawyer, a guy named Mazinski. Somehow all those cases went to the same couple of prosecutors, including this big beefy guy named Theil."

I recalled the man. An incompetent fool.

"Time after time, evidence got lost, witnesses weren't called, cops didn't testify." He leaned forward. "The court calendar was arranged so all the cases got put before the same few judges."

We locked eyes.

"Each time, Kearney let Mazinski's defendants off with community service, house arrest, a fine, and a suspended license. Then everyone got to go home. The judge and lawyers cashed their checks, throwing some money to the clerks who controlled the schedule. The drivers kept drinking and driving."

My eyes returned to the midday sunshine on the trees out the window.

Then he said, "No doubt you know Stinson had a record before he killed Bethany."

I startled, shocked to hear my granddaughter's name come out of his mouth.

He saw it register. He continued. "Stinson's family had some money. The first time it happened, the person he hit was undocumented. No family. A Juanita Doe. Stinson's uncle had connections. They hired Mazinski and managed to sweep it under the rug. He got charged with 'failure to yield to a pedestrian in a crosswalk' and fined. It was easy enough to bury it. But he learned how to get off easy and who to call."

He went on, "After he hit your granddaughter, Stinson followed the same pattern as before. He hired Mazinski—and lo and behold, Kearney got the case. I was deep into the investigation at that time, and I attended the sentencing. I saw how devastated your daughter and her husband were." His tone shifted a little. "I don't remember you, though."

I didn't owe him an explanation. I had no obligation to tell him how I was afraid Iris wouldn't allow me to sit with her. About how I showed up and tiptoed quietly inside, sitting as inconspicuously as possible in the rear, my eyes glued to the back of my daughter's head. About how I could only watch it as if it were happening to someone else. There really is no explanation for my weakness—my inability to figure out how to help my daughter. And if I had an explanation, he wasn't the person I owed it to.

When he realized I was going to remain silent, Evan said, "Eventually Mazinski and a couple of the prosecutors ended up in jail. But we couldn't get Kearney. I had to accept that. Flash forward, and there I was in the Ridgewood dining room, tasting my mushroom soup, when Kearney and his wife walk in. I almost choked. I sat there, once more stuffing down the anger at these assholes who get away with horrible things, and get their publicly funded pensions, acting so high and mighty. Insisting on everyone calling them by the title they dishonor."

I looked at him and his eyes burned back. He went on, "I fantasized about publicly denouncing him in the dining room, like in some cheesy movie. But what proof could I offer? The guy had been investigated and had managed to slip under the net. I tried to let it go. One more time."

He shifted. "Then, when I recognized you and Iris, and saw you spending time with them, I began to wonder."

"So that's why you've been staring at me for the last month like I'm a specimen in a petri dish?"

"I've been watching you longer than that. You simply didn't notice."

I recalled all the times he had just happened to materialize. My mouth went dry. "And what have you concluded from your study?"

He placed his hand over the top of his mug, as if warming his fingers over the cooling tea. He pinned me again with his eyes. "I remember one evening, my daughter took me for ice cream, and we got back late. When I walked through the lobby I happened to look down the hall and saw you bending over the medication cart outside your door. I talked to you, remember? I didn't think anything of it." He shrugged. "But then Katherine died suddenly, and you switched tables so quickly, and started picking at your food and looking pale . . . and I remembered your medical career." He tilted his head. "Let's just say, the coincidences seemed suggestive. And you seemed to be so miserable." He cleared his throat. "I thought you might have something to say."

I turned to him, and he was smiling at me. The same way a cat would smile at a mouse he thinks he has cornered.

CHAPTER

18

I SIPPED MY TEPID Lipton's and swallowed. He was fishing. He couldn't possibly know anything. No one, including me, knew with absolute certainty what had killed Katherine. I would force him to say whatever he was thinking, plainly and out loud. "What in the world are you are implying?"

He faced me, again with the intense level gaze. He would have been a hell of an interrogator. "I'm wondering why you seem so miserable and look so haunted. It isn't simply grief at losing a friend. Did you find something out? Do you know something?"

"What are you talking about?"

"I think you know more than you're letting on. Even maybe had something to do with it . . . though I'm not sure why."

"That's absurd! Katherine was my friend. She was sick, she was old—like all of us here. What makes you think it was anything other that?" I summoned all my self-righteousness. "How arrogant can a person possibly be? Or—are you having some sort of delusion? Losing your mind?"

I peered into his face, performing concern. I knew all too well how charged my suggestion was for people our age. How all of us live in fear of that very possibility.

He barely blinked.

I gestured toward the door. "I think you should leave. I can't imagine you would want to stay anyway, given the sort of person you apparently think I am. Aren't you afraid I will do something to you? Slip some medication into your tea?"

He pushed himself up. He was quite tall, and his uneven tufts of curly silver hair made him look a little crazed. "That's an interesting comment."

"What comment?"

"I never said you slipped anybody anything." He tilted his head thoughtfully.

I exhaled shakily. "You implied it."

"Really?" He shrugged. "Okay, I'll leave. But I want you to know . . ."

"What? That you think I am capable of hurting my friend? Please go." I crossed my arms and stared at him. "In fact, I honestly think you should see a doctor."

He flushed bright pink, which surprised me. I watched his Adam's apple bob. "I obviously misjudged the situation." The look he gave me was complicated, weighted with significance. It left me chilled. He limped stiffly to the door, leaning on his cane. He pulled it open awkwardly and walked out without closing it or looking back. I got up, shut the door, and let out a shaky breath.

I brought his mug back to the kitchen. He hadn't touched it. Good. Maybe it meant he was afraid of me. I stood at the sink for a time, letting warm water run over my hands.

What did he suspect? And more to the point, whom would he tell?

I lay down on the couch, wrapped myself in a blanket that Iris had knitted, and stared at the woods where his brother-in-law had revealed a secret.

The knock brought me out of my reverie. I heard a muffled voice. "Hello? Mrs. Greene?"

"Graciela?" I had completely forgotten about my lunch. I pushed over and opened the door.

Graciela shifted from one leg to the other, looking nervous. "I'm so sorry. I forget your sandwich." She held out a Styrofoam container. "But I made them add some French fries."

"Thank you." I took the container. "To tell you the truth, I forgot about it myself. It wouldn't hurt me to skip lunch one day."

She inhaled sharply and looked panicked. "No! Please don't say that. I'm sorry. I won't forget again."

Her tone caught my attention. I studied her face. She was drawn and looked distressed.

"Graciela? What is it?" I stepped back and gestured her inside. "Would you like to come in and sit down?"

"Oh no! I can't. I mean, thank you, but I better not. I'm on duty. Just . . . I hope it's okay about your lunch."

"Of course. Are you sure you're all right? "

She glanced quickly down the hall. "I'm . . ." She stopped and gave me a brief smile that didn't cancel the worry in her eyes. "Everything is fine. I'm just tired."

I wondered what, or who, she was looking out for. I said, "You know you can tell me if you need something, right?" She nodded, but there was apprehension there. She attempted a reassuring glance before hurrying away.

I reheated the French fries in the microwave while I chewed the turkey sandwich, unsettled by the whole ridiculous morning and rattled by Graciela's puzzling behavior. She was nervous about something. Afraid, almost. Again, my stomach knotted.

Graciela had been on duty the night of "my intervention." The thought chilled me.

I realized I didn't really know anything about her. I saw her character, that's true enough. She was clearly an empathetic person. It was obvious from the patience she showed Mrs. Collier and the other kindnesses she routinely performed—like bringing me French fries, even though she probably had to convince the cook to do them special.

But the details of her life? I was pretty sure she was from Mexico. I knew she spoke Spanish anyway. And that she had a child. Did she wear a wedding ring? I couldn't remember. It was disconcerting to realize how little I knew. I suppose it is always that way—workers always know more about the bosses. It behooves them to pick up on the preferences and desires of those who have power over them. To know where the bodies are buried. So to speak.

No—she couldn't possibly know anything.

I was too tired to think.

I went back to my favorite chair and closed my eyes.

*   *   *

When I opened them, the sun was gone from the windows, and late afternoon shadows were slanting through the nature preserve. Disoriented, I shifted, feeling what the chair had done with my arthritis. Thank goodness my walker was still nearby. I pulled myself up and hurried, as much as I could with that contraption, to the bathroom. It was when I emerged after taking care of business that I saw it. An envelope had been slipped under my door. I grunted as I picked it up.

I assumed it was one of the newsletters the Ridgewood staff periodically put out, or a notice of a menu change or special event they'd added to the schedule. But when I turned it over, I saw "Francine Greene" neatly printed in green ballpoint pen. Someone's idea of humor. My mouth went dry. I opened the flap and found a note written in the same green ink:

Dear Francine,

Please forgive me for imposing on you earlier. I was not trying to be mysterious.

I guess an explanation is in order.

I mentioned my work, and how I started the investigation into the crooked attorneys, and how we almost got Kearney. Like I said, I helped put one of the lawyers away. The bigger truth—and one that I should probably feel great shame over but that I can't honestly summon any for—is that I goosed the evidence.

Mazinski was without a doubt guilty. That much I *know*. We had enough on him to indict, and probably enough to convict, but I didn't want to take any chances. So I decided to make sure. I located a guy who used to booze it up with Stinson. The drinking buddy said that maybe he remembered Stinson talking about the deal with the lawyer. Then again, maybe not. But it was easy enough to coach him on what to say. I found him a decent apartment for a couple of months, cleared up some minor trouble he had with his ex, and made sure he would testify on how Stinson had bragged that Mazinski had an inside track with the judge, and with the right amount of money, could get him off.

We hoped Mazinski would help us against Kearney, but I'm convinced Kearney pulled strings to make sure Mazinski was tried before a lenient fellow judge. He refused to flip. After the trial, a large sum suddenly appeared in Mazinski's wife's bank account. Untraceable. He got a light sentence and is probably kicking back on some Caribbean beach by now. We never could get enough evidence on Kearney for an indictment to stick.

There's more I could add, but I've said enough. Now you have it. In writing, an admission that I tampered with a witness. What you do with this information is up to you. But I hope you will believe me when I say, I know the difference between guilt and innocence. What I'm trying to tell you is, I am an ally. Whatever is troubling you, I am on your side.

Evan Landrum

19

I HID EVAN'S NOTE between my mattress and the box spring. I didn't want Iris or Charlie or an aide to accidentally see it. But clearly I needed to hang on to it. Not that it made me trust him any more, but still. You never know what will prove to be useful. This confession might help discredit him if—well, if I ever needed to.

I headed to the chapel, hoping to still my swirling thoughts. I kept trying to pray, even though it didn't seem to be working. Some small spark of belief—or perhaps hope for comfort—instilled from all the years, still flickered. But the words escaped me, and any sense of intelligence or spirit at the other end of the prayer had evaporated. My pleas echoed, unabsorbed by any outside force, reverberating through a disinterested universe. Still, the chapel was the one place where I was able to tap into a feeling I can only describe as emptiness. Not in a despairing sense. Rather, calmness. A loosening of the tight knot inside me.

I sat in a pew and closed my eyes, concentrating on my breathing the way I'd heard one was supposed to do in meditation. Moments slipped by. Then the sound of a deep sigh caught my attention. It was infused with what seemed like despair. Or exhaustion. I opened my eyes.

In the gentle light I saw a woman kneeling on the other side of the chapel, her shoulders slumped. She sighed again, in what seemed like pain. Without thinking, I got up and approached her. I cleared my throat so she wouldn't be startled and gently touched her shoulder. "Forgive me for interrupting. But are you all right?"

She turned to me with a pallid face, drained of color and moist with perspiration. I realized with a shock that it was Geri, Lottie's friend. But she was much changed. I remembered when we'd first met at that initial book group—the same time I'd met Evan. I had noticed that Geri had held her side stiffly and moved with caution. But not like this.

She said, "I'm sorry. I didn't know anyone else was here." She held a hanky to her mouth, and the thought sprang to my mind: this person is at the end of her rope.

I sat down. "Please, don't apologize. But—are you okay? It seems like maybe you could use some help."

She swallowed again and with effort shifted from her knees, pushing herself up to sit next to me in the pew. "That is very kind of you." She blotted the perspiration from her face. "I'll be all right. It is just—I'm having a lot of pain today. Sometimes it gets to me, and I need to drop the brave face. If my kids or grandkids saw me like this . . ." She looked down and spun her handkerchief around her fingers. "Maybe this is just what getting old means for me."

She chewed her lip, and the handkerchief became a knot. "To tell you the truth, sometimes I'm not sure life is worth it, if it's going to be like this. That's when I come here. It seems ridiculous, but a few minutes of not having to be brave, but giving in to feeling sorry for myself, helps."

"I know," was all I could say. I reached out my hand and she took it. We stayed silent for a moment, succumbing to emotion. I said, "It is so hard . . ." My husky voice revealed my own fears.

She nodded as she took her hand from mine and pulled herself up. I saw her wince as she stood.

"Thank you. For your understanding."

"May God give you strength," I replied. It seemed appropriate, since we were in a chapel.

She nodded, collected her walker at the end of the pew, and slowly pushed out of the door. I sat in the quiet, thinking of all sad things. I knelt and tried to pray, for her, for all of us, and my eyes kept filling. I thought of Bethany, but now my memories of her bled into memories of Katherine, my comforting images of Cal were overlaid with the images of Nathaniel's crumpled despair. I had stained my own memories, making even sources of comfort smudgy with guilt. I layered my hands on the back of the pew in front of me and put my head down on top of them.

That's how I was when Iris found me. She touched my shoulder.

I pulled up, startled and disoriented. "Huh, what?"

There was alarm in her eyes. "Mom? Are you okay?"

"Iris!" I blinked and rubbed my face. "What are you doing here?" I struggled to get up.

She lifted me into a hug. "We got back early."

I reveled in her warmth. Then my mind raced. What would this look like to her? In the years since her father had died, I had made no secret of my doubts about organized religion, and yet there I was, asleep on my knees in the chapel. I'd convinced her to go on vacation and begin building her new life, not to worry about me, and this is how she finds me?

I squeezed her tightly, feeling the sting of tears. "It's so good to see you."

We sank onto the pew. "Oh, Mom. It's good to see you too." We simply smiled at each other for a moment. She'd been in the sun, and the freckles that marched across her nose were subdued under a tan. She looked healthy. Then she scraped her upper lip with her teeth. "I hope you haven't been too lonely? I mean . . ." She gestured around the chapel, acknowledging the irony. "We worry about you, you know."

I reached out and took her hand. "Don't you worry about anything." I leaned forward and used the pew in front of me to pull myself up, suddenly cheered. "Let's go to the patio. We can sit outside. I want to hear all about your trip!"

She stood, kissing my cheek. I leaned on her elbow, and we slowly made our way out and through the lobby. Hallways radiated off the main lobby, some went to the music room and library, others to the dining room. But in between there was a short hall to a sunroom and adjoining patio.

We found a wicker bench.

"So, how was Yellowstone? Do you have pictures?"

She pulled out her phone and began swiping through images of gorgeous scenery; Jimmy mugging for the camera in front of a mountain lake; Iris in a wide-brimmed hat, eating an ice cream cone. They seemed so lovely, so entirely normal, somehow. So—dare I think it?—like images of the old Iris.

"Oh, honey!" I heard the emotion in my voice. "It looks like you had a great time.

"We did. It was great to get away. Gain some perspective." Iris set down her phone. "Mom?" she swallowed. "I know Jimmy talked to you about our—well, our possible plan. About moving."

She took my hand, and I stroked the back of her hand with my thumb.

I said, "I think there is a lot to be said for it."

She shrugged. "I think so too. Sometimes. But then I'm not sure. Am I just running away? I don't know anybody in the city. Maybe it will be worse." She frowned. "I don't want to always be the woman whose kid died. But in the city, I'll be just another person, and *nobody* will know. I don't think I'd like that either."

"It will take some time, but you'll meet new friends. Just like other things, as you get to know people, you learn about one another. And then your friends will know."

She lifted her head, eyes moist. "But none of them will have known *her*."

I bit my lip and nodded. There was nothing I could say to that. We sat in silence.

Finally she said slowly, "And I'll be farther away from you." Her voice cracked. "I don't like that, Mom. I feel like we'd be leaving our family behind." She pressed her lips together.

"Iris, it isn't the end of the earth. I lived hundreds of miles from my mother."

"Right. And you always used to say how much you hated that."

"Yes, but my mom lived nine hours away. This will just be a . . . small inconvenience." I pushed hair off her forehead. "Look. It's been a blessing that all of us have lived so close to each other. But seriously, it might even do me good. Force me to get out. I always meant to get into the city more."

"We don't know for sure we're doing it yet."

"I know. But I want you to do what's best for you."

She evaluated me, her gaze suddenly sharper. She pulled back to run her eyes down my frame. "Well, here I've been yammering on about our trip, and moving, and you look so thin."

"I'm fine."

She exhaled, like the old Iris. "Really? Even though you're hanging out in the chapel?"

I smiled. "I know." I nodded in recognition of the absurdity. "But everything is okay. Honest. I just go there to think sometimes because it's so peaceful and no one ever bothers you. I guess it was so quiet I fell asleep."

She looked me up and down. "I feel like I should worry."

I waved her comment away. "Sweetie, I'm fine."

"You always say that. You said that after you fell—right before we had to take you to the hospital."

I lifted my shoulders in acknowledgment. "I know. But I truly am fine. Not that I don't get blue sometimes. I do. And then I go to the chapel. I just needed a place to think. To remember."

The apprehension in her eyes softened, and she nodded. "I understand." If anyone could understand, it was Iris. "But I mean it. I refuse to even consider a move if it will hurt our relationship. I couldn't handle the guilt. Please. You have to promise you'd tell me if something was going on, if you were worried about something."

This was one promise I could never make, not to Iris. I squeezed her hand. "Oh, sweetie. What would I worry about?"

*   *   *

That evening I went down to the dining room early, seeking distraction from my own thoughts, and also because tonight there was a "cocktail hour," when the staff put out little bowls of peanuts and offered alcohol before dinner; I'd decided to allow myself a glass of wine. Also because Evan tended to eat later, and I didn't want to encounter him. Those stories—his wife, her cancer, his brother-in-law, the other woman who Stinson had killed . . . It felt like opera buffa, complicated and messy, a story that kept widening and pulling people in, a time line that was more like a spiral. Who knew what was true and what was conjecture or even paranoia?

Although he had been right about the names. I'd double-checked my clipping file about the investigation. The lawyer who'd defended Stinson *was* named Mazinski. The prosecutor *was* Theil.

But still. I had not seen Evan since receiving his note, and I had no desire to. I was pretty sure he'd want to talk again, and I did not want to discuss anything to do with Katherine, the trial, or the judge. At all—ever. I had no reason to trust him—that letter he'd shoved under my door, which was supposed to put me at ease, was meaningless. The statute of limitations had long since run out on any of his illegal acts. And what did he care if his reputation was ruined now, so long after his retirement? That note offered me no real security.

Though, in a weird way, some aspects of Evan's visit *had* reassured me, a little. Whatever could be said about him, Evan was an unusually observant guy. A professional noticer. If it took a person like him to be suspicious, and even then, he couldn't prove anything—well, it made me feel that I could avoid any repercussions. The smartest thing to do was to keep my head down. It had been weeks, and the more time that passed, the less likely it was that anyone would think anything was amiss, or even remember the circumstances of Katherine's death.

That was only in terms of legal consequences, of course. Emotionally, I felt more vulnerable than ever. Like a layer of skin had been removed. I was raw. Prone to crushing sadness, feelings of despair. Fear of death, even more than usual. My thoughts had grown more kindly toward my fellow residents, as if my own particular guilt had merged with the more generalized sorrow.

But one of the best things about my table in the dining room, half hidden behind the door, was that it was near the coffee station and the nook where the staff hung out and chatted as they prepared to serve the meal. I could listen to them, especially when I came down early, as they prepped dishes and talked while waiting for the rest of the residents to arrive. It reminded me of my old working life during the occasional slow times when we would gather in the break room or hang out at the desk and gossip about who was sleeping with whom, and who was getting engaged or divorced, or which patients were the most difficult. Some might say I was eavesdropping, but that implies an intention. I simply let their conversation wash over me and savored memories of when I belonged somewhere and contributed to something.

Behind me, Jannah was talking about her son, Shaun. I had seen a picture of Shaun: a bright-eyed seven-year-old with brown skin and curly hair, wearing a Spiderman T-shirt and eager grin. Jannah glowed when she talked about him. Last month she told me how he'd gotten all A's on his most

recent report card. Now Jannah was saying, "He'll be starting Little League next week."

The person she was speaking to sighed. There was longing
in it, and sadness. Then Jannah spoke again. "Don't worry.
You'll be able to visit him soon." There was no response that
I could hear, and then Jannah's voice again, soft and sympathetic. "I can't imagine how you must miss him."

"It's two years. He's getting so big . . . He won't remember me." The mournful voice was familiar. It was Graciela.
"He was so little when I left."

"But you talk with him every night, right? And I'm sure
your auntie tells him about you. Keeps you alive to him."

Another sigh. "But she has so much to do. She's still
working when she can find something that pays. I can't send
enough back."

Tears sprang to my eyes. Like I said: I'm raw.

"Aren't you up for a raise?"

"Yes . . ." There was a pause, and the change in her voice
was palpable. "Thomas has to approve it." Then she dropped
into a whisper. I couldn't make out the words, but her tone
was so upset it chilled me. Thomas was a manager that I
knew all the staff disliked. He was oily and obsequious to residents, but I had seen him be short-tempered with the staff.

Jannah replied, "I know. He accused me of forgetting to
take Mr. Dion his dinner last week."

Graciela stammered her answer. "He knows that I was
on duty . . ."

What was this? I bent my head to listen more closely.
Her weeping was barely contained behind her whispers, but
I could make out a few words. Including "ICE" and "sent
back."

Jannah's whisper was outraged. "But he's Ramon's
cousin!"

I risked a sideways glance. Jannah had her arm around
Graciela, whose normally carefully plaited hair was coming
loose and untied. Jannah was patting her shoulder, the way

you comfort someone at a funeral. There was a crash in the other end of the dining room, and I spun around. Mrs. Hanson had driven her motorized wheelchair into the corner of a table and sent a place setting clattering to the floor. "Oh dear," she cried. When she pulled on the controller to back the beast up, she banged into the chair occupied by Mr. Ron Gilliard.

"Watch what you're doing, for God's sake." Gilliard began pushing on the arms of his chair, trying to get up while ranting, "Damn women drivers! Even in here, I can't get away. Who gave you a license for that thing anyhow?"

Gilliard's daughter, seated next to him, took command. "Dad, please sit down before you fall. She didn't mean anything."

Mrs. Hanson looked mortified. "Oh dear. Oh, I'm so sorry. I just got this chair and I . . ."

By now Jannah and Graciela had arrived. Jannah said, "It's okay, Mrs. Hanson, no harm done. Everything is fine." I saw Graciela wipe her eyes before tucking the Kleenex into her pocket.

I don't remember what I had for dinner. My mind kept circling back to what I'd overheard. Was I being a nosy old lady? Very well, maybe I was a nosy old lady. But what had she been talking about? The small voice I kept ignoring murmured, she might know something or have seen something.

I had to keep my ears and eyes open. I had to get to know Graciela and Jannah better.

*　　*　　*

The opportunity to act on that intention presented itself only a few hours later. Graciela was on medication duty on Monday nights, so I waited with my door cracked open. As I heard her round the corner, I stepped out into the hall. I played with my phone, proceeding very slowly, till she was close enough to help me, and then I accidentally on purpose dropped the rosary I was carrying.

Graciela, always kind, noticed. She seemed very quiet and heavy-spirited, but she lifted her lips in a small smile and said, "It's okay Ms. Greene. I'll get it for you." She picked up the rosary. "This is so pretty." Then she weighed it in her hands. "And heavy. No wonder you dropped it."

"It's hand carved, from Rome. That rosary was blessed by the pope himself."

Graciela lifted an eyebrow in curiosity and stroked a bead with her forefinger. "Really? Did you see him?"

"Not me. My mother-in-law. Her cousin was a priest who worked in the Vatican, and when she visited him, she managed to go to one of those masses with the pope where he walked by and blessed people. She held it out as he passed. It was one of her treasured possessions." I watched as Graciela examined the lovingly carved crucifix affixed to the end of the rosary. I asked, "Are you Catholic by any chance?"

She nodded. "I am. Everyone is where I come from." She paused. "Here is not the same. I didn't even know which church to go to when we first get to this place." She'd been rolling the beads between her fingers this whole time.

"Where are you from?"

"From Guatemala. Very different from here." An expression at once nostalgic and hopeful slanted across her features like a passing shadow. "But it's better here. I work and I send money home. My husband and me, we go to school, and our life will be better and better."

Her face lit up as she spoke. In her voice I heard the echoes of generations of people from all over the world who arrived here with hope and fear, saying almost exactly the same thing with a thousand unfamiliar accents. For some of them, maybe it had come true.

I asked, "Do you have children?"

The light dimmed. She dropped her gaze. "Yes. But my son is in Guatemala. He stays with *mi tia* until I can bring him."

I changed the subject. "What are you studying?"

She lifted her chin and gave me a quick smile. "I want to be a nurse. It is why I work here: I can learn more." She hesitated. "I began my studies in Guatemala before we came. I almost finished to be RN. But my husband got a job here, and we had to come then. So now, in two months I take my test to go to the university. But first I need more English, to pass the exam."

I perked up. "Graciela, did you know I was a nurse?"

She nodded. "Jannah told me." And she added, again with a hint of shyness. "Was it good work?"

"I loved it. In fact"—I hesitated—"I mean, I would be happy to help you study for your exams. If you'd like."

Her eyes widened, but then just as quickly, she moved back the tiniest bit. "It is not allowed. We are not supposed to be too much friends with the residents."

"Well, that's ridicu—" I stopped myself. She was obviously feeling vulnerable. I didn't want to diminish her fears. "Well, maybe there's a way. Think about it. We don't need to do it here."

She nodded.

I gestured toward my door. "Would you like to come in for a cup of tea?"

She blanched. "Oh no." I saw anxiety veil her eyes before she shifted to a tone more distant and official. "I need to go. The people need their medicine before they go to bed."

"Of course," I said, "but I really would love to sit and chat with you a little bit more." I was reluctant to let our connection go. I said, "I've always been interested in Guatemala. And I've never been able to visit." I was fully aware of how false that sounded, like stilted dialogue from a bad travel commercial played late at night. So I decided to add the sympathy card. "It gets boring here. A lot of the people, their memory is gone . . ." I just let the implication hang, not wanting to explicitly brag about how much sharper I was than some of the other residents, even though maybe it was true.

I could tell she was struggling with what attitude to take. Sympathetic? Humoring? In the end she settled on distant and professional. "That would be nice. But the work makes me very busy." She patted my arm with a touch of apology and a smidgeon of the condescension the young commonly display toward the old.

From the apartment across from us, I heard my confused neighbor calling, "Hullo? Is that you? Amanda?" Graciela heard it, too, and sighed down at her cart. "I better get Mrs. Collier her medication."

And then, from down the hall, a sharp voice sounded. "Graciela! You're behind schedule. Is there a problem?"

Both of us turned and beheld Thomas, bearing down on Graciela like an ocean tanker on a rowboat. I stood up a little straighter and stepped forward to intercept him.

"I needed Graciela to help me." I explained. "I dropped something."

He immediately slipped into the gooey officiousness that he adopted around the residents. Especially around residents like me, who still have our wits, our memories, and our hearing. He reminded me of a mean fifth-grader, the one who picked on kids smaller than him, sucked up to kids bigger than him, and always appeared to be perfectly angelic when the gaze of the teacher turned his way.

"I see. Well, I'm glad she was here to help." Then he turned to Graciela. "But you better get back to work."

Graciela kept her face down, but I saw a flush on her neck. "Yes, sir." She wheeled the cart a few paces away and began to check the contents of the little cups against a clipboard. He spoke sharply, "Without further delay."

Graciela hurried the few paces to Mrs. Collier's door, looking like she couldn't get away fast enough.

I cleared my throat to get Thomas's attention. "I didn't mean to delay Graciela."

He turned his oily condescension toward me. "She needs to make sure that people get their medications on time. Even though we appreciate that our residents might like to chat, that is not really the role of our help."

My chest felt hollow. What had led to this rigid adherence to the schedule? It seemed new. I thought of Evan. I suddenly regretted throwing him out of my apartment before I could suss out exactly what he thought about Katherine's death.

I said, "I understand. In fact, I have been meaning to commend you on what a good job Ridgewood does in hiring its *staff*." I emphasized the last word and edged closer to him as I spoke.

He backed away slightly. I could tell he was trying to work out what exactly I was driving at. His smile didn't reach his eyes. "Yes. Um, thank you."

"Timely medications are something I appreciate. You know I was the chief surgical nurse at St. Mary's until a few years ago. So I'm especially impressed by the excellent staff you have."

He nodded, still uncertain what my intention was, unsure if he was being praised or put in his place. For Graciela's sake, and Jannah's and the others', I hoped maybe he took it as a warning. Whatever he was doing to make them feel afraid, I wanted to somehow extend a bit of protection their way.

Thomas said goodnight and walked off, but I was left unsettled. I resolved to keep my eyes open. For one thing, it worried me that Thomas seemed to be paying special attention to the evening medication rounds. For another, focusing on helping Graciela and the others would make a nice change from worrying about the state of my soul.

20

WHEN I ARRIVED in the dining room for lunch the next day, it had been rearranged. The tables were in new positions, and folding screens blocked off one corner. I peeked behind them and saw ladders, toolboxes, and spools of wire. Holes were cut into the ceiling, exposing pipes and conduit.

I watched as the staff explained patiently and repeatedly why people had to sit in different places because of the construction, and the reasons for their newly positioned tables. Apparently, if you want to make old people cranky, there is no better way than to mess with anything that has to do with their mealtimes.

"I know, Mr. Herman, we apologize. We are installing a new sprinkler system, and the workers need to get into the pipes over in the corner."

"We understand Mrs. Maclelland, it is a terrible inconvenience. We are so sorry."

"Yes, of course Ms. James. Of course, the same people will be sitting at your table. And look, now you'll be closer to the window."

Seriously, how do they manage to hire such patient workers? If I had to describe, over and over, that the screen in the corner was to hide the tools and equipment, and the ceiling panel was cut open so they could access the sprinkler system; and yes, the system is in place to keep us all safe; and yes, it is required by law; and well, no, I can't really say whether this is another example of the government interfering, I'd lose my mind.

My regular spot was blocked off as well. I looked around the room for a place to land and saw Geri sitting by herself.

I approached her. "May I join you?" It occurred to me that I should mention our conversation in the chapel, but I didn't want to remind her of the distress she'd been in. "I, um, I hope you're feeling better?"

Our eyes locked and she blushed. "Yes. Nice to see you under better circumstances." She gestured to a chair. "I'm sorry I imposed on you."

I waved her words away and sat down. "We've all had tough moments."

As we spoke Lottie arrived, leaning on her cane. She pulled out the chair next to Geri, clearly her regular place. "Francine! I haven't seen you in forever." She dropped the final few inches onto the seat, before letting out a small *uumpf.* Her heavy necklace, made of silver and what looked like carved bone, clacked.

As the server, a shy-looking teenager I didn't know, filled our glasses, we began to chat. I sipped my water, said yes when the waiter asked if I wanted salad, and began to relax. I had forgotten how enjoyable it could be to participate in conversation over a meal. We were discussing the challenge of remembering the plots of old movies when both Lottie and Geri stopped speaking and shifted a curious gaze over my left shoulder.

I jumped when someone kissed my cheek. I turned, surprised. Iris had her hair brushed into a ponytail and wore makeup. I caught a breath of scent and realized she'd even put on some perfume. She grinned down at me. "There you are! I dropped by to take you to lunch. But I see I'm too late." Obviously she was making an effort: to look good, to be upbeat, to spend time with me. Only those who knew her well might sense some brittleness behind the good cheer, notice that there were still shadows under her eyes. She looked around the table with friendly expectation. Geri and Lottie smiled back. Their glance bent toward me.

I froze. Ever since I'd discovered who Nathaniel was, I had been careful about keeping Iris away from any possible interaction. Before Katherine's death, my main tactic was simply managing logistics: if Iris was taking me somewhere, I always waited at the front of the lobby, pushing through the revolving doors as soon as her car pulled into the lot. I told her it was so she didn't need to park, but really it was to keep her out of the building. If she insisted on coming by my apartment to visit, I made sure to tell her I was "busy" during the times when I thought Nathaniel would be practicing his piano in the room off the lobby, to avoid the possibility they might see one another in passing. Even so, I was full of anxiety whenever I knew she was stopping by. Fortunately, Nathaniel was a man of rigid habits. It was nerve-racking, though ultimately not too difficult, to avoid the dining or music rooms any time he was likely to be there.

But since Katherine's passing, the task of protecting Iris had become exponentially more complicated. To begin with, I now had to keep her away from any people that might pique her curiosity or say anything that might open a can of worms—any circumstance or situation that might require me to talk about Katherine, both because I was afraid I couldn't hide my anxiety and because it might lead to talk of Nathaniel or referring to him as "the judge." I also had to make sure Iris never found out I was going to the chapel so much, to avoid triggering the worry she'd expressed when she found me there. Further, I had been telling her that I was involved in all sorts of wonderful Ridgewood activities, like the book group with Lottie and Geri. The same people who now sat across from me, one of whom had just announced she hadn't seen me "in forever."

I swallowed, trying not to panic.

Iris said, "Mom? Can you introduce us?" As she slid into the chair next to me, I desperately tried to think of something to direct conversation away from any dangerous topic.

"Um, yes. I'm sorry. This is my daughter, Iris." My voice came out tight and weirdly high. I gestured to our tablemates. "Iris, these are my friends Geri and Lottie." They visibly relaxed. Probably they thought I'd forgotten their names. Then, thank goodness, I remembered something. Hurrying to nudge the conversation in a safe direction, I added quickly, "Iris, you and Geri share a passion—she also loves horses and riding."

Geri lit up and turned to Iris. "You're a rider too? I used to love it. Do you own a horse?"

I relaxed as I saw Iris engage. She smiled, warming to the memory. "I wish. But when I was younger, my friend's dad had a hobby farm, so I could go over there to ride anytime." Her face grew animated. "I adored it. For a while I thought about competing, but I could never settle on what that really meant." She shrugged. "I couldn't decide if I was a cowgirl or *National Velvet* material. How about you?"

Geri smiled. "I owned a horse for a while. Gingertoe, because she had a splash of red on her fetlock. She was a mixed-breed filly. No special pedigree or background, but she was sweet as could be." She brightened at the memory. "Fast too." As Geri glowed, I noticed Lottie watching her with a familiar expression. It mingled boredom at a story she'd heard many times before, fondness, and pride. The way an affectionate lover looked at their partner.

"Gingertoe!" Iris grinned. "Did you race?"

Geri shrugged. "Not really. Though Ginger was always chomping to kick into a gallop. I used to enjoy going all out, flying over the hills as fast as we could." Her face grew pensive. "One of my saddest days was when we had to put her down." Lottie covered Geri's hand with hers and squeezed, and Geri sent her a small smile.

"Did you get another horse?"

Geri sighed. "No. I got hurt right after that. In fact, you could say I'm still paying for my love of horses."

Lottie explained. "Geri took a bad fall. It's what injured her back."

Iris made an appropriately sympathetic noise.

Geri nodded. "It was ridiculous—one of those rides you do on vacation out west. Tamest horses imaginable."

Iris smiled, and her freckles seemed to glow under her tan. "I just got back from a road trip. We went riding too."

Geri leaned forward. "Then you know. We were pacing through a canyon, very sedate, a ride for people who don't ride. I got lulled into not paying attention. But it just goes to show you. I dropped the reins to take a photo, and right then we surprised a snake. The horse spooked and reared. Put a quick end to our vacation, I'll tell you." She added, shaking her head, "The thing I really hate is how people's reactions to it have changed as I've gotten older. My pain is now because I'm old, not because I was injured having fun on vacation."

Lottie jumped in. "It's as if people assume we're suddenly a different species or something when we hit seventy." She lifted her shoulders and looked at Iris. "I feel more 'myself' than ever, actually. If that makes sense. Like the years have worn away all the layers of stuff I don't really need or think. Though I resent having less time to do things, and less energy."

Before I could chime in on this, both Lottie and Geri's attention shifted again, this time to look at the door. Iris and I turned.

There was Lisa, walking in with Nathaniel.

They were heading directly toward our table.

Oh God.

Lisa aimed her smile at me as they approached. "I'm afraid we've been displaced by the construction. May we join you?" At her side the judge frowned, but he didn't say anything. His eyes stayed focused out the window.

Before I could make some excuse, Iris piped up, friendly as ever, "Please. Have a seat," and motioned to the last two empty chairs. Lisa eased her father into one and then took the other. They all looked at me expectantly, since it was clear I knew everybody.

My mouth was so dry I didn't think I could speak. I hadn't had to converse with the judge since that night at the door of his apartment, much less introduce my daughter to the man who had done such damage.

I dug my nails into my palms and cleared my throat. "Lottie and Geri. This is Nathaniel and his daughter, Lisa." In a normal situation I would have mentioned Katherine when introducing Lisa and Nathaniel, but to have to pronounce her name in this context was torture. My voice wavered and cracked. "Lisa, this is my daughter, Iris." I could not bring myself to actually introduce her directly to Nathaniel, to say their names in the same sentence.

But Geri, eager and a little nosy, had scarcely let me finish before she addressed Lisa. "Didn't I see you earlier with our friend Katherine?"

My stomach shrank. Next to me I sensed Iris's heightened attention. She glanced over at me, wondering, I'm sure, why I hadn't mentioned this.

Lisa smiled sadly, one of her many earrings flashing when she turned her head. "Yes, did you know her? She was my stepmother."

Lottie's voice warmed. "She was a sweet lady. I'm sorry for your loss." She leaned in, clearly about to launch into a story. "I remember what she said about a book we were reading . . ."

At that point, Nathaniel, who hadn't even spoken to greet anyone, huffed loudly and turned to openly glare at Lottie, his pale eyes magnified by his glasses. It was so surprising and so hostile that both Geri and I pulled back in our seats. But Lottie, so intent on sharing her story, didn't notice. Lisa flushed bright pink and spoke loudly, deliberately talking over Lottie. "Yes, yes. Now what are they serving this evening? Oh good! I like their chicken."

Lottie stopped speaking and tilted her head, her mouth still open. She looked confused. Nathaniel continued to stare at her, radiating disapproval.

Despite Nathaniel's obvious unwillingness to talk about his wife, Iris, sweetly clueless as ever, didn't pick up on the signals either. She chirped, "Yes, my mother told me so much about Katherine. I'm sorry I never got to meet her." Nathaniel shifted in his seat, about to turn his indignant gaze on Iris, when Lottie, apparently no more observant than my daughter, or perhaps just refusing to be silenced by his rudeness, pressed on. "How long ago was it that she passed? We miss her at the book group. She always had such an interesting take on things."

Nathaniel's eyes glowered under his thick eyebrows. He drew himself up. "Yes, she did. But I would prefer not to discuss my late wife, if you don't mind." By now Lisa's cheeks were flaming. Iris, sympathetic as always, seemed—to my intense dismay—like she was about to say something comforting to the judge. Thank goodness, the server arrived and began distributing our plates of chicken and rice.

Geri elbowed Lottie, who looked down at the table, apparently contrite. "My apologies. I know it must be painful."

Nathaniel spoke imperiously. "At our age, and given our faith, both Katherine and I always considered death to be one of the Lord's mercies." He lifted a finger as he quoted, "'Through the tender mercy of our God; whereby the dayspring from on high has visited us.'"

Geri stared. Lisa's face was deep red. Lottie blinked, clearly discomfited. Dropping any attempt to make conversation with Nathaniel, she turned toward me. "Am I right in remembering you were a nurse?" Her eyes signaled a desperate plea for a topic to move us away from the awkwardness of Nathaniel's pronouncements. This time Iris picked up on Lottie's clear desire to change the subject and, kind as always, jumped in. "My mom was the surgical nursing supervisor at St. Mary's for years," she said proudly.

Geri grabbed hold of this conversational lifeline. "You must get asked about people's ailments all the time. My sister, may she rest in peace, was also a nurse and complained about people wanting to consult her about their ailments at parties." Some humor came into her eyes as she reminded me of our chapel meeting. "Or complain to her about their pain."

I nodded. "I worked mostly in surgery, so my patients were usually pretty out of it. But believe me, I understand. And as I get older, it isn't just academic, though personally I've been pretty lucky. My aches and pains are relatively manageable."

All this time Nathaniel had begun methodically chewing, seemingly oblivious to our conversation, but Lisa had been listening. Now that the topic seemed safer, she tried to draw her father in again. "See, Dad? Everyone has pain once in a while. But it seems like your new medication is working. Do you feel more like yourself?"

He cut through his chicken breast and seemed at least to try to be sociable. "Yes. The medicine seems adequate. Thank you for asking."

Adequate. Oh God.

Iris looked at him peculiarly. She tipped her head, examining him.

Oh Jesus God.

The judge crossed his silverware on his plate without looking up. "I think I will be retiring now."

Lisa, who had just begun to eat her own dinner, looked at his food. "But you've only had a few bites."

"Yes," he said, and pushed away from the table, still without looking up. "Good evening everyone." Obviously, Lisa's dinner was over as well.

She sent all of us an embarrassed, conciliatory glance. "Yes, thank you for your company," she said, her face reddening again. She helped her father out of his chair and handed him his cane. Her own food was scarcely touched.

We watched them leave. Lottie said, "Well. That was awkward."

Geri lifted her eyebrows, "Not sure what to make of that. He must really be grieving."

Eager to put a stop to this line of discussion, I jumped in, "Let's change the subject from sickness and sadness. Weren't we discussing new titles at the library? We really need an infusion of new books." We chatted about what to read next and about maybe starting a movie group. But Iris was uncharacteristically quiet.

Later, as she walked with me back to my apartment, she said, "What a strange man."

"Yes. He's very . . . trying. I feel sorry for him. He's not really 'all there,' if you know what I mean." I tapped the side of my forehead, to indicate mental impairment. In truth, he was always curt, so I didn't think his behavior meant a cognitive decline. But Iris didn't know that, and I was trying to position him as someone not worth paying attention to. Not worth bothering about.

"Oh really? He didn't seem disoriented. Just very angry."

"Well, you know that's a sign of dementia. Especially in men, sad to say. They're confused, and so they lash out. Sometimes I think he doesn't even know who he is."

She nodded, thinking. "What did he do for a living?"

And there it was. I had been dreading her asking. Somehow we had gotten through dinner without anyone referring to him as "Judge," thank God. Because that might have given the game away.

"He was a . . . professor." I figured his imperiousness and ego matched well with that profession. Lie begat lie. "But as he's losing his grip, he's beginning to think he is his father, who was a judge. In fact, sometimes he makes people call him that." I had to know. "Why do you ask?"

"Oh just curious. Something about him seemed familiar."

That did it. Iris and Nathaniel simply could not ever run into one another, ever again. It absolutely could never happen. I had to make certain of it. Somehow. I said, "Well, he's from Louisiana, so I'm sure you've never met him." Finally, a sentence that was at least partially true.

"But did you bring the pictures you promised? Of the tiles for the condo bathroom?"

She immediately switched gears, eager to talk about the redecorating, fishing a brochure out of her purse.

We drank tea in my apartment and browsed through all the various options and plans for the new bathroom. I enjoyed talking about this almost as much as she did. But when she left, I collapsed in my chair by the window.

I was exhausted. Lying was exhausting. Anxiety was exhausting. That dinner had been ghastly beyond measure. The thought that I still had to deal with Nathaniel, to keep him away from Iris, was like a punch in the gut.

It had grown dark. I stared out at the preserve, visible in rising moonlight. There was a stack of books by my chair, and they reminded me of another nagging thought, another lingering reminder. Before Iris and Nathaniel and Lisa had shown up, my conversation with Lottie and Geri had been so nice. Somehow I had forgotten the pleasures of chatting with friends.

A crushing sadness filled my chest. The sound of Katherine's voice, soft but superior, came back to me.

If I was being honest with myself, I had to admit that even while we were getting to know each other I had sensed no-go zones, topics about which our differences would have proven too significant to overlook. Our lunches had reminded me of some of the friendships of my youth—the ones that came on strong and were almost like an infatuation or crush in their intensity. Like a crush, they didn't necessarily mellow into long-lasting relationships. At one moment or another, the new friend would say or do something that revealed some aspect of personality that I couldn't fathom or that demonstrated some attitude I couldn't forgive. I thought about our conversation during that soap opera.

Still—the fact was that in this late stage in life I had found someone I could learn from and have fun with, a real actual friend. The pleasure of new company, the connection with a person very different from myself, had been real.

And I had ended it. I couldn't push it away any longer: I had destroyed the last friendship I might form in this life in a misguided quest for revenge. And on top of that, because of my actions I had to keep my daughter away from my home. Karma bites back, it seems.

21

Now that Katherine was gone, if I took a morning stroll, I did it mostly alone. Iris sometimes joined me, but she wasn't really interested in whether Mr. O'Neill and Miss Baxter were flirting with one another or if Mrs. Schwarz's son was really as big a shot as she claimed. But when Katherine was alive, we used to make a perambulation around the facility and notice things. Gather impressions. Then we'd spin our theories about our neighbor's activities over coffee. But if I tried this with Iris, I never got very far. She said it wasn't like me, that I was becoming a busybody in my old age. She was right, but I found I had enjoyed being an occasional busybody. What else did I have to do?

*　*　*

But since she returned from her trip, Iris seemed determined to spend time with me at Ridgewood, maybe to convince herself that I'd be okay when she moved, or perhaps to take advantage of her proximity. Fortunately, the huge upside of walking in the morning with her was that I could simply relax and enjoy her company, because neither Evan nor Lottie or Geri, and certainly not the judge, were ever seen before lunchtime.

One morning after our stroll, we landed in the front sunroom. It was the perfect place to observe the world of Ridgewood. From there, we could watch the comings and goings in the lobby and hear almost everything as well. Including Thomas buttering up his boss, Mr. Alfred, the supersized executive director. They were standing outside the door to the office. As usual, Thomas wore an ingratiating expression. His body was pitched forward, looking up at Mr. Alfred's chin. Alfred pointed and nodded at the patio, visible through the lobby windows, where a number of residents were sitting. I had noticed a similar exchange yesterday. When Alfred went back into his office, Thomas immediately reached for his phone and made a call, his face a stern mask.

"Mom? Mother?"

I realized Iris had been talking to me.

"Earth to Mom. What in the world is so interesting? What are you are looking at?"

"Let's go out to the patio." I pushed myself up off the bench. "I want to sit outside. It looks beautiful out."

"Great idea!" Iris said with too much zest. There seemed to be a lot of intentional enthusiasm lately. She stood and put her hand under my elbow. "Let's get some fresh air."

As we headed past Thomas, I offered him my brightest hello. He was frowning into his phone, looking out at the patio, but he gave me a fake smile and a thumbs-up sign. I leaned on Iris as we stepped outside, and lifted my hand against the sun to let my eyes adjust. Chevron paving stones outlined a dappled courtyard lined with benches. Pots of begonias and impatiens hung all around. At the far end, past the flowers, a trellis framed a path to the wide lawn, which sloped down to the preserve—the same preserve I saw outside my window.

Next to the trellis was a folding table with a paper sign taped to the front: "Nature Walks and Critter Watchers." Iris and I looked at one another and headed toward it.

As we neared the table, Marta, the activities director, appeared, looking flustered. She slipped her phone into her pocket and smiled at me. "Francine! Nice to see you again."

Shoot. I hadn't talked with Marta since I'd stopped attending the book group. I had to head her off before she announced my lack of attendance, because I wanted Iris to think I was super busy and engaged. I replied loudly, "Yes. We missed you while you were away."

She looked at me, confused. "I wasn't . . ."

I picked up the clipboard that was lying on the table and interrupted her, "What's this about? Looks interesting."

She switched gears immediately and leaned forward. "Would you like to sign up for a Nature Walk? Be a 'Critter Watcher?' You would love it. Last week we saw deer, a raccoon, and an egret." She pushed a pen toward me eagerly. Nervously. Her eyes flashed for a moment to where Thomas stood in the lobby.

So he was making her jittery too.

Iris jumped in. "Mom! That's a great idea. You've always loved the outdoors."

I've always loved cheeseburgers too, I thought, *but that doesn't mean I want a behind-the-scenes tour of MacDonald's.* But I did not want to alienate anyone. Instead, I smiled. "Thanks for asking." I patted Iris's arm, upon which I was leaning, "but I don't think I could handle the uneven terrain. Even on this patio, if Iris weren't here with me, I'd need to use my walker, or at least my cane."

"Oh, no need to worry about that," Marta said. "We've put in a special path for wheelchairs and walkers, and we always have plenty of staff and volunteers on hand."

Iris was enthusiastic. "I was just reading in the newspaper about how we're all suffering from 'nature deficit disorder.'" She turned to me. "Mom, sign up! I'll try to come along, if it works with my schedule."

Marta held out the pen. "Francine, I think you'd be a wonderful example for some of our other residents who aren't as active as you. Or as curious and informed."

I knew she was trying to flatter me. At Ridgewood, there were several areas the residents got competitive about. A big one was health: either how much pain they were in or how bad their rheumatism/heart palpitations/knees were; or, conversely, how great they were feeling, how they still golfed or swam or power-walked. Another arena for bragging rights was how fabulous their kids and grandkids were, or how much the younger generation ignored them or sponged off them.

But Marta was trying to engage me in a different sport, a competition about acuity: reminding others—and ourselves—how good our minds, memories, and hearing still were. This was a weirder competition and more ambiguous, since the gradual erosion of memory and cognition was not always recognized by the people who were affected. Perhaps that was a mercy. Being "still sharp" was harder to brag about, since it wasn't necessarily connected to getting old. Some people have been idiots their whole lives, and in my experience a lot of stupid people don't know they are stupid. In fact, for some people a symptom of their stupidity was that they were proud of their own faulty thinking.

But clearly, it was in this arena of competence and intelligence and memory, of having capacity and wit to think and put two and two together, that Marta figured I was vulnerable to flattery. And she was right.

Iris saw the crack in my resistance. "Mom, come on. You should do this." Then she lifted a brow and got a glint in her eye. "Remember all those hikes you and Daddy used to make us go on?" Her voice was teasing, but I knew she'd be relentless. "I seem to recall you harping about how important getting out in nature was and how good for us it would be." Iris had always complained about those hikes. Her grin told me she was enjoying this. Turnaround is fair play, I guess.

I sighed. It wasn't like I had anything better to do, and I had the sense signing up would help Marta. She was obviously trying to placate Thomas.

"I suppose I could give it a try. When is the next outing?"

Marta's face radiated approval. "Tomorrow morning, as it happens." She offered the clipboard, and Iris handed me the pen. Clearly, I was not going to get out of at least signing up. I took the pen and put down my name.

Iris winked at me. "I wonder how many of those chickens you'll see?"

Marta said "Chickens? I don't think—"

Iris ignored her and continued to grin at me. "You know. All those 'you need to get out in nature' chickens, coming home to roost."

I groaned. "Your father always said you were the family champion of bad jokes."

* * *

Later that evening I sat by my window and looked out at the preserve, feeling my old resistance kick in. My impulse has always been to avoid participating in group events, even in activities I consider pleasurable. But why? After all, these sorts of opportunities are why I pay rent here rather than living in some dark institution with no access to nature or staff to help one experience it. Was it because I thought it meant I was somehow giving in—drinking the "old person Kool-Aid"? That doing organized activities with my peers signaled I had lost self-awareness, that I had become just like all the other old folks following along and giving in to some sort of groupthink? Couldn't I plan my own outings, thank you very much?

Right. Because I had so many other options. I was holding myself apart because of my vanity. *"Bloom where you are planted, Francine,"* my mother's voice came in dimly.

So, I could pretend I was not really an old person living at Ridgewood because I had fallen too many times in my condo—the condo I moved into to begin with after the stairs in my old house got too tall. Or I could try to find enjoyment even here, even now.

* * *

The knock came at my door early, but I was ready for it. I had on sunglasses, bug spray, and a wide-brimmed hat. Ridiculous, perhaps. I wasn't going to the equator. Still, I figured, "in for a penny, in for a pound."

I pulled open my door and was happy to find Jannah, wearing a smile and sunglasses. I hadn't seen her since the night I'd overheard her conversation with Graciela.

"Seeing you makes me happy that I let my daughter talk me into this," I said.

"Good morning! The feeling is mutual. I was surprised to see your name on the list, but I was glad." Sweet. The way she said it made me think maybe she really meant it. "Do you want to use a wheelchair, or do you think you can manage with a walker?"

I considered. "How long is the trail?"

"Maybe a half mile, all told. But we go only as far as you want. What do you think?"

Suddenly I was unsure of my strength. It's one of the worst parts about getting old. I find myself second-guessing my own abilities, constantly having to balance my sense that I can still do anything with the fear of embarrassment if I fail.

"I think you'll be good with your walker," she said. "If you get tired, we can stop."

I really liked Jannah.

We made our way through the lobby and joined a small group on the patio. Most of them were in wheelchairs. Marta was there in a yellow hat and with her omnipresent clipboard. She grinned as she saw me. "Glad you could make it."

Then she turned to the others and spoke loudly, "Welcome everyone. Today we have a special treat. We have a guest from the local Audubon Society. He says there has been a sighting of a Cooper's hawk in the area." A short-legged man dressed in a green "Birders Are Beautiful" T-shirt and khaki pants a smidge too tight stepped in front of us.

"Good morning!" he boomed. "I'm so happy to be here! We're going to see some exciting things today!" He canted forward on his toes like a kindergarten teacher.

I thought, *Uh-oh. Here it comes.* This is why I avoid joining things: I hate being treated like a child. He spoke loudly and enunciated as if we were tourists just learning English. He held up a laminated photo of a hawk. "Can anyone guess what this is?"

Let me think. A Cooper's hawk?

"No one wants to venture a guess?" His head rolled on his neck like he was a toy figure. "It's a Cooper's hawk! This pretty boy has been seen in your woods, like Marta mentioned. Isn't he something?"

By now even Marta looked uncomfortable. She stepped in, clearing her throat. "Yes. Well. Thank you." She eased the man to the side. "Perhaps we should set off and try to see it."

"You don't want me to give my presentation? I brought visual aids—"

"I think it's better if we get going before the day gets too warm. If you don't mind?" Seeing the man's crestfallen demeanor, she added, "Perhaps you could walk along with us and let us know if you spot something?"

I sent a quick "oh God, rescue me" glance to Jannah, and to my great relief, I saw her smile twitch and her eyes signal understanding. She mouthed, "No worries."

We set off. After the group crossed the side lawn, we came to a path that sloped gently downward, into lovely, dappled shade. Jannah let the others, along with Marta and the Audubon volunteer, go in front of us. After we crossed into the wood and let our eyes adjust to the filtered sunshine, Jannah slowed even more, and the group got further ahead. They passed out of sight when the path curved around a small rise. By unspoken agreement Jannah and I stopped and took in the green light and smell of moss and leaves and moist soil. A small white butterfly danced by.

Jannah had her arm looped under my elbow, supporting me. She said, "It's beautiful here. Just steps from the lawn and it feels like an enchanted forest." Then she seemed to be embarrassed. "I guess that sounds childish. It is what I used to think whenever I played in woods when I was a kid."

We started walking again, slowly. I asked, "Where did you grow up?"

"Right by here. In fact, I remember when they built this place."

I turned to her in surprise. I had always taken her to be an immigrant because of her slight accent and patterns of speech. "You're from here?"

She stiffened. "My family is from Jamaica. But we came here when I was young." Her voice had lost its warmth.

Embarrassed, I flattened my hand against my chest in a gesture of apology. "Oh, please don't think badly of my question." I added, "My parents were immigrants too."

She pressed her lips together and nodded. "I know you didn't mean anything by it. It's just some here aren't very nice."

I spoke deliberately. "People are being difficult?"

Her eyes flicked away. "It's fine. Please, I shouldn't say anything."

I thought of what I overheard between her and Graciela. "Do you mean Thomas?"

She stopped and there was concern in her eyes. "I'm not complaining. They pay okay, and most of the residents are sweet." She inhaled and put on a professional face. "Like you!" Then she added, "Besides, it's a great job while I'm in school."

"For nursing? Like Graciela?"

"Maybe. I'm in night school now. I have to see if I get decent grades in chemistry before I can apply to the program."

We proceeded slowly along the path. It was packed crushed limestone, easy enough to negotiate with my walker, and not slippery. As the sun filtered through the trees, Jannah and I fell into a comfortable silence. I had to admit it was pleasurable. Feeling the green all around me and smelling the earth was better than watching from my window.

Suddenly Jannah tightened a grip on my arm and stopped me. She held her finger to her lips and motioned her head to the left.

There, more still than the trees surrounding them, froze a doe and her fawn. Jannah and I were perhaps fifteen feet away. For a charged moment, neither of us moved. The doe stared at us and seemed to be weighing her options. Then, from far ahead of us on the path, someone cried, "Hawk!" The doe sprang away, bouncing off into a thicket with her fawn.

We both exhaled. Jannah said, "I loved how she looked at us. Do you think they were afraid?"

"Probably. Although I've seen deer become unafraid when they learn that no one hurts them. In the forest preserve I used to go to, the bucks got to be so brazen they wouldn't even get off the road when I drove up to them."

"You mean they were tame? Did you feed them?"

"No, not at all. It seemed almost the opposite of tame . . . it was like they were in charge. Like they knew nothing would happen. In fact, there were so many deer, they were destroying the wood. Too many animals eating the plants." I hadn't thought about it in years. "It really bothered me, the first time I had to honk and honk to get a deer to move off a roadway. Something about it made me think of all the ways we have altered the world, how messed up the balance is. It wasn't right."

We proceeded a few moments. Then Jannah asked, "Where did you grow up?"

"On a farm. Way up north, near Canada."

"Is that where the forest preserve was?"

"Oh no. The forest preserve I was referring to is around here. I used to take my kids. The deer where I grew up acted a lot different. Up there, the deer were definitely afraid of people. They were right to be. There was a lot of open land, and everyone hunted."

As we rounded a curve, there was a bench discreetly placed next to the path. We could hear the enthusiasm of the Audubon volunteer echoing through the leaves ahead of us. We glanced at each other, and instinctively we both sat down.

Jannah sighed. "It seems sad for the deer, in a way. So hemmed in. Their lives are controlled, even if they are safe."

I sensed she was going to say more, to explain. But in a moment she asked, "Where were your parents from?"

"My mom's family was from Czechoslovakia. My dad was Sicilian. My mom got in a lot of trouble for marrying him. He had dark hair and a dark complexion, and people where they lived called him a WOP."

"A what?"

I looked at her. "A WOP. You mean they don't use that expression anymore?"

"I've never heard it."

"Good. It's an insult. It means 'without papers,' but it was only used against people who weren't considered quite as good as others." I swallowed. "People would use that term to imply they didn't belong here."

Jannah met my eyes, and there was a wordless exchange.

I tried to raise the topic again. "At one hospital where I worked, there were people who took advantage of immigrants. Asked them to do things others didn't have to do, gave them the worst shifts, and didn't promote them or give them raises. I know it happens."

She turned away and wouldn't look at me. I decided to risk it. I cleared my throat. "Jannah . . . I-I overheard you talking with Graciela the other night. About her son, and I wondered, I mean, I don't know, of course, but . . ."

I was blathering. Jannah lifted her eyes to me, her expression unreadable. I knew it was none of my business. But I also knew that sometimes people could stop unfair things if they were willing to stick their nose outside of their own business once in a while.

So I bit my lip to stop yammering. I sat up straight, looked her at her directly and said simply, "Please forgive me if I'm out of line. But I wanted to tell you that if there is anything I can do for either of you, please let me know." I could hear the rest of the nature walkers drawing near us: they must've turned around after seeing their hawk. Jannah had still not answered, but she now shifted her gaze up the path toward the sound of them coming.

She stood. "It seems like we're returning." She leaned down to assist me to my feet. But she still wouldn't make eye contact. She helped me up, holding my elbow. I cleared my throat and said, "Jannah?"

She kept her face turned away for another second. Then she turned to me, consternation in her expression. "I understand you mean well. But it's complicated. Please. It's better if you just keep out of it."

We had only a moment before the others arrived. She still was supporting my elbow, and I pressed her hand with mine and spoke so she couldn't mistake my meaning. "Okay. But if I can ever help, please just ask. Really. I may be old, but there is freedom in that. It means I can say what needs to be said. I'm not intimidated by bullies."

Her solemn eyes held mine for a moment. Then her mouth became soft, and she nodded.

CHAPTER

22

THE NEXT EVENING Charlie and Pam and the kids were taking me to dinner. I was in the lobby, waiting for them to pick me up, when someone thumped down onto the bench next to me.

Evan.

He smiled. "Finally. If I had to put money down, I would bet you've been avoiding me."

A spark of anxiety prickled my neck, but I answered blandly. "It has been awhile. But you'd lose your bet."

"If you say so." He lifted a knowing eyebrow. "So, how are things? Why do I never seem to run into you?"

So he'd been on the lookout for me. I shrugged. "You just don't travel in the right circles, I guess."

He laughed at that, leaning back. Then he rubbed the top of his cane and turned toward me. "Maybe we could have lunch together again sometime."

"Maybe. Sometime." I glanced past him and saw Charlie's car enter the far end of the parking lot. I leaned forward and got ready to push myself up.

Evan said, "How about Monday?"

I frowned with irritation. Didn't he understand when he was being put off politely? He added, "I promise, not to talk about . . . anything you don't want to discuss."

The car was not Charlie's after all. Darn. For once it would be really nice if my son were early. I slumped back against the cushion.

Evan persisted. "Frannie, come on. Don't you just wish you had someone to gossip about this place with?"

"Is that what you think? That I'm a gossipy old woman?"

"No! That's not what I meant." He held up his free hand. "Maybe 'gossip' was the wrong word. I just . . ." He shrugged. "You know what I mean. You see things. Like me. You know who's flirting with whom, whose kids are resentful or greedy, which couples are arguing. Who's pocketing the silverware. You notice things about the staff and wonder about their stories. But you don't have anyone to chew it over with. If your kids are like mine, they aren't interested."

When I didn't answer, he waved his hand, gesturing around the lobby. "And what else are we going to do—go jogging?"

This made me chuckle. "Well, no. But we could play shuffleboard."

"I'd beat you. I'm good at shuffleboard."

The exchange was almost flirtatious. I thought that had been settled, but I wanted to make sure. I asked, "Evan, this isn't some backhanded way of asking for a date, is it?"

"No!" He blanched. "I-I-I wasn't thinking of it like that." He looked panicked. "Not that you aren't— But I, well, if you want to think of it that way, um, well. I-I . . ."

His discomfort was answer enough. And though it was fun to watch him twist in the wind, I lifted my hand to quiet him. "Good. I am not interested in romance."

But I *was* tempted to accept the invite. I realized I'd been foolish when I made him leave my apartment without forcing him to tell me exactly what he thought about Katherine's death. I'd let my fear and anger and panic get the best of me when I should have found out what his suspicions were and how he came to them. And now, with Thomas's increased scrutiny of Graciela and Jannah . . . Evan was so observant.

Having the chance to get his take on things might be helpful. In his letter he'd said he was an ally. Very well, I would
at least for the moment treat him that way. Not that I would
let my guard down or reveal anything. Allies aren't necessarily friends.

I still didn't trust him, but it had been more weeks since
Katherine's death—enough time that it seemed clear he
wasn't going to act on any suspicions or make them public.
It also occurred to me that if I gave him something else to
chew over, he would leave off thinking about Katherine and
her passing. He really was, as he said, a noticer. So maybe I
could give him something else to notice.

I turned to him, suddenly decisive. "Okay. Monday it is.
But you're buying."

Beyond the lobby doors I spotted another silver Toyota,
and this time it really was Charlie's. I didn't want my son
and Evan to have another annoying male-bonding conversation like they did when they both invaded my apartment
and negotiated over who would clean up the spilled cookies. So I hurried—if you could call my progress with a cane
hurrying—toward the exit. I hit the "Door Open" button,
and as I waited for the glass doors to slide apart, I said, "See
you Monday."

*   *   *

I was more animated with Danny and Adam than I had been
in a long time. Halfway through dinner, Danny nudged me.
"You're in a good mood, Grandma." I realized it was the feeling that at least I was taking some action, not just stewing in
misery.

I reached over and pulled my grandson's ear. "It's just so
good to be with you."

*   *   *

Then, on Sunday afternoon, what had been a vague concern,
perhaps born of nosiness, became more urgent.

The construction was finished. I once again sat at my regular table, tucked in the corner by the coffee station and staff area outside the kitchen. I heard whispering and looked around.

Graciela was murmuring urgently into her phone. This in itself was a violation of the rules, and something I'd never seen her do. Her back was to me, so I couldn't see her face. But her voice was frantic, and it sounded like she was crying. I moved my head to listen and strained to follow her words as she switched between Spanish and English.

"Please Ramon. *Pide a tu tia. Por favor. Puede hablar con* Thomas." She was desperately upset. "*Mi acusó* . . . he say I make *un error con la medicina.*" Her voice broke. She swallowed and then she whispered with urgency "*Y si llama* ICE *o la policia . . .?*" The brewing coffee gurgled and hissed, drowning out her voice.

My stomach dropped. She turned and I quickly leaned my head on my hand so she wouldn't see I'd been eavesdropping. She rushed out of the dining room, a Kleenex pressed against her mouth. I had studied Spanish years ago when we had an exchange student from Bolivia stay with us. I was far from fluent, but it didn't take a genius to figure that the words *un error con la medicina* or *la policia*, spoken with such trepidation, did not bode well. My stomach tightened.

"How are you tonight, Mrs. Greene?"

I jumped. The young man who had materialized at my elbow was Lucas, one of the part-time aides.

"Oh! Hello." I blinked. "Hello. Nice to see you."

He smiled. "Great to see you too, looking as bright as ever." Lucas was a university student with a friendly disposition.

I turned to address him. "Come to think of it, you haven't been around much lately. Studying for exams?"

"Not exactly." He shrugged. "He's only giving me a few shifts a week."

I lifted my eyebrow, questioning.

"You know." He glanced around. "Thomas."

I lowered my voice. "Is he difficult to work for?"

Lucas shrugged and offered a knowing smirk. "I can't complain. He's not too hard on me." He indicated the staff area behind me with a movement of his head. "He's tougher on some of the others, who depend on this place more. You know—who have fewer options." The look he gave me was freighted.

After he brought my lunch, I lingered as long as I could over my wedge of iceberg lettuce with blue cheese crumbled on top and my beef barley soup, keeping watch for Graciela. I even asked for dessert, which I almost never do. But she didn't return to the coffee station behind the door, and I waited until my ice cream melted before I finally gave up and made my way back to my apartment.

All afternoon the implications of Graciela's phone call churned in my stomach. Until now it had seemed that everyone assumed Katherine had died of natural causes. Evan had indicated an intuition, born of knowing my family's history with Nathaniel and the fact that he'd seen me by the med cart. But even he had said he had no idea what really happened.

But now, all these weeks later, questions seemed to be emerging.

I stood at my window, fear gnawing at me. I spent the rest of the day formulating some seemingly innocent but revealing questions for when Graciela came with the meds that evening.

When the knock came, I flung open my door. But it wasn't Graciela.

"Oh!" My voice betrayed my surprise "Um. Hello."

The young woman blinked at me and swung her gaze from me to the apartment number above my door and then down to her clipboard. She had mousy overgrown bangs and dark lipstick. Though reason told me she was an adult, she looked like she was about fifteen. She said, "Francine Greene?"

"Yes, that's me."

She lifted the pleated cup that held my blood pressure medication. Then she looked at her clipboard and checked my apartment number again. Finally she offered it to me tentatively, like it was an explosive.

I smiled as I took the offering. "You're new, aren't you? What's your name?"

"Dorrie." She pulled her lips upward like a kid whose mom had reminded her to smile. "Nice to meet you." Her mouth again fell into a flat line. Then she just stood there looking at me, her left foot bobbing.

"Nice to meet you too." I added, "Is Graciela out sick today? I hope everything's okay?"

Dorrie flushed. "Graciela is here. But she can't do meds anymore."

"Oh . . ." I decided to attempt to prompt her. "Do you know why?" I hurried to add, "Not that it isn't a pleasure to meet you."

"I don't know." Still, she made no move to continue on her way, and peered at me, scraping her lower lip with her teeth. She offered nothing more.

"Well . . ." I nodded at her, giving up on getting any information. "Have a good evening," I said, and began to close the door as she stared at me.

"Wait." Her arm shot out to stop me. "I'm supposed to watch you swallow it."

"Swallow what?"

She looked at the pill cup in my hand.

What was this? In the past I would sometimes take the cup of water Graciela offered just to chat a bit longer. But it had never been required. I said, "Are you saying you have to watch me take my medicine? Really? Since when?"

The poor thing blushed. "I don't know. That's just what they told me. They said that a few weeks back somebody didn't get the right medication. Thomas said I need to be certain."

All moisture drained from my mouth. I didn't trust myself to speak. She poured a few sips of water into a Dixie cup and watched as I choked down my pills. Then she leaned over the cart to make a note on the clipboard.

I thought of Thomas's attention to Graciela when she was on med duty.

What—*exactly*—was Graciela being accused of?

I was unable to sleep that night and stared into the dark until the wee hours. I was glad I'd be talking to Evan. If only I could figure out how to frame it without revealing anything.

* * *

The next day Evan and I went back to the country club. This time when we ordered, I included a glass of sauvignon blanc. His eyebrows shot up at that. "That's a good sign. Last time we were here, you were as guarded as a nun in a saloon."

"Ah . . ." I let my voice trail away before pursing my lips. "Let's just say I didn't know you so well then."

After our drinks arrived and we ordered our sandwiches, he lifted his beer in a toast. "To lunches without anxiety." He clinked my wineglass with his beer bottle.

"That would be good."

I sipped the pale, green-tasting wine. It had been a long time since I'd indulged in alcohol at lunch.

He tilted his head. "So? What's new, Frannie?" He adopted a slightly ironic, "what shall we talk about now?" tone. "What are you doing these days, since you have abandoned the book club?"

I decided I might as well just jump in. I leaned forward. "What do you know about Thomas?"

"Who?"

"You know. The manager."

He looked puzzled. "The one with the stick up his you-know-what? What about him?"

"What do you think of him?"

"Like I said. He acts like he has something stuck firmly in his behind. Tightly wound. He's nice enough to me, of course, but he has to be. Why?"

"I think he is semi-abusive to the staff. They all seem afraid of him."

"Semi-abusive?" He tilted his head. "What does that mean?"

I exhaled and pressed lines into the tablecloth with the tines of my fork. "I'm not sure. But the staff seems really apprehensive. Like, frightened."

"You mean physically?"

"Noooo. I mean, I think he manipulates them. Lords things over them."

He shrugged. "So the guy is a petty tyrant. He likes power, but doesn't really have much. So he pushes around folks with even less power than him."

The waiter appeared and set down our plates. I took a sip of wine as he walked away. Suddenly I could hardly breathe. The trepidation was overwhelming, like a band around my chest. I blinked to keep tears away.

"Frannie? What is it?"

I bit my lip and inhaled to calm myself. After a moment I slowly said, "I overheard something. I think he's up to worse than merely making his underlings miserable. It might even have some—legal aspects."

"Legal aspects?" He picked up his fork.

I swallowed the lump in my throat. "Do you know Graciela?"

"Of course. The nurse's aide. Short, kind, long dark braids?"

"She's the person I first noticed it with. In fact, it was the day you . . ." I paused. "The day you stopped by my apartment and met my son."

"Oh sure. The day with the cookie spill." He cleared his throat. "When we had the coffee klatch with Ida."

He was honoring the fiction he'd created about that day. I gave a quick smile in recognition, but I couldn't maintain the eye contact. I resumed scraping the linen with my fork. "That was when I first picked up on it. She brought me my lunch after you left. She was super-nervous. She kept glancing around, and seemed panicked that I might complain because it took so long and the lunch was cold. I figured he was just a run-of-the-mill asshole boss. But I decided to keep an eye out and intervene if I could, because I hate bullies. So I started watching him. And he is, as you say, a petty tyrant. It seems like the entire staff gets nervous and flustered and fearful when he is around. Marta, Jannah, even that student—Lucas, I think his name is. All of them."

He opened his napkin. "So where does the legal aspect come in?"

"You notice how many of the staff are immigrants?"

He nodded. "Yeah. That might make people more vulnerable." He sipped his beer.

"You know where I sit in the dining room?"

He chuckled. "Of course. You hide yourself away in that corner. Makes it very hard to observe you, I have to say."

I smirked. "Well, it also makes it easy for me to observe everyone else. And to listen in on what the staff are talking about." I paused. "And I've heard a few conversations that . . . made me worry."

"Like what?"

"Well, to begin with, a while back I heard Graciela and Jannah talking, and Graciela was really upset. She was talking about her son, and it became clear he is not living with her and that she is sending money back to her family. Then Jannah tried to comfort her, pointing out she'd get a raise soon."

"And?" He slipped the pepper shaker out of the holder and lifted the top off his burger.

"And then Graciela whispered something about Thomas having to approve the raise, and she was almost crying. And from the way she said it, and from Jannah's reaction, it wasn't just about the money. Like they were really frightened of what he might do. And then she whispered something about 'ICE' and Ramon—I think that's her husband—and Jannah said, "But isn't Thomas Ramon's cousin?' and Graciela, who was in tears by this time, said, 'Yes, that's how he knows.'"

I took a bite of my patty melt. Evan watched me and didn't say anything.

"Well?" I finally asked.

"You think he's somehow using her immigration status against her."

I nodded.

He wiped his mouth. "So, you mentioned legal aspects?"

"I just told you . . ."

He opened his hands. "Look, this kind of thing pisses me off too. And I'm as sympathetic as you for Graciela, and Jannah and everyone who works to take care of us. It's what makes Ridgewood a nice place. But without knowing anyone's immigration status, there's not much to go on. Do you know her status?"

I shook my head.

"Plus . . ." He exhaled. "I'm afraid there isn't much protection people can claim if they don't have a work visa. It's the reason immigrants are so vulnerable to begin with."

"There must be something we can do. It's getting worse. Just a couple days ago, I overheard her talking on the phone. She was crying. She said he was accusing her. He can get her sent away. She mentioned the police . . ." I cut myself off. I didn't dare say more—not yet. Maybe not ever.

I kept my face down, struggling for composure. I felt the weight of his eyes on me, but I had no idea what he was thinking. Neither of us spoke for a moment. I could see his left hand, twiddling the frilled toothpick that had speared his sandwich.

Finally he cleared his throat. "Let's think about this for a minute. Why is this happening now?"

I shrugged. I hadn't told him about the charged confrontation between Thomas and Graciela over the med cart.

Or the fact that she wasn't working the medication cart anymore. I couldn't bring myself to.

He sipped his beer and exhaled. "Look at us, chewing over tidbits. I guess we have to take what excitement we can get."

I flared at him. "It isn't a game. These are the people who care for us. We should care about them."

His eyes widened, and to my surprise he blushed. "You're right. I didn't mean to sound flippant. It's just that trying to stop a bully isn't quite the high stakes of a criminal investigation or life-changing surgery."

I couldn't meet his eyes. *Please God,* I thought, *please let it be as he says.* A case of workplace bullying. Awful, but nothing to do with untimely death. Please don't let anyone think Graciela messed up the medicines and killed Katherine.

There it was. The thought that I had been fighting off ever since I overheard her phone call. My real fear: that my meddling had caused Katherine's death, and Graciela was being blamed.

The self-deception of my supposed concern for the staff hit me with full force. Thomas may be an asshole boss, and he might not be sympathetic to immigrants' concerns, but the real crux of my worry was that Thomas suspected something had gone awry with the medication cart and that an investigation could result. Or that a blameless person would be blamed.

I could somehow, maybe, justify to myself taking revenge on people who had hurt my family. But ruining the life of an innocent bystander was something else entirely.

Oh God. Oh God.

23

I couldn't sleep. At three am, after hours of tangling up my sheets, I finally took half a sleeping pill. It knocked me out, but I didn't feel rested when my alarm went off. Bad dreams. I stumbled to the kitchen. Worse, the calendar on my refrigerator reminded me, in large letters written in orange marker: *Check-up, Doctor Rudd, 11:30*. Darn it. That meant Iris was supposed to pick me up at eleven. Which meant she'd be here at ten thirty because, unlike her brother, Iris is always early. Ugh.

Of course, of all mornings this would be when I ran out of coffee. I put water in the microwave and rooted around for the packets of English Breakfast I had grabbed from the dining room for just such an emergency. I added a bunch of sugar to make it drinkable and fortified myself with a few sips.

But man, did I need a shower. Tossing and turning and sweating and worrying will do that to you. I carried my tea into the bath and turned the tap on full blast. A shower would wash away the grogginess and clear my fuzzy head. I dropped my pajamas and stepped in. No sooner had I lathered up my hair than it happened.

I didn't exactly fall, as much as tilt too far when I went to pick up the dropped bar of Dr. Bonner's peppermint soap. I leaned too much to the right and ended up off-kilter, bumping against the shower wall and slipping, slowly and evenly, like a little mound of suds trailing down the tile. The slide came to a halt as my body curled into an awkward half sit, half sprawl in the bottom of the shallow tub.

I took stock of the situation as the water, still running, began to cool. If I stretched I could just reach the emergency call button on the side of the shower. But I didn't want to do that. I wanted to avoid the humiliation of having someone come in and rescue me out of my own bathtub, thank you very much. Plus, I knew they were required to call the paramedics and Iris and Charlie, and it would be a huge big deal. The expression I would see on Charlie's face floated in my mind's eye and gave me the strength I needed.

From my position in the tub, I managed to grab the handles on the sliding shower door, and with great effort pulled myself up. The door slid open and water began splashing everywhere, but I maneuvered till I was perched on the tub's edge, my legs inside the enclosure. I turned off the faucet. Still holding on to the shower door handles, I managed to stand.

I stepped out of the tub and looked around. There was water all over the floor. Shampoo suds dripped down my neck from my half-rinsed hair, and the bathroom rug was sopping in a puddle. The guilty bar of soap was a goopy lump on the bottom of the tub. I had avoided the embarrassment of having to be rescued naked and dripping, but I still had to figure out a way to clean up. Not to mention get the soap out of my hair.

I inspected my body. My slide down the shower wall hadn't been violent or jarring, and it didn't seem like I'd hurt anything. I might even get away with no bruising. I grabbed my walker, which I had parked nearby for after my shower, and put on my robe. Then I pulled towels off the shelf to unfurl over the floor.

First stop, the kitchen. I dropped the robe off my shoulders and used the sprayer in the sink to rinse the soap out of my hair. I had to wrap a clean dishtowel around my head, because all my big towels were soaking up the water on the bathroom floor. Then I pushed over and got the wheelchair they gave me when I moved in after rehab out of the little nook it was parked in. I put a blue plastic bucket on the seat and leaned a mop on the footrests and over the back: a makeshift cleaning trolley. I rolled it into the bathroom, locked the wheels, and carefully hoisted the sopping towels and plopped them into the bucket. Then I used the mop to wipe up, swabbing the floor as best I could.

Eventually, the place looked presentable enough, and it certainly smelled clean, since shampoo-scented water had splattered everywhere. The floor could finish drying on its own. The last thing I did was to reach in and scoop up the offending slimy bar of soap. I almost slipped again doing it, but I didn't want it to harden onto the bottom of the tub, ready to sabotage me next time. I took hold of the back of the wheelchair, and pushed my way out. I parked the loaded wheelchair out of sight in the closet.

Already tired, I slumped into my bedroom and sat at my dressing table. I pulled the dishtowel off my head. My hair has never been my best feature. It is schizophrenic: simultaneously wispy and straight, curly and limp. With the help of a decent cut, bobby pins, and hairspray, I can normally plaster it into a reasonable appearance. But that morning, by the time I got into my bedroom and began to get ready for Iris to pick me up, it was half dry and settling into the worst version of itself . . . sticking out in some places, flat and flyaway in others. I tilted my head at my reflection and sighed.

In spite of my hair, when I was younger I didn't avoid the mirror. Though I was never given to much experimenting with makeup and hairdos and all of that, I'd had my share of vanities. People always commented on my long eyelashes, which I augmented further with mascara, and my smooth skin, which I supported with expensive moisturizer (an expense I have fought with myself about my whole life).

When I laughed, I looked like I meant it, because of my dimple. I used to draw attention to my smile and my white teeth with deep red lipstick.

But I am not crazy about the view in my mirror now. Even the most expensive moisturizer doesn't keep skin from creasing or lines from forming around one's eyes. Those lashes I was so proud of have grown thin and sparse. My teeth are still my own, so I guess that's good, but I had to switch from my old Scarlett Promise lipstick to something milder, since it ends up blurring into the wrinkles around my mouth. Supposedly human noses continue to grow throughout life. In my case, it must be true, since mine has begun to take up rather more than its fair share of facial real estate.

I am accepting of all these changes, or at least resigned to them. Better wrinkles than some other effects of getting old, like pain or dementia. Thank goodness I have never made my looks the measure of my self-worth. But sometimes I catch sight of myself unexpectedly in a mirror or window and I wonder, who is that? before the realization sets in. The picture doesn't line up with my inner image.

I sometimes think it would make a good research project for a psychology student to ask old people what age their self-image defaults to. How old are they in the picture of themselves they carry around in their mind? Do they hold the image of when they were a prom king or queen, with unsullied skin and shining eyes; or that graceful and sexy twenty-something dancing at the wedding? Do some people see themselves frozen at a happy and fulfilled moment—when their kids were young or they got their first big raise? Or do we simply carry around an idealized version of the self we are now—maybe fifteen years younger, healthier, stronger?

Whatever it is for other people, all I know is the person who looks back from my mirror now is somehow not exactly me. But of course, that old woman with the wrinkles is me. Exactly me.

And at the moment, an old woman with messy, disordered hair. I grabbed bobby pins and some Aqua Net and went to work. I like to look put-together when Iris arrives, and it is even more important for me to appear on top of my game when we go to the doctor. At my age, I approach every trip to his office with foreboding, and the slip in the shower had rattled me. I needed all the self-confidence I could muster.

The clock chimed ten. Shoot, I hadn't even eaten yet. I rushed, pulling on a dress, one with buttons down the front to make changing at the doctor's office easy. In the kitchen I smeared some peanut butter on a piece of whole wheat and forced down an orange. Then I sat. I took out a mirror from my handbag and reapplied my lipstick. I inhaled and closed my eyes, cultivating a mindset of calm and poise.

Iris knocked right on time, which is to say, a half hour earlier than she needed to be. "Come on in, honey," I called. She let herself in with her key.

"Hey, Mom." She bent to kiss me. Then she said "Oh, my. It smells nice and clean in here. I thought the cleaning service came tomorrow."

"I, ah, my shampoo tipped over and half the bottle spilled in the tub. Can you believe how fragrant it is? It's making the place smell like a hair salon."

"I'll clean it up for you."

"Nothing to clean up. I just rinsed it all down the drain."

But before I could stop her, my well-meaning daughter charged into the bathroom.

"Mom?" I heard from behind the door. "What's with the towels?"

Shoot. I thought I had put the bucket full of wet towels in the closet. My mind raced for an explanation when Iris emerged holding a shampoo bottle. She waggled it back and forth, and thank goodness, it really was nearly empty. "We can pick you up some more of this after the doctor's appointment. But I think you need to call housekeeping and have them do your laundry. Your towel cabinet is empty."

"Oh, right. Thanks for noticing. I'll phone them as soon as we get home." I pushed up with my cane, feeling suddenly pleased with myself and ready to face the doctor. "Let's go. Maybe we have time to hit the drive-through and get one of those Frappuccino things."

"Mom, Dr. Rudd wants you to use your walker. You know that."

I waved her away. "Come on, Iris, don't start." I smiled at her, suddenly full of gratitude for this irritating, loving daughter. "I want to lean on you today." In my best Hollywood Western imitation, I said, "We don't need no stinkin' walker." She sighed at me, but indulgently. She tucked my arm around hers as we walked out the door.

*   *   *

Dr. Rudd's office did not have the most welcoming reception room. A television glowed down at us with the sound turned off. For some reason it was tuned to the weather station, so pictures of neon-colored fronts whorled across the United States, while at the bottom, crawling text kept us informed about the temperatures in Utah. Outdated copies of *Golf Digest* and *National Geographic* completed the options for patients trying to distract themselves while they waited. In the corner there was a forlorn kid's play table. Long habit made me wonder how often it got wiped down with disinfectant. But it must be the other doctors who were seeing younger patients. Alex Rudd had been my doctor for a long time, and most of the people he cared for were oldsters like me. He stopped taking new patients about three years ago and was talking about retirement. I was not happy about this. I didn't want to have to break in a new doctor, and I was planning on being around for a while yet.

When my name was called, I rose, sprightly. Iris stood to join me, but I gave her my look. We'd been through this before. "Iris, I don't need you to come with me."

"But . . ." She lifted her eyebrows, frustrated. A couple years ago, after my first fall, I took the doctor's advice and gave Iris medical power of attorney. Since then, she seems to think it has entitled her to all information.

"No. You can ask some questions afterward, but that's all."

She exhaled at me and crossed her arms. But she sat back down. I walked tall into the examining room, not even leaning on my cane.

The nurse had me remove my dress, even though, as I pointed out, when unbuttoned, it offered at least as easy access as one of those stupid tie-on gowns. But she made me put on one of the stupid tie-on gowns anyway. She noted my weight and blood pressure, asked me the same questions I had answered on the forms in the waiting room, and left. Then there was a knock at the door, and Alex came in.

"Hello, Francine. Good to see you. How are you feeling?" He checked my blood pressure again, thumped my back and chest, examined my toes and feet, asked me about my daily routine, lectured me about eating right, looked into my eyes and ears and throat, studied my nails, had me stand first on one foot and then the other to demonstrate balance, and asked me about the knee I injured when I fell, about my meds, my sleeping, my bowel movements, my routine, and everything else under the sun.

Then he said, "You seem to be in pretty good shape. Can we call Iris in now for a quick check-in?"

"Can't I just tell her I'm fine?"

"Are you?"

I rolled my neck. "What do you mean? You just said everything looks good."

"It does, except for the bruises."

I swallowed. "Bruises?"

He crossed his arms and leaned against the desk. "When did you fall?"

"What? I didn't."

"Well, if you didn't, then I'm really worried. We'll definitely have to get her in here, because I'm going to have to run a lot of tests to rule out lupus, Hodgkin's, leukemia . . ."

I held up my hand. "Okay, okay." I sighed. "But I didn't exactly fall. I sort of slid down the wall of the bath while I was reaching for a bar of soap. I dropped it, tilted sideways when I bent over, and just . . . gently curled into the bottom of the tub. I didn't land hard or anything. Really, I'm surprised I even have a bruise. I didn't see one when I checked."

"It's on your backside. Just beginning to show up." He indicated my cane with his chin. "And I see you are refusing to use your walker."

"I'm not refusing. I just don't need it today. I have Iris to lean on, remember." He uncrossed his arms and leaned forward, obviously about to make a point, but I jumped in quickly. "Listen, Alex, I am normally just fine. Really. But the last few days I've been worried and I couldn't sleep. I finally got up today at three in the morning. But I was so tired I took half of one of those sleeping pills you gave me for emergencies."

"And?"

"And it worked. I went back to bed and conked out. But it must not have been completely out of my system when I got up and took a shower."

He regarded me for a minute. "What are you so worried about?"

Oops. I opened my hands. "A friend is going through some difficulties, and I'm trying to figure out how to help. I sort of owe her."

He stood and went to the door. "I'll go get Iris."

"Are you going to tell her?"

He tilted his head. "Frannie, she loves you and wants to be kept up to speed. It is hardly a bad thing for her to be involved."

"But she'll worry. Please, Alex. You know what she's been through."

"Does it ever occur to you she needs someone to worry about, to care for?"

Of course it had occurred to me. I looked down.

He said, "Frannie. It might seem like a little thing, but it could have been bad. And you know that. You can let her in a little."

I nodded, "Can we . . . not tell her everything?"

He inhaled. "Leave it to me."

When Iris entered the room, she looked scared. Uncertain. My heart went out to her. I saw just how much she must dread getting bad news. Bad news about my health would be even worse for her than for me, I think.

"Everything looks pretty good." Alex began, and I saw Iris's shoulders relax, "but there is some bruising. I think she might need some vitamin B supplements."

Iris's eyes sharpened. "Bruising? From what? Mom, is everything okay?"

"I'm fine."

Alex interjected, "Her balance is pretty good. Sometimes just a slight bump we don't even notice can cause it if the B12 is off. I'll give her some supplements." He turned to me. "But please use the walker when you're feeling shaky."

I nodded, knowing he was doing me a favor. I was in no position to argue.

He was feeling around in the pocket of his lab coat, looking for a pen. "Remind me, where did you move to again?"

"The senior apartments at Ridgewood."

He looked up and bumped his hand to his forehead. "Oh that's right! I forgot to tell you. I'm one of their doctors on call now. Filling in for a friend. I could have saved you a trip. I come in once a month to hold office hours and approve meds."

I felt my mouth drift open. What? That meant he had access to the med room and records. Was this good or bad?

I was still processing this information when he tore off a sheet from his prescription pad and started to hand it to me, but stopped himself. "In fact, Ridgewood has a pharmacy service. They can get this filled for you and keep it in their med room, so you won't have to go to the drugstore. They've got your insurance info, right?"

Before I could reply that I liked going to the pharmacy to get my own medicine, Iris interjected, "That would be great. Save us a trip."

He made a note in his chart, saying, "Ridgewood is a nice place. I'm glad you're there." When he finished writing, he glanced at me very briefly before looking away quickly. He turned to Iris. "Residents can request staff assistance to help them bathe, right?"

What? He was sabotaging me? No wonder he couldn't meet my eyes, the coward. I said sharply, "I don't need help. I am perfectly fine on my own."

But Iris interrupted, "I think that's a great idea. I've been trying to get her to do that for months."

Alex pressed his lips together and then faced me. "Look, Francine. Some of the meds you're on can make you dizzy. And you know what a fall can do . . . it's the whole reason you ended up at Ridgewood to begin with, remember?"

"No, I will not agree to this. I am capable of bathing myself."

"Mom, please. At least consider . . ."

I crossed my arms and stared at Alex, then Iris.

After a second she said, "Okay. How about this? How about if we ask a staff member to be there, just in case? They can stand outside the shower and only help if you need it?"

I wanted to scream. I was looking at two people I trusted, and one who loved me more than almost anything, and yet I was feeling furious, betrayed. And a tiny irritating part of me knew they were right. My outrage at the injustice of getting old and helpless felt like a mountain inside of me, a glacier shearing off and crashing into the sea. To my horror I felt tears behind my eyes. I swallowed and looked away.

"Fine," I managed to croak into the silence. "But they sit outside. I'd like the dignity of washing my own bottom for as long as I can."

24

WE WERE QUIET when we got in the car. The ride started off in an icy silence, but after a couple of miles my anger leaked away. It wasn't Iris's fault. It wasn't anybody's. I might as well rail against the snow or the rain. When she went to adjust the radio at a red light, I reached over and squeezed her hand. She squeezed it back, and her eyes were moist. "I'm not trying to cramp your style, Mom. I just want you to be safe and sound and healthy as long as possible. I love you."

"I know, honey. I know." Why am I so hard on her? I could not ask for a kinder or more loving daughter. I patted her hand and nodded. "I love you too."

She flicked tears away quickly before the traffic surged. As we made our way through the intersection, she said "How about lunch? We can go to that Lebanese place you like."

It wasn't until I got home and could sit by my window that the full impact of the morning caught up to me. By then, my backside was definitely sore. No wonder Alex had seen a developing bruise. By morning it would be purple, and judging by how it was feeling at the moment, very tender. I must've also banged my elbow, because it throbbed. I was irritated with myself and irritated with the situation. Now

I had to follow up and schedule someone to bathe me. Or rather, I reminded myself, a person to be on guard in case I needed help, which my daughter and doctor clearly believed I did.

I twirled my wedding ring and reminded myself that everything else had been good. No bad blood pressure news, no worsening arthritis or hearing, no symptoms of anything except getting old.

Getting old. The ever-present cliff in front of me. How many more doctor visits before I heard, "I'm sorry, but the tests came back positive"? Before Alex or some specialist he'd referred me to said, "I'm afraid there's nothing more we can do." How many more times before a small miscalculation, like bending to pick up a bar of soap, had major negative consequences? I'd recently read that one out of three people over the age of eighty-five has dementia. Would I continue being able to recognize Danny and Adam?

I try to focus on the positive. I may have less time left in my life, but I have more time during each day, since I'm not working or raising a family. I can read books I've always wanted to tackle, go out to lunch with my daughter, get together with friends.

Except most of my friends are gone. And my Cal is gone. And Katherine.

So much for focusing on the positive.

I stood, thumping my cane. Enough. There may not be many upsides to getting old, but it's all I have. I am here. Every day in my right mind and without pain is a good day. I remembered Geri in the chapel, praying for strength. And Lottie grunting when she lowered herself into a chair.

I called the resident services office. "Yes, hello. I would like to schedule some bathing assistance. Starting later this week."

"Certainly, Mrs. Greene. What day would you like this to begin?"

Sigh. "I guess, um, how about Thursday?"

"That's fine. And did you have a particular aide you would like to request?"

What was this? "You mean I can request who I wish to help me?"

"Yes. With our more personal or private services, we try to connect residents with staff they are familiar with, if we can. We find it can make a resident more comfortable. We can't always accommodate personnel requests, of course," she cautioned in an officious tone.

"Well, in that case, I would appreciate it if Graciela could help me."

"Oh, I'm sorry. She doesn't work this Thursday."

"What about Friday? I don't really need to wash my hair before then anyway."

In the ensuing moment of silence, I could feel the woman frown and raise her eyebrows. Maybe she thought I'd be too stinky if I waited.

She cleared her throat. "Let's see, Friday . . ." Her voice trailed off, and I heard her nails clacking on a computer keyboard. "Graciela does work that day. We usually schedule bathing assistance for the morning. Would eight thirty be okay?"

"Yes. That's perfect. Thank you for your help."

*　*　*

I had leftover kebab from the Lebanese restaurant for dinner. I was restless and couldn't concentrate on television or my book. I fidgeted from one distraction to another until I heard the knock at the door for my meds. I realized I'd been waiting for it ever since we got back from the doctor's. I hurried to answer.

It was Dorrie again. I said, "Hello. How are you this evening?"

She looked more at ease than the first time, but still very serious and almost formal. "Fine," she responded. But nothing more. She handed me my medications.

I held the little paper cup, now including vitamin B12, and plopped the pills in my mouth. I swallowed with the Dixie cup of water she handed me. I wanted to prolong the encounter and establish a connection with this intimidated and solemn creature. As unforthcoming as she was, she had earlier proved she could be revealing once I got her talking, and at the moment she was my main conduit of information.

I pretended to have something caught in my throat. I patted my clavicle. "Could I have more water?" I croaked.

She reached for the pitcher. As she poured, I glanced at the clipboard she'd left sitting on top. It was not much changed from how it had been when Graciela was doing this duty, if memory served. A simple chart that listed the resident's name, the type of medicine, the dosage, and the time delivered. But now there was an additional column squeezed in where the aide had to indicate that they had observed the medicine being taken.

I said, "This reminds me so much of my early jobs, when I was studying to be a nurse." I put my hand on the cart. "Are you in school, by any chance?"

"No," she said baldly. It was so curt as to be almost rude. Which, given her nervousness about being reprimanded, I decided to exploit.

"Well. Sorry I asked. I was just trying to make conversation."

She blushed so intensely I immediately felt guilty.

"I'm sorry," she blurted out. "It's just I get anxious. That's why I've decided I can't be a nurse. After what happened, I hate doing this part of the job." Then she pressed her lips together. "I didn't mean to be rude."

I nodded, as grandmotherly and nonthreatening as I knew how to be. "It's okay. Believe me, I understand. Having done it, I know it's a big responsibility, and I applaud you for taking it so seriously." Dropping my voice and trying to impersonate a gossipy old lady I said, "But what happened? Graciela wasn't careful enough, eh?"

Her eyes grew troubled. "I-I really don't know. I guess someone got the wrong medicine. Now Thomas scolds her whenever she gets near the medication room. He hardly lets anyone in there now, just me and Tabitha along with him."

Tabitha was the other aide who did this duty, in the morning. Since I don't receive any morning medication, I didn't really know her. In our few interactions she had struck me as a disinterested, cog-in-the-wheel type, no better than she had to be. She did what she was told, gathered her paycheck, and went home. Her blasé remove told me she neither liked nor disliked her job. Work was work, one job no better than another.

Dorrie stuck out her hand, gesturing for the empty Dixie cup. "I need to get going. They don't want me to take so long." She winced and glanced apprehensively at Mrs. Collier's door.

I smiled at her. "Well, I think you are doing an excellent job. And if you'd like me to say so to your bosses, I will."

"Oh no!" She blushed. "I just want to get done. Thomas is going to hire someone else, and then I can go back to my regular job."

"Oh. Of course." I stepped back. "I hope I haven't kept you too long. Have a good night."

Back at my window, my brain churned. *You're making too much of this,* my inner voice said. Wouldn't it be better to stay quiet and assume all is well? Katherine died almost five weeks ago. Why would anything come up now?

Another voice rose up, this one dark and authoritative. *Maybe something already has.*

I had to find out, somehow.

CHAPTER

25

IT WAS EARLY. I woke at dawn and went to walk the hall, stretching my legs while my coffee brewed. There weren't a lot of residents around, not to mention staff, and I moved slowly, reveling in the quiet. But when I caught a glimpse of a blue uniform, a chill zipped down my spine, my body reacting before I consciously understood it was a policeman, standing outside Mr. Alfred's office.

I tried to squelch the queasy dread that filled my chest. It was probably just something routine. Maybe one of the residents had left their wallet somewhere. Or maybe someone had a son or grandson who was a cop. *Guilt is making you paranoid,* I told myself. But still. Anxiety clogged my throat as I forced myself down the hall.

I stopped just at the top of my corridor, where my hallway spills into the lobby. Now I could see there were two policemen, one standing on each side of Thomas and Mr. Alfred. No one noticed me. Thomas looked clammier than usual, and Alfred's face was grim. But focused. His eyes stayed on the officers' faces, taking in every word while Thomas's eyes darted from Mr. Alfred to the cop who was speaking and back again.

Mr. Alfred gestured toward his office. The cops and Thomas filed inside.

What was going on?

I stood for a few moments, considering what to do. I began to head into the lobby, weighing whether I would be able to hear anything if I went and sat by the office door, when it suddenly opened again, and they quickly came into the lobby. I pulled back, out of their angle of sight, and held my breath, hoping to pick up what they were saying.

I needn't have worried. One of the cops said in a booming voice, "Thank you for the information. If anything else occurs to you, give us a call. Tobias will probably be following up with the staff that was on duty."

What had happened?

And further, what to do? I slipped down the hall to my apartment and made a phone call.

Evan's voice was blurry, foggy. "Hullo? Who is this?"

"Evan? It's Frannie."

"Wha—? Frannie? You're calling me?" I heard him grunt as he moved—I imagined he sat up in bed. "Do you know what time it is?"

"We have to talk. It's important."

"What? Did a manager say something mean to somebody with an accent?"

That infuriated me. "Sorry," I said coldly. "I guess I made a mistake." I hung up, shaking.

What now?

Within a minute the phone rang, displaying Evan's number. I almost didn't answer, but I had no idea who else to talk to about this. I picked up.

"I'm sorry, Frannie. It was just my crankiness at being woken up. Really, I apologize."

I was torn between wanting to chew him out and then never speak to him again, and blurting out my questions. I just cut to the chase. "Do you still have contacts in the police department? You wouldn't happen to know somebody named Tobias, would you?"

I could sense him come to attention. "Tobias?" He sounded confused. "Um, yeah. I know someone by that name." He cleared his throat. "Why?" Then more sharply, "Are you in trouble?"

I told him what I'd seen.

For a moment he was quiet. He said, "Let me look into it. It might take a bit. I'll see what I can find out and get back to you."

The tone of his voice made my stomach drop.

I paced my apartment, unable to eat, my mouth lined with sandpaper.

Then I remembered it was Friday. The day Graciela was going to help me bathe. How does one greet someone who is about to help them bathe? With cookies? I was nervous, but not because I needed help with my shower. It was because I knew I had to get information from Graciela, and I didn't know how to go about it. When the knock on the door finally came, I almost jumped.

"Come in," I rasped, my throat tight as I headed toward the door.

The key turned in the lock, and Graciela opened the door partway, "Mrs. Greene? Good morning. Are you ready for your shower?"

I smiled. "Yes. Please, come in." I gestured to a couple of mugs I'd set out on the counter. "Can I get you some coffee?"

Graciela spoke quickly. "No. Thanks."

She was more curt than usual. I wondered if she knew about the police visit. I sat at the counter. "Are you sure? Would you mind if I have a little? I really need my coffee this morning." She hesitated and glanced at the clock. I added, "I promise, I won't be long. And I take very quick showers."

She nodded. "I'm sorry. I shouldn't rush you. And it's early yet."

"Join me. Please?"

"Well . . ." She hesitated. "All right—just a little." I poured her a cup.

She sipped. Silence descended.

"How are your studies going?" I asked.

Her eyes widened, alarmed. "Why do you ask that?"

"I just wondered. You mentioned earlier you were studying to be a nurse."

Her shoulders relaxed. "Oh yes. I forgot I told you." She paused. "I-I am taking a break from studies."

"Can I ask why?'

The apprehension came back. "It just, it seems like maybe it isn't a good choice for me after all. Maybe I . . . maybe it is too hard to do it right."

I could bear the game no more. "Graciela, can I ask you something?"

She lifted her face, curious but guarded.

"Why are you afraid of Thomas? Why did he take you away from your duties?"

She stood, alarm sparking in her eyes. "I think we need to do your shower now."

"Graciela, I can help."

"No, no. Please. Everything is okay. I shouldn't be speaking about this." She gestured to the bathroom, her expression opaque, her voice brusque. "We start on the shower."

Her tone rebuked me. Who did I think I was? Chastened, I slowly stood. Without warning, I felt tears rising in my eyes, and I swallowed as I made my way to the bathroom.

Graciela noticed. She softened her manner slightly. "It's okay," she said, and put her hand under my elbow as we entered the bath. She sat me down on the bench built along the wall while she positioned my newly acquired shower chair in the tub. She put my shampoo and conditioner and soap within easy reach. Then she turned to me. "I understand that I am here only if you need me. So, I will help you into the tub. We'll close the door and you can slip off your robe and hand it to me. I'll be here if you want help to wash your hair or if you drop something, and when you're ready get out." Her shields were still up, but her eyes held kindness too. I nodded.

She turned on the tap, adjusting the water as it came out of the faucet. I removed my slippers and leaned on her as I stepped into the tub. She slid the frosted glass door most of the way closed, giving me privacy. I unsnapped my housecoat and handed it out to her. I sat on the shower chair, flipped the lever and the water began to flow from the shower head above me. I had to admit, it felt very secure and nice to be sitting while I washed. Graciela asked, "Everything okay?"

"I'm fine, thanks." Though I would never have said as much to Iris, my slide down the shower wall had spooked me. It was good to have someone there in case I needed help.

I would have sat there for a long time, enjoying the hot water, but I didn't want to lose my chance to feel Graciela out about my questions. I finished quickly and turned off the water. "Graciela, could you hand me in a towel?"

The door opened slightly and a hand appeared, holding a towel. I wrapped my dripping hair with it.

"Another please? A big one?"

Her hand appeared again, buried in thick pink terry-cloth. I dried off, wrapping the large towel around myself securely and opening the door. "Ready for my entrance!" I said, smiling.

Graciela helped me out and held up a clean housecoat the way men on dates used to hold women's coats at restaurants in the old days. I slipped my arms in, pulled it closed, and let the towel slide to the floor as I snapped it shut. I turned to face her.

"Thank you. You made that easy and comfortable."

She smiled. "I just sat here. I'm glad it went so well."

She helped me to sit and straightened the bathroom, picking up the towel and setting the shampoo and soap in their place as I put on my slippers.

Watching her competent, efficient movements, I decided to try again. And this time, to simply let her know I was in her corner.

"Graciela?" Despite my resolve, my voice was tentative.

She straightened but didn't look at me.

"I . . . I just want you to know that I'm not simply being nosy. I have my own reasons, and I have a feeling they might impact your—" I stopped and tried again. "I want you to know that I notice things. That I might be able to help you. Maybe ease your worries."

She half turned toward me but kept her eyes on the towel she was folding and unfolding.

I went on. "Sometimes I think the people who work here forget we're people too. That we hear things and see things." She tilted her head as if she was about to say something. I held my hand up to stop her. "Okay. Okay. I know. Not everybody here notices very much or can hear very well. But some of us can. And do." I hesitated. But my instinct about her was very strong. So I took a deep breath and went on. "I want you to know I am on your side. I am an ally."

Those words are almost exactly what Evan had said to me. And I had not trusted him for one minute. The difference was, of course, that I had actually done something wrong, and I was pretty sure Graciela hadn't. Another difference was that for someone Graciela's age, I was unimaginably old, and therefore not anyone to fear. Her large eyes were dark, but I saw she understood.

*   *   *

The next morning I heard a knock at my door. I wasn't expecting anyone, so I hobbled over and rocked onto my tiptoes to peek through the peephole.

It was Graciela. Surprised, I pulled open the door.

She was brusque, almost nervous, and she spoke before I could say anything. "Today is the day of the nature walk. I thought you might want to go?"

Her expression was peculiar. What was going on? I said, "Um . . . but I'm not . . ."

She gestured toward my closet. "Don't you want a jacket?"

There was a knot forming in my stomach. Clearly, she had decided we needed to go for a walk. I swallowed. "Sure. Ah, let me get my sunglasses too."

I glanced at the wheelchair she was holding. "But I can walk. So long as we take it easy."

"I think it might be easier to talk if you were seated."

I looked directly into her eyes. The glance she returned was pleading.

I sat down in the wheelchair. Only as we were on our way to the lobby did it occur to me to wonder if I should be frightened. I was an old lady heading into the woods to discuss murder, after all. I exhaled and cleared my head of such ridiculous thoughts. I had been reading too much P. D. James.

Near the exit to the patio, I saw Marta gathered with a number of other residents. "Oh, I'm glad you were able to come. Graciela told me you might want to join us."

*　*　*

We made our cumbersome way out to the path. Just as had happened with Jannah, Graciela slowed to let the others go ahead. Obviously she wanted to talk.

Once the others were sufficiently distant, I turned over my shoulder and asked directly. "Graciela? What is going on?"

I felt her tense. She looked as if she wanted to say something, but she kept pushing the wheelchair for another minute. When we reached a shaded spot, she parked me to the side of the path near a bench and sat. She took a breath before she said, "Jannah told me you talked with her. That . . . you might be able to help."

I nodded.

She pressed her lips together and went on. "You know the lady that was married to the judge? I think you were friends with her."

My heart began to pound. "You mean Katherine? Mrs. Kearney? Of course."

She didn't speak.

"Graciela?"

She bent down and plucked a strand of clover nearby and sat on the bench. "I love the smell of this little white flower." She held it out to me. I took it and inhaled its subtle sweetness. She looked around.

"Graciela?" I said again.

She plucked another clover and twirled it between her thumb and forefinger. "It happened when I noticed something wrong with her medicine. It didn't look right." Her voice was clogged, fearful. "So I put those pills aside."

My mind flashed back to the night I changed the medicine, and the arrangement of the cart—the pills destined for the apartment, marked "Kearney." So my fears were correct. I must've switched Katherine's medicine, rather than Nathaniel's. My chest contracted.

I managed to swallow. "And?"

She got up and began pacing. I could sense her fear, her agitation.

"I meant to give it to her." Her voice cracked. "I delivered the rest of their medicine—but held those back. I was going to find the doctor on call and send them a picture of the ones that made me worried. I told Thomas. He said to mind my own business, that I didn't know what I was doing. Said I had to give her all the medicine." Her voice rose. "But Thomas is not a doctor or a nurse! He didn't know."

There was only the pebbly sound of her feet on the path as she returned to the bench.

"And?"

She exhaled shakily. "Thomas yelled at me, made me go back to their apartment. But when I did, Mr. Kearney got upset and said Mrs. Kearney was already in bed. I told him she needed the medicine, but he said not to worry, that she had taken them late or skipped them sometimes before. He closed the door and didn't even take her medicine inside the apartment."

I twisted in the wheelchair to look at her. She returned my gaze, and her voice became earnest as she pleaded, "Something was wrong with the pills—I know it. It was too much. They were too strong for her." She pressed her lips together, and the silence stretched on while she regained her composure.

Her voice dropped to a strangled pleading. "Then she died. Thomas says it is my fault because she didn't take her medicine. Thomas is family—my husband's cousin. He says if I tell anyone, we will lose our visas. Now he won't let me near the medication room or anything. He says we have to be quiet and that if I tell, he'll keep me from applying to nurse school. But I heard the police are asking about Mrs. Kearney."

She stopped speaking for a moment to collect herself. "I need this job. I don't have my green card yet, and my visa . . ." There were tears in her eyes. "You were a nurse, you know people . . ."

So there it was. Someone else's life, someone innocent, was being harmed because of me. Was I any better than Stinson, pursuing my own needs and not caring about anyone who got in my way? I summoned every bit of resolve I had to stay calm, to communicate to Graciela that not delivering that medicine could not have killed Katherine, when it hit me. Suddenly, like a truck careening around a corner, it hit me.

If Katherine hadn't taken the medicine, then I hadn't killed her either.

I began to hyperventilate. Adrenaline surged through me, and sweat gathered on my lip. I gulped. I couldn't hear Graciela's voice over the roaring in my ears.

She was in front of me, stooping to put her face level to mine. "Mrs. Greene? Mrs. Greene?" Her words came through the thunder in my head, faint but persistent.

I started laughing. Hysterically. I saw Graciela's face move from appalled to concerned, to downright frightened, like I was I was having some kind of fit. I knew I had to get ahold of myself. If only I could stop shaking.

She crouched in front of me, staring directly into my face and gripping my elbows. Half shouting, she repeated, "Mrs. Greene! Mrs. Greene!" Somehow the panic in her voice was like a slap to my cheek. It knocked me out of my hysteria. I got a grip on myself. We looked at one another, her face appalled and astonished.

I swallowed. "I'm sorry. I apologize for reacting that way."

She stood and inhaled. Her eyes were indescribable. Fright, anger, confusion all seemed to register there. "I should not have told you. I thought you could maybe help. You could tell Thomas I am a careful worker."

I reached out. "No, no, it's good! It's good you told me." I focused, inhaling, exhaling. I squeezed her hand. "Graciela, listen to me. You do not need to worry. Katherine would not have died by missing one dose of that medicine." She was standing directly in front of me. I grasped both of her hands in mine. "You did not do it. Missing one dose of that medicine would not have killed her."

Though her eyes were fearful, I could see in them a desire to believe me.

I went on. "That medicine builds up in the body. Dangerous overdoses can happen easily, so you were right to not give it to her." I swallowed, thanking God for this conscientious, observant woman. "But for that same reason, missing a dose is not fatal." I leaned forward, eager to make her understand. "I know this for certain. Not only because I was a nurse but also because my husband was on the same medicine, and sometimes he forgot his. And I remember Katherine telling me that she often forgot her meds and would end up taking them late."

Her wide brown eyes became moist with hope.

I repeated, needing her to hear me. "You don't need to worry, and you can tell Thomas that too. In fact, you can tell him to talk to a doctor if you want. Talk to Dr. Rudd.

Or I will, if you prefer. I can have him to talk to Thomas."
I ducked my head to catch her gaze. "You did not hurt her."

Tears flooded Graciela's eyes. And mine.

Not only had she not killed Katherine, but, as affirmed by the sudden lightness flooding my disbelieving, grateful heart, apparently neither had I.

26

WHEN I RETURNED to my apartment, everything appeared different. Awash in light. The place looked welcoming, hopeful. It was a new beginning. I was free. I paced my apartment, lightness and joy buoying me like warm ocean waves. When the phone rang I fumbled it in my eagerness to talk to my daughter. At seventy-two years old, I suddenly had a fresh lease on the future.

But the voice on the other end was Evan's, not Iris's. The gravity in his manner was entirely out of alignment with my new-found innocence. "We should talk," he said slowly.

The lightness faded as I took in his tone. The air went out of my balloon.

Evan went on, "Frannie . . . I talked to Tobias. He told me the cops were here because they had some questions." He stopped speaking. The silence was loaded.

I sank into a chair, cold fear rising. "Questions?" I squeaked.

"About Katherine's death. Irregularities. We need to talk. Sandra is coming over in a few minutes. She can drop us at a diner somewhere."

I was so relieved at finding out my plan had failed, I had forgotten that the cops were poking around. I paced from my living room to the kitchen, pounding my cane against the carpet.

Katherine *must* have died from natural causes. Mustn't she? After all, she was old, she was sick, her heart was bad. Was it too much to hope that she had simply slipped away in her sleep? And that she had done it on the same night I'd tried to kill her husband and meddled with her meds by mistake? Okay, granted, quite the coincidence. But stranger things had happened. Hadn't they?

When Sandra knocked a half hour later, I flung open the door. She must've wondered what was wrong with me because, despite my best efforts, I could hardly contain my agitation. She dropped us off at a local greasy spoon, and Evan steered us to a table in the far corner, so no one could overhear, I assumed.

We gave the waitress our order and made tense chitchat until she delivered our coffee and sandwiches. As soon as she went back to flirting with the cook at the far end of the restaurant, I grilled Evan. "Okay. What is it? What happened?"

He looked tired. Like he hadn't slept. "Frannie . . . they did an autopsy on Katherine."

"An autopsy? Really?" My voice came out louder than I'd intended. I cleared my throat. "I mean, that surprises me, that they'd do an autopsy on an eighty-year-old with heart trouble."

He shrugged. "They do them occasionally when a death in assisted living is a surprise, just to make sure everything is on the up and up. Nathaniel was sedated, so they asked the daughter, and she said yes."

I didn't respond, just stared down at my hands. My cuticles were a mess.

Evan said, "Frannie?" I glanced up, and he pinned me with that evaluating gaze. "They are viewing her death as suspicious."

"Suspicious!" I croaked. "No! But, how can that be?"

He exhaled. "I don't know. Maybe you could tell me?" Evan's gaze was level, and his tone brooked no nonsense.

I understood. It was time to be honest, finally. I spread my hands but then collapsed them together. I suddenly realized how crazy it was all going to sound. I inhaled. "I guess I'd better start at the beginning."

"That might be a good idea."

I took another deep breath and plunged in. "You . . . guessed correctly. I was acting guilty because I did try to hurt someone. I *did* meddle with the medications. Heaven help me." My voice failed, and I bit my lip.

"Go on."

I looked at him square. "You were right. I knew who Nathaniel was. But not at first. I became friends with Katherine before I realized. Then after I found out, I just . . . well, I don't know what I thought. I wasn't planning anything." I looked at him. "Really."

He nodded.

I swallowed. "But one night, I thought Iris had taken another bad turn. And just then he was so horrible and vain and mean, and—and I was angry." I exhaled and licked my lips. "I had some of Cal's leftover pills, and on an impulse I switched his meds with some of Cal's." The words came out in a coarse whisper. I tried to look at him, but I couldn't meet his eyes. Instead, I dropped my gaze to watch my hands twist in my lap.

"Then Katherine died that same night." I paused. "I realized I had messed up and switched the meds for the wrong Kearney." My voice trembled and my mouth was completely dry. I took a sip of water,. There. I had said it out loud. Finally.

I had to take a moment to compose myself. The dim clatter of dishes in the unseen back of the restaurant filled the silence. Finally he said again, "Go on."

I squared my shoulders. "Remember when I told you how I overheard Graciela on the phone with her husband? And I thought it was something to do with her immigration status?"

He nodded.

"Well, I didn't tell you the whole story . . ." I fiddled with the saltshaker. "It turns out that Thomas isn't some bully. He's related to Graciela. He thought she had messed up Katherine's medication. That's why he was so hard on her and why she felt so vulnerable—they thought it would impact all of their futures. And she was afraid that she'd made a mistake that caused someone's death." My breath shuddered as I spoke. "I was afraid she was being blamed."

"For something you did."

I looked up quickly. I started to nod, but then I declared "But that's just it. I didn't!" My voice was squeaky.

"I don't understand." He leaned forward, eyebrows drawn together. "What do you mean, you *didn't*?"

The bright thread of absolution glimmered, and I lifted my chin. "I finally got Graciela to talk to me, just today. It turns out she noticed the medicine was too big a dose, so she held those pills back, meaning to check with the doctor." My words were drenched in emotion and relief. "But before she could check on things, she mentioned it to Thomas, who insisted she deliver the pills anyway. So she went back to the Kearney's apartment. But by the time she got there, it was late, and the judge sent her away without taking the medicine. Told her to come back in the morning. You know how imperious and nasty he can be. She got intimidated and she left."

Evan nodded, and I continued. "So when Katherine died, Graciela blamed herself, thinking that it was because she didn't get her medicine. Thomas thought so too." I looked at him, pleading and fear coming through my words. "And the immigration fears were real—I didn't just make that up. Thomas is related to her husband, and he worried it would put the whole family and their visas at risk. But, like I explained to Graciela, missing one dose of that medicine wouldn't have killed Katherine. So she had nothing to feel guilty over."

My voice quickened. "And because of what she did, Katherine wouldn't have gotten my overdose either." I felt myself blush. "So I didn't do it!"

He didn't respond, simply tipped his head slightly and evaluated me.

"Evan?" I finally asked.

"So. Let me get this straight." He cleared his throat. "You wanted to arrange an overdose for Nathaniel. Of a medicine he was already on."

I nodded.

"But you made a mistake and arranged the overdose for the wrong Kearney." I looked down and nodded again.

"But Graciela noticed and was going to check on it, and because of her delay, Katherine didn't receive the medicine that evening. Then when she died, Thomas blamed Graciela, and she blamed herself because she didn't know missing the medicine would not have killed Katherine. And just this morning you discovered Katherine didn't get the medicine after all, so you couldn't have killed her either." I nodded again and bit my lip. It sounded even more ridiculous when said out loud.

He turned and stared out the window, and didn't respond.

"Evan?" I finally asked.

He exhaled and turned to me, leaning back. "Right. Which brings us to the real point of this meeting, as delicious as my burger was."

I had forgotten that he had brought me here for a reason. My stomach clutched all over again.

He ran his fingers across his chin. "Frannie—I'm not sure how to tell you this." With his fork he smashed a lone fry into a glop of ketchup on his plate. "Even though Katherine didn't have any prescriptions for pain medication, her blood work showed high levels of prescription painkillers. They are what killed her."

I stared at him. "Are you sure?"

"Tobias wouldn't get into the details, but he let the painkiller part slip."

I felt my mouth open. "But . . . how? Why?"

"They are trying to work that out. But the obvious answer is a mistake with the medications she was given." He raised his eyebrows and pursed his lips. "You, of all people, should know how easily things are manipulated."

I blinked. This was some sort of nightmare. His voice came through dimly. "Walk me through it, step by step. What is the protocol?"

I tried to slow down, to think, but my brain felt doused in murk. I forced myself to form the words. "Um. The way the medicines are distributed is that two people—usually Thomas and an aide—count out the pills and make sure they match the prescriptions on file. Having two people do it is supposed to keep them accountable. They even sort the most dangerous medications—the painkillers—into special blue cups. Then the meds are delivered. It used to be they just handed the pills to the resident, and we could take them then or bring them into our apartments, but after Katherine's death they started watching as we swallow them." I ignored the burning in my cheeks. "After rounds, any undelivered pills are counted again to make sure that everything is on the up and up."

"So—where's the hitch? What might have happened?"

I paused, trying to make sense of this. Then it clicked. I remembered what Dr. Rudd had told me. It was simple, really. I leaned forward. "The staff are supposed to make sure residents take their medicine. But people have their prescriptions sent directly to Ridgewood, and most people have no idea what their medicines actually look like. So, even if a resident knew they were supposed to take, say, four pills, anything could be substituted and most people wouldn't know." I opened my hands, palms up. "Once the cart leaves the med room, there's nothing to stop anyone from substituting a pain pill or two. And those pain meds are powerful. It wouldn't take much."

"Is that what you used?"

"What?" I frowned at him in shock. "No! No, I just told you!" My hands lifted in objection. "I mean—I switched medications. But it would never have occurred to me to use a pain medication like that. That would have been too much like . . ." I let the sentence hang. In a stab of insight, I saw now that I had allowed myself the luxury of thinking I had just increased the odds of Nathaniel dying. The fact that I'd left just enough to chance was my subconscious effort to enable me to live with myself. Meddling with medication Nathaniel was already on had left the door open to the possibility he would survive. Even in attempted murder I'd been a coward.

I swallowed in shame and told Evan the absolute truth. "In honesty, if he hadn't been on digoxin, I don't think it would have occurred to me."

He looked exasperated. "Why?"

I explained about digoxin and how it works. "It was because I had some leftovers from Cal that I even thought of it." I swallowed. "I guess it seemed like I was leaving a little bit to chance. Like it wouldn't really be . . . murder." My face felt hot. "And like I said, it wouldn't trigger any suspicion in an autopsy because the drug was *supposed* to be in his system." I gulped and hurried to remind him—and myself—that I'd been saved from my own action. "Besides—since Graciela intercepted the pills, it doesn't matter."

"Oh. Right." He stared at me. He was not letting me off the hook. "So, you're telling me that what *you* did had no effect, but that anyone could have cribbed the medicine that actually killed Katherine." Evan looked at me with barely suppressed skepticism. "Rather convenient, wouldn't you say?"

I blinked back my sudden tears, my voice husky. "But why would I kill Katherine? And besides, why would I tell you all this if I had something to hide? It wouldn't make sense for me to admit to *anything*."

"It makes as much sense as trying to kill someone but leaving the door open to them not actually dying."

I stared, horrified. He was right. My half measures, and the intellectual and moral outs I'd allowed myself unspooled before me. I gripped the table, fearful I might faint.

Evan signaled the waitress at the far end of the restaurant, and she lifted her chin in acknowledgment.

"Evan?" I asked. He didn't answer. "Evan?" I repeated, my voice panicky.

He ignored me, flipped open a battered cell phone with extra-large buttons, and called Sandra to say we were ready to be picked up. I tried not to scream as he handed the waitress some cash and grunted as he slid out of the booth. All without saying another word about what I'd told him or responding to my obvious distress. I glared at him as he helped me out the door.

When we got outside, I pulled my arm away. "I didn't do it, Evan. You have to believe me."

He held up his hand. "It's okay. The cops are inclined to assume it was staff error, since there seems no apparent motive."

"Staff error? Does that mean they'll still blame Graciela?" I couldn't make sense of it. All this and now I was back to right where I began? "But you believe me. Right?"

"I'm not sure how . . ."

Sandra cruised in and tooted her horn. I hobbled as quickly as I could to the car. Evan got in the front. I let Sandra talk while I stayed silent in the back seat, steeped in panic and fear and fury. When we arrived at Ridgewood, I asked her in a choked voice to drop me at the entrance, and got out of the car. I hurried, to the extent that I was able, to get through the automatic doors. But Evan got there before me.

"Frannie? Please, don't be upset."

"Just go. Leave me alone."

I hit the button to open the door and walked through the lobby with as much dignity as I could muster, praying I would see no one. I wanted to make it to my apartment before I started bawling.

MY CHAIR LOOKING out at the preserve offered no comfort. I saw it all. Just because a conscientious person had foiled my attempt didn't mean I was any less guilty. I had tried to kill someone, and ruined the peace of mind, and possibly the career, of Graciela. If there had been a medication error, it would land on her . . . and it would be my fault. My meddling had interrupted her routine, disrupting the established procedure. Nurses know all too well how a break in one's attention can lead to mistakes. I had no business claiming innocence.

Another realization hit hard and burned through my chest with shame. I'd told myself I wanted to avenge my family. But I hadn't given any *real* thought to Iris or Charlie or my grandchildren. I'd been so absorbed—first with my anger, then with my guilt—that I'd ceased being present in the moment, enjoying the people I love. I covered my mouth with my hands when I realized I had actually tried to keep Iris—my beautiful, loving daughter—away from visiting me, in case the judge was around. I had ceased honoring the memory of Bethany or Cal, only wanting to feel their presence in the chapel as a sign of forgiveness. I had worried Iris, pushed Charlie away, curtailed my presence in my grandsons' lives, and derailed the closeness with them that I'd forged with Bethany. I had so few years left, and I'd turned my life into ruins.

Out the window, the white butterflies that had danced around Jannah and I made another appearance, barely discernible, showing only when they darted in front of a deep shadow, the darkness framing the flash of light on their wings.

It couldn't be too late.

I made a plan.

I called Charlie first, then Iris. I invited them to dinner the next day.

Charlie was so happy to hear from me. How long had it been since I'd just called him to chat? "Sure! I'd love to. Where do you want to go?"

"Well, here of course. I'll make your favorites!"

Silence. "You're . . . going to cook? I didn't think you did much of that anymore."

"I don't, mostly because I don't need to. But that doesn't mean I can't. Besides, I'm paying for an apartment with a nice kitchen, and I sort of miss using it."

"Are you sure?" He sounded hesitant. "It won't be too much for you?"

When I called Iris, she had the same concern. She offered, "Should I come by beforehand to help?"

I assured them both I was more than capable. It irritated me that they seemed to think I had forgotten how to make a meal. But I reminded myself that they loved me and I loved them, trying to stay focused on the moment and not think about what I was planning for after. At least one more time I was going to make their favorites, and we were going to enjoy one another's company.

Then I called a cab. I had to get to the grocery store.

*   *   *

I hated to admit it, but they were right about it being a lot of work. I'd forgotten just how taxing it was. And the dirty dishes! But penance was supposed to be hard. Thank God, I had decided to keep it simple: I roasted a chicken and even cheated and bought some already-cooked rice I just had to heat up. It was easy enough to sauté some garlic and slivered almonds in butter to toss with the rice, so it approximated the pilaf I used to make when they were young. All I had to do with the bagged salad was add some cherry tomatoes and dressing. Easy peasy.

I thought the real challenge would be the lemon pie. But even though my baking muscles were rusty, the instinct for how the pastry should come together and just how much sugar to add was still there. It turned out beautifully. I decided I would take Iris up on her offer to help, and told her to bring whipped cream.

They arrived right on schedule. Iris and Jimmy, Charlie and Pam and the boys. I could feel myself glowing. How had I allowed myself to miss out on this?

"Wow, Mom, it smells great in here!" Charlie gave me a kiss and a huge smile.

Pam came in and handed me flowers. "It smells wonderful. But I hope you know you didn't have to go to all this trouble."

If there was a touch of the resistance I sometimes sensed from her, I ignored it. I am mindful I am not always an easy mother-in-law. I nodded. "I know, but I was feeling energetic, and I miss doing this. Thank you for indulging me on such short notice."

Iris was carrying wine. She bent to kiss me, and then she spied the pie. "Oh, Mom! Your lemon tart!" She turned, grinning.

It was her special favorite. She used to request it every birthday. Seeing my daughter's face light up brought tears to my eyes. Jimmy leaned down to kiss me and whispered, "Not sure what brought this on, but thank you." He clearly had a hunch that there was more behind my invitation than simply reclaiming my ability to host a family meal. Jimmy was one of those people whose surface seems bland and easy—but his waters run very deep. In some ways, I think he understands me better than my own kids do.

Adam and Danny ran in. Adam was always reliably goofy and fun, but Danny was at an age where you don't always know what you'll get, cute kid or crabby preteen. Tonight, thank God, they were both funny, cooperative kids. Adam gave me a huge hug. Danny kissed my cheek and said, "You look pretty tonight, Grandma."

"You smell good too!" said his brother.

I laughed. "Thank you for noticing!" While at the grocery store I'd visited the Health and Beauty aisle and bought some new lipstick and cologne. I figured if I was going to be a hostess, I should look the part.

At the end of the hall from my apartment, a door led to a little grassy area with a picnic table, and we decided to enjoy the beautiful evening and eat outside. We ate and chatted, and the boys played Frisbee, and Jimmy and Iris compared notes about their western trip with Charlie's and Pam's from the trip they had taken a year ago. And I took it all in. Family dinner, a happy summer evening. I sipped wine and watched my beautiful grandsons play among the fireflies in the growing dark.

* * *

After they left, I spent all night thinking. Now that I had remembered what growing old happily was supposed to be about, I asked myself, why throw it all away? After all, I hadn't actually done any harm. I was an upstanding person, retired from a respectable career, a grandmother. And considering everything my family had gone through, the universe owed me a little slack. I'd had one lapse of judgment, one moment of weakness. One time when I hadn't wished Satan behind me.

And Katherine?

I turned my thoughts aside. Let it go, for Pete's sake. I had no idea how she'd died, and frankly I was exhausted worrying about it. Hadn't I earned a respite, just to enjoy myself and my family? But trying to convince myself that I deserved to be let off the hook didn't quite work. I tossed and turned, unable to sleep.

That logic, the siren song of being easy on myself, completely fell apart the next morning when I passed through the lobby and glanced into Mr. Alfred's office. Sitting in front of his desk was another policeman. Next to him sat Graciela, her face pale as chalk and her dark eyes enormous. When she turned and saw me, her expression shaped a terrified and accusatory plea.

And then I knew. I knew my lightness and sense of joy earlier was only partly because of a nice dinner with my family. It was also because I had felt free from guilt for the first time in months. If I was ever going to know peace again, I had to make this right.

I turned back to my apartment. I canceled my bathing appointment for later in the week, because I wasn't going to be here. Then I made another call.

"Precinct twenty-four. How can I direct your call?"

"I'd like to report a crime."

The voice sharpened with a sense of urgency. "Ma'am, Is there a crime in progress? Are you in danger? Please hang up and dial 911."

"No, no. It already happened."

"So you want to report a crime that's already occurred? Call 911, they can take your—"

"You don't understand. I want to *confess* to a crime. May I speak to Tobias, please?"

There was silence on the other end. Then, "I see. Please hold." I heard her whispering, then "Ma'am? I'm going to transfer you."

After a few minutes a man picked up. "Detective Tobias. How can I help?"

"Yes, Officer. Good morning. I, um, I would like to confess to a crime."

Silence again. "I see. Who is this? Can I get some more information?"

"Of course. My name is Frannie Greene. Francine. I live in the Ridgewood assisted living facility."

"I see. And what crime are you saying you've committed?"

"Murder."

This time the silence was weighted. "You . . . you killed someone?"

"Yes. And I am ready to face the consequences."

"I see. Um, I think I should come and talk with you in person. Give me your address again?"

"588 Ridge, Ridgewood Assisted Living, Apartment 119. My name is Francine Greene. That's Greene with an 'e' on the end."

"I'll be over in a few minutes."

He hung up. I exhaled and pressed my knuckles over my mouth.

*   *   *

Detective Tobias was a man in his fifties with thinning short hair. His stiff posture gave off an impression of discipline and fitness, but there was a hint of a belly spreading beneath his pale sports jacket. That small paunch made it easier to talk to him somehow.

I let him in and offered him tea.

"Ah, no thanks." We stood there awkwardly.

I said, "Well, I guess you should come into the living room."

I balanced on the edge of my favorite chair and remembered when Evan had sat there and basically accused me of trying to kill Nathaniel. And of my self-righteous denial.

I cleared my throat.

Tobias took a seat on the couch and leaned forward. "Now, what is this all about?"

"I . . . killed someone."

"Yes, so you said. But I'm afraid I need some details."

"Her name was Katherine Kearney. She was another resident here at Ridgewood. I deliberately tampered with her medicine. Since I'm a former nurse, I knew what I was doing."

He gave me the same sort of look Evan did.

"What did she die from?"

Oh. Shoot. I suddenly realized the flaw in my plan, not knowing exactly what drug killed her. "I, uh . . . well, I'm sure the autopsy told you."

He moved his head sharply. "Where did you hear we'd done an autopsy?"

Oops. I didn't want to get Evan in trouble. "I saw some police officers here," I dithered. "I asked around. Someone mentioned something . . ." I felt increasingly stupid.

His mouth pulled to the side as he evaluated me.

"So. You say you were a nurse? And that you know medication? But you don't know what she died from?"

"Yes. Well, it's just that I don't remember. Specifically." He must have thought I was an idiot. I stammered, "It was, um, some weeks ago. It was a painkiller."

He paused and nodded. "I see. So you're saying you deliberately tampered with the medicine, but you don't remember which medicines. But you're sure it killed her."

I nodded, trying not to blush as I heard in his voice how ridiculous I sounded.

"And why did you want to kill this person?"

This was a sticking point. I had been so focused on making myself follow through with this plan, that it was only after I'd made the call that I'd realized I'd need to address this. Of course he'd want motive.

While I'd been waiting for him to arrive, I had decided to simply level with him. To explain that I had meant to kill the judge and to be honest about why: that he'd been a participant in corruption that led to the death of my granddaughter, but that in pursuing my plan, I'd screwed up and tampered with the medicine for the wrong Kearney.

But as the officer stood in my living room, with his crew cut and a badge pinned to his belt, I realized he was a part of the same system. Not likely to be sympathetic to claims about crooked cops. Plus—absurdly—I wanted him to like me. I figured that if cops were anything like front-line nurses, what happened during this initial encounter could determine a lot of what followed. I didn't want Graciela to be punished, but I also didn't really want the justice system to get too invested in punishing me. I was doing a fine job of that by myself.

And perhaps most importantly, I wanted to keep attention as far as possible away from Iris and Bethany and my family. Which meant I couldn't tell him everything. I just wanted to confess, with a quick arrest, no trial, and a sentence that showed mercy to an old lady.

So, mind racing, I punted. "Katherine and I, . . . we had a falling out." I made myself taller in my chair and tried to seem as imperious and haughty as I could.

He continued to stare at me. "I see. A falling out."

I nodded. "I was very angry."

Then he stood up. I held out my wrists.

He looked at me. "Mrs. Greene, I am not going to place you in handcuffs."

I felt my cheeks go warm. "Of course, how silly of me . . . as if I could run away."

"Mrs. Greene, I am not going to arrest you."

"But I am confessing!"

"I am afraid I don't quite believe you."

I was incensed. "Why would I lie?"

He sat back down and exhaled. "I have no idea. People confess to things all the time for all sorts of reasons."

"It's because I'm old," I snapped. "You think I am a foolish old woman, making things up."

"Not at all. If you are indeed a murderer, we will find you out. You are right, we are looking into Mrs. Kearney's death. But I am not of the mind to squander police resources, or to be made fun of in the local paper for hauling a senior citizen into the station." He checked his watch. "You seem like a sharp person. But, no offense, I think you are confused about this. I assure you, we will get to the bottom of anything suspicious." He stood and started toward the door, but then he turned back to me. "Just in case . . . what's that phrase they always use on television? 'Don't leave town'?" He winked and smiled. "Have a good day."

I was infuriated. And angry with myself as much as him. How had I bungled things so badly? I'd been so intent on my aims that I hadn't thought it through: so intent on my hopes for atonement and redemption and protecting Graciela that I ended up making myself look like an idiot.

Ugh. In the old days when I was upset, I would power-walk around my neighborhood. Today, the best I could manage was to hobble around my living room, pounding the carpet with my cane. Anger propelled me from one end of the room to the other. It wasn't just that I'd made myself look like an idiot. Appearances were the least of it: I had acted idiotically. Why had I needed atonement to begin with? Because I had failed to think things through. My failure to exercise even the most basic judgment, not to mention moral discipline, extended to the entire sorry episode. Beginning with when I tampered with the medicine and up to this very moment. Perhaps beginning even earlier. Perhaps all the way to when I'd first discovered who Nathaniel was. I could have confronted him. I could have denounced him. I could have avoided him and cut off my friendship with Katherine. I could have told her why and held her to account for her complicity and then kept myself separate from them, recognizing that justice does not always happen. I could have simply lived my life. And if I couldn't bear it, I could have insisted on moving. But instead I played some sort of psychological game, observing them, burying my darkest impulses and simultaneously choosing not to see her complicity for the sake of my friendship. Was that any different from what she had done? Maybe even worse, was my weakness—my brand of foolishness, denial, and idiocy; of stumbling from one impulse to another—any different from Stinson's?

Or perhaps—the thought chilled me—perhaps it indicated some sort of incipient cognitive failure? Cold fog filled my chest.

I was probably ten minutes into this self-chastisement when there was a pounding on my door. It almost made me lose my balance, it was so loud. I limped over. I barely had turned the knob when Evan came charging in, his anger filling the foyer.

He glared at me. "What is wrong with you? What were you thinking?"

"Hello to you too. What are you yelling about?"

"You tried to confess?"

I backed up and sank onto a kitchen stool "How did you know?"

"Tobias knows I lived here. He stopped by."

"He told you?" I couldn't believe it. "He should be more discreet. Isn't there some pledge of secrecy?"

Evan looked at me like I was nuts. "What do you think he is, a priest?" He wagged his head at me. "He told me some lady was trying to confess to the murder of a resident." He leaned against the counter. "Really, Frannie, what in the world got into you?"

I looked away. I didn't want to explain. I wasn't even sure I could. Finally I swallowed and said, "I wanted to protect Graciela. I saw her being questioned in Alfred's office, so I came back here and called Tobias."

He sighed. "What did you expect would happen?"

"I guess I thought he'd just take my word for it. My plan was to plead guilty, so there wouldn't be a trial. I'd make something up to tell the kids and take the punishment. I didn't think I'd have to prove anything." I shrugged. "If I'm being honest, I was hoping they'd take pity on me and give me probation or send me to one of those country club prisons or something."

He glared at me like I had grown horns or an extra pair of ears. As if I was a creature the likes of which he'd never seen before. "But why? You didn't do it."

I gaped at him. "So now you believe me? You might have said so earlier." I bit my lip and looked away. "But believe me or not, everything I told you is true. I honestly have no idea how Katherine got that painkiller. But if I hadn't messed around with things, interrupting the normal work flow, a mistake with the pain meds wouldn't have happened. So ultimately it was my fault."

I couldn't meet his eyes.

He sat on the stool across from me, and his voice turned gentler. "Look, I get it. You tried to do something horrible. Now you want to be punished. But please, figure out another way. If you involve the cops, a lot of people will be impacted. Including your daughter. Because you won't be able to contain it. The connections will come out, and the press will love it—an old-lady avenger? They'll eat it up. It will all come roaring back to the headlines, and Iris will have to go through it all over again."

I rejected that. "If there wasn't a trial, no one would figure it out."

"Frannie?" He bent forward, his voice soft. "Tobias already knows who Nathaniel is. He recognized his name." He paused. "It won't take much to put two and two together."

I lifted my face in horror. What had I done? Iris was finally putting it behind her, and I was dredging up all the pain again?

I leaned my elbows on my counter and covered my face with my hands. I didn't want to cry in front of him, but I couldn't stop. Whether it was in disgust at my stupidity, or the obvious fact that I was losing my mind, I couldn't say.

Evan rounded the counter and put his arm around my shoulder as I sobbed. "It's okay, Frannie." His voice was kind. "It'll be okay. I told Tobias we were friends. That you were super-sharp most of the time, but sometimes you got confused. That just last month you went to put sweetener in your tea and became convinced someone had substituted laundry detergent for the Splenda."

I turned away, wiping my face on my sleeve. "Thanks a lot."

He handed me a tissue. "What happened to the tough lady that sat in that living room and shot down my questions?"

I blew my nose in misery. "I don't know. I think that when I found out I hadn't done it . . . it was like a block of ice melted inside me. I could finally look at it head on, and how horrible and awful . . . I really think I *am* losing my mind."

He scoffed. "You? You're about the last one in here I would accuse of that."

I sniffed and lifted my chin. "So what now? Do the cops have any idea what happened?"

"I think you don't need to worry. Like I said. He isn't going to send you to jail."

"And what about anyone else? Graciela?"

He tilted his head. "I think they might let it go." He tapped the counter thoughtfully. "It's funny. Tobias is usually pretty dogged, determined to get to the bottom of things. But today he said something that struck me. He said, 'All told, it's probably a tender mercy anyway.'"

28

I DIDN'T KNOW WHAT to do. After Evan left, I tried to read but ended up staring out the window as the shadows in the woods purpled and lengthened. I couldn't concentrate, thinking of how foolishly I had acted and how I had messed up my life. The accusations in Graciela's eyes floated in my mind, and the knot of anxiety in my stomach tightened. I set aside my book.

Something was not right.

What had Evan said? "Tobias was usually pretty dogged, determined to get to the bottom of things." If he was so determined, and he knew that Katherine's death had been caused by a medicine she wasn't supposed to take, why in the world had he been so quick to dismiss my confession? Even if he thought I was senile, it seems like a basic desire to dot every "i" and cross every "t" would require him look into it, at least a little.

Of course, maybe he was. The thought chilled me, but I had to admit it was possible. Perhaps he *had* taken me seriously and just didn't want to let on. Keeping his cards close to his chest.

A movement caught the corner of my eye. A deer had ventured from the adjoining woods to nibble at the base of the tree where my birdfeeder hung. My breath caught in my throat. Remembering, for once, that nowadays phones have cameras, I slowly slipped mine out of my pocket. Miraculously, I located the camera icon, tapped on it as my grandkids had taught me, lifted it and took a photo of the doe as she nibbled at the fallen grain. A cardinal landed above her, showering more millet. I tapped the screen again. The bird bobbling the feeder seemed to bother the deer. She pulled her head up, glanced around, and bounded away.

I peered down at the photos, proud of myself for having remembered how to use the camera. I swept my finger across the screen, looking at the few other images I had captured with the device.

And there it was. The photo I'd taken of the top of the medication cart.

It all came back so clearly now, framed in hindsight and without the self-deception I'd been embracing. Looking back I realized how my interest in the med cart, and in which spices the judge used, was just the preamble, the unexamined roots of my half-baked plan; the hesitant, half-considered, indirect way I had allowed vengeance to permeate my mind, growing unchecked till it had weight and shape, till it had become an inevitability. Unable to admit it to myself, I had allowed it to take hold as if I were a bystander in my own thinking. Scorched with shame, I looked at the photo again.

But this time I noticed something I hadn't before.

Oh my God. I enlarged the picture.

I peered out again at the forest preserve, my hand covering my mouth. But I wasn't seeing the woods or the pond or the birds.

"All told, it's probably a tender mercy anyway." Now I knew where I'd heard that phrase before.

I thought of that last real conversation I'd had with Katherine. Her opacity, the sense she was trying to say something

I just wasn't picking up on. I thought of Lisa and our talk in the lobby.

You never know when it's the last time you'll see someone, I've always thought. After Bethany died, it became sort of a mantra for me.

But Katherine knew. In our last conversation, she'd been trying to tell me. Her opacity, her good manners kept her from saying so directly. But she knew. She'd been saying goodbye. I remembered my talk with Lisa, "Oh so you know her trouble is not going to get better."

At the time I assumed Lisa was referring to some generic challenge of old age . . . none of our heart troubles, rheumatism, or eyesight were going to get better. I'd been too irritated to sense the more specific truth behind the words. And after Katherine died, I'd been so focused on my own guilt, and the simultaneous fear that my actions might be exposed, that I could think of nothing else. I peered into the screen again, spreading my thumb and forefinger, making the glowing image as large as I could, and examined it more closely.

I thought of Nathaniel's back trouble. And the night that I'd rushed to their apartment. And how Graciela had also gone there. And how he'd taken his meds from Graciela but sent her away when she tried later to deliver Katherine's.

How could it not have occurred to me? I'm a nurse, for God's sake. How could I not have seen it? And the answer, immediately: the same reason no one else did. We are old. We have pain, we have anxiety, we have sleeplessness. We are sick. And what's more, we have prescriptions, the bottles of which we never see. Prescribed by our doctors, paid for by our insurance, and kept in a med room. To be prepared by unseen hands and delivered to us.

I was certain. I had no direct proof, but I also had absolutely no doubt.

I knew what I had to do. I pushed myself to my feet and went the bathroom. I took a quick look in the mirror and put on lipstick. I wasn't entirely sure why, but it seemed like I should be a little bit spiffed up when confronting a killer.

*   *   *

I rode the elevator to the third floor. I hadn't been there since Katherine's death. That night I had been in a panic, desperate and frightened. Now I was cloaked in calm.

Piano music slipped into the hall from the Kearney apartment, and I recognized the same jazz tune I'd heard Nathaniel play in the music room, so long ago, it seemed. Marty Paich, I think he'd said the composer was. I rang the bell.

The music stopped, and after a few moments, the door opened. Nathaniel's appearance shocked me. He had bags under his eyes, and his face was ashen. But despite his diminished state, he still managed to be imperious. "I'm afraid this isn't a good time."

"There is something I need to talk to you about."

"I am not receiving visitors."

I let my manner match his formality. "I'm afraid I really must insist. It's important." I pressed forward as I said this. I could see the confusion on his face when he realized I was not going to stop. He backed into the foyer. I got all the way inside and moved into the living room, past the gleaming grand piano he'd bragged about, which was stationed in front of large windows framing a view of the trees and the pond. I lowered myself onto a settee on the opposite side of the room.

Suddenly, the certainty and the energy that had been propelling me shifted. I realized I had no idea how to begin, and although I was certain I knew what had happened, I didn't have anything more than the vaguest notion of what I was going to say.

Nathaniel stood in the door to the room and frowned at me. "May I ask what is so important that you feel entitled to invade my privacy?"

"I know what happened, Nathaniel. I know."

He stared at me for a moment, blinking. Then I saw understanding come into his eyes. He drew himself up into full imperiousness. "I'm not sure what you are speaking of. You must be confused. Perhaps I should call the reception. They can send someone up to help you back to your apartment."

"I know what happened. There is no need to pretend." I took the phone from my pocket and enlarged the image it bore, spreading my finger and thumb. On it was the photo of an aqua blue cup holding a little gray pill, familiar from my hospital days. The cup sat on a card labeled "N. Kearney."

"Do you know what this photo shows?"

He seemed determined not to face me. He walked stiffly to the piano, dropped onto the bench, and cleared his throat. I was reminded once again of the afternoon when we met and when I first encountered Katherine.

"What was it? Was she having a lot of pain?"

Instead of answering, he lifted his hands to the keyboard and began stroking the black keys lovingly, but without sounding them.

I went on. "She didn't seem to be suffering. But you were worried. Was she losing the ability to care for herself?"

He played a chord, softly. I saw his Adam's apple bob in his throat before he said, "Katherine was very dignified. Very proud." He slowly sounded middle C, then rippled a few keys. He tilted his head. "She was always very private, you know. In fact, even with me, she changed in a separate room, always had her hair and makeup in place before we . . ." His fingers slid gently over a few keys before finding a soft remnant of the melody. "They found a tumor, pressing on her brain." He paused. "She would have hated needing help with the toilet or bath. Not to mention diapers." He played a few more bars.

So I was right—she had been saying goodbye. I waited for the notes to fade away. "It was your medicine, wasn't it? The pills for the pain in your back?"

He leaned over the instrument. Softly a melody flowed into the room. It was an old Fred Astaire song, "Let's Face the Music and Dance." The darkest, slowest, most dirge-like version imaginable.

I spoke over the music. "This photo shows the medication. Very powerful. With her heart trouble it wouldn't have taken much."

He stopped abruptly and looked at me, cool and dispassionate. "I didn't want to see her lose her sense of herself, her ability to take care of her body . . . to become so dependent. She wouldn't have wanted it either." He stroked a piano key with one finger. "We thought we had a few more weeks at the very least. But that night she took a turn. Could barely move. I had to help her from the toilet to the bedroom. It seemed the time had arrived."

"So you simply took the pills you'd saved and then gave them to her." It was a statement, not a question.

He lifted his head to look out the window again. Then, instead of replying. he resumed softly sounding keys on the piano, and something about his entitled silence made me furious.

I slapped my knee. "Judge Kearney!" The change in my tone seemed to get through to him. He turned to me, and his face was no longer so vacant. His eyes sharpened. Proud. Haughty.

"Do you know who I am?" I asked.

He shrugged. "You're Katherine's friend. She liked you. You were a nurse."

"How about Roger Stinson? Does that name ring a bell?"

He drew his brows together and looked at me again, actually seeing me this time. Suddenly his eyes widened. He knew who I was. Or at least who Stinson was.

But he didn't let on. "I have no idea what you're talking about."

"Maybe I should go down to my apartment and fetch an envelope I have. It's full of press clippings—newspaper stories. Perhaps they will jog your memory."

He shrugged, turning away. Feigning unconcern. But I could see a vein jumping in his temple. "Why should I care about your scrapbooks?'

"Not scrapbooks. Evidence. Newspaper stories. Investigations into dishonest lawyers and a corrupt judge who took money to give drunk drivers absurdly light punishments."

He still wouldn't face me, but I felt him stiffen, every cell attuned to what I was saying.

I spoke slowly but without raising my voice. "Do you recollect now? You let Stinson go with barely a slap on the wrist. And then he got behind the wheel, drunk again, and plowed into a teenage girl."

He lifted his chin, his profile strong against the window light.

"Her name was Bethany. She was my granddaughter. I bet you remember her mother. That ridiculous farce of a trial and the insulting 'punishment' you gave Stinson for killing Bethany nearly destroyed her. You had her escorted out of your courtroom. As if *she* was the problem."

His eyes narrowed as he faced the front of the piano.

He finally turned his gaze to me. "Those rumors were slander."

"You killed my granddaughter."

"You just want someone to blame. You're not strong enough to accept that life can be hard, so you are blaming—"

"Stop it!" I demanded, sharp and loud. He pulled back, surprised.

I lifted my chin. "You are a corrupt judge. You dishonor the title."

"How dare you?" he barked. He turned toward me, bringing one hand down, hard, on the piano, sending forth a discordant clang. "I am a respected member of the bar."

There was a shuffling, and from down the hall, a door opened and I heard a muffled call. "Dad? You okay?"

Nathaniel inhaled, nostrils flaring. He answered, "Yes, Lisa. All is fine. Please, go back to your work."

He was still glaring at me. I leaned toward him, my voice lowered. "I know everything. The question is, what do we do about it?" I settled back. "Perhaps I should tell the police."

He sniffed. "They won't believe you. They know me." He lifted his brows, full of arrogance. "Katherine's death was caused by error—simply a regrettable medical error." He sent me a chilly smile.

Fury threatened to derail me. I dug may nails into my palms. "And what about the person who will be blamed? You are ruining her life, her reputation."

He lifted one eyebrow and shrugged. "Sometimes these things happen. But I'm sure if she moves to a new position at another facility, all will be forgotten."

I saw it now. He knew that Graciela could figure it out, and he wanted her gone. He'd engineer it if he had to.

My voice rose, ragged and outraged. "But she may be deported. How can you—" I caught myself. It was all too obvious. But what leverage did I have?

And then I realized a possibility.

I sat back and folded my hands in my lap, lifted my voice and called, "Oh, Lisa?"

It wasn't quite loud enough for her to hear, but he got the idea. His head whipped around, and alarm flashed across his face. "No," he hissed, pushing himself up. "I will not have it."

I scoffed at that. "You have no authority to stop me, Nathaniel." The self-satisfaction was gone now. Instead I saw fear, real fear. And I saw I had guessed right. Now that he was living with the devastation of having lost Katherine, the only person keeping him from being bereft of any human connection was Lisa. The daughter he'd never developed "heartstrings" with was the only person he had, the only one keeping him from dying alone and unmourned. He needed her goodwill at all costs.

It was the only play I had. I had no real power to make him confess. He was right, the cops would much rather call Katherine's death a medical error than deal with the messy consequences of an elderly judge with a compromised history who'd killed his wife. Even in mercy. Or not.

I leaned forward and continued, watching his face, feeling my way. "Maybe Lisa never read the newspapers during that time. Or perhaps she did, but she listened to you, your version of things." I lifted my brows. "But I wonder if hearing the story from the point of view of a family member of one of the victims, along with all the clippings and interviews—would bring it all to life? And surely she doesn't know you killed her beloved Katherine?"

He was vibrating with umbrage. I went on. "I'll make sure she knows everything. And that knowledge will be in her mind every time you need her, and you will see it in her eyes every time she looks at you."

His eyes grew wide. He couldn't face it, the unraveling of his image.

That was it. The key. I saw it clearly. His vanity—which is probably what had made him so susceptible to corruption to begin with—animated what was left of his life force. Which also made it his weakness, his Achilles heel. It wasn't only his need for Lisa. Yes, he depended on her and her goodwill. But perhaps just as strong was his desire to protect his bloated self-image, to preserve his appearance as an upstanding individual at all costs. This was where I could apply pressure.

I went on, feeling like I was gaining the upper hand. "And it isn't only Lisa I'll talk to. You know how news travels around here. I'm sure many people would love to hear about the details of your career. It would make for juicy conversation in the dining room." I added ominously, "And in case you think people will discount me, you should know I am not the only one here who realizes who you are. Who knows your history."

The judge half rose. His eyes bulged, and he looked so enraged and red that for a moment I thought he was about to have a stroke. "I . . . I . . ."

"You have a choice." I lifted my hand, to still him. "Talk to the police. Say you did it by mistake or that Katherine made the mistake. But if you don't, I will tell. Not just about the pills. About your career. I know the investigators. I can get access to their records, the statements of your collaborators. I'll make sure Lisa knows everything. I will make her *feel* what you did to my family, and others. Every time she has to take care of you as you grow old and helpless, she will be thinking, '*This man enabled killers.*'" I tilted my head. She'll think, "'*This man killed my stepmother.*'"

"You have no right to talk about my relationship with my wife," he spat. "I loved her. I did it out of mercy."

"Did you? Or was it that you couldn't bear to be the one who had to be the caretaker, not the center of her attention?"

"How *dare* you?" His eyes were wild. "I loved her more than anything. I couldn't stand to see her suffer."

I shrugged. Even in this absurd situation, I realized I was hardly in a position to question someone else's self-deceptions. And it didn't matter.

"Maybe. Either way, you enabled killers as a judge, and now you've killed your wife." Confident in having landed a defining blow, I stood. "Somehow or another, you must make sure Graciela or any other staff person isn't implicated in any way."

He raised his hands and banged them, hard, on the keyboard. "I will not be impugned by the likes of you."

I stopped and started toward the hall, calling, "Lisa."

"*No!*"

I turned toward him. "Then for once in your life do the right thing. Live up to Katherine."

I paused before heading to the door. "I'll let you think about how you want to handle this. If I don't hear from you by tomorrow, I will start letting the cats out of the bag."

His face collapsed like a bridge falling into water. He glared at me, and I felt the impotent fury in his gaze as I headed toward the hall.

THE NEXT MORNING there was a knock on my door. When I rocked onto my tiptoes to look out the peephole, I was shocked to see the judge. He looked shrunken, but stiffness permeated his entire posture.

I opened the door. He lifted his chin, "I would like to speak to you."

I gestured him into my foyer. He was pulsating with discomfort. Even so, it was habit as much as hospitality that prompted me to offer, "Can I get you something? A cup of tea?"

"No." He straightened his spine. "I won't have a seat either. I won't be staying."

I nodded in acknowledgment. This was not a social call.

"I . . ." He pressed his lips together and squared his shoulders. "I have been considering your suggestions from yesterday. I have decided you are right. It certainly isn't in anyone's best interest for the young woman—the nurse's aide—to be worried. After all, these are difficult jobs, and my recollection is that Katherine thought she was very competent and personable."

Part of me wanted to point out I hadn't made a suggestion, but rather an ultimatum. And that I doubted whether he had any idea what Katherine thought of Graciela, since I was quite certain he did not pay the slightest attention to the people who worked at Ridgewood. But antagonizing him would not be productive.

I crossed my arms, uncertain what he was offering. "So, what are you saying?"

At this he dropped his head, and when he looked up, his eyes suddenly misted. "I . . ." He swallowed again. "I was hoping that you could be the one to handle it."

What? I frowned in confusion. "Handle it how? As you have already pointed out, the authorities won't believe me."

"No." He paused. "But they would believe Lisa." His voice cracked with the same strained, strangled quality I'd noticed when I'd overheard him talking with Lisa in the music room. I realized now that conversation had been shortly before Katherine's death. This was his voice under extreme emotion. When he glanced up at me, his eyes framed a fervent plea. He said, "I had hoped you could talk with her. Explain things." For a dreadful second I thought he might cry. "Explain that . . . Katherine took my pills by mistake."

I took a moment to consider. He was right. The cops would believe Lisa. She had authorized the autopsy in his stead, after all. But why should I make things easier on him? He did it, and he should at least have to acknowledge his wrongdoing. Not to mention his disgusting plan to allow Graciela to take the blame.

I was about to upbraid him when I realized—with hot shame—the absurdity of my own position in this. What moral high ground could I claim, for goodness sake? Some might think that my actions were less justifiable than his. Take the branch out of your own eye before pointing out the sliver in someone else's, Sister Marie-Clotilde used to say. *"He should at least have to acknowledge his wrongdoing?"* For goodness sake! I blinked in appalled disbelief at my own blindness and felt my face grow flushed. I'm sure he wondered why I turned away for a second.

"All right," I finally managed to say. "But I'll frame it as I see fit. I will get Lisa to make sure Graciela suffers no consequences."

He nodded and seemed even more shrunken. I suddenly saw how much the fact that he had come to me, a concession of defeat, had cost him. He raised his chin, "And . . . about our other history?"

I stared at him, deliberately focusing my disdain into my gaze. He couldn't meet my eyes and looked away. Slowly he said, "I acknowledge some decisions I made during my legal career did not . . . lead to the best outcomes." He drew himself up, and some of his native haughtiness started to creep back in, though he still wouldn't look at me. He said, "No judge can always predict how things will turn out. After we show leniency."

What? I felt a spark of rage. "Are you saying letting drunk drivers off easy was simply an error in judgment? Sort of like the 'medical error' you were okay with Graciela being accused of?" I leaned forward, voice rising.

He immediately stepped back and lifted one arm. "No." He wavered. "No. Clearly I . . ." He paused. I detected some small shift . . . perhaps now it was his turn to be appalled at himself? He cleared his throat. "I made poor decisions about things that seemed at the time relatively small. I didn't think through what the impacts might be. I allowed myself to be . . . used." He lifted his eyes to mine, and I realized the mixture of embarrassment and confusion I read there was as close to an acknowledgment as I was going to get. "Please. Can you not tell Lisa?"

*   *   *

An hour later, Lisa was the one who knocked on my door. I invited her in, and she sat in my kitchen as I made tea.

I put our mugs on the table and settled across from her.

She sipped. "Dad is upstairs looking as shaken as I've ever seen him." She tilted her head. "Can you explain? What happened?"

"He didn't tell you anything?"

"He just said I needed to come down here. That you had something important to talk with me about. But he's so . . . overwhelmed." Her eyes were worried. When she spoke, her face seemed like it was made of mismatched parts. "I don't have any idea what is going on."

I chose my words carefully. "Do you remember mentioning to me that Katherine had some bad news when she was last in the hospital? She alluded to it too. But neither of you ever said exactly what it was."

"I thought you knew. She said she'd told you."

Perhaps for Katherine, that last elliptical conversation *was* her way of letting me know. Or perhaps she'd just told Lisa that as a way of putting off hard discussions.

"No. She hinted at something, but she was so oblique and vague, I didn't realize what she was trying to tell me."

Lisa gazed into her tea. "During that last hospital stay, they discovered there was a tumor in her brain. It was beginning to affect her speech, her movement . . ." She shrugged. "But they thought she'd have some time yet. She was dealing with it, trying to enjoy every day she still had." She glanced at me. "I know she wanted to read at least a few more books with the group and spend a little more time with you."

"And your dad?"

She sighed. "He was terrified. I told you how he hates to lose control and how much he relied on her. He was veering between complete denial and overprotective panic."

I thought again of the conversation I'd overheard between Lisa and Nathaniel in the music room. He'd been in refusal mode, avoiding her need for help, her desire to acknowledge their dwindling time. I thought of Katherine's quiet acquiescence to what I had thought was bullying.

I said softly, "Did you know the autopsy showed she had prescription painkillers in her system? That they are what killed her?"

She nodded mutely. "My father said it was a mistake by the aide."

"Lisa . . ." I spoke deliberately. I waited till she lifted her face. I looked directly into her eyes. "Your dad gave your stepmom the pills. They were his."

"No!" She stood up and went to the window with her back to me. She was silent for a moment. Then she bowed her head, and her next words were almost whispered. "You're sure? How did you . . . how do you know?"

I wasn't certain how to answer, but when she turned, I could tell by the light in her eyes that she believed me; that as soon as the words had been spoken, she'd understood they were true.

In Greek mythology, Morpheus lived by the river of forgetfulness.

"Lisa, you have to tell the police."

She came back to the table but wouldn't look at me. I reached out and put my hand on her forearm. "I'm not saying you need to tell them everything. Just make sure no one else gets blamed. Say your mom made a mistake and took your dad's medicine. That you didn't realize it till the autopsy. Or anything. They'll believe you. But if you don't, innocent people will pay."

She inhaled shakily and covered her face. "What if they think she did it on purpose? She would hate that."

I almost pointed out that it didn't matter, but I stopped myself. I understood her wanting to be true to Katherine's feelings, even in death. I remembered the fraught conversation Katherine and I had had over the *Young and the Restless* and her horrified reaction to the idea of suicide.

I took Lisa's hand. "You can shape what they think. Say you are certain she didn't do it on purpose. They have no reason to doubt you." She looked away. I whispered, "Lisa, please. You must at least tell the police that no one else was responsible."

"Why do you care?"

There it was.

I took a deep breath. "Look. There are things you don't know . . ." I stopped and looked down, pulling my hands into my lap. *Why do I care?* How to untangle the threads? How to weave the narrative so I don't need to tell her I tried to kill her father? So I protect her from the reality of what he was? And what Katharine was?

What *I* am?

I began again, facing her now.

"Because . . . karma. It's only fair. Life has treated your dad well. But the people who will be blamed don't deserve this." I didn't trust myself, and I had to stop for a second. I wanted to add at least a hint—*you know as well as I do that some of your father's good fortune came by questionable means*—but I didn't. At this point maybe none of that mattered.

"No harm will come to him. You know that. He has friends on the force. It will be ruled an accidental death, only slightly premature. But you must make sure no one else is blamed."

She was quiet. I pressed on. "The aides are good people who take care of us. They helped Katherine." I saw her waver. "Your stepmom was a kind woman. She would not have wanted anyone to be harmed. If nothing else, for the sake of common decency. You know that's what Katherine would have said."

Tears trembled in her eyes. "My father loved my stepmother more than anything. More than . . ." Her voice cracked now. "More than anyone."

There were tears in my eyes too. I took her hand, "I know. That's why he did it." It was the kind thing to say. And one way or another, likely true. Depending how you looked at it.

* * *

A few days later, I perched on my kitchen stool as Evan opened a bottle and poured what was probably too much wine into my glass. He had called me after hearing from Tobias that the investigation had been closed as an accidental overdose, with no indication of an error by the staff. He handed the glass to me and then lifted his own in a toast. "To Frannie, investigator extraordinaire."

I laughed. "That's something, coming from you." I turned to look out at the preserve, the backdrop onto which I had projected so many fears and which had reflected back so many truths.

He asked, "How did you figure it out?"

It was very expensive merlot, and I let the wine play on my tongue before answering. "A few things. You mentioned Tobias was usually pretty dogged, but for some reason he seemed like he might let this case go. Then you mentioned he had used the phrase, 'tender mercies.' That struck a chord. It isn't something you hear every day."

"No, it sure isn't. I'd never heard it before."

"It's from the Bible. It was also the exact phrase Nathaniel used when talking about Katherine's death. Tobias knew Nathaniel, after all. That might explain why a typically tenacious detective might be less than aggressive in this case." I shrugged, "Anyway, the phrase tripped a switch in my brain. It occurred to me that maybe Tobias was echoing Nathaniel."

Evan sipped his wine. "That's all? You figured it out because you remembered that phrase?"

Remembering. Once again that word, with all its baggage. The imperative I felt to avenge Bethany was due in part to my unwillingness to forget the way she'd died. I had kept pressing on the bruise, keeping the pain alive. I weaponized my memories. But sharp edges cut both ways. What I should have done was to shift the focus. To set aside how she died and free up space for memories of how she was when she lived. I lifted my head suddenly, as out of nowhere a joyful burst of her singing flooded my mind's ear, almost as if she were next to me.

"Frannie?"

I shook myself, trying to refocus.

"Right." I cleared my throat. "It fell into place when I happened to see the photo I'd taken of the top of the med cart way back when I was first thinking about . . . my plans." I blushed, remembering that night and the beginnings of my disastrous choices. If only I had stopped there. I looked into my glass and spun the wine. "I was so focused on Katherine's meds I hadn't noticed it before. But when I came across the photo, I looked more closely—and saw that Nathaniel was on Vicodin." I felt the heat crawling up my neck, and knew I was turning pink.

"Look, we don't have to talk about this if you're not ready."

"No, I want to." I straightened on my stool. "The main thing is that—it all made sense when I thought about my final conversation with Katherine. The last time we talked, she was clearly grappling with something, trying to explain why she'd been so withdrawn. And why she needed to spend time with Nathaniel. But I didn't really understand what she was trying to tell me. It left me a bit irritated, to be honest. At the time it seemed opaque and confusing, but looking back, I wish I hadn't been so stupid. I should have known. I feel bad that I didn't pick up on what she was hinting at."

He lifted his eyebrows. "Which was?"

"She'd been to the hospital and gotten some bad news. She had a brain tumor." I cleared my throat. "Not that she was explicit. I only found this out later, after she was dead. But now I realize she was trying . . ." I had to stop, take a breath. "She was telling me how much I had meant to her." My voice cracked. "And that she didn't have much time." I once again felt soul-shriveling remorse. I had been so preoccupied with anger that I hadn't recognized what Katherine—what *my friend*—had been telling me. How much mortification it must have cost for someone as private and self-contained as Katherine. And how much she valued me, to have entrusted me with that. Opening up, as far as she was capable, telling me she had embarked on that final, most mysterious turn. All

I had perceived had been cloudiness and vanity. And I'd been irritated with her for it.

Evan looked away, to give me a moment. Then he asked, "So she had cancer?"

"Apparently moving was getting more difficult, her speech was slipping. It was becoming harder for her to cope. She would have been an invalid, unable to care for herself." I examined my blurry reflection in the dark wine. "I was too dense to pick up on it. But Katherine was trying to hint that she wouldn't be herself for much longer, without being alarming or making me feel obligation or pity."

We both were silent. Everyone our age lives with the unspoken fear hovering over our every day, that we may soon have to make that kind of confession.

"Poor Katherine." He twirled his glass. "I hope when I go, it happens fast."

I looked at him, surprised. "You don't want a little warning? To say goodbye, settle things?"

He waved his hand in front of his face.. "I'm seventy-nine. How much warning do I need? I'm trying to live my life now so that everything is ready. I don't want to linger."

I realized the jury was still out for me on this. Evan had seen his wife slowly sicken. I had seen Cal diminish over time. But I had also seen the effects on the family when death comes suddenly.

Obviously, I'm no spring chicken. Unlike for Bethany, when someone my age dies, it isn't quite as shocking. But I still had a lot of energy and zest for life, and a lot left to do. Is anyone ever ready? And as difficult as those last few months were with Cal, I wouldn't have traded for anything the opportunity to hold his hand and tell him, as many times as I could, that I loved him. I was thankful he hadn't wanted to rush to a departure despite his pain and his embarrassment when the home health worker had to help him to the bathroom and he couldn't make it, or the bad smells from the wound that wouldn't heal. He let me have every day with him that God, or whoever was in charge of these matters, allowed.

But maybe Nathaniel could only love Katherine on his terms. Maybe he just wasn't as strong as I am.

Evan's voice brought me back from that brink. "Finish your story. How did you figure it out?"

I sat up. "Right. The final piece fell into place when I got to thinking about what must have happened that night. Graciela and I each had gone to their apartment, at different times. Not surprisingly, I was easily brushed off, since I couldn't come up with a good reason to be there. But Graciela went back there specifically to deliver Katherine's medicine. And yet Nathaniel not only didn't take it from her, but he also told both of us separately that Katherine was already in bed. I remember he still had his clothes on—and Katherine had told me they *always* went to bed together. Once I heard about the autopsy and saw the photo, I remembered that night and realized the obvious. He had given Katherine his pain pills and turned away the medicine from Graciela because he knew she wouldn't need it anymore."

Evan was quiet for a moment. "Maybe he didn't want to see her waste away. Or couldn't stand the idea of her losing her dignity."

I refrained from voicing the more ungenerous possibility: that maybe he was just so selfish he couldn't stand having to play a supporting role in someone else's drawn-out death.

"Frannie?" I knew from his voice he was going to ask me the question I'd been haunted by. "Do you think she was aware of his plans? Or did he take it upon himself?"

In the space between his question and any possible answer lay a million bits of shattered glass. Shiny, sharp, jagged. The whole world stretched between those two poles, of knowing and not knowing, love and mercy. Sacrifice and letting go. Selflessness and pride. Suicide and murder.

I closed my eyes. Old age imposes certain requirements. Letting go of questions that are too painful to ponder is a big one. After a certain point, getting old becomes a winnowing process. We focus on the small stuff because in the end, that is what we have. Of course, I had no way of knowing what Katherine knew, or intuited. Whose idea it was. Or how much agency she'd had.

I was in my sixties when Cal first got sick. Our dreams of eating our way across Paris, hiking through England, or exploring Alaska by boat began to pale, peeling away like pages on a calendar in old movies. Fading to nothing in the times between one test and another, in the months between when he didn't have pain and when he finally had too much. Gone were any other ambitions, our lives and energies condensed to what really mattered: time with one another, with our kids. Our grandkids. In the space of a year and a half, what had seemed exciting and doable became frivolous and forgotten, relics of an imagined future in the recessed corners of my brain.

When I finally emerged from mourning Cal, and partly through my closeness to Bethany, I returned to myself—those things didn't seem interesting anymore. I felt like I'd been cured of any ambition beyond spending time with my family. And then when Bethany died, my only desire—or so I thought—was for Iris to come through the other end of it in some version of intact. To become Iris again, to know joy again, or at least peace.

In nursing, there is something called the Mid-Range Theory of Chronic Sorrow. It often applies to people who have lost children—who suffer "the periodic recurrence of permanent, pervasive sadness or other grief associated with a significant loss." My desire was to cure Iris of this. To help her heal. I assumed it would be my last ambition, my last mountain. And after that, I would rest. I assumed I'd never again be tempted by anything other than celebrating life with my family.

But I am apparently a susceptible creature, easily inflamed. It didn't take much spark for anger to be rekindled.

A slowly burning desire for revenge. It wasn't like the thunderclap of attraction I'd experienced when I met Cal, or the ferocious terrified love I'd experienced for my children, or my determined ambition to become a nurse. It appeared slowly, like heat shimmering on a distant landscape, disappearing, mirage-like, when I looked too closely. And it cost me a lot. Luckily, I'd been saved from the consequences of my worst impulses, but I'd paid. In lost confidence, lost self-respect. In shame, both for my actions and self-delusion. But most of all, in lost time with my family. I had squandered my most precious resources, time and energy. And thanks to this, first anger and then fear had dragged me out of bed in the morning, and guilt had ruined my nights.

I had loved Katherine, after a fashion, in a complicated, on-again, off-again way, and she had loved me. So once again I stood where I had stood before, reckoning with the future after a loss.

Nathaniel had loved Katherine, absolutely and poignantly—very likely the only love he'd ever really extended in his life. Whatever else he lied about, to others, to himself, to Katherine—and clearly, all three of us were masters of self-deception—that much was definitely true.

It suddenly occurred to me, maybe self-deception is the last, the final thing we let go of.

I remembered the old saying about how the truth sets you free.

I opened my eyes and blinked at Evan. "All I know is he did it because he loved her. Whether he was motivated by a selfish wish to avoid witnessing her decline or because he wanted to spare her indignity, I have no idea. To tell you the truth, he probably couldn't have parsed the difference."

In Greek mythology, Lethe is the river of forgetfulness and oblivion. It flows through the cave where Morpheus sleeps, surrounded by poppies. Getting old is like standing on a grate over the water. Things drop out of our pockets, slip through our grasp. And rather than reach to catch them, we watch them fall, almost thankful that there is one fewer thing we have to carry.

I looked away and heard a *plink*. The answer to Evan's question, and any key I might have had to unlock the mystery, went falling into the deep.

I swallowed the rest of my wine and held out my glass. "Could I have some more?"

CHAPTER

30

Dear Ruth,

Finally! I hope you didn't give up on me. Please forgive me for my neglect. I received your postcards saying you were worried and imploring me to tell you what was going on. I am so grateful for your concern. Your guess that something was troubling me was correct.

Let me begin by reassuring you that now all is well. However, you were definitely right to guess that something was going on. In fact many things were, and whenever I tried to write, I didn't know where to start. But now that I am out the other side, I can fill in at least the broad outlines.

To begin with, I think I might have mentioned that Iris went through a rough patch a while back. She is doing better now, but I don't mind telling you I was worried. Then, after she began to recover, she and Jimmy seriously considered moving to the city. They even put in an offer on a condo. I might have written you they were thinking about it. As much as I would have missed her, I understood the reasoning. It was an effort to turn over a new leaf in new surroundings, to make new friends with people who were not parents of kids Bethany's age, etc., etc.

But it was very hard on me, and I had to make an effort to not feel abandoned, as childish and selfish as that sounds.

Now I am (selfishly?) happy to report that in the end they decided against it. They opted instead to stay and became foster parents. She has so much to give, and they have the means to create a nice home and plenty of love and patience and support to offer. At the moment they have a pair of ten-year-old twin boys living with them. It is a challenge, but they are really committed to doing it, and so far it is going well. Do you remember Danny and Adam—Charlie's boys? They've been welcoming to the twins, and it seems like some tentative friendships are developing. They are all playing soccer together, and every other Saturday, Charlie and Pam pick me up for breakfast with the boys, and then we go watch their games. Everything about it makes me very proud.

Speaking of real estate, another thing that was going on was selling my old condo. We had the place repainted, got the kitchen updated, and redid the baths. Charlie and Iris organized the work. They did a good job, so it wasn't on the market very long, and we got a decent price for it.

I continue to go to the book club I told you about, and am becoming closer friends with some of the other members. We've convinced the Ridgewood folks to start a movie club, and at least once a month we go to the local multiplex for a matinee. Oh—do you remember me writing about the young aides I'd become friendly with? One of them just got her green card and is now reunited with her son. I am happy for her—she's had quite a journey. They both occasionally bring their sons by to visit, and we have cookies.

* * *

Okay. Now, comes the hardest part. The real reason that I have taken so long to write.

Ruth, something occurred in my life that knocked me off balance . . . and I reacted in a way that I still can hardly believe. I should have known better, and I have been turning over and over in my mind how to tell you. How to begin, how to explain? I have decided to keep it simple. So here goes:

It all began with a horrible coincidence, that someone who I knew had done something awful also was living here at Ridgewood. When I realized who this person was and what he'd done . . . well. Some very terrible notions took hold in my mind. If I told you, you would not believe me, and to be honest I can scarcely fathom it myself.

In any case, God, or good fortune, protected me from my own poor judgment, and my actions had no ill effect. However, I didn't realize that for a while. And during those weeks, I went through hell. I could hardly eat, I couldn't write or talk to anyone. I couldn't even hear Cal's voice. I ended up going to the chapel often, trying to find peace, but there was none. But— thankfully—I discovered that I wasn't very competent at doing bad, and my misdeed bore no poison fruit. Thank goodness. Before you say anything, of course I realize that being ineffective doesn't absolve me from guilt. I had to spend significant time and energy and worry and ingenuity cleaning up various messes I'd made.

Like I said, things are now returning to normal.

Ruth, I know the above is vague, and I worry that in your imagination it might become even worse than it was. I hate that, because I want you to think well of me. I'm also worried that you might get the impression that my unwillingness to describe it more fully means that I am not truly sorry. But believe me when I say that I will live the rest of my days in huge gratitude that I escaped the consequences of my own worst impulses. Now, every day I try to reconnect with my best self. I also promise to avoid getting on my high horse (which, as you have often pointed out, I have a tendency to do), knowing just how easy it is to stumble. I promise.

Maybe someday, when it is further behind me and I am not so mortified at myself, I can tell you more. But this is the best I can manage at the moment. I hope you will forgive the mysteriousness, and also the delays in getting this to you.

Write back! I promise I won't take so long to reply. From now on, I expect life to be blessedly boring.

With much love,

Frannie

AUTHOR'S NOTES AND READERS GUIDE

I WANTED TO WRITE a morally complicated story—a story about a good person who has succumbed to their worst impulse. What prompts someone to stray from the straight and narrow? What if they were convinced justice was on their side?

And when my mother entered an assisted living facility, I realized such a place could offer a perfect setting for that kind of story. I imagined a protagonist whose buried heartache and anger—which she thought she had dealt with—reemerged with new urgency. Throw in the paradoxical freedom of being near the end of life—and the sudden sense such a protagonist might have of being both above suspicion and beyond consequences—and the story glimmered into view.

Frannie's story and the actions she pursues raise several themes.

Relationships Between Women, and Friendship

- Frannie's friendship for Katherine is real, but as time goes on, she develops doubts about Katherine's values and priorities. Have you experienced losing respect for a friend? Or had a friend whose partner you disliked or disrespected?

- Frannie recognizes that Iris needs to focus her anger on someone. She understands that, as her mother, she is the safest target. But at one point Iris's anguish leads her to reject Frannie, even though she clearly needs her mother's support. Iris's grief also impacts her relationships with her brother, her nephews, and her friends. Have you observed tragedy driving people apart instead of bringing them together? Or someone's grief being so intractable they are impossible to be with?

Justice, Revenge, and Complicity

- Once Frannie realized who Nathaniel was, what should she have done? Ignored him? Denounced him publicly? Avoided both him and Katherine, with no explanation? In a place like Ridgewood, how would that have played out?
- While the seeds of her action are taking root, Frannie does not look too closely at her own thinking. Have you ever done something (big or small, consequential or not) for which you realized (in retrospect) that you'd been preparing, even if, at the time, you would not have acknowledged it?
- In addition to the central action, there is another question that percolates in the background: What evils might a person deliberately overlook in someone they love (as Katherine overlooks Nathaniel's misdeeds)? And what might other people in their lives make of that complicity?

Belief

Several times Frannie recalls her religious upbringing (quoting sister Marie-Clotilde, referencing going to church, her mother-in-law's rosary.) But her faith has deserted her.

"I fingered the rosaries, remembering all the years of prayer. For a long time I'd hoped fervently that there was some sort of accounting on the other side of the divide . . . a pit of suffering and retribution. Now the idea that there might be such a place filled me with dread. . . . What a horrible irony: imagining a happy afterlife now that I'd lost the right of entry."

She even seeks solace in the chapel:

"I kept trying to pray, even though it didn't seem to be working. Some small spark of belief—or perhaps hope for comfort—instilled from all the years, still flickered."

Think about the emotional stakes of losing one's faith, especially late in life—after decades of belief.

Place and Situation

- Ridgewood is almost a character onto itself. When people move into senior housing, there is a cultural tendency to write them off as no longer in control of their own lives. How accurate or inaccurate is that? Frannie is not cute, doddering, quirky, or irascible—or warm and fuzzy. What are some other stereotypes of older women? Of older men?

- Have you ever been surprised by someone asserting themselves in unexpected ways? What prompted it? Why was it surprising? What assumptions or patterns did it disrupt?

Status, Hierarchies, and Class

- The first time Frannie goes to lunch with Katherine, she notices how easily Katherine gives direction to the staff.

"She did it graciously, but she was definitely comfortable giving orders. I, on the other hand, was not used to these sorts of hierarchies. One of the biggest challenges

> *I'd had in Ridgewood was talking with the staff. I didn't know what was appropriate. The aides didn't work directly for the residents, but still, they took care of us: personally, intimately. And I knew I would sometime need to make demands, but the lines felt blurry to me."*

Think about and discuss the interplay of dependence, privacy, autonomy and interactions with family the residents and staff negotiate in a place like Ridgewood.

- Early on, Nathaniel emphasizes the fact that he has a grand piano in his apartment. Frannie realizes *"Just like every other community, Ridgewood had hierarchies some people were very invested in reinforcing."* Think about how markers of status, attitude, and class (wealth, kids, travel, clothes, careers, current health) are registered in various ways among the residents. Why might people cling to them? Perhaps more tantalizingly, why might people not?

- Graciela's background and immigrant status, as well as Jannah's race, might make them vulnerable to the attitudes and biases of some residents, a fact Frannie is sensitive to from her work as a nurse. How might issues in the outside world play out in places like Ridgewood?

ACKNOWLEDGMENTS

LOVING THANKS TO my family: My husband Mark, my daughters Simone and Isabel, for always believing in me, to my siblings Marty, Kristin, Matt and Hugh, and to my wonderful in-laws, especially Marguerite whose encouragement means so much.

My deepest gratitude to my writing posse: Kristin Ginger, who shared her gifted ear, remarkable insight, and discernment every step of the way; to Melinda Rooney, beta reader extraordinaire; to Stacy Tolbert and Tammy Matthews for their encouragement, ideas, humor, and support.

To Abby Geni and Rebecca Makkai for their enormously valuable feedback, along with all the folks at Story Studio for their work on behalf of the Chicago writing community.

To Simone Boutet for her generosity and advice.

Thanks also to my brilliant editor, Tara Gavin, and to Rebecca Nelson, Melissa Richter, and the entire team at CLB.